B

Bad Bones

LINDA LADD

KENSINGTON
Kensington Publishing Corp.
www.kensingtonbooks.com

KENSINGTON BOOKS are published by

Kensington Publishing Corp.
119 West 40th Street
New York, NY 10018

First electronic edition: September 2014

ISBN-13: 978-1-60183-052-4
ISBN-10: 1-60183-052-1

First print edition: September 2014

ISBN-13: 978-1-60183-328-0
ISBN-10: 1-60183-328-8

Printed in the United States of America

Prologue

Blood Brothers

Years Ago, When Innocent

His chest heaving with fear, the little boy cowered under his bed and hid his eyes. The crowd of men was outside in his backyard. They were yelling and screaming and guffawing and drinking beer out of red Solo cups, and their chants were getting louder. *HIT 'IM, HIT 'IM, HIT 'IM*. He pressed his palms over his ears and tried to block it out. Scooting farther back into the dark corner, he pressed himself up against the wall. He did not want to go outside, not ever again. He hated what was going on out there.

Trembling, he clamped his eyes shut and didn't move a muscle. Maybe his pa wouldn't come looking for him. Maybe this time Pa would forget about returning to the house and dragging him outside. Maybe he was too drunk this time to remember. Maybe Pa was passed out somewhere, and then the boy and his twin brother would be safe until everybody went home. He entwined his fingers tightly to stop them from shaking. He felt sick to his stomach, as if he were going to throw up.

It had to be very late now; he'd been hiding under his bed ever since it started. Maybe even past midnight. His room was full of shadows because he'd switched off his lamp, but he could still see pretty well because all the pickup trucks had their lights on out there. Smoky beams were flooding through his bedroom window so he pushed deeper back. All he wanted was for his mama to come back. He wished she hadn't gotten cancer and died and been buried down in the ground over in the graveyard on the back hill of her family's property. That's where he had lived with her. That's where he wished he was now.

But after she passed away, his pa came and got him, and then he brought him back to live in this house with all his big brothers. He didn't know any of them, and he didn't like any of them. Except for his twin. That one was all right. He had never even met him before that day, didn't know he had a twin or any brothers, either, until after Mama had flown on angel's wings up to join the heavenly host. He had been shocked when they had first come face to face because they did look so much alike, not exactly the same, but still a whole, whole lot. In fact, all the brothers looked a lot alike, and they all looked like their pa. It was almost like staring at his own face in a big bunch of mirrors.

One difference was that his twin was a little taller than he was, and had more muscles, too, and sure was plenty braver. Pa said that his twin had gotten that way because of hard knocks and tough training and being around his older brothers who didn't cut him any slack. He said he trained his sons to be men, just like somebody he called the ancient Spartans did. He said he wanted them all to be great warriors and defeat any enemies they ever came up against. He said that his boys were hard as nails and had been ever since they'd taken their first baby steps.

Thinking about all that made the little boy start sobbing again. He just wasn't as hard as nails, and he wasn't as tough as the ancient Spartans, either, whoever they were, because his mama told him that he shouldn't never fight and hit people because that was a bad thing, a real awful sin. Maybe that's why Pa didn't cotton to him as much as his twin and the other bigger boys, who were always hitting him and pushing him down in the mud and spitting on him and stuff like that.

Mama had liked him the best, though, that was for sure. He was the only one she'd taken away when she left Pa's house and went back to live with her parents. But now she was gone forever and buried deep in the ground far away across the cow pasture on that high hill. Sometimes, when he was really lonely and scared, he ran all the way to the end of his pa's land where it overlooked the rushing river that fed the lake and tried to see her headstone, but it was way too far off in the distance.

Suddenly, he heard the footsteps coming down the hall, clomping, loud, boot-heavy, heading swiftly toward him. Oh, no, his pa was coming after him! His little muscles grew completely rigid, and pure dread overwhelmed him. He was gonna get hurt again. They were gonna hurt him real bad, just like last time. Then he was gonna cry and beg for them to stop, and then Pa was gonna give him a whupping for being such a sissy, right in front of everybody. But no, wait, oh, thank you, God, it wasn't his pa. He let out a relieved breath when his new twin brother squirmed in under the bed with him. The other kid wriggled his way back to him and lay down so close in front of him that their noses almost touched. It still shocked the boy sometimes to see another person that looked so much like himself, almost like he was having a dream.

"Pa said you gotta come out there and do your fight. You hear me, bro. You gotta do it, or he's gonna drag you out there and beat your butt black and blue in fronta all those guys. Then they's gonna laugh at you and throw rotten tomatoes and slap you around. You know that, don't ya? That's what he always does if any of us wimps out and acts like big babies, 'cause then he looks stupid in front of his fightin' buddies. He's done it to me, one time, when I lost my fight to this bigger kid, and all the rest of us have got beat up, too. It ain't fun, let me tell you. Goin' out there and gettin' hit on by another kid is better'n that."

The frightened twin's throat clogged up. "I don't wanna fight nobody. I'm scared to. I'm gonna get hurt again and my nose's gonna start bleedin'. They hit me in the face last time and then my head hurt so bad that I couldn't even stand up. I just kept fallin' down."

"Hey, now, kid, you think I don't know how it feels to get slugged up the side of the head with a big ol' fist? You think he ain't beat me near to death, afore I started winnin'? Tell you one thing, it's gonna be a lot worse if you hide under here like a little scaredy cat sissy. And he been sayin' that you can wear my boxin' gloves this time and we can play it tag team-like since we're so much littler than the other kids fightin' tonight." His twin stopped then, took a deep breath, and listened for a moment to the shouting going on outside. "Okay, now listen up good. All you gotta do is go out there with that other kid and start the fight goin' and do your best not to fall down as long as you can, and then I'm gonna come in there and take over right after that big kid knocks you down the first time."

"Please don't make me," the frightened twin whispered. "I gotta crack in my skull the last time. That doctor said so, I heard him say it. I had to go to the hospital and everything. Don't you remember that? When Pa told the doc that I fell off the barn roof. He lied and lied to all of those nurses, and everybody down there."

"Yeah, but your head got healed up good and fine, now didn't it? You okay. You fit to fight, and you gotta do it. Pa's probably not gonna let 'em hit you up the side of your head anymore, anyways. I heard Pa tellin' 'em they couldn't punch you in the head. I heard him sayin' it to that kid waitin' out there for you."

"But I still got those bad headaches, so bad I can't even remember nothin'. I don't like fightin' like you do. I hate it! I hate him!"

"That's just 'cause you be so new at it, and stuff. Ain't done it much yet, that's all that is. None of us liked it at first, neither, not when Pa made us start out hittin' each other. You just get used to beatin' on other kids after a time, and then someday you'll get as good at it as me. You thinkin' that I liked it at first, huh? Damn right, it hurts when they beat you up with their fists, but then I figured out that it hurts them when I hit them, too, just as much. Listen good, bro. What you just gotta do, is hit 'em first and hit 'em so hard that they back down and get scared or fall down and end the round. Then you jump on their bones and beat the holy crap outta them. Got that? That's all you gotta do. So quit bein' such a big crybaby and come on out there."

He just lay there, and then his twin grabbed his arm. "Hey, c'mon now, you gonna get better at this, I swear you will. You gonna get good like me one of these here days. Then you gonna be the one breakin' kids' bones and givin' 'em headaches, not them givin' 'em to you. You gonna beat 'em up so bad, and all you gonna get is some skinned-up, cut and bloodied-up knuckles. Then you gonna like fightin' as much as the rest of us do and then Pa's gonna be proud of you, too."

"I don't wanna hurt nobody. Ma said that we shouldn't never hurt people. She said the Bible says we gotta turn the other cheek."

"Well, she ain't here no more. She shouldn't've ever told you that kinda stupid stuff, anyways. She shoulda made you tough like Pa made me and the rest of us. I'm glad Pa kept me here when Ma ran off with you."

"I'm glad Ma took me. She loved me. She did. Grandma and Grandpa love me, too. I wish they was here. They'd make 'em stop hurtin' me. They'd take me away from here." More tears welled up and rolled down his cheeks. He wanted to just lie on his stomach and moan and groan and roll up in a ball for a long, long time, forever, until he died. But he smeared the wetness off his face and tried to stop crying. If his pa saw him crying, he'd put him back in the punishing cage, and for sure.

"C'mon, we gotta go. You hear me, kid? Everybody's been waitin' out there for you to show up. If Pa's gotta come in here and drag you out again, you'll get what for."

"No. I ain't gonna do it."

That made his newfound twin angry. "You just listen to me, you little punk kid. I'm tellin' you that if Pa's gotta come in here and drag your ass out there again in front of his drinkin' buddies, they gonna laugh him off this farm and call you a sissy boy from here on out. And you know what happens then."

"I ain't gonna go out there. You can't make me."

"Look, you dumb jerk. I'm on your side. I'm gonna help you, I swear it. Just let that other kid hit you one time, just once, and act like you can't get up, and then I'll come in and beat the hell outta him. I know that other kid; he's the tall one with the skinny legs and big feet. You 'member him from last time, right? The one they like to call Hardnose. I can take him. I'll beat him up so bad that you won't never have to come back in the ring. I'll put him outta commission for a week. That's what he's gonna get for puttin' that crack in your skull."

"Promise? Really? You promise to God and all his angels?"

"Yeah, sure, I do, I guess. Don't I always help you out when Pa's all pissed at you? I ever let you down since you showed up here? We gotta buddy up, just the two of us, like the older boys do. We gotta stick together and then we gonna be okay."

That was true. His twin hadn't ever let him down. He had been real nice since they met each other that first day. And he did help him steer clear of Pa, especially when Pa was drinking whiskey and getting all mean and scary and cussin' up a storm. And he'd taught him what to do and where to hide when his pa got out his punishing whip.

"What if I wet my pants, like last time?"

"Hell, kid, you don't wanna do that. If those guys out there laugh at you and call you a baby and say stuff 'bout wearin' diapers, Pa'll go apeshit. Just do it like I do until I get to come in. You know what I'm a talkin' about, don't ya? Stare 'em down. Look like you gonna kill 'em and skin 'em alive and eat their bones, like you can't wait to hit 'em and knock their teeth out. Like you hate their guts."

Then his hard-as-nails twin squirmed out and grabbed his legs and jerked him out from under the bed. Desperate now, the little one pulled and struggled against his brother's tight grip, all the way down the steps and out on the back porch. Then he saw his pa coming. He was striding toward the house to fetch him, looking all big and frightening and pissed off. His face was all red, and his breath smelled like spilled beer.

"You get the hell out here, you little sissy. Good God, your ma made you as soft as a li'l baby girl. Hell, I oughta put you in a dress and parade you around. Quit bein' such a sniveling little punk. Hell, that's what I'm gonna call you till you show me some gumption. Punk. Damn right, that's a helluva good name for you, you little crybaby. You need to be more like your big brothers. They ain't afraid of nothin'. They all got some guts, by God. So, get your tail out here and show 'em what you're made of."

Pa grabbed Punk and pushed him down on the back steps and then he squatted down and shoved some boxing gloves on his hands. He jerked the laces tight. "Now listen up good, boy. You can't just stand out there and let that other kid beat you bloody, you little turd. You gotta weave around and dance your feet some, like I've been tryin' to teach you every day for a month now. You gotta protect your face with your gloves, and not let him hit you in the head. You gotta fight him like all your brothers do. I got money on you this time. You got that? You better not let me down, you listenin' to me, boy?"

Punk nodded. He looked out at the cars and pickup trucks, where they were parked in the circle that made up the fight ring way back beside the cow pasture. All the headlights lit it up like it was daytime, but the ground was kind of smoky and foggy and strange. He could see the kid who was standing out there in his underwear and waiting to beat him up. Hardnose was only nine years old, older than Punk and his twin were. But he was bigger and taller, and he still had a black eye from his last bout. Punk looked over at the picnic table where they always put the loser kids. There was a boy lying there on a blanket, and he was groaning and his nose was bleeding all over the place. Nobody was paying any attention to him because he lost his fight. His pa called that picnic table Loser Land.

Punk's heart began to pound again, but somehow he walked on wobbly legs out into the ring of lights. His pa kept his hand clamped hard on his shoulder, hurting him and pushing him along. He began to quiver all over, and he kept searching everywhere for his twin brother. But he couldn't see him. Okay, he was gonna have to do it. He had to. He would just have to fall down real quicklike and let his twin come in and save him. He could do that. Maybe. As they neared the ring of cars and pickup trucks, everybody started yelling and jeering like they always did, and the boy in the ring started pounding one fist into the other palm. He was growling and snarling and stamping his bare feet and saying some really bad cuss words that Ma had taught Punk never, ever to say.

Pa pushed Punk toward the boy waiting to bloody him up. Somebody hit the old cow bell with a steel hammer, and Punk desperately tried to remember what he was supposed to do. The other kid was already charging straight at him. He put up his gloves in front of his face and tried to dance around with his feet like his twin brother always did in his own fights, but he couldn't do it without stumbling. He ducked down when the other kid took a big swing at him, but he wasn't fast enough to get out of the way. The blow hit him in the side of his neck and sent him staggering sideways, and all the dads and grandpas and uncles and other kids sitting around in folding chairs yelled and hooted and yelled out for Hardnose to hit him again.

Then he heard his twin brother yelling, too, and telling him to punch the other kid in the nose, so he tried to. He jerked back his arm and hit out as hard as he could. To his surprise, it connected and blood flew out all over the place and got all over his pajama shirt, warm and wet and bright red, but it just made the other kid madder than ever and he charged at Punk again, both his gloves pummeling blows all over Punk's arms and chest. When a real awful blow hit him in his head right over his right ear, he went down on his knees in the grass, a piercing pain stabbing him behind the eyes.

But then, his twin was there beside him, tagging him out, and Punk crawled away and collapsed between a car and a truck and watched how his twin charged at the other kid, yelling shrilly, his head down, and pounded on him with both his bare fists, screaming and cussing and growling like a mad dog or something. He kept it up, too, kicking the boy and finally knocking him down on the ground. He kicked him some more, and then he jumped on top of him and sat on his chest and punched him in the face until it was all red and slick with blood that looked almost black under the smoky headlights. He kept on doing it, too, like he was sort of out of his mind, twisting the other boy's arm backwards until it got all quiet and everybody heard the muffled pop the bone made, and Hardnose screamed and howled with agony and cradled his broken arm.

After that happened, Pa ran out and pulled Punk's twin off the other kid who had turned over facedown now, trying to protect himself and groaning as if he were dying. Pa hugged Punk's twin like he loved him so much and told him that he was a good boy, a brave fighter, and that he'd get a special treat for winning the fight. Then he lifted up his twin's right arm and yelled, "Meet our new champ, my favorite son! He wins again! I christen you Bone Breaker!" All the onlookers laughed at that and clapped their hands and put their fingers in their mouths and whistled long and hard.

Punk just shut his eyes and sighed with relief, glad it was over. He wished his ma was there to take him away again, but she wasn't. And she wasn't ever going to be. He was stuck forever in this awful, scary place where he had to fight other little kids, and there was nothing he could do about it. Nothing at all. He was trapped there forever.

Chapter One

Lake of the Ozarks looked like a winter wonderland, or the North Pole; take your pick. Everything was pure white and mounded up and pristine and shining with ice. In fact, so much snow had fallen thus far in the month of January that all precipitation records had been blown away, both in accumulated inches and serious vehicle collisions. From where Canton County Homicide Detective Claire Morgan sat inside her partner's white Bronco, heater on and blasting hot air on her frozen hands and feet and face, she watched Bud Davis taking his turn working outside on the slick streets, directing slipping, sliding, out-of-control vehicles around yet another traffic accident. This one was snarling traffic near the entrance to the Grand Glaize Bridge, and that was not a good place to line up impatient drivers.

At the moment, Bud was gesticulating traffic signals so wildly that he was having trouble staying on his feet atop the thin sheet of ice covering the roadway. The snowplows were still out and clearing county roads, but nowhere close to finishing the job. A silver BMW ignored Bud's urgent gestures to stop and thereby started a sideways skid down toward one of the mall's entrances. Excited, Bud slipped again and fell on his knees but had barely hit the ground when he was back up, trying to veer off to one side and warn a new white Camry that was now entering the street in the path of the out-of-control vehicle taking a rapidly accelerating backward slide toward a steep embankment. Both vehicles managed somehow to stop before the worst could happen. Claire had to laugh a little under her breath at Bud's wild antics and wished she'd had a video camera running. The other guys down at the office would've had a ball watching it. She started to pull on her heavy gloves and get out to help him, but then she realized that he now had everything under control.

Actually, Bud was very good at traffic control. Claire had done a few similar gymnastics herself while on today's beat, including skinning up her knees. Her backside was also sore from going down hard on the ice more often than she liked to admit. She decided to get out and help him anyway, even though her thirty minutes of heater heaven wasn't up yet, but her smart phone chose that particular moment to vibrate alive.

Quickly digging it out of her brown departmental parka's pocket, she was expecting yet another call alerting them to yet another traffic smashup. They had been summoned to one after another all day long, the accumulated layers of ice and snow on the county highways causing all kinds of havoc around the lake. In fact, all of Missouri suffered the same inclement conditions and the state was hard-pressed to get the interstates cleared for travelers wanting to go anywhere at all.

Caller ID said her boss, Sheriff Charlie Ramsay, was on the line, so she picked up in a hurry. "Yes, sir?"

"You and Bud still down at the bridge?"

"Yes, sir. We're directing traffic around a pretty bad fender bender. The ambulances haven't shown up yet but they're on their way. I can hear the sirens coming. We got a couple of patrol cars out here with us, but they're working traffic down at the mall entrances."

"Well, I've already got another patrol car on the way to take your place. I need you both at Ha Ha Tonka, and ASAP. Park ranger found a body out there."

Shocked, since that was the last thing she had expected him to say, Claire remembered all too well one other time they'd investigated a murder in that same rugged Missouri state park, a horrendous case that she wished she could forget. "Is it a homicide, sheriff? Or an accident?"

"I'm gonna let you and Bud determine that. Just get out there in a hurry. This's all we need with everything else going haywire today."

"Where's the body?"

"At the bottom of a cliff, somewhere up around the Castle ruins, I think. Apparently, he went off one of those sheer drops out there. They told me to tell you to take the tourist boardwalk to the area, but then you're gonna have to get off it to find out where he went down. Be careful. The ranger said it was as slick as glass up there along the edge."

Well, that was just great, just about as hunky-dory as it gets. Climbing around on straight-to-the-bottom craggy cliffs the day after an ice storm was just what they needed to end their otherwise hellish day on the job. "Yes, sir. We're on our way."

"Well, make it quick. If it is a murder, keep me posted. Hell, keep me posted whatever the hell it is. Dadgummit it, I hate these blasted ice storms."

"Okay. It might take us a while to negotiate these roads. It's crazy out here and it's startin' to come down hard again."

"The park guy said the best bet is to come in by car at the main gate. I'm sending Buck and his forensics team out there by boat because, as I understand it, the victim landed fairly close to the water and that way'll be easier for them to carry in their equipment. All our patrol officers are working traffic, so you'll probably need to string the crime scene tape and make sure the park's shut down. Not that anybody in their right mind would go out there in this kind of weather. And be careful, for God's sake."

Claire had to agree with him. Ha Ha Tonka was a beautiful and wild place, a siren's song for hikers and explorers and geologists, but it was rather remote once you got inside, with lots of high craggy cliffs and gorgeous views and foot trails winding through woods and streams and rocky outcroppings. Still, it could be a treacherous place if visitors stepped off the wood-planked walkways or ignored the safety barriers and warning signs. Heavy snow was going to make it even more so, and the Park Service had already closed it, as soon as the storm had been predicted. But the victim had gotten inside somehow, whether on foot, car, or by boat, and it was their job to figure out how and why and when.

Beeping the horn a couple of times, she finally got Bud's attention and waved him back to the SUV. Another uniformed officer was already out on the street with him directing the slow-moving traffic. Bud trudged his way back through the deep snow at the side of the road until he reached the Bronco and got in with a rush of cold air and fluttering snowflakes and one rather inventive curse. His lean face was ruddy with cold and windburn, which really emphasized his ashy-gray eyes, and he grumbled around as he pulled off his gloves and held his fingers up against the heat vents. "Man, this sucks so damn bad. I bet I lose some fingers to frostbite this time. I wish I'd never left Atlanta."

"I told you to wear more layers, Bud. It's six degrees out there."

"Tell me about it. And if I put on anything else I couldn't walk two steps. You have the constitution of a damn Eskimo, Claire."

"No, I just put on lots of layers, and some Polartec underwear and a fleece pullover and then a Down Tek jacket that Black got me from L.L. Bean, and then my parka. I dress a lot warmer than you do, but enough about the weather. Charlie says we've caught a body out at Ha Ha Tonka."

That got his full attention. He turned his head and stared at her. "Are you freakin' kiddin' me? Today? Please tell me it's not a homicide. And I do wear insulated underwear. And it's the good stuff that I get over at Bass Pro Shop in Springfield."

Claire shrugged. Bud was Southern. He was always cold in the winter months, but this weather was extreme, she had to admit. "Don't know yet what it is. Charlie wants us to go in down there and tape it off at the gate. The body's up somewhere around the Castle ruins. Not sure exactly where. You've got tape in the back, right? And flares?"

"Yeah. If it's a homicide, we'll be out there 'til midnight. The temperature's supposed to drop ten degrees below zero again tonight."

"Well, that does suck, I have to agree. But Charlie wants the top of the cliff taped off before we climb down to where the body is."

Starting the engine, Bud kept up the grumbling under his breath. "Climb down there? How the hell are we gonna get down those cliffs in this ice? I can't even walk across the pavement without goin' down and slidin' ten feet."

"Guess we'll figure that out when we get there. Buck's bringing in his team by boat. The lake's gonna be iced up around the bank, too. At least it is in my cove."

"Well, I guess anything's better than standin' around and watchin' idiots crash their vehicles into each other. Morons, all of 'em. Out shopping. Really? Today? Come on. Why don't they just stay home and watch the soaps and give us a damn break?"

Used to Bud's grousing, Claire said, "Amen to all of that."

Bud inched his way out into the highway intersection and took a wide slow left turn that avoided the wrecked cars still blocking the roadway. "God, I'm hungry. Starving. You got any of those Snickers bars left over?"

"Yeah. I got some hot chocolate in my thermos, too."

"Well, pour me some and get me those Snickers quick. I can't believe we didn't even have time to eat lunch. I gotta keep up my energy levels. It's gonna take a long time to get to that damn park."

"You'll live, Bud. All you ever think about anyway is food."

"So? You got something better to talk about when you're hungry?"

Claire handed him a couple of candy bars, wondering how the hell they were going to work a crime scene in this kind of weather if the victim was located at the bottom of a cliff. She usually loved falling snow and ice and warm fires and sitting in hot tubs with her honeybun, Nicholas Black, but not this time and not today. She didn't think she'd ever been this cold for this long in her entire life, and she had a bad feeling that they were still going to be working this crime scene well after dark and in the predicted blizzard that was coming in from the southwest.

Suddenly, Black's idea of spending the winter months down in New Orleans, where there was little snow and no ice and where he had a spacious walled mansion in the French Quarter, sounded more enticing than residing in the current frigid Missouri climes. She figured that he was already back from Los Angeles by now and that he was smart enough to stay inside and was as warm as toast no matter where he was working. Too bad she and Bud didn't have that option. But if Black had made it in before the snow had started again, that was a very good thing. He had been gone almost a week this time.

Fortunately, she and Bud made the drive to the state park without going into a ditch and/or getting slammed into by helpless motorists sliding around in recently dented and damaged automobiles. The length of the ride and Bud's super-hot, magnificent heater managed to thaw both of them out to some degree, but that wouldn't last long once they got outside and into the wind and tromped around in ridiculously deep snow drifts for four or five hours. The front entrance to the park was wide open, but the smooth white mantle cloaking the road was unblemished by tire tracks. They pulled up and stopped long enough to stretch the fluorescent-yellow crime scene tape at the front entrance. They didn't want anybody to cross that line, especially media or ambulance chasers, which would only disrupt footprints and trample evidence, if there even was anything left behind that hadn't already been covered with the heavy snowfall.

When they got back inside the car, Bud turned to her. "No tire tracks. So how did he get in here?"

"Snow could've already covered it up. It's been falling on and off all day long. Last night, too."

"Yeah, true. Wonder how the park ranger found him."

"I'd say he came in down by the water like Buck's gonna do. It'd be easier than climbing down there like we've got to do."

Bud frowned. "Yeah, it's a tough job, and all that crap."

The parking lot was situated on a hill, as was most of the park, not to mention the rugged cliffs and craggy rock formations. They left the Bronco there, and headed up the road on foot to what was left of the old stone mansion. It was called the Castle by the locals, but had once been a magnificent family home overlooking the lake and Niangua River, constructed of white granite blocks, and no doubt full of rich furnishings. But fire had destroyed it at some point, leaving barren outer walls and open cellars and empty arched stone window frames. Still, it was quite a sight to behold and brought in even more tourists and hikers and botanists to explore its surroundings, not to mention lovers looking for a dark place to make out with one heck of a light-spangled romantic night view out over the lake. She and Black hadn't tried it out yet, but maybe they should.

Bud and Claire struggled along the edge of the pavement, through the deeper drifts, but it probably didn't matter where they walked. No footprints were going to be found anywhere in the park, not with the six more inches that had fallen since daybreak.

Bud stopped at one point, hands on his hips, and looked disgusted. The wind was picking up where they stood, now very high on the cliffs, almost howling around the Castle ruins, like in a horror movie. Maybe it was. Maybe those nasty walking dead or super sexy vampires were going to jump out at them, unaffected by the frigid temps since they were already cold and dead. Bud said, "We aren't gonna find a shred of evidence up here, I can tell you that right now. Look around. It's like a barren landscape. Looks like the surface of the moon, or something."

Bud was right, of course. Claire already had a bad feeling about the case, and she hadn't even seen the body yet. How could they find any usable evidence in such deep and undisturbed snow? Maybe that's why the killer, if there was a killer, chose such a remote spot in which to dump the victim's body. On the other hand, there might be something underneath the snow, signs of a struggle perhaps, or the murder weapon or a bloodstained shirt or another body or a road map to the perpetrator's hideout. Who could tell? But to find it, they'd probably have to either melt off three tons of icy precipitation with a flamethrower or wait until the sun came out in April and did it for them. No telling when the storm would break, either. It had been snowing almost nonstop for the last week and a half, except for some lovely hours of sun that very morning.

When they finally slugged a path through the trees and to the cliff extending just past the Castle ruins, a brisk, bitterly cold wind stung them square in their already wind-burned faces, but they continued to make their way along the high precipice, but not too close, uh-uh and no way, until they could see the lights down below where three police boats had gathered in the water below them. Buckeye Boyd, Canton County's trusted medical examiner, was already on the scene. They could see him standing out on the prow of one of the boats, bundled up to his ears and directing his top-notch technicians around the crime scene. The other boats had portable floodlights focused on the victim in the falling winter gloom, and she craned over as far as she safely could and tried to locate the body. As far as she could tell from so high above them, the victim had probably tumbled down the open area under the boardwalk and then slid right over the cliff drop and landed far below. She couldn't really make out anything yet, but it was a pretty good guess that the body had to be frozen stiff. Everything else in the park was, including Bud and her.

"Looks to me like he went off somewhere around here, all right," Bud called out to her over the whirling wind, clapping his gloved hands together for warmth. "Probably bounced around some on the rocks and scrub trees before he tumbled to a stop down there somewhere."

"Yeah. Our problem is how we're gonna get down there without killing ourselves. Any bright ideas?"

Bud stamped his feet and clapped his gloved hands together some more and pulled the drawstring on his brown fur-lined hood tighter around his face. "Man, what a god-awful way to die, especially if the fall didn't kill him. Just to lie down there alone in the dark, all broken up and slowly freeze to death."

"If it makes you feel better, they say that when you freeze to death, it gets to the point where it's sorta like just drifting off to sleep." Claire took out her camera and started clicking photos of the outlook platform on which they stood. It didn't have any disturbed snow or signs of footprints leading to or from it, except for the ones they had made in their approach. Several feet of snow had completely covered one side, sloping all the way up to the top of the handrail. "Maybe he didn't go off from up here, Bud. Maybe a killer dumped him down there and wanted it to look like he fell."

Bud blew into his gloved palms. Stomped some more. He hailed from Georgia, poor guy. Snow was an anathema to him, certainly not his favorite thing. Winter, either. Or hypothermia. Or thermal underwear. Or electric socks. "Or he might've just jumped and ended it all. Got all despondent for some reason and decided to make the hurting stop. Could've been because of this stupid frigid weather. I think I want to end it all, too, now that we've got to stand out here all night."

"I feel your pain, Bud."

"Maybe he bought it even before the storm hit. The ranger probably wouldn't've seen him down there right off the bat. He might've been down there for days. All winter maybe."

"Well, there've been suicides out here. He wouldn't be the first."

"Makes sense to me. Still, he chose a hard way to go. Most guys just blow their brains out when they want to end it all. Faster, easier, manlier. Takes guts to put a gun in your mouth."

Pulling out her phone, Claire considered Bud's theory as she punched in Buck's cell phone number. From her high vantage point, she could see Buck grab his phone out of his pocket. She hoped the call would go through, considering the weather. It did. "Hey, Buck. We're up top. What'd you got down there?"

Claire watched as Buck bent his head way back and gazed up at them. He gave a wave when he picked out their position on the outlook platform. "It's a male victim, I think, completely encased in ice. Looks like a damn grape Popsicle. From what I can tell, appears like he's got some broken bones and abrasions, but we can't see him all that well yet. The ice is clouded. But I'm pretty sure it's a man by the size of the body. Can you see where he went off?"

"Could've been anywhere along here. No signs of struggle or footprints. The snow's covering up everything. Maybe we can find something underneath, but it's gonna take days to shovel all this out."

"I don't think we'll get much down here, either. Looks like he might've been here a while. See any clothes or a coat up there? Any suicide note?"

"Nope. Nothing. Unless it's hidden under the snow. We'll scrape around and see if we find anything where he could've gone off. I'm taking some photos, but there's not much to see up here. Just smooth pure white snow, untouched."

"Then he must've come out here in his underwear or swim trunks or something. It looks like he's almost completely nude, but with the body in this condition, it's hard to tell much yet. We gotta get him back and thawed out under the heat lamps."

"So you think he's been down there a while? Maybe nobody noticed him because of the storm fronts coming in and dumping snow on him?"

"The body looks fairly fresh, but like I told you, there's at least an inch of ice covering his entire body. He's lying half in the lake and the other half is frozen to the rocks. I've got to get him back to the morgue and do the cut before I can tell you anything for certain."

"Okay, we're gonna look around up here some more and then

head down there along the boardwalk. We might find something along the way. How long are you gonna stay?"

"A long time, it looks like. We've got to have a blowtorch to melt him off those rocks and then cut him out of the ice. He's stuck tight from neck to waist. We've been trying to knock him loose with a sledgehammer, but it's not working so far."

They hung up, and Claire glanced around. "Well, let's tape off the edge along here and get the rest of the photos. I am so cold I can't even feel my toes anymore."

"Tell me about it." Bud grumbled some more, mostly under his breath, but he unwound the tape and walked along the edge, hooking it around the handrails.

Claire shot pictures of everything along that area of the drop, most of which ended up as bare white landscapes that showed exactly nothing except undisturbed deep snow. No help that, not for a murder investigation, and that was for damn sure. She also checked out the area inside and behind the Castle for low mounds of snow that might indicate wadded up clothing or weapons or another corpse or any other hidden evidence. They dug off snow anywhere that looked promising but found nothing but more snow. If the guy wasn't wearing clothes, Claire was pretty sure he'd been murdered. Why would he commit suicide in the nude? Who would do something like that? Especially a man. In her experience and unless the decision had been made on impulse, suicide victims usually went the other way and tried to make themselves look as presentable as possible to whoever discovered their body. On the other hand, a killer would not want to leave anything behind, no evidence, no clue to the victim's identity. It would be to his advantage to take any clothes that might be identifiable. Or the victim could've escaped his assailant and tried to flee, but in his panic had run right off the edge and fallen to his death.

After half an hour of searching, they gave up and attempted unsuccessfully to follow the steep boardwalk down in its meandering switchback trail to the lake without slipping and sliding and plummeting themselves down to the crime scene. It was almost impossible to keep their footing on the steeper inclines and they both fell and slid on their backs multiple times. Claire ended up getting snow down inside her boots and up her pant legs and in her gloves, and so did Bud. So by the time they finally found their way to Buck and Shaggy and Vicky and the other technicians, they were not only cold but wet and miserable, too.

There, they found their good friend, John Becker aka Shaggy, Canton County's ace criminalist, where he was being supported by a couple of other techs while he used a small blowtorch to melt through the ice holding the corpse against the rocks. The bottom half of the body was still encased in the frozen water just off the bank. Buck had ordered the lights to be focused on the victim, but dusk had fallen fast and hard now, and it was difficult to see as the snow turned to sleet and began to come down harder and in swift, slanted arrows that felt and sounded like BB pellets.

Shivering like crazy, Claire made her way closer to Buck, where he stood supervising the extraction of the body. There was little she could tell about the victim's face, except that his skin looked purple. As Buck had said, the murky ice distorted his face and made his features unrecognizable. The scene in its entirety looked a lot like textbook photographs she'd seen of wooly mammoths being dug out of Arctic ice. The victim seemed to have frozen to the spot where he had landed in a relatively upright sitting position, head down, chin frozen tightly against his chest. The ice casing followed the contours of his body and made an ice effigy of a human being that created a very surreal and awful tableau of death in those smoky lights and windblown sleet.

"My God, Buck, what'd you think happened to this guy?"

"I'd say murder. There are better ways to commit suicide. But could be that he was on drugs, high on PCP or something like that. Had a bad trip, went crazy, stripped off his clothes and tried to fly off that cliff up there."

Claire considered that scenario and then shook her head. "Sounds reasonable. Except there aren't any clothes up there. No car, either. No tire tracks. No footprints. No nothing. And this place is pretty much off the beaten path. I doubt if he would've walked out here buck naked in freezing winter weather and then decided to jump to his death. That's just too farfetched."

Buck glanced at her. "Yeah, but who knows what a suicidal crazy's gonna do?"

"True."

After another ten minutes, Shaggy turned off the blowtorch and helped the others hack out the lower portion of the frozen corpse with a couple of axes, and then load him on a stretcher, still in a sitting position.

"I guess we can't identify him until he warms up," Claire said, already knowing the answer.

"Not unless he's got ID on him, but that doesn't seem possible, given what he's not wearing. I'll take him back to the morgue tonight and put him under the lamps. You and Bud might as well go home, get some rest. Nothing else you can do until we get his name and I can go to work on him. And I hear that a second front's movin' in later tonight."

"That means more idiotic people travelin' the roads tomorrow," Bud said. "And some more dents in my SUV. Great. Can't wait."

"Well, at least this gives us a reason not to have to direct traffic for a few days," Claire cried out above the rattle of sleet pellets striking the rocks. "Come on, let's take another look around topside and then go home. My gut tells me this isn't suicide or drug-related, but we won't know anything until tomorrow anyway. I'm about to freeze to death, and I'm not exaggerating."

So they switched on their flashlights and trudged through more frigid drifts, slipping and sliding all over the damn place. Oh, yeah, she should definitely have listened to Black and taken a leave of absence and stayed in New Orleans for the rest of the winter. Or better yet, they should have flown to Tahiti and some serious sun and fun on some pristine and private golden beach paradise, which had been Black's second suggestion and quite an enticement that had been, too. Oh, yeah, at the moment, that sounded like the perfect place to be, all right. She was beginning to hate winter, almost as much as Bud did. If that was even possible.

Chapter Two

A little over two hours later, Claire found herself knee-deep in the icy white stuff again, this time trekking down the road to her own place, boots squeaking in the deep snow, panting with exertion, more than ready to step into her own warm and snug little A-frame house after a very long and bitterly cold workday. Bud's Bronco couldn't make it through the windblown drifts across her road so he let her out at the end near Harve Lester's house. Harve had been her partner in Los Angeles, and was one of her best friends, but he was not home, having caught a ride with Black out to California on Black's own personal little Learjet and was probably now having a good old time visiting with their former LAPD cronies. So she didn't even have a place to stop and warm up. Oh, yeah, the day had been pretty damn crummy thus far. On the other hand, she was almost home, and her dear one, Black, was supposed to be there already, so she increased her footsteps. Yes, indeedy, the idea of him and a very warm hot tub at the end of the road, both just waiting for her to show up so the fun could begin, did register awfully high on her whoopee scale at the moment.

When her cabin finally came into sight, all lit up and warm and welcoming, Black's Cobalt 360 was indeed tied up at her ice-clogged little dock. He had the top up and buttoned down to protect him from the wind and weather and keep in the heat, and she remembered fondly the previous summer when they had frolicked just off her dock in the hot sun. Winter sucked; Bud was right on. Forging on, she just hoped Black had brought something good to eat, too, because lunch had not happened, not with the dozens of snow-related vehicle accidents that she and Bud had worked all day long. But first things first, she was freezing. Minutes later, she stomped across the front porch, kicked caked snow off her heavy fur-lined boots, and thrust open the front door. Black was standing at the kitchen counter, dressed in a tan thermal shirt under a plaid black-and-tan, fleece-lined flannel shirt that was unbuttoned and rolled to the elbows. He had on jeans, and was drinking a cup of coffee that smelled absolutely wonderful, and looking as hot as hell as usual, with those ice-blue eyes and thick black hair and killer dimples, especially the dimples because he had a big welcoming smile on his face.

"Well, it's about time you got home. You hungry? I've got T-bone steaks. Still nice and warm and juicy. Medium well, just the way you like it. French fries, extra crispy, and Caesar salad on the side. Peach cobbler for dessert."

Claire slammed the door behind her, unzipped her parka, shrugged out of it, and threw it on the floor. "No time to eat. I gotta get these clothes off."

Black appeared startled. He put down his cup. "I do believe I've had this dream before."

Claire had to laugh. "Stop, Black. I'm freezing, I kid you not. And that hot tub's gonna warm me up faster than anything else."

"I take offense to that," Black said, but he wasted no time pulling off his shirt. "But we'll see. I like a challenge."

By the time Claire sat down on the couch and pulled off her gloves and jerked off one crusted snow boot, Black was already undressed and sitting in the hot tub waiting for her. He said, "Bad day, I take it. You're usually incapable of turning down French fries for this long."

"Yep, pretty damn bad. Unless you enjoy standing in sub-zero weather, directing traffic and avoiding cars slipping and sliding all over the ice."

Claire pulled off her sock hat and unwound her scarf and threw them both aside, hurrying now, ready, willing, and able to get into that nice warm bubbling water with her guy. Her little white poodle, Jules Verne, had other plans. Not to be ignored, he suddenly came barreling down the steps from the loft bedroom and jumped acrobat-ically onto the couch and then up into her arms. She took a minute from tugging off her clothes and snuggled him close and momentarily suffered his excited face licking.

"That dog always gets to you first," Black said, watching her push down her snow pants and kick them off. "So it was pretty brutal out there, huh?"

"Yeah, and I'm tired and very ready for some downtime. And black and blue from falling on the ice."

"Is that sunburn on your face?"

"More like windburn, and maybe a tad of frostbite."

"Well, hurry it up and get those clothes off. I've been waiting for this all day long."

"Ditto, believe you me."

Claire quickly unzipped her flannel-lined hooded fleece sweatshirt, her eyes latched on Black. He looked pretty damn good bare chested, eyes flashing blue in the lamplight as he watched her strip off more clothes. At least he did until he frowned and said, "And I can't help but notice that you're not wearing your engagement ring."

"Yes, I am."

"Well, I don't see it on your finger, Claire."

"No. But it's right here on this chain hanging around my neck, right alongside the St. Michael's medal that you gave me to keep me alive and kicking." She pulled it out of her thermal underwear top and showed him, and then looped both it and her badge chain off over her head.

"Right. Guess I haven't seen all that many engagement rings worn quite that way."

That remark was edged with a very mild degree of sarcasm, so Claire thought it best to ignore it. He stared at her, apparently rather unhappy with her choice of ring display, and not willing to hide his irked feelings. Since she happened to have a perfectly good reason for the chain thing, she decided to share it with him.

"Don't get your back up, Black. I don't wanna lose it since it cost you plenty, the market value of this house, probably. That diamond's so big that I'm afraid it's gonna get caught on something if I have to pull my weapon real quicklike. I know you wouldn't want that to happen."

"So you shoot with your left hand now?"

Claire unzipped her jeans and kicked them off. "Sometimes, I do, if my other hand's busy punching somebody in the gut."

"Hope you're not referring to me." But Black was not one to hedge when he had something to say, and he didn't this time, either. "So what's this all about, Claire? You having second thoughts about getting married? Is that it?"

Claire stopped undressing and gave him her most highly exasperated, and yes, annoyed gander. "Well, no. Come *on*, Black, give me a break here. I'm cold and tired and not in the mood for some silly argument."

"You were ready enough to commit before that snowstorm hit and grounded the plane on Christmas Eve. Or we would've been married that night in Las Vegas. Now it's the end of January and still no wedding."

Claire pulled off her insulated undershirt. "Yeah, but the plane *did* get snowed in. Hey, you're the one who wants a great big, flashy wedding. That takes time to plan, you know."

"At this point, I just want a wedding, period."

"And you're going to get one, trust me. And something else you need to think about, Black. I deal with criminals all day long every day. What if one of the creeps I have to hassle notices this big expensive ring I'm wearing and decides to follow me home, mug me, maybe even kill me, and take the ring so he can retire. Ever think of that?"

He hadn't, judging by the concerned expression on his face. "I'll tell you one thing, if anybody ever touches you or that ring, I'll kill them."

"Aw, how sweet. Promise? Problem is I'd still be dead."

"All right, I get it. I see your point. I just like to see that ring on your finger, that's all. Looks good there. Tells the world how it is."

"And you will. I do love it, and I do want to marry you, or you would have it back by now. So, we good now? No more talk about that damn ring?"

"Yes. You just said what I wanted to hear. So, hurry it up. Your skin looks a little blue, almost Smurfette-ish, in fact. Good God, how many clothes do you have on?"

Pulling down her thermal underwear bottoms, she kicked them

off, too, and hopped her way to the tub, stripping off her heated socks and everything else along the way.

"Enough *not* to keep me warm." She stopped beside the big hot tub and laid her phone on the edge. She took her engagement ring off the chain and held it up for him to see. "Okay, see this. Watch closely now, I'm putting it on my finger right now, where it belongs. Happy?"

His eyes slid down over her slightly blue and half-frozen body. "Oh, yeah, you bet I'm happy. Now get in here with me and show me how glad you are to see me. It's been a very long week."

Down to naked skin now, rather goose-bumpy naked skin, to be sure, and shivering all over, she eased down into the warm and silky water and felt as if she'd submerged herself into a slice of heaven. Black watched, smiling at her long sigh of pleasure. Claire sat there across from him, relaxing and allowing her frigid limbs to slowly thaw out a bit, and vowed never to step foot outside the house again. "So, tell me, Black, how did your day go?"

"I saw a couple of patients, swam some laps, worked out in the weight room, tried to get over my jet lag from the flight back from LA, all the while waiting for you to get home so we could enjoy several hours of slow, inventive lovemaking. So, I guess it was pretty uneventful. It's looking up now, so come over here and let me say hello."

"All in good time. So everything's cool and copacetic at your Los Angeles clinic? You did go to Los Angeles like you said you did, right? Do I need to call out there and verify your story? Sure you weren't in New York partying it up with your buds at the Ritz-Carlton?"

They'd had a bit of a tiff not so long ago when he had lied about where he'd been, but that was long over. He'd had a good reason at the time and had squared it with her satisfactorily. Still, it had rankled a little and made her wonder where he really was every time he flew off to distant locales.

Black didn't bite. He usually didn't when she was baiting him. He was a crack psychiatrist, after all. He probably knew her better than she knew herself. In fact, she was pretty sure he did. "Everything's fine in California, and when Harve's cop friends showed up at the airport to pick him up, he was very glad to see them. And right now? I'm glad to be back home with you. So, one more time, why don't you come over here and let me show you?"

This time Claire decided to do his bidding, having missed him rather a lot, too, and they quickly entered into their usual slippery, sliding, slick and lovely, skin-to-warm-skin, mouth-to-mouth explorations. They did so love their nifty hot tub and therefore used it often and well.

"You feel so damn good," he muttered into her hair, his hand sliding up her bare back to grip the nape of her neck. "I love kissing you more than just about anything I can think of."

"Yeah? Well, keep it up. I'm getting halfway warm for the first time all day."

"My temperature's been up ever since you took off all that sexy thermal underwear and those battery-operated socks."

Claire laughed at him again, but the sound died away as he turned her around and pressed his mouth down on her naked shoulder, and in a very warm and eager way, too. Black knew full well where to find her major and most titillate-able erogenous zones, especially that spot on her shoulder that always made her go weak in the knees and in other places, too. Oh, yeah, he used that knowledge often and expertly in order to get her all turned on, and as fast as possible, at that. It was working admirably, yet again. She moaned with the keenest sort of pleasure, could not help it, as his lips moved up the side of her throat and settled over her mouth again. Thus and therefore, they had at it with lots of feeling and a plethora of it's-been-way-way-too-long carnal enthusiasm. He pulled her onto his lap facing him, and she slid her arms around his neck and entwined her fingers into his hair. His mouth attacked hers with renewed interest, and she responded with equal alacrity, or at least she did until her telephone started ringing.

"Don't even think about it," Black murmured against her throat.

"Sorry. Got to," she muttered, reluctantly disentangling herself, not exactly thrilled about the interruption herself, and yes, just when it was getting good. She left Black muttering under his breath and grabbed her phone off the ledge and looked at Caller ID. "It's Bud. What the hell? He just dropped me off. Something must be wrong."

"Damn it," Black said, seriously not lark-happy anymore. "Tell him we're busy."

Claire ignored him. "What's up, Bud? You okay?"

"Buck just called. We definitely got us a homicide. He says it looks like every bone in that poor guy's body is broken and in ways that couldn't be caused by any kind of fall. He said it's god awful what somebody did to him."

"Man, that's just sick. Is the body still frozen solid?"

"Frozen solid? What body?" That was Black, moving up behind her and pulling her back up against his chest.

Claire concentrated on what Bud was saying, but it took some effort as Black took some more than welcome liberties with his hands. Bud was still talking and she tried her best to listen. "It's still frozen, but Buck can see compound fractures, and he says it looks like there's gonna be a ton of 'em. He can't perform the autopsy until tomorrow. He's gonna call us. Just wanted you to know we're back on homicide for sure. Charlie already pulled us off traffic for good. Thank God."

"Okay, great. Thanks for letting me know."

Black stopped what he was doing and said, "Please tell me that you're not going out again tonight."

"I'm not going out again tonight."

"Did I hear something rather unpleasant about somebody's body being frozen?"

"Yeah, we found a homicide victim out at Ha Ha Tonka. Frozen to the bottom of the cliffs, half in and half out of the water. Wanna hear the gory details?"

"Later. I'm not finished warming you up yet."

Claire was feeling pretty damn warm by now, hot even, but she wanted him to touch her as much as he wanted to, which was their usual state of affairs. She turned around and pressed herself up against him. "Okay, now, where were we?"

He showed her where they were, and it felt very good, and she felt very happy that he was back home and things were heating up so well. Because tomorrow was not going to be quite as pleasant as tonight. In fact, it was probably gonna be downright ghoulish and stomach-turning and horrible. Yep, just another typical day at work.

Blood Brothers

After the fight was over, they carried the poor kid named Hardnose to Loser Land, and just left him lying there, groaning and bleeding and crying. He had to stay there alone a while and suffer some pain to teach him a lesson, and then his father would take him to the doctor, if need be. That was the rule. Punk dragged himself to the back porch and lay down on the bottom step. His head was spinning around and around and making him sick to his stomach. He was seeing two of everything, and he couldn't make them come together. He squeezed his eyes shut because he felt like he was going to throw up. Everybody was leaving now, climbing into their cars and pickup trucks and pulling out on the road with lots of revving engines and roaring motorcycles. And then it was dark and quiet and he felt very alone.

After a while, Pa stopped beside him, his boots planted apart and his fists on his hips. He looked furious. "You know what I gotta do now, don't ya, boy? You acted like a 'fraidy cat out there. It's downright embarrassin' what that woman made you into. You got in one good punch but that's it. Maybe after you spend a coupla nights out in the pen with the dogs, you won't act like a big baby anymore. Now git on out there with them dogs and don't you come outta there 'til I come git you out. You hear that, Punk? You hear what I'm sayin'?"

"Yes, sir."

Punk staggered his way out to the dog runs alongside the barn, and then he felt so completely exhausted that he fell on his hands and knees and crawled the rest of the way. His pa raised coon hounds and beagles to hunt and to breed, as well as some really vicious pit bulls and Rottweilers that he used for the bloody dog fights they had every Wednesday night. Punk hated the way Pa made his older brothers go down into town and steal other people's little poodles and other fluffy little dogs that he called "poms," so that he could use them as bait dogs to rile up the killer dogs. Punk never could bear to watch those tiny little sweet ones get torn apart inside the ring. It made him sick, and he wished he could save them, but there wasn't anything he could do but go off by himself and cry for them.

When he reached the chain-linked gate of the closest dog run, he opened it and crawled inside. The dogs were no longer barking, not now after all the cars had driven away and all the yelling and cheering was over. They were back inside the barn, sleeping, probably. He looped the rope around the post again, and made his way to the swinging dog door. Crawling inside, he lay down in the straw. Most of the dogs were lying around inside, snuggled up close together. Truth was, Punk didn't mind so much being with the dogs. He liked them a lot better than he liked his brothers, except for his twin, who was okay and tried to protect Punk when he could. But he was the only one who did. The rest of them liked to slap him up the side of the head or shove him hard in the back so that he'd fall down in the mud.

It wasn't long before his favorite puppy, a little beagle named Banjo, roused up and left the other pups in her litter, stretched lazily, and walked slowly over to him, her tail wagging. Punk was so tired now that he couldn't sit up any longer, so he collapsed down and lay on his back. Banjo licked his face like she always did, and her little rough tongue felt so good on his cuts and bruises. It was nice that somebody was showing him all that love, almost like his ma used to. That sweet little dog loved him, even if nobody else did. The summer night was cooler now, and after a little while, more of the beagles and coonhounds moved over and settled in close around him, too. They licked his face and kept him warm, just like they always did when Pa punished him and put him inside their pen. He sure did love them, each and every one.

All through the night and every time he roused up, afraid, and not knowing where he was, Banjo licked him and made him feel better. Punk loved it so much that he decided to lick Banjo back and see how that felt. So he started licking the little puppy's nose and found that it felt really good. He closed his eyes and pretended it was his ma he was kissing, that she was back down from Heaven, and all beautiful again with her white hair and pale skin. He wondered if she still looked so pretty underneath the dirt they had shoveled in on top of that plain pine box they'd put her in. He'd like to know that. He wondered if he was strong enough to dig her up and see how she was doing down there all alone. Maybe he would someday. Yeah, he sure would. She was probably awfully lonely, even if she was still sleeping so peacefully while her soul went up to be with God.

After he had licked the dog all over her pretty little head and velvety ears, his nose finally stopped bleeding and he fell fast asleep. He slept for a long time, snuggling closer to the dogs. But then around dawn he was startled awake when his oldest brother came inside the barn. He was tall and strong and had a little beard. He was standing in the middle of the barn and looking into the dog pen at Punk. "You ain't supposed to get no food today, got that, Punk? Pa said no food, no water, and you stay right where you are till he comes gets you out. And you better not, or he'll whup you. He'll whup you good."

Punk didn't say a word. His pa would whup him all right. His whip was hanging right there beside the loft steps, handy for when it was time for him to beat the killer dogs. He knew that from the last time he lost a fight. But he was relieved his big brother didn't drag him out and throw him in the creek to wash off the dirt and sweat and the stink of the dogs. The water was spring fed, and so icy cold that he could barely stand to put his hand in it. Even now, in late August, it was that cold.

Still tensed with dread, he watched the bigger boy move down to the other end of the barn where his pa kept the Rottweilers and pit bulls. Pa usually made his oldest boy tie them up to a post every morning on a very short leash and whip them to make them mean. Punk couldn't stand to see that whip hit those poor animals or hear their yelps of pain and fear, so he quickly pushed his way out of the plastic dog door and into the cool morning air. Banjo came outside with him, and they snuggled up together using the lean-to shelter that shielded them from the hot sun.

They stayed there, huddled together for a time, dozing and keeping each other company. Then Punk began to feel so hungry that he could barely stand it. His stomach was growling so much that he could hear it, and Banjo perked up her ears and cocked her head at the sound it made. He peeked out to see if Pa was around anywhere, and then he crawled back inside the barn and grabbed two handfuls of dog food that his brother had poured into the feeding dishes. He took it back to the shelter and shared the food with Banjo. When he got thirsty, he dipped water out of the trough the dogs used. Back inside the shelter, he fell asleep again, glad that nobody was bothering him.

"Hey, you, Punk, come on over here," came a loud whisper from outside the fence.

Punk's muscles tensed up, but then he saw that it was his twin brother. Pa called him Bone Breaker now. He had a big flaky biscuit and a red apple in his hands. "C'mon out, before I get caught, would ya? I stole you some breakfast. Hurry it up, c'mon! Pa's gonna see me!"

Punk looked around for his pa, but he was nowhere to be seen. He scrambled out and grabbed the apple through the holes in the fence and took a giant bite. He ate it as fast as he could.

"How's that nose feel? You oughta see it. It's all swollen up and black and busted up good, and you know that your eyes are black as old Midnight, don't ya?"

Old Midnight was his pa's favorite pony, a beautiful and sleek animal that nobody got to ride except for Pa. "I figured I was messed up. I can't hardly see nothin' this mornin'. Everythin's all blurry, and stuff."

"Here's some salve and stuff that Pa puts on my bruises. Don't you tell him that I gave it to you, you hear me, Punk? He'll tan my hide for helpin' you."

Nodding, Punk took the little metal jar and rubbed the greasy medicine around his eyes. It hurt to touch the swelled up parts.

"I have to call you Punk, you know," Bone Breaker said. "Pa said so. All of us have to. And they're all callin' me Bones now, too, 'cause I broke that bone in Hardnose's arm. Pa's givin' us all fightin' names now."

"Okay." Punk looked at the only brother who had ever been nice to him. Bones was awfully brave to come out and defy their pa. "You did good last night. Thank you for comin' in and beatin' up that Hardnose kid for me."

"No problem. I like to beat up kids like him. He acts all rough and rowdy until you hit him hard as you can in the face. Then he ain't so tough no more." Bones grinned, very pleased with himself.

"You're real good at fightin'."

"Yeah, I know." Bones looked around. "I better git outta here 'fore Pa comes out. He'll whup me, even if I won and broke that guy's bone. He says he's gonna whup you today, so be ready for it. And remember, don't you yell and cry, or he'll keep it up until you stop."

Punk nodded, but inside he trembled with fear. He had gotten whuppings before, and it really hurt. Pa always used the whip that he used on his fighting dogs. So he went back inside the shelter and gave Banjo half his biscuit, and then he hid there for the rest of the day, hoping his pa would forget about him. But his pa didn't forget about him.

Just when the sun was almost all the way down and it was hard to see anything in the gray light, his pa called out his name from outside the dog pen. Punk cringed down in the straw and held his breath.

"You better come out here, you little sissy punk, or I'll take the hide right off you!" Pa was yelling now, loud and scary. All the dogs got real restless and started barking and howling, afraid, too.

Punk crept out the dog door and stood beside it in the dusk. He began shaking all over, like the leaves on the oak trees around the dog pens. He was terrified. His pa did all kinds of bad things to his boys, and especially to Punk.

"Git over here. Now!"

Swallowing hard, Punk obeyed and walked slowly to the end of the dog run where his pa stood waiting with the whip. He was slapping it in his open palm, hard enough to make a clapping sound. He always did that when he was waiting to punish somebody. Punk moved up to him and stared down at the ground.

"You know why I'm doin' this to you, boy?"

"Yes, sir."

"Why then?"

"'Cause I lost that fight."

"No. Because you are a sissy little punk coward, that's why. And

I'm gonna beat you until you show me some backbone like my other boys do. Give me your hands."

Punk held them out, and Pa tied them to the fence post. Then he hit him once very hard on the back. Punk clamped his jaw, trying not to scream, like Bones had told him. But it hurt. It hurt him so bad.

"Good boy," said Pa. "Now you're bein' a man and takin' it like you oughta."

The crop came down hard again, this time at his waist. He bit his lip until it nearly bled. But tears came out of his eyes, and he tried to wipe them on his shirt before Pa could see them.

"You cryin' now, that what you doin', you sniveling little pig."

When his pa raised the crop again, little Banjo inched closer and started growling at him. When she bared her teeth, Pa laughed. "Hell, lookee look, that damn little pup has more courage than you do. At least, she's got some guts."

But then Pa brought the whip down on Banjo's back as hard as he could, and the little beagle fell on her side, bawling with pain. Horrified, Punk didn't even think about it, he just turned as far as he could on the ropes and kicked his pa's legs as hard as he could. He kept it up, too, yelling cuss words at him until Pa stepped back out of his reach. Pa started laughing.

"Okay, now. That's more like it, kid. Showin' a little spunk now, aren't you, boy? That's what you gotta do, show me some grit and I'll leave you be. Maybe I oughta beat that little puppy there every time you turn coward. Maybe that's what'll light a fire under you and get you as tough as the rest of us. Nothin' else's done it."

Punk said nothing, just ground his teeth together so he wouldn't cry. But inside he was angry, so angry that he could barely stand it. He wanted to grab that whip and beat his father in the face with it. But Pa was untying his hands. Then he turned around and walked off toward the house without another word. Punk fell to his knees and grabbed up Banjo and held her tightly against his chest, licking the little dog's face, comforting her just like Banjo had comforted him the night before. That's when Punk decided that Pa wasn't never gonna hit Banjo again, never. Even if he had to beat some other kid to death in a fight, Pa wasn't ever going to whip poor little Banjo again.

Chapter Three

By the time Claire and Bud arrived at the medical examiner's office late the next morning, the rest of the team had already assembled around the corpse. Fortunately, the forecasters had been wrong and the storm front had not materialized, at least not directly over the lake. Outside, the sun was actually bright and shining and making the mountains of snow sparkle in the balmy nineteen-degree weather. Not a lot of melting going on, however, and that was unfortunate. As they entered the autopsy room where Buck still had the victim's body warming under heat lamps, the first thing Claire noticed was the ultra-serious expressions on her colleagues' faces. The second thing she noted were the x-rays on the light boxes attached to the back wall.

Buck saw her repulsed reaction. "That's right. Every damn bone in his body is either broken or cracked or chipped. Some have pierced through the skin, causing severe compound fractures. This poor man endured a beating like none other that I've seen or heard of in all the many years I've worked here."

Bud moved closer and stared at the x-rays. "So he didn't fall, I take it? He was just dumped down there?"

"Some of the damage could've come from the fall, I reckon. There are lots of cuts and abrasions and bruises. But certainly not to this degree, and certainly not incurred by that kind of fall. The skull is fractured in three different places. If I had to guess, I'd say an aluminum baseball bat or a piece of pipe, maybe even a tire iron or crowbar, something on that order."

"Good grief," Bud muttered, still staring at the films. "I've never seen anything like this, either."

Buckeye nodded. "Certainly not this extensive. I believe this victim was slowly and methodically beaten to death, no question in my mind."

Claire stood beside Bud and studied the skeletal fractures, her mind hovering on the very edge of disbelief, too. "How could anybody do something like this to another human being?"

"The victim probably didn't stay conscious very long, unless the perpetrator saved those blows to his head for last. The pain he suffered would've been excruciating. And look at the body. I've never seen so many bones actually broken and piercing through the skin, except maybe in the very worst car crashes. Look how many there are, and all over the body. This took some time and effort and know-how."

"A crime of passion," Claire said. "Whoever did this hated this guy's guts, no doubt about it, not to my mind."

"Yeah. Or maybe there could've been more than one assailant," Bud said. "It would take a long time to inflict this much damage. We got overkill here. Big-time."

Claire moved back to the body and felt the heat from the lamps warm her cold face. There was water on the steel table under the body from the thawing process. She stared down at the sharp, splintered ends of broken bones sticking out of both forearms. There was another huge wound where about six inches of blunt bare bone from the broken right femur was visible. Some of the victim's fingers and toes were smashed absolutely flat; others had metacarpals protruding. Some of the breaks jutted out at impossible angles. Lord have mercy. It was a horrific sight. She finally averted her eyes, something she usually didn't have to do at an autopsy. Shivering, she shook her head and turned away, not wanting to examine the body further. "You think a fistfight might've gotten out of control?"

"Maybe it could've started that way, but it looks to me like the victim didn't do much to defend himself, or he couldn't. Maybe he was too drunk to hold his own or there were too many assailants. There are rope burns around his wrists that look as if he were bound, maybe hung up somehow. Take a look at his hands. No defensive wounds. All those injuries have been inflicted by the killer."

Buckeye was right. She didn't think the poor man had been able to defend himself because he had been strung up by the arms. They needed to go back to the park and look for any evidence of that. Suspended from a tree limb, maybe. "Any idea yet who this guy is? Any tats or identifying scars?"

Buckeye shook his head. "Nope. No ID or clothing or jewelry, either. Shaggy's in there right now running his prints through our databases but hasn't got a hit yet so he's probably not gonna get one."

"What can you tell us?"

"Caucasian male. Twenty to twenty-five years old, I'd say, maybe a little older. In good physical condition, good muscle tone. Looks like he was healthy and well-nourished before he was killed. Some scars, but nothing noteworthy. Looks like he might've gotten them in fistfights. I'll have to wait until I get inside to see what kind of internal damage was incurred, but it's gonna be extensive. I'd be pretty comfortable saying there is lots of internal bleeding, probably ruptured liver and stomach and other internal organs, certainly collapsed lungs, one or both, probably both. More than one rib is protruding. You can see some of the damage right here." He pointed to the frontal x-ray of the victim's chest.

Claire grimaced. She could see it all right. Every rib was cracked or broken in two. "This killer is brutal and thorough. He knew his physiology and didn't stop until nearly every bone in this man's body was splintered. Looks almost like a ritualistic killing. You know, method to his madness, something like that. I bet this isn't the first person he's beaten to death. God, I'm afraid we're gonna turn up some more homicides with similar MOs."

Buck said, "He probably just hid the others better."

Bud frowned. "Then why did he leave this one out in the open where we could find him?"

Claire looked at Buck. "Could be he dumped the body when it was dark and snowing hard. The wind could have been swirling up so that he couldn't see the bottom of the cliff. Truth is, we probably would never have found him this soon if he hadn't landed sitting up in the water like that. That's pretty hard to miss. Maybe not even until the spring thaw. Maybe not even then, if the animals got to him first. Or, it could be that he did him and dumped him out in the lake somewhere and the wind and waves pushed him in against the shore, right down there where we found him."

They all stood around the table in silence, staring down at the broken and battered body of the unknown young murder victim.

"We might ought to order a full search at the bottom of all the cliffs throughout the park," Claire said at length. "Serials usually have their favorite dumping grounds. Maybe the park is his. Maybe he sinks them to the bottom, and this one got loose and came up, or maybe the ice shifted and pushed him up."

Bud wasn't convinced. "Doesn't make sense to me. Tourists are everywhere around there, taking pictures, and so are the park rangers. Too dangerous for him."

"Hey, Claire. Bud, my man. 'Sup?"

That was their resident hippie, Shaggy, back from his office and the running of fingerprints. He was decked out in his usual surfer garb, despite the winter weather outside. But he did have on long-sleeved white thermal underwear under his black-and-white-and-red orchid-flowered Hawaiian shirt. He had recently cut off his dread-locks, or at least they didn't hang all the way to his shoulders any-more. But he still had his earrings, all eight of them in each ear. But, despite his bohemian fashion sense, he was absolutely top-notch at his job and probably the best criminalist in the state of Missouri. Canton County got him because he loved the lake and everything that went with it. Claire adored the guy. He was one of her best friends, although they didn't spend as much time together since Black had come along and tended to monopolize her off hours.

"You get a hit on those prints?" Buckeye asked quickly.

"Nope. How's he cookin'? Done yet?"

"He's thawing quickly now."

"When you cuttin' him, boss?" Shaggy asked, staring down at the broken corpse. Then he leaned closer to the victim's face. He stood up and shot a startled look at Bud. "Hey, you know what, man? I think I might've seen this guy before. Wow, and just the other night, too. Dudes, I can't believe this. I think I know this dude."

Claire couldn't believe it, either. But she sure hoped to hell that

Shaggy could ID the deceased because they certainly didn't have any other way to get his name. She watched Shaggy lean down close to the victim's bearded face again. It was still bluish and pale and smooth as marble, looking almost like a clothing store's mannequin but he'd been a nice-looking guy. The whole body was pale, in fact, except for some faded tan lines around the neck and the upper arms, as if he had always worn a shirt when out in the sun.

"Well, who is it?" she prompted.

"Well, I tell you what I'm a thinkin'. This dude here? He looks an awful lot like one of those cage fighters I saw over at the Lake Inn Resort a coupla nights ago. You know the ones, don't ya, those mixed martial arts guys that beat the crap outta each other inside a chain-linked cage. God, they are stinkin' beasts, I tell you. Blood sprays out everywhere and runs down their arms when they hit each other. It's great stuff, man."

"Yeah, that's the MMA guys, all right. I've seen them on the tube," Bud said. "They're crazy, those guys. They box, wrestle, use their feet to kick, and everything else you can think of. And then there's the bare knuckles guys. Talk about savage."

Claire looked down at the body again. "Well, that certainly fits our victim's injuries."

Bud said, "They don't use baseball bats, but just about anything else goes. I doubt if this was a sanctioned match, if it even was an MMA fighter. Maybe a black market bout like they do out in the boonies where nobody can find them. I've heard of that going on around here. Practically everywhere else nowadays, too, or so I've heard. You know kids wantin' to be like the heroes they watch fight on TV."

"How stupid can somebody get," Claire said, irritated. "Who would agree to get into a ring without any rules and just beat up on each other?"

"Hey, Claire, there's big money in the cities for winnin' bouts. It's a big deal in St. Louis, with fights held in the arena and everything. Kansas City, New Orleans, lots of places have 'em now."

"Any fight clubs or karate places around here that would cater to a guy like this?" Claire asked Shaggy.

"Yeah, lots of 'em."

"Where's that place where you saw him fight, Shaggy? We need to pay them a call."

"It's the Lake Inn Resort, over off Highway 54, down in a hollow right on the lake.

You know, it's got a big flashy red-and-green neon sign that moves like a fisherman catching a bass. 'Member? The bass looks like it's jumpin' up the line and into the boat with him? You've seen it. I know you have."

Buck said, "Yeah, they have bass fishing contests out there, too. It's pretty redneck, but they've got a great golf course. I played there once. Best round I ever played."

Claire didn't remember the place, but why would she? She spent all her time at Black's hotel and resort, quite a honey of a place by the name of Cedar Bend Lodge, which was way too classy and up-scale to host any sort of a bloody fight night. Nobody dripped blood on Black's elegant décor, uh-uh, a very big no-no. Except for her, oh, yeah. She'd come home bleeding a time or two, much to Black's chagrin. Hers, too, actually. "Well, we'll just have to pay them a visit. Can we get a picture of his face, Buck? Maybe somebody can give us his name."

"Sure. Shaggy'll get it for you. You need it now?"

"Yeah. We've got time to get out there before dark. I want to interview everyone involved in that fight you saw, Shaggy. Was it held on the property?"

"Yeah. Lake Inn's got a big convention center kinda place out back for parties and dances and whatnot. They put up this cage thing right in the middle of it. First time I'd ever been down there. Wow, it's awesome to watch. You just can't sit on the front row or you might get some blood spatter on your clothes, especially if they start pushin' each other's faces up against that cage. I tell you, it's awesome, dudes."

Claire frowned. "That's not awesome. That's gross."

"Nah. They mop up any spilled blood quick enough. Haven't you ever been to a prize fight, or nothin'?"

"No, and I won't be going to one anytime soon. Like I said, they are stupid shows put on by stupid people."

"Well, I sat way back on the bleachers, but I sure do think this's one of the guys who was fighting that night. Not positive about it, but pretty sure."

"Did he win or lose?"

"He won. Bloodied up the other guy pretty bad. He was bigger and looked stronger, but this guy here, well, he was like some kinda whirlin' dervish, or something. Quick as all get out. He just didn't ever stop until his opponent was pinned down and called for an end to it. Never seen anything quite like it. He had some wrestlin' skills, oh, yeah, you shoulda seen it."

"Well, I still think it's dumb. Two grown men getting inside a ring and punching each other until one is knocked unconscious. Just plain ignorant."

"I thought you liked to kickbox."

"I do, but I do it for my own self-protection, not to entertain a crowd of bloodthirsty people holding their thumbs up or down like in the gladiator days."

Nobody disagreed with that, but Claire had a feeling all her male colleagues liked boxing and fighting and bloodletting just fine, and the bloodier, the better. Black certainly did. Men and their testosterone jollies. Jeez.

"Hold on, I'm gonna pull up that place's site on the net and see if I got this right. Don't move." Shaggy ran off toward his office with his usual boyish enthusiasm.

Claire looked at Bud. "Guess we need to do some research on cage fighters in this area, and anybody else connected to this so-called sport."

"That's gonna take us till summer."

"I'm right!" yelled Shaggy from the other room. They watched him through the window as he came rushing back into the autopsy room. "His name is Paulie Parker. Ring name is Parker the Punisher. He's a real tough kid, who's been comin' up fast in MMA circles. He fought last week, too, up in KC. I saw it go down on the tube but didn't put that together till now. That's how I knew about him comin' down here. He won up there, too, beat up the other guy real good. Broke his nose."

"Maybe we'd be better off getting the names of his opponents. All of them probably have some issues with this Parker guy," Claire said.

"The guy Parker beat over there at the Lake Inn? Name's Frankie Velez, but he calls himself Pancho Villa, you know, after that Mexican guy who did somethin' down in Mexico once upon a time. Don't remember what. But Parker's from down around here. They say he lives somewhere out around the lake."

"Any address on him?"

"No, but it says he got his start at a fight club over around Lebanon. They called it the Knock Down Drag Out."

Bud laughed. "Well, that's highly appropriate. Pretty much nails what goes on in those places."

"Okay, Bud, let's go. Shaggy, you got a location for that place?"

"Highway 54, too. That's all it says. Can I go, too, Claire? Maybe we could watch some of the guys spar? Get some autographs, stuff like that?"

"Don't think so."

"Okay, but if you see that Pancho dude anywhere, tell him that I'm a big fan of his. He just had a tough night, and the Punisher's an all-out beast."

"Oh, yeah, sure, can't wait to meet him," Claire said, letting her unenthusiastic tone do the talking.

Shaggy just grinned. "Want me to see what else I can pull up on those guys?"

"Sure, and print it out. That would help us big-time. Thanks."

"No problem. I do love me that MMA stuff. I'll e-mail you anything else I find, too."

Buckeye said, "Well, first, you're gonna finish processing this guy. Then you can play on the Internet."

"No problem. Not much to process, except his DNA."

And there lies the problem, Claire thought, but at least they had some good leads now. Mixed martial arts was a new concept for her, new and alien and absurd, at least from her point of view. But to each his own. And Parker's fighting connections matched the kind of wounds found on his body. It wasn't going to be a slam dunk, but it was a start. So square one, here we come.

Afterward, they stood by, breathing masks in place, and reluctantly viewed the autopsy, and then they took off, fairly eager to get out of the morgue and away from the horrifically injured body and into the interviews. They were halfway out the door to the parking lot when Shaggy came running down the hall after them. "Hey, Bud, dude, wait up. I got something to tell you!"

They stopped, came back inside, and waited by the door for him. Shaggy skidded to a stop in front of them, but then started hemming and hawing around like he was big-time nervous or had forgotten what he was going to say. But that was Shaggy for you. Nobody ever knew what he was going to say next, even him.

"Bud, I'm just gonna have to say it, man. Brianna's come back home. She wants to see you."

Mightily startled by that little tidbit of news, Claire darted a quick glance at Bud. His face had blanched as white as their beaten and broken corpse, mouth open a little, if only by the pure shock. Nope, he had not been expecting that to come out of Shaggy's mouth, either. Brianna Swensen was Shaggy's sister, and an old girlfriend of Bud's, one who had been involved in one of their homicide cases and had been terribly injured as a result. Bud never mentioned her anymore, but Claire was pretty sure he had never gotten over her, either.

"Bri's here? At the lake?" he finally got out after a few seconds of stunned silence.

"Yeah, she's stayin' out at my house. She wasn't sure you'd even want to see her, or nothin'." Now Shaggy really looked uncomfortable. "You know, the way she just took off on ya, and all that crap."

Awk-ward, Claire thought. Then they stood there in a very uncomfortable silence and waited for Bud to say something. He didn't. Still flabbergasted, she guessed. They waited some more.

Finally, at long last, Bud said, "Sure. I want to see her. Sure I do."

Despite the double amount of *sures*, he didn't sound the least bit overeager, oooh, no, not at all. It sounded more to her like Bud was dragging his feet or being overly polite or mumbling out something that he wouldn't remember later. But it was enough for Shaggy to don a great big wide grin. "Awesome, man. I'll tell her. Maybe she'll give you a call. Or you can call her. You got my home number."

Bud nodded, turned around, and headed out the door. He didn't say a single word more, just climbed into the driver's seat and started up the engine. Claire joined him, waiting for him to want to talk about it. He backed out and drove out of the parking lot in silence. Okay, he was mulling it over in his head and didn't want to get chatty about his old love. Claire could relate. There were people she didn't want to talk about, too. People she didn't want to think about, either. A lot of them, in fact. Bud knew she was there any time he wanted to talk about anything. He was her rock at times, and vice versa. So they rode on in silence, Bud no doubt mulling over in his head all the ramifications of Brianna being back, meaning the good, the bad, and the ugly. Claire spent the quiet time thinking about Black and wishing they were back in that hot tub again with all that water sloshing over the sides.

Chapter Four

In the bright afternoon sunshine, The Knock Down Drag Out looked as if more than a few people had been knocked down and dragged out, all right. Ramshackle, rusted, seedy, it definitely needed a care-taker or two by the looks of the four feet of snow on the sagging cor-rugated tin roof. There was a house trailer on the same lot, held up on concrete blocks and of equally squalid description. A car's motor was hanging off a giant oak tree limb in the front of the trailer and a chicken-wire dog pen holding six snarling pit bulls, who all, to a dog, looked cold, miserable, and murderous. They started barking and salivating at the sight of Claire and Bud as soon as they climbed out of Bud's Bronco. Probably thought they were lunch on the hoof.

Out on the shoulder of a two-lane highway running through Lebanon, four old beat-up pickup trucks sat unoccupied because the parking lot had not yet been cleared, even after two full days of heavy snowfall. A copper-colored Mercedes sat alone across the road, late model and shiny and expensive, all of which Claire found highly in-teresting. Hmm. Maybe a scruple-empty somebody was making beaucoup money off the young idiots who went inside a chain-link cage and beat each other to bloody meat each and every night. Maybe she wanted to talk to him.

Bud glanced over at the yapping, howling critters who probably considered both of them delicious-looking Whoppers with Cheese. "Well, these guys can't be all bad. They're dog lovers."

"Or they run a dog fighting operation," Claire said. "Hope so. There's nothing I like to bust more than jerks who abuse animals."

They slugged their way through knee-high drifts to the front of the building and stared at the dented front door. Maybe they used it as a battering ram for practicing their head butts. That wouldn't surprise Claire. The snow had been shoveled slightly around the entrance, but only in a narrow path from the ersatz fight club to the seedy trailer and highly agitated dogs. So they climbed over some more impressive snowbanks until they reached the cleared-off part.

"This bites, all right, but not as much as standing out in intersections dodging out-of-control cars," Bud said. "I hate winter. I love summer. I love Florida. I love the tropics."

"Just think of the good things about winter, Bud. You know, Christmas and snowmen and sleigh bells and hot tubs."

"Yeah, right. All that's fine and dandy, but Christmas is long over, and we're freezing our butts off day and night. And we don't all have hot tubs in our living room."

"You can use mine anytime you want. I told you that."

"Yeah, that'll be real cozy. You and me and Nick. I hate to think of what I'd have to witness."

Claire laughed. She couldn't imagine him being in the tub with them, either. Not after their little romp last night. "Okay, just remember what we're here for. Somebody around here might've beaten that poor kid to death, possibly with various and sundry deadly weapons. The perpetrator could very well be inside. Don't start anything. They're bruisers and trained fighters, and we're too cold to be on top of our game."

Bud looked at her, highly incredulous. "Me, start things? Ha! You're the one who usually throws the first punch."

"C'mon, I only do that when I have to. And I can tell you right now. I'm not going to incite some ultimate fighters into a bout of fisticuffs. I'm not that dumb, and I don't want to have to shoot anybody this early in the case."

"Hey, I know. Just hit 'em with that big ring Nick gave you. That oughta put out their lights, if the glare doesn't blind them first." Bud laughed at his own cleverness. "Maybe we shoulda brought along a Brink's truck to keep it safe."

"Ha-ha. You're just jealous, is all." But Claire shouldn't have worn it on her finger. That's all she'd gotten all day long from her colleagues at the office, jokes about the size of her glaringly giant diamond solitaire engagement ring. She knew better, of course. She'd only put it on her finger that morning in order to please Black, who was surreptitiously watching to see where she'd wear it and all the while trying to hide his keen interest, but interested he had been. However, there were limits to how long she could endure being the butt of engagement ring jokes, even good-natured ones. She was quickly reaching hers. The hidden-on-a-chain-around-her-neck idea was sounding better all the time.

Unfortunately, Bud was not finished with his jabs, probably trying to get his mind off the beauteous and newly arrived Brianna. "Yeah, I guess all I need is a rich girlfriend. A female version of Nick, maybe. Now that's a scenario I could go for. Bud Davis, adored by a filthy rich woman and loved to death in a hot tub. Do I ever like the sound of that, man alive, whoo-hoo."

Well, that hit pretty damn close to home. "Very funny. And it's not my money, if you recall. It's Black's money. I have to earn a paycheck, just like you do. Long hours, cold hours, cold-blooded murderers, the whole nine yards."

"Yeah, yeah, I've heard all that before. Hell, I could buy a brand-new house with that rock you're wearing. Or a brand-new designer wardrobe. Something Italian maybe. Outta Milan. Oh, yeah, Milan duds. That's what I'd buy first with it, if my rich lady gave me her credit card. And she would."

"Would you just shut up about the damn ring already, or I'm gonna take it off."

Bud laughed. "Better not. Nick'll get mad and not shower you with cash anymore. He might even ban you from his private jet. Oooooh, how could you stand it?"

"Just shut it, would you?" Claire usually just ignored his friendly joshing, almost getting used to it by now. Down deep, though, she didn't like those kinds of jokes. She usually didn't like snooty, filthy rich people, either, avoided them like the plague, in fact. But Black was different, sort of. At least he was generous and not stingy and uppity like most of them, and he had earned every dime of the money he had. But she wasn't rich or entitled or anything else remotely re-sembling it. She worked hard for a living, just like Bud and Shaggy and Buck and everybody else she knew. Black worked hard for his money, too, damn it.

Thankfully, Bud changed the subject back to work. "Something tells me this isn't the primo address for the A-list cage fighters that we watch on TV."

"No kidding."

"Ever been in this kind of place?"

"Nope. Thank goodness."

"Okay, take a real deep breath. I think you're gonna need it once we walk in that door."

As it turned out, he was dead on. It was steamy hot inside, which was the only good thing about it. It smelled bad, of sweat and testosterone and the two big bloodhounds lying on the floor beside the door. Something was cooking. Some kind of meat was frying in a skillet, smoky, unappetizing, at least to Claire. The club was comprised of one big room with two round cages inside, both with padded floors and plastic wire sides. Two morons were now inside, practicing their craft by pummeling the hell out of each other sans boxing gloves or shoes. Lord have mercy, and thank God she had been born with a brain.

"Hope I don't get blood on my jacket," Bud said. "I just got it dry cleaned. Twenty bucks and change."

Bud worried about such eventualities because there was indeed a lot of blood flying around. Nobody seemed to notice that or the fact that two law enforcement officers had entered the building. All were merrily intent on the bloodletting. If this was practice, Claire would hate to see the real thing. She had a feeling that she was going to have to watch a lot of this stuff before they solved their case. Wonderful.

"These guys are crazy," Bud said softly. "I wonder how many of them end up with brain damage. That's what I'd worry about."

"Yeah, you and me both."

At one side of the room and behind a long bar made out of carpenter's trestles and wide wood planks, a man was cooking something in an electric skillet. It smelled like beef steak, maybe, sizzling in serious amounts of lard. The chef was watching the sparring young men, too, incongruously turning the meat with a long fork while wearing an expensive three-piece black suit. He had a white towel over his arm à la the waiters at Two Cedars, the fancy-schmancy restaurant in Black's Cedar Bend Lodge. When he noticed them, he stared at them a moment and then gave them a big smile. "These guys are always hungry for meat after they fight."

Yeah, probably raw hamburger. She was surprised he was cooking it. She glanced at the cages, in one of which was a kid sitting on the other one's chest, hitting him in the head. She frowned. "Yeah? If they have any teeth left to chew it with."

The man laughed, unfortunately not offended. He looked to be around forty years old, graying at the temples with wavy salt-and-pepper locks that hung to his collar. He had a thick accent which indicated that he did not grow up within a thousand miles of mid Missouri. Oh, yeah, he definitely hailed from Brooklyn or the Bronx or Poland, maybe. He wasn't that bad looking, except that both ears slightly resembled cauliflower blossoms, both in size and color, thus indicating a healthy knowledge of all things brutal. But he was pleasant enough when he said, "What can I do for you officers on this cold bright beautiful day?"

"How'd you know who we were?" Bud asked, always the curious detective.

"You got the look."

Claire didn't inquire further, because she didn't give a damn. She pulled out the chain with her badge and held it up for him. "We're Canton County Sheriff's detectives. I'm Detective Morgan. This is Detective Davis."

"That can't be real," he said and gave her an amused little smirk.

Claire frowned. She didn't quite cotton to that remark. "The badges are real all right. We got real weapons, too, if you'd like to see them pointed at you."

"I meant that ring you got on. God, it's the size of a freakin' Fig Newton. What's a matter wit' you, girl? Everybody's gonna know right off that it's a fake. It's goddamn gaudy. You gotta tell your guy to get you somethin' real instead of that glass trinket so you ain't embarrassin' yourself like this in front of people who know the real thing when they see it. Better for you if it's real, I'm tellin' you, even if it's little bitty. You're hookin' up with a cheapskate, trust me. That thing must be twenty carats, at the very least, all fake and made outta glass and silver plate, probably."

Bud barked out a genuine laugh and then cut it off and looked warily at Claire.

Claire fought the urge to pull her weapon on the smug, ring-appraising imbecile. Hell, she probably couldn't get her Glock out without her cheap, Fig Newton-sized trinket obstructing her draw time. And Black had told her that it was only fifteen carats, anyway, which showed how much that moron knew about flawless white diamonds, and it sure as hell wasn't as big as any Fig Newton, either. A Cheez-It, maybe, or a Frosted Miniwheat, or probably more like a Peanut M&M squared off some, but no cookie or cracker any bigger than that. And Black said it was set in platinum, not silver plate anything. So why did everybody she meet find it necessary to exaggerate about Black's damn ring? It was getting downright ridiculous. With some effort having to be exerted, she restrained herself. She presented him with a tight rendition of a false smile. He was just stupid. She had to remember that. It was almost cute how stupid he was.

"We're not really here to discuss your opinion of my jewelry, sir. We're here concerning a homicide investigation."

That obviously took him aback. "Homicide? Who got killed?"

"Is now a good time to ask you a few questions?"

"Like what?"

"Like what's your name and your business here?"

He took plenty of time turning over another steak before answering. "Name's Sonny Randazzo. Dazz, for short. And I own this place. Keep it running out here in the sticks so my scouts can find my fight company some raw talent to develop."

Claire watched him fork up a huge sirloin steak and carefully transfer it to a paper towel covered plate. Behind her, one of the contestants in the ring screamed. It sounded rather painful, and she tried not to look, but couldn't help herself. The fighter was writhing around on the mat, moaning and groaning and a good amount of blood gushing out of his nose. The other guy was being glad-handed by his handlers. High fives even. Sick, sick, and more sick, oh, yeah. But back to business.

"Well, Dazz, by the looks of that Mercedes outside, I'd say you can afford to buy your boys over there a pair of boxing gloves. Maybe even a face guard and mouthpiece, to boot. You know, just to cut down on broken bones and black eyes."

"What are you, anyways, detective, a softie? Just like a girl to say somethin' like that. My fighters are as tough as nails. Those kids don't need a goddamn thing inside that ring except their hands and their feet. They got those four deadly weapons. Don't need nothing else."

"Wow, somehow the term *blatant exploitation* occurs to me."

"Don't kid yourself, lady. They beg me to let them fight."

Claire narrowed her eyes. This guy was seriously chewing up her reserve of police politeness. She fought an urge to smash him in the face with Black's gaudy, cheapo, embarrassing glass ring.

Bud said, "I wouldn't provoke her like that, if I were you. She's not as soft as you think she is."

"Ha! What's this sweet little lady gonna do, hit me with her big fake ring?"

Okay, that did it. The ring was going back on the chain and around her neck and hidden under her sweatshirt, as soon as they got back in the car. But hey, this guy was just asking for it. "Well, I tell you one thing this little lady's gonna do to you, Dazz, she's gonna run you in to the Canton County Sheriff's Department so that you'll cooperate in a homicide investigation or sit in a cell until you do."

"Uh-oh, now I'm shakin' in my Italian loafers. And unlike that ring, mine are the genuine article. Straight outta Rome, Italy."

Bud jerked a look down to see if they really were real, no doubt, and then he looked at Claire and shook his head. "Those are cheap knockoffs, man. Somebody took you for a ride."

"No, they're not. I got them in Memphis last week, right out of the box."

"Yeah, right."

Oh, for God's sake, Claire thought, *can this interview get any more stupid?* "Is there somewhere we can sit down and talk, Mr. Randazzo? Or do you need to turn off your skillet and get your coat on?"

"Okay, okay, we can talk back in my office. Hey, Woodrow, come up here and finish cooking these steaks for the boys. I got business."

A little old guy came rushing up. He looked like he probably had cauliflower ears, too, under his knitted dark blue sock hat. He was wizened, to say the least. She didn't use *wizened* much in official descriptions, but he fit that moniker big-time. He looked around ninety plus, grizzled as all get out, faded blue eyes, gold front tooth in an otherwise rather nice smile. He didn't say anything but he nodded an acknowledgment of their presence and started checking on Randazzo's meat.

"Follow me, officers," Dazz said.

Well, at least he didn't call himself Dazzle or Dazzler—that would've been a little much, even for a guy of his obnoxiousness level. His office was walled off from the bloody beat downs going on at the moment, which probably occurred every instant the establishment was open. Inside Dazz's personal space, it looked like a showroom at Pottery Barn, especially when lined up against the hillbilly setup and sawdust on the floors outside his door.

"Please take a chair. And that's real leather, by the way."

They all sat down. Nobody said anything. Nobody was very impressed with the leather, either, real or otherwise. Nobody wanted to be there. Especially Claire.

Loafers Aficionado Dazz said, "Can I get you a drink? Bourbon? Scotch? Beer?"

"We're on duty, sir." Claire hated him. She really, really did. Even after five minutes, her you-loathsome-pig-you barometer was pushing its needle into the extreme disgust and annoyance range. She bet he beat his wife, too. "Is your wife well, Dazz?"

"My wife? Yeah, I guess. I ain't seen her in couple of weeks. Been out on the road with my fighters."

"What fighters?"

"Not those guys outside. They're just training for bare knuckles, tryin' to get a start in the legit business. I decided to give 'em a chance, if and when Woody thinks they're ready."

"So you do train your fighters?"

"Oh, yeah. They need to know all sorts of moves. It's mixed martial arts, you know. Not just street brawling. There's a real art to it."

Could've fooled me, Claire thought, but she said again, "What fighters?"

"Well, I got three or four that I usually travel with out here in these parts. A few other guys come along sometimes. I've got a big operation outta New Jersey. Top-notch. Lots of contenders."

"Right," said Claire, going in for try number three. "What fighters?"

"Paulie Parker, Frankie Velez, Malachi Fitch, Shorty Dunlop, to name a few of the best. I got a second tier, too."

"Where are these guys now?"

"They've probably already landed in St. Louis. We got a gig there on Friday and Saturday. We were in KC last week, won all our bouts, too. I gave them time off to, well, you know."

"To what? Heal up? Get over their concussions? Buy themselves some boxing gloves?"

Bud laughed.

Dazz shook his head. "You don't like our sport much, I take it?"

"I don't care to watch exploited young men beating each other up, no."

"I take offense to that, detective."

"You should. It was meant harshly."

He frowned. Claire frowned. Bud frowned, probably because she was frowning and he knew what that meant. She wasn't in a good mood anymore. Her joy at the sunshine and bright day and Black being home was long gone. Gone to hell, in fact. Something told her that her loathing was starting to show. But the phony jerk sitting across from them made her feel woozy with disregard. Bud decided to take over, which was probably a good thing.

"Okay, Randazzo. Let's cut the crap. Do you know where Paulie Parker is right now?"

"No, I sure don't. But he's a big boy. He don't need no chaperone to baby him." He looked directly at Claire. The self-satisfied smirk was back. "I bet the guy who gave you that rock has his hands full with you, huh, sweetie? I bet you give him what-for."

Claire stared at him without blinking and let Bud handle him. Randazzo seemed adept at pushing her buttons so she wouldn't give him the satisfaction. Said buttons were now on lockdown. Bud saw and knew the score so he'd deal with this guy. That's the good thing about partners. Sometimes it was the other way around, and she had to intercede before Bud threw some irksome guy through a window. They couldn't help it. Neither of them was patient and/or fond of nasty, in-your-face creeps. It was just a thing with them.

Quiet for a moment, she calmed herself and got her second wind. "Your big boy? Paulie Parker? Guess what? He's dead. Beaten to death with a baseball bat or similar weapon."

Claire watched the blood drain out of Randazzo's face. He started stammering. "W-w-what? No way. You're lyin'. Don't do that to me." He placed his hand over his heart. "Now don't be makin' jokes about Paulie. You wanna give me a coronary, or somethin'?"

"I'm not lying to you, sir. So now maybe you should try to be a little more forthcoming."

"He won his last match with Frankie over there at the lake, but he wasn't hurt all that bad. What happened? Where is he now?"

"We found his body in Ha Ha Tonka State Park," Bud told him. "Did you know he was still in Canton County?"

He shook his head, no more smirks, no sirree. "He was supposed to fly out with the other boys. I know he was born around the lake somewhere, but I don't know exactly where. He fought down there before he got to the top tier." Randazzo sank back into his swivel chair and rocked back and forth. "Oh, shit, I can't believe this. Paulie's my top draw."

Disgusted, Claire shook her head. "That's cold, Dazz. Even for you. You really are a dirt bag, aren't you?"

"No, no, uh-uh, I love the guy, 'course, I do. But I got a business here to run. Who beat him up? Tell me."

"That's what we want to know. How about your other guys? Velez, maybe? He have a beef with Paulie Parker since Paulie beat him bloody at the lake the other night?"

"Nah. They get along okay. All of these guys are from around these parts. They're pretty tight. You oughta be able to find most of my fighters at the Holiday Inn in downtown St. Louis. That's where I'm puttin' 'em up until they fight this weekend. Except for Shorty Dunlop. He's still in the hospital up there in KC. Broke his damn ankle falling on the ice, but not before he won his bout fair and square against Ike Sharpe. Good win, that was. Nothin' but a freak accident, falling down the wrong way on that left foot, so he's gonna be laid up a while and off the circuit. I talked to Shorty just this morning, just to make sure he was gonna be okay. Doctors want him to stay off that foot for a while."

"Do any of your fighters have any reason to harm Mr. Parker? Any bad blood or death threats? Anything like that?"

"No, no, no." He jumped up and started pacing around. "They get along just fine, I'm tellin' you. They're all fierce competitors, but they're great friends outside the ring. They're all buds, I'm tellin' you. All my assets like one another. You ain't gonna find any killers in my stable. Forget about it."

Randazzo pronounced it *fergeddaboudit* like Tony Soprano and other New Jersey mobster characters. Claire wondered for the first time if this Ultimate Fighting thing could be mob-related. That could explain the kid being beaten to death with a baseball bat. *The Sopranos* were in reruns now, and she was pretty sure she remembered a baseball bat scene. Bats were always such readily available deadly weapons. Even she had one in her backseat.

Dazz was still rambling on. "I cannot believe this. I *cannot believe* this. Parker could take care of himself. He was good, one of the best. Fought like a demon inside the cage. Quick as lightning. Oh, God, this is just awful, awful." For the first time, he looked and sounded human. Almost. "How am I gonna break this to his wife?"

Bud and Claire perked up. Bud said, "We can make that notification for you. Can you give us his wife's name and address?"

"Her name's Blythe, Blythe Parker, and she lives over at the lake. They got them a nice big house over there up high on one of those hills. Lake view, and everything. I pay my boys good, just like I told you. Tell her we'll take care of her. Tell her not to worry 'bout anything."

"What's that address?"

He gave Claire one that she wasn't familiar with so she wrote it down in her notepad. "We're gonna need to talk to those other fighters. Can you arrange interviews?"

"Yeah, but you're gonna have to come to St. Louis to do it. I got contractual obligations over there this weekend and all next week, too. No way can I break 'em."

"Tell us about your other fighters."

Randazzo began to list them, basically by their adeptness in the cage and their whereabouts on the rankings. "All of 'em have probably made it to St. Louis by now, except for Shorty. Like I told ya, he's still in the hospital up there in Kansas City. Ike got him pretty good in the noggin a couple of times, too. He'll come through, all right, though. I told him to take all the time he needed to get over the dizzy spells and get to walking again. You know, he's got blurred vision and all that kinda stuff. Won't take him long to recover, though. He's a little guy, but he's a hard case."

"You're a prince," Claire said, trying not to grit her teeth. She envisioned getting him out back in an alley and showing him what the little lady could do with her own hands and feet. Maybe while wearing brass knuckles. She'd give him all the time he needed to get over his dizzy spells and blurred vision and inability to walk, too.

For the next thirty minutes, they questioned him at length, got quite a bit of nothing else out of him. But, nevertheless, enough for the next round of interviews. Despite his fast talk and sociopathic-like lack of true feelings, Randazzo turned out a lot like the three monkeys of legend. He saw nothing, he heard nothing, and he spoke of nothing that would help them one iota except for the name of Paulie's wife. But he was not off Claire's hook. Claire would just love to arrest him, and took the time to look around his office for a bloody baseball bat on her way out. She didn't see one, but hey, maybe she'd still get the chance. He wasn't off her list of suspects, not by a long shot.

Blood Brothers

On the same day that Punk learned all about hatred and protecting his little beagle puppy, his pa held another fight out in their cow pasture. But this time only Punk and his brothers fought, and they fought one another. They started with his oldest two brothers first. Pa made them strip down naked and fight with bare knuckles. He pushed them out into the dirt ring, shouting degrading and humiliating things the whole time.

"Okay, boys, let's see some blood now," he called out. "You ain't stoppin' till one of you is lyin' down there on the ground and beggin' for mercy. Do it, or I'll do it for you, by God."

Punk sat beside Pa and watched his brothers go at it. It was hard to watch, the way they were kicking at each other and biting and trying to jab fingers into each other's eyes. He averted his gaze, unable to watch, and wished that Bones was there with him. Then there came a terrible jolting blow to his ear, hard enough to knock him off the bench. He held his head and whimpered as Pa leaned down close.

"You keep them eyes open, you hear me, boy. Then maybe you'll learn somethin' from your big brothers out there actin' like men."

So Punk kept his eyes open, but he tried to think about other things as the fight went on and on, until the younger one fell half-conscious and exhausted in the dirt. His pa jumped up. "Good job, Tiger. You're the best fighter by far. Go on inside now and grab yourself a beer. The rest of you drag that loser over to the table. I'll deal with him later."

"Want us to doctor him up, Pa?" said his next oldest son.

"No, let 'im bleed out for a while. Teach him to try harder."

So they left him in the dirt under the picnic table, bleeding from his nose and mouth and his cut-up fists. The second set of boys walked into the ring, and his pa hit the bell with his hammer. "Now let me see some spilled blood, or I'll whup you both myself. Hear me, do you hear me!"

It was then, in that moment, that Punk truly began to hate his father's guts. He hated him with all his being, with all his heart and soul. Pa was evil, just like his ma had always whispered to Punk. He was cruel and mean and horrible.

The second fight was even worse than the first one. The boys were still too young to have developed big muscles and were skinny and uncoordinated. They whaled on each other for as long as they could until they both fell onto their knees in the dirt, exhausted and bleeding and crying.

"You weaklings, just look at you, out there blubberin' like little freakin' girls. What? A few blows and you give up. Good God, you oughta be ashamed of yourself. Now git on out there to that dog pen and stay there, you little shits. Now you both is gonna have to answer to me and the business end of that whip o' mine."

Angry, Pa stood up and paced around the dirt circle, shaking his head and ramming his fist into his palm. "I'm a telling you, I've never seen such a bunch of sissies. Hell, when I was little, littler than you, boy, my pa'd put us in the ring oldest to youngest and we never cried and took on like little babies. You gonna cry there, Punk. You gonna cry, too. Go ahead. Cry, crybaby, cry your eyes out."

Punk didn't know what to say. He didn't know if his pa wanted him to say no or yes or just listen and say nothing at all. He was afraid to say anything wrong or Pa would hit him again.

"Well, are you or not? Cat got your tongue, you sissy punk?"

Afraid, Punk finally said, "No, sir. I ain't gonna cry no more. Not never."

"Well, guess we'll see about that. Git up and git in that ring. Now!"

Punk looked around for Bones, but he couldn't see him anywhere. He hadn't shown up for the practice bouts. Pa was gonna kill him if he didn't come soon. Where was he, anyways?

Dragging himself out into the center of the dirt ring, he looked around again, hoping that Bones would show up soon. He couldn't fight long without his tag team partner. He didn't know how to win or duck the punches or evade the jabs. And who was he gonna fight with, anyway, if Bones didn't come?

"You ready, kid," Pa said, and then he put up his own fists in front of him like a boxer. Oh, God, no, he was gonna have to fight his pa! That was the worst thing of all. He had seen his pa beat up his oldest brother until he couldn't get out of bed for a week.

"I—I—don't know. I just started learnin'—"

"You are a sissy, ain't you? Don't you worry none. I ain't gonna kill you, unless you won't fight with me."

Punk just stood there. His pa frowned and came over and slugged him hard in the stomach. He bent over double, holding his gut, the breath knocked out of him, but then his pa was back, picking him up bodily and throwing him down on the ground. He kicked him in the side, and Punk cried out with pain. "Well, you sure didn't last long, now did you, Punk? C'mon, git up on your feet and hit me. Hit me as hard as you can. I'll let you. Go ahead. Do it, or I'll knock your teeth plumb down your throat."

So Punk dragged himself up and weakly doubled his fist. He swung out at his pa's stomach, but missed entirely. Laughing at him, Pa slapped him up the side of his head with his open palm, one side and then the other, until he fell down again. He groaned, and this time he didn't get up.

Then suddenly, out of nowhere, here came Bones, flying to the rescue, attacking their big pa as if he wasn't twice his size. Fists pummeling, yelling the most awful obscenities, he hit his pa between the legs, hard with his fist, causing him to lurch over and fall to his knees. Punk sat back and watched as Bones began to kick Pa in the side, harder and harder, with the toe of his leather work boot. Then he pushed the big man down onto his back, grabbing him around the throat and riding him like a cowboy as Pa tried to buck him off.

Punk smiled to himself, thinking that Pa deserved to get hit like that, but now he was afraid for Bones. His pa was surely going to kill him for messing him up so bad. And that was against the rules of the ring, anyways, to kick anybody down there in the crotch. For that, Bones was gonna be punished so long and hard that he might even die.

But then, after a few minutes, Pa rolled over and held his arms up in the air. To Punk's shock, he was laughing, even though Bones's blows were still landing all over his chest and face. "Now, that's what I'm talkin' about," Pa cried out, pleased. "You boys need to be more like old Bones here. Bones is gonna be a champion someday, and that's for sure. Bones has no fear. You don't see him cryin' and snivelin', now do you? He's the best of the lot of you. The rest of you just suck. So you can all go without dinner tonight because Bones and me, we're goin' into town to McDonalds and then to the movies."

Then he stood up and picked up Bones and boosted him on his shoulders and carried him away like he was the winner and the best fighter in the world. Punk lay back in the dirt and stared up at the clear blue sky. He pulled in a deep breath and tried to stop the bleed-

ing of his nose with his fingertips. He didn't care where his pa was
going, he didn't care what he did there; he was just glad he was gone.
He hoped he had a wreck and died and never came back again.

But Pa eventually did come back and all the brutality continued
for a long time to come. As the years passed by, Punk toughened up
more and more. It took lots of bruises and injuries and bloody noses,
but he got stronger and braver and better. Pa rarely whupped him
anymore, or any of the other boys, either, because they were all now
as big and brutal as Pa was. One time, they got a visit from a police
officer, and he told Pa that his boys had to start going into town to
attend school. But Pa said he was homeschooling them, and the cop
left and had not come back again. So they had their school lessons
every morning, and the rest of the day, they sparred in the new
chicken-wire cage that Pa had constructed inside the barn. They
practiced all week for the Saturday night matches out in the pasture,
and they all had begun to win. They were famous in the neighborhood. Famous for winning cage fights and for Pa's cruel dog fighting
business.

One night when Punk was out in the barn, feeding the dogs, with
Banjo at his heels, Pa came inside and shut the door behind him. He
had his whip in his hand, and Punk looked at it and then at his pa's
face. Pa was frowning and looking at Punk out of very mean eyes.
Punk could smell the booze on his breath, lots of it. Pa let them all
drink with him now, even the youngest ones. He let them do whatever they wanted to do, smoke, drink, stay out all night hunting and
fooling around and knocking mailboxes off their posts, but only if
they fought hard on Saturday and won their matches.

"Time for you to learn how the dog fights go, Punk Boy."

"Okay." Punk put down the pail of dog food and waited. Pa was
unpredictable when he was drinking so early in the day. He got real
nasty and ugly and cruel. That's when he was the scariest. That's
when he lost control and hurt them the most.

"Git over here, boy. Wassa matter wit' you?" Pa's voice was
slurred. His face was red and flushed and his eyes were watery. He
had really hung one on that day. He was smashed.

"Yes, sir." Punk was beginning to wish Bones would show up and calm Pa down. He was the only one who could, but he had disappeared again, off somewhere by himself, doing whatever he did when he went off alone. Punk always felt a lot safer when Bones was around to protect him. Bones was Pa's favorite kid by far. Bones hardly ever got in trouble or was punished for anything, no matter how bad it was. Pa said that Bones was his golden goose.

Punk stood silently and watched his pa open the gate and grab a big Rottweiler named Demon by the collar and drag the whining dog out to the beating post. He put him on the short leash, and the dog whimpered and moved nervously from side to side, well aware of what was coming. Pa beat his best fighting dogs daily to make them mean. It made Punk want to vomit, and he always tried to comfort them when Pa was done and left them lying there, all cowed and pitiful and snarling at any kind of human contact.

"Okay, boy, it's your turn to learn to whup these curs into shape. You ain't near good enough in the ring as Bones is. You ain't never gonna amount to nothin'. You hear me, boy. You ain't worth spit."

Punk looked down at the whip in his pa's hand and then at the cowering, terrified dog. He set his jaw. "I ain't gonna do it. I ain't gonna whup no helpless, tied-up little dog."

First Pa looked absolutely stunned, and then Punk could almost see the terrible rage gushing up out of him, like it always did when one of the boys defied his orders. "What did you say to me? What did you say, you little turd?"

"I ain't gonna whip no dogs. Not ever. And I ain't gonna let you do it, neither."

Another shocked stare, and then Pa threw back his head and laughed down deep inside his gut. But then he sobered and the mean look came back. "That so? How you gonna stop me, boy?"

"Just go back in the house and go to bed, Pa. You're drunk. Sleep it off. Let me be and go about finishin' up my chores."

When he turned around and picked up the bucket again, his father came at him, raining down blows with the leather whip. He hit Punk in the face before Punk could dodge the assault, and blood oozed from the long red weal down his left cheek. He kept on hitting Punk with the whip, and Punk tried to catch it in his hand and pull it out of his grasp. He finally shoved his pa and got the whip away from him, but then Bones was there, his guardian angel flying in to the rescue, and he grabbed the heavy pail and swung it forcefully against their pa's skull. It hit with a sickening clang, and Pa went down on his knees and then fell face-first in the straw.

"I'm getting' out of here before he wakes up," Bones said. "Come on, run."

Punk took the time to put poor quivering Demon back in his pen, and then he headed out to the woods at a run in search of his twin. There was gonna be hell to pay for knocking their pa out, but it was worth it to see him lying there bleeding on the ground. He deserved it. In fact, Pa deserved to die for all the beatings and cussings and mean things he did to all of them. And maybe he would. Maybe Punk and Bones could kill him together and free all their brothers from his constant cruelty. Maybe that's what they should do. Happy at that thought, he ran out across the pasture after his brother, whom he could just barely see now, way far ahead of him. Yeah, they needed to kill him. They needed to do it together. Punk laughed out loud. He had never been so excited.

Chapter Five

"Man alive, I can't get enough of this sunshine. I almost forgot what it looked like. You know, blue sky, glitter and sparkle off the snow, and the water in the lake actually moving."

"Well, don't get used to it, Bud. It's supposed to drop below zero again tonight with more snow on the way."

"I can never remember the weather bein' this cold and snowy since I moved up here. Think I'll just move back down to Atlanta where the weather gods are kinder and love Southern accents."

"Oh, no, you don't. I've got way too much invested in you. I'm not gonna break in any new partners, believe me." Besides, she probably couldn't find another guy in his right mind willing to take her on, considering her record of attracting vicious serial killers and lunatics.

Bud shot a quick look at Claire. "Aha, you do love me, Morgan. C'mon, just admit it. I knew it all along, to tell you the truth. And tell you somethin' else, you're never gonna find another guy like me to have your back. I am something special."

Claire smiled. "True, all true. You're one of a kind, all right, but what kind? That's the pertinent question."

Bud grinned. "You just don't wanna admit how much you rely on my sense of calm and my good common sense. Hell, you might've slapped old Dazz up the side of the head about that ring thing, if I hadn't taken over and brought everybody down a notch."

"You're probably right. I still might, if I ever get another shot at him. The jerk."

They were driving up into the hills surrounding the lake, searching for Blythe Parker's address, but not having the best of luck. "Do you even know where Sky View Ridge is?"

Bud said, "You know good and well that I know everything about everything. I read books. I watch the Discovery Channel. Be patient. We're almost there. And I can tell you one thing, we're workin' our way up into some verrrry pricey neighborhoods about now."

"Yeah, I can tell."

And Claire could tell. All she had to do was peer out the passenger window at the passing pricey scenery. Large wooded tracts, each and every one, all with fancy lantern-lit brick entrance gates and paved driveways that wound up through big snow-laden oaks and elms and ended at veritable mansions barely visible from the road. "I find it a tad hard to believe that a puny little cage fighter lives up here with the Trumps and the Buffets."

"Maybe he's manor born. Or more likely, maybe she is."

"Guess we'll soon find out. There's his mailbox, right there, see it? Over on the right."

Bud pulled up and stopped beside it, a fancy white lacey thing that probably cost mucho buckeroos. They were on a rural lake road now, one too isolated to suffer a lot of traffic. None, to be exact. Claire had certainly never been up there before. The sun had melted off some of the snow and ice on the side of the road, so they turned in the driveway without any trouble. The entrance road was pretty much scraped clean, unlike most of the others they had passed along the way. Walls of snow lined each side. "Man, I do not want to do this to this poor lady," Bud said. "So you're gonna do the talkin' this time, right, Claire?"

"Thanks for nothing."

"Hey, I do my fair share. You're just better at this sort of thing. Bein' a woman, and all that."

"Yeah, right. I suspect I can do it better than Dazz would." But the fair share part was right on, especially since she'd spent several months down in New Orleans with Black, and not so long ago, either. Bud was her best friend, for sure. Bud and Harve both. She could always depend on them. No questions asked, just like Black. Well, Black asked a lot of questions, no doubt about that, but he was always there when she needed him. "I know you do your share of the work. You're the best, Bud. I depend on you."

"That's what I'm talkin' about." But Bud looked happy, noticeably pleased as punch as he started driving up through the snowy woods. He slowed down the Bronco when the house came into sight. He stopped and they both just stared at it. "Whoa. Good grief. Remind me to take up cage fighting. Then I won't have to marry that ugly rich gal."

Claire thought the house looked more like an estate. Big and sprawling and modern, with dark cypress wood and miles of shining glass and angular clean lines. Lots of walls made entirely of plate glass, and dozens of doors and windows faced one sweet view of the lake from as high a vantage point as Black's penthouse. Claire glimpsed a woman in one of those giant windows, wearing a short white dress and standing motionlessly as she stared out over the lake. A wife worrying about her husband? Probably so. And for very good reason.

Bud followed the circular drive to a little decorative oval fish pond which probably held some seriously chilly goldfish and stopped at the bottom of a flight of steps that led up to a front porch covered by a fancy pergola made out of huge cypress beams. Somebody had shoveled off the snow up there, too. They both got out and clunked their doors shut. They gazed up at the house looming a good three stories above them. And yes, they were slightly in awe. It was a very unusual structure, more than impressive, really. Like something Black might buy for its architectural interest but that Claire would hate because it looked cold and empty and soulless to her. On top of all that, it was plain bizarre looking.

The ground floor appeared to be a spacious garage, similar to the one at Black's house on Governor Nicholl's Street in the New Orleans French Quarter, which had been built up high in case of flooding. But there was no way in hell that this place could ever flood. It was up way too high on the cliffs, cliffs that were very similar to the ones in Ha Ha Tonka State Park and in other parts of the lake. It occurred to Claire at that point that their victim could've been thrown off that very selfsame cliff and later dumped at the park. But why? She couldn't think of a good reason. She walked the short distance to the edge of the cliff, which really wasn't all that far from the front porch, and looked down, way down. Far below, the ground was covered with deep snow and barely visible brambles and thickets and bushes, all of which could hide a body forever. Claire moved away from the edge and walked back to Bud where he waited at the bottom of the staircase. He didn't like heights so he tended to let her check them out. Suddenly very interested in meeting that pensive lady in that upstairs window, they started climbing the steps.

Claire didn't have to wait long. Before they were halfway up the steep staircase, the same woman appeared above them on the landing. She was hugging herself, her arms crossed over her chest, apparently cold sans a coat in that very short dress. "You're the police, aren't you?" she called down to them. Her voice was trembling a bit, and each excited breath she took looked like smoke in the bitterly cold air. She started wringing her hands and shivering all over. She looked as if she were teetering on the precipice of a nervous breakdown, one of gargantuan proportions.

Claire glanced at Bud and then looked back up at the woman. "Yes, ma'am. We're detectives at the Canton County Sheriff's Office. We'd like to talk to you, if that's okay."

"He's dead, isn't he?"

"Are you Mrs. Blythe Parker?"

"Yes. Yes, I am. My husband's dead, isn't he? Tell me, tell me the truth!"

"Maybe we could come inside and talk to you. Would that be all right?"

The woman did not look good. In fact, she looked like hell warmed over. She pressed both hands over her mouth and gave a strangled sob. She knew all right. Women's intuition? Or maybe if you had a cage fighter for a husband, you had a tendency to expect the worse. They clomped their way up to the porch, trying to stamp snow off their boots along the way. Mrs. Parker stood back and allowed them to precede her through a pair of eight-feet-tall French doors made of beautiful stained glass etched in the design of a majestic leaping buck.

The inside of the home was about what Claire expected. Purest of luxury, to be sure. Nicholas-Black-Luxury, in fact, and that meant

pretty damn luxurious. Dark shiny hardwood floors that looked like
wide planked bamboo, maybe, dark iron chandeliers dripping with
crystals, low black leather couches, teak tables, damask easy chairs,
original paintings, framed photographs consisting mostly of shots
of the lake and the beautiful Ozark hills. Yep, the whole bit. Somebody in the Parker brood had beaucoup dollar bills and didn't mind
spending them. No doubt about it. Something told Claire that the
poor guy lying all broken up and lifeless downtown on that cold autopsy table had not forked out the dough for such a place. If not him,
then who? Again, her distrust of the super wealthy began eating a
hole in her comfort zone.

The woman had started crying now and was hiding her face in
her open palms while she boo-hooed. She was tall, even taller than
Claire, who stood around five feet nine. She was extremely pale,
EXTREMELY needing capital letters to describe it, with unreal-
looking porcelain white skin, platinum white hair, cut very, very
short, almost buzzed, and gelled up slightly on top near her forehead.
Almost albino-ish, in fact, except that her eyes were green, a bright,
piercing, artificial green manufactured by tinted contact lenses, bet
on it. So green, in fact, that both she and Bud were in danger of
becoming mesmerized by them. Sort of Wizard-of-Oz-Emerald-
City-greenish. Who knew, maybe the woman was hiding some weird
pink eyes under those lenses. Or was that an old albino wives' tale?

Truth be told, the woman's flesh looked so white, especially in
that white dress, that Claire suspected that if she were to lie down
on the snow, all one would see would be those magnetic X-Men eyes.
She was thin, too, wafer thin, and in need of a Quarter Pounder with
Cheese Value Meal, Supersized, and a full bag of Snickers bars and
an M&M McFlurry, all in the worst way imaginable. All of which
also gave Claire some vivid hunger pangs. However, their hostess
was indeed slight with very small, sharp features, very canary bird-
like, in fact, which pretty much described every other part of her,
too. A gorgeous, rare bird that seemed fragile and ethereal and in
need of a hearty refill of her seed bowl. A bird that looked terribly
frightened at the moment and close to losing all vestiges of composure. Claire couldn't have thought up a better name for the woman

standing in front of them, either. She looked exactly like a Blythe should look.

"They killed him, didn't they? Paulie's dead, isn't he? They finally got him! Tell me, tell me, tellllll mmmme!"

Whoa there, doggie. That last part was shrilled out and echoed up through the wide wooden spiral staircase behind them. Claire frowned a little. Okay, this wasn't going according to plan, or smoothly, even. Paulie Parker's wife was not going to let Claire ease out a slow and tender homicide notification. She apparently already knew, and had been expecting bad news. She hadn't asked for their badges. She hadn't asked anything but that one pertinent question. So, so be it. "Yes, ma'am, I'm very sorry to have to tell you. We found your husband's body yesterday and did not identify him until today. We came here as soon as we could. We are both just so sorry for your loss."

Now the woman just stood there and stared at them out of wide, shocked, and scary-as-hell green eyes. If Blythe Parker had somehow known in her heart, she sure didn't want to believe it now. They all remained standing, just inside the front door, in a stilted silence, a pretty horrible stilted silence at that. No sounds came from around them in the house at all, not even a clock ticking. At length, Bud said, "Maybe you should sit down, Mrs. Parker. This has got to be quite a shock for you."

Blythe Parker seemed to awaken from a trance and stumbled her way over to a deep and soft, blue-and-white-and-gray chevron-patterned chair with a matching hassock. She just dropped down into its depths, as if her legs had given out from under her. Tears were gushing out big-time now, streaming down both pale cheeks, but she made no sounds of grief or horror or despair, as if she had learned long ago how to weep in complete and total silence. Creeeepy, you betcha.

Still, Claire could see that the absolute grief overwhelming the other woman was quite real, which made her slightly unsure on how to proceed with the interview. She also sensed something very peculiar was going on inside that spacious and frigid-cold-looking mansion atop the hill. "Again, let me say that I'm so sorry about your husband, Mrs. Parker."

Claire gave the poor lady a few moments to compose herself. Claire needed a few more moments herself. She took a deep breath, thrown for quite a loop, which was not something that happened every day, or ever. She considered Blythe, who had become calm now and had turned her head to stare out the windows at the sky, which was now dark with snow-threatening gunmetal clouds lining the horizon like layers of gray agate. Blythe had not asked her what happened, as if she already knew. But what did she think? What the hell was going on? She hated to be intrusive, but the woman did not speak again, but sat silently, looking all heartbroken and collapsed in upon herself, like a whipped puppy or a flopped soufflé. It was hard to watch. Claire and Bud exchanged a significant glance. Said glance told her that Bud was not going to say a word, not on a bet. So neither did Claire.

Complete quiet reigned for almost five minutes, which seemed more like five hours. Then Blythe Parker spoke up, her eyes never leaving the windows. "I knew they'd kill him. Sooner or later."

Okay, a remark like that was always interesting, especially to two hard-nosed homicide detectives who had found a dead body beaten to a pulp with lots of bones protruding through the skin. "I guess we're gonna have to know exactly who you're talking about, Mrs. Parker."

"My ex-husband's people. I guess he finally got to him."

Bud and Claire stared at her. A very bad feeling began to take shape inside Claire's gut, sorta like the first twinge of nausea that heralded a horrendous three-day stomach flu. Things were sliding downhill very fast and very hard. She had to ask a lot more questions of this very white lady, all of which were going to complicate their case, but she had to do it.

"Forgive me, but are you accusing someone of murder, Mrs. Parker?"

Somehow that was the question that brought the woman out of her funk, and she turned back to them, dried her wet cheeks with the backs of both hands, and became all business, and real quickly, too, as if her five minutes of grief were enough, already. Weird lady, no doubt about it.

"Yes, I am. That's exactly what I'm doing. They did it. I know they did. They have threatened to do it, over and over and over, ever since I left him and came out here."

"And he is?"

"Ivan Petrov. I suspect you've heard of him."

Oh, terrific, and damn it to hell, too. Claire had heard of Ivan Petrov, all right. He was the purported godfather of the East St. Louis mob, and the defendant in many a deadly criminal case, which happened more often than not. Whatever followed now was going to be sticky and complicated and dangerous, all right. "Are you sure you want to accuse him of murder, ma'am?"

"It wasn't just murder. It was an execution. Ivan ordered it done. You can bet on that. He wouldn't dirty his own hands, but he was behind it. He just wants to drag me back there into that filthy hellhole he calls a compound."

Holy crap. Doubled. Maybe even tripled. Claire tried to remember everything she had heard about Petrov. She had heard the name lots of times before but not much else about the man. Just that he was known for slitting throats from ear to ear on anybody who crossed him. Word was he did it himself to instill fear. "Do you have proof that Ivan Petrov harmed your husband, Mrs. Parker?"

She released a cold and humorless laugh. "What do you think?"

"I don't know. But you've just made a very serious accusation that we will need to follow up on. Can you tell us anything else?"

"Paulie and I ran off together several years ago, just tried to disappear. I stay up here, alone, and wait for him to come home from those god-awful, terrible fight shows. But that's what Paulie loves to do, that's how he makes his money, and that's how we got this place. Ivan's cousin gave me some money when I left him without a cent to my name, God bless her. She told me that she knew how it was to be trapped inside his compound with no freedom at all. It was her velvet box, she always said. And it was for me, too. That is exactly what it was."

All very interesting, true, but it didn't tell Claire much. "I'm afraid that you'll have to come downtown and identify the body. Are you up to that, Mrs. Parker?"

She stood up, stared down at them, almost accusingly, and then she resumed her place at the windows with her back to them. She had on spiked white heels with no hosiery, just those ultra-white legs. "Tell me what they did to him. Did Paulie have to suffer?"

Claire hesitated. Bud shook his head, adamantly. He did not want that vulnerable girl to know; she was teetering on the edge of going to pieces anyway. But she had to know the truth, there was no way around it. "He was brutally beaten. His body was found at the bottom of a cliff in Ha Ha Tonka State Park. Near the Castle ruins. We're not sure how long he has been dead."

"Was there a gunshot wound to the back of his head?" Blythe Parker asked Claire without turning around, and then she quickly covered her mouth with her hand as if feeling sick.

"No. The medical examiner believes he was beaten to death."

"His throat wasn't slit, either? You're sure?"

"Yes, ma'am."

"Then it wasn't my ex-husband himself. That's his calling card, and he's proud of it. He brags about it. Says his knives are handmade and so sharp that it just takes one swipe of the blade to rupture a man's gullet."

Now that was a sharp knife, all right. However, all Blythe Parker's deadly words were spoken calmly and casually, as if family-perpetrated dagger murders were as commonplace as Saturday barbeques. Death and blood and gore. No big deal. We're the Petrovs. We've been there, done that.

Blythe said, "Well, Ivan's always been resourceful. Just so his victim ends up dead. The end justifies the means, that's his motto. He did this, trust me."

Claire wasn't willing to take Blythe's word for it. There were lots of other questions, and Claire needed to ask them. "Paulie Parker was a cage fighter. From what I understand, that's a very rough business. I suspect he was beaten up before, maybe had some bones broken. Could he have suffered fatal injuries from a cage fight?"

"He was too good for that to happen. He usually wins his matches. And he promised me. He put his hand on my grandmother's white Bible, and swore that he'd stop any fight in which he felt outclassed. That he'd call default and get out of the cage and walk away. I told him I'd leave him if he ever came back as bludgeoned up as he did that first time. He nearly died. It was in the beginning before they had the rules they have now. It happened up at the farm where he was born. His brothers and daddy and lots of other men fight up there. Just for the fun of it. God, you should've seen how he looked that first time he came home from there. I thought he was already dead when his brothers carried him in."

And now he really was dead. "Do you know anybody else who might want to harm him? One of those people who fight up around that farm, maybe?"

"Maybe. Or some of the other fighters. He said that some of them are jealous. And some of them are just cretins, animals, savage and stupid and obsessed with beating on people. I don't understand it. I never did understand it." She sighed, long and drawn out and helpless. "He wins a lot. He's that good. They don't like that. And he makes good money on the circuit. That's how he supports me. He's an honest man, a good man. He works hard. He bought this place for me."

She was still in present tense. She hadn't accepted it yet. "Has Paulie received threats that you know of?"

Blythe shrugged a delicate shoulder. Claire could see how her collarbone stuck out of flesh that seemed almost transparent. She had to be anorexic, had to be, bulimic, at the very least, and her skin had never been uncovered out in the sun, either, believe it. The albino thing was getting more and more probable. "But he wouldn't tell me if he got threats. He's always protective of me, always worried that my family or my ex-husband would come and force me back into that compound. He put in a lot of security devices so that I could call the police if they came for me while he was gone." She stopped, and sighed deeply. "He was fighting all the time and trying to earn enough money for us to get out of the country. He wanted to live in Peru. Somewhere far away like that and out of the sphere of Petrov influences. Ivan finagled around until he could legally take my children away. He thought that would make me stay there with him. I haven't seen my sons since I left the compound. Either one of them." She stopped, appeared to be steeling herself, sorrow taking over her delicate features.

"I'm sorry." Claire knew how it felt to lose a child, but she couldn't let herself think about Zach. Not ever. She still couldn't bear to remember him, even the sweet little day-to-day memories, even after all the years that had passed. But he was there, still an adorable blond-haired, blue-eyed toddler, hidden away inside her heart, always. Sometimes she missed him so much that she wanted to put her gun to her head and pull the trigger. She took a deep and cleansing breath, banishing thoughts of her beautiful little baby boy behind the wall in her heart where she kept him safe in a way that she hadn't been able to do in real life. She sat still a moment, forcing him down, and then she tried to gather her thoughts on the job at hand.

Thankfully, Bud chose that moment to take over the interview, God love him. "Can you give us any names? Anybody that you think might have done this, other than your ex-husband? Among the fighters? Anybody who's capable of beating him in such a brutal way? Or from up there around that farm?"

"Malachi was the most belligerent, but Paulie said he was mainly bluster and that they were friends outside the ring. It never seemed that way to me, though. Malachi's got some brothers who fight, too. One's supposed to be a real badass, but apparently he retired or quit or something. Nobody's ever seen him, not that I know of."

"Malachi who?"

"Malachi Fitch." She hesitated briefly, seeming to be considering her next words. "You haven't heard about the Fitches yet? Well, let me tell you. They are all crazy. One-hundred-percent certifiable. Believe me, I know."

"Anybody else who might want to harm your husband?"

"Any of them, I guess. They were all jealous of Paulie's titles. He won most of the time, but he paid a price. In pain and broken bones, but he still could beat them all. And legitimately. He would never have thrown a match."

Broken bones was right, Claire thought. This woman was in for a horrible sight down at the morgue. She hoped that Buckeye would keep the battered body covered at the identification viewing. This case had already turned into a nightmare, and it was only Day Two. One thing she did not want to do was go calling on the Petrov compound, aka Gangsta Land, over in East St. Louis, but she was going to have to, damn it.

Claire took the interview reins again. "Do you have a way down to the sheriff's office, Mrs. Parker? Or would you like for us to take you with us? I'm afraid that you'll have to identify the body. We will be available to take you down there right now, or at any time you wish. All you have to do is call us."

Blythe's swallow went down hard. "Thank you, but I can drive myself. I need time to . . . prepare myself. Is that all right?"

"Yes, ma'am. Just give us a definite time and we'll make the arrangements for the viewing. Here's my card. You can call me at that number any time that you feel you're ready. Or any time you feel the need to talk about what happened to your husband."

Blythe looked away from them again, out the windows at the darkening sky, and was silent for a moment. "I will call you tomorrow, if that's all right." She looked back at Claire. Claire nodded. Then Blythe said, "Will all of this have to be in the St. Louis newspapers, detectives?"

"We're trying to keep it under wraps. The media's preoccupation with the bad weather should help us do that. I can't promise you that they won't get wind of it eventually. But we'll try our best. I promise you that."

"Thank you. I know that you can find your way out. I need some time alone now. I'm sure you understand."

After that, she left them where they sat, walking swiftly down through the silent house, her white stiletto heels clicking loudly on the hardwood floors until the staccato sounds finally faded away. Claire and Bud stared at each other.

"Charlie's gonna shit a brick," said Bud.

"This's gonna be a bad one, all right. Talk about poking a hornet's nest. But we don't know if the Petrov family is involved yet, not in the actual murder. I don't think we can rule out the fighters yet. C'mon, we need to fill Charlie in on this mess."

"Well, I sure as hell dread that little face to face."

"You and me both," said Claire.

They took off, drove back to the office pretty much in total silence. Both of them knew this case was getting ready to blow up in their faces, engendering enough headlines to cause a feeding frenzy across the state, if not across the country. Damn, why did trouble always seem to follow her around? Well, at least it wasn't snowing.

Not yet, anyway. And she did have an ace in the hole. Nicholas Black had a couple of underworld connections that nobody knew about except for her and a select few. And if that knowledge of his included the throat-slashing bad boys in St. Louis, he was going to tell her, whether he liked it or not. And he probably wouldn't like it. Nope, he sure as hell wouldn't like it, not in the least.

Chapter Six

As Claire had expected, Sheriff Charlie Ramsay did not take the news with a stiff upper lip. In fact, that was the understatement of the century. "Are you shittin' me? Are you telling me that this case is possibly related to the Petrov family? My God, she's Ivan Petrov's ex-wife? Do you two have any idea what kinda stink this is gonna blow up? The feds are gonna want in on this, for God's sake."

Claire and Bud nodded slightly but kept their mouths shut. Charlie's questions were rhetorical, or at least, Claire hoped they were. She sure as the devil didn't want to explain anything else. Actually, and believe it or not, the sheriff had taken the news much better than she had expected. He had yet to drop even one F-bomb, which was his wont in days gone by, but the day was young and she prepared herself for oncoming sharp and stinging ire. Truth was, however, she was more anxious to have her little tête-a-tête with Black and pick his brain about certain Russian wiseguys going by the name of Petrov. But alas, and after his recent trip to California, he was busy shrinking his patients in the private bungalows at Cedar Bend Lodge, and she was trapped in an office with her irate boss. Not good. Not a bit good. And certainly not a skip down any primrose path, either. She just hoped it all ended soon, and all ended well.

"Okay, here's the deal." Charlie stopped, breathless and red-faced in his outrage. He pulled in a deep inhalation and grabbed his trusty pipe off the desktop. She was used to that, too. He always smoked his pipe when he was upset. The NO SMOKING signs in the building did not apply to the sheriff. Nobody dared call him on it, either, because all the staff was halfway intelligent. He continued with his regular routine, knocking packed ashes out of the pipe's bowl into a clean glass ashtray. "Now, listen up. Davis, I want you in Kansas City today, talking to that guy who's still laid up over there. That Shorty Dunlop fella. Interview him and everybody else in his retinue, if he has one. See if he can provide you with any new information on the other fighters and their relationships with our victim. Somebody must of knocked him around pretty good if he's still banged up enough to end up in that hospital bed. Maybe some of his buddies took umbrage to that and went after revenge. Also check out the arena over there, or wherever the hell they hold those kinda fights. And contact the KCPD before you do any of it. Got it, Davis? Don't go off half-cocked and get yourself in trouble up there. And the highways are supposed to be clear now so you can drive. Save the department some money on a plane ticket."

"Yes, sir."

Sheriff Ramsay turned his intense gaze upon Claire. He was wearing his bulldog look, the quivering jowls one, the one that indicated snarls and sharp teeth and heavy gnashing. She waited on edge and wondering why she wasn't assigned to go with Bud. They worked together. She hoped he wasn't assigning her to a desk, a fate worse than death, in her opinion. She didn't have to wait long for the answer. "I want you in St. Louis, Morgan. I want you to talk to every dadgum one of those fighters over there, bar none. And their sports agents. And their families. And anybody else they've ever spoken to since they were in diapers. I want you to research their backgrounds and see if you can find any connection to the Petrov family." Charlie stopped there, lit his pipe with a great deal of ritual, and then he sighed heavily. "And I guess you better pay an official visit to Ivan Petrov while you're there. Find out where he's been the last week or so. Got all that? And take Nick Black with you, if he's available to go. I value his input, as you well know. Maybe he'll offer to use his Learjet and save us the cost of another ticket. Thanks to the blasted snow and ice, our budget is already shot to hell with overtime this year, and it's only January, for God's sake."

"Yes, sir."

"Any questions about anything?"

"No, sir," they singsonged together. Something they'd learned to do through the years. She and Zee Jackson, her temporary partner once upon a recent time down in New Orleans, had gotten pretty good at doing that, too, when answering to Sheriff Russ Friedewald down in Lafourche Parish in Louisiana. Even though she hadn't spent much time working there, all hell had broken loose on her watch. Murder and mayhem following her south, no doubt.

"Then what are you waitin' for, and keep me posted on everything, and I mean every single detail, dadgummit. You heard from Mrs. Parker yet? She comin' down here today?"

"No, sir. I haven't heard from her. She's probably working up the nerve to identify the body. She was pretty torn up when we left her."

"Okay, but wait . . ." He paused, frowned around some, and then continued. "Before you leave the lake, I want the two of you to go over to that resort where they held Parker's last fight. What was it, the Lake Inn, that correct?"

"Yes, sir."

"Go down there and see what they can tell you. Maybe there was an argument behind the scenes that somebody bore witness to. Doubtful, but sometimes we get lucky. So get goin'."

After that, he waved them away, like two pesky little moths annoying his green-shaded reading lamp, and they fled his office in a big hurry. They did stop politely and listen to his sweet little munchkin secretary named Madge tell them about her grandkids' snowman that looked just like Jay Leno, and then they trudged out to the parking lot and climbed into Bud's Bronco.

Bud fired the ignition and turned up the heater. "Want my opinion? I don't think Petrov ordered it. I think one, or maybe more, of those fighters messed up Parker. Beat him to death. Payback, probably. They know how to use their fists and break bones. I suspect they know how to use bats and crowbars, too. Judgin' from the ones I've seen fight."

Claire nodded. "Could be right. But I suspect that Petrov's thugs are pretty good with bats and pipes and weighted saps, too. Death by Louisville sluggers is more their style. At least, that's what I hear." And maybe Black could tell her more. He had proven himself buddy-buddy with a couple of godfathers that she'd had the misfortune to meet up close and personal. Unfortunately. But fortunately, too, because at times it opened doors to her that other law enforcement personnel would have to kick down with a signed warrant and a black-clad SWAT team. Black had never mentioned any mobsters/personal friends that he knew in the St. Louis metropolitan area, but on the other hand, he didn't discuss his secret association with bad guys all that often. Never, actually. Especially now. All he ever wanted to do now was look through *Brides Magazine* and talk about wedding veils and guest lists and receptions and ask her questions like: So, have you set the date yet or not?

By the time they reached the Lake Inn, a light snowfall was spi-raling down to delight the denizens of the lake area. Yeah, as if. As they drove down the hill and onto the cleared tarmac road that led to the front entrance, she decided the hotel had a pretty good layout. Waterfront properties like Black's huge luxury resort were money-making gold mines when they were located right on the shores of Lake of the Ozarks. This one was okay, but not even close to Cedar Bend Lodge in classy digs, primo location, basic grandeur, or any other kind of wow factor. It looked as if it had been around a couple of decades. There was a good deal of lake frontage and what looked like a nine-hole golf course, and in the back she could see a fairly large convention center. There was no giant marina full of speedboats like Cedar Bend had, but it looked like it was doing a brisk business, probably guests left over from attending the recent and bloody cage fight.

Bud pulled up under a wide canopy and parked behind a taxi with a driver loading beat-up brown baggage into the back. No handsome black-and-tan-uniformed valet came running, as was the case at Black's joint. So nobody was around to complain about them block-ing the front door, which was large and made of dark polished wood. To the right of the door, there was a large glass advertising box. It had a poster of the busted-up guy on Buckeye Boyd's autopsy table. Paulie Parker was posed in the typical boxer stance, fists up in front, legs apart, one in front of the other for balance. She knew that from her old Bobby Blanks kickboxing tapes. He was a fairly nice looking guy when he had been alive, with lots of curly brown hair and a beard cropped close along his jawline. He was wearing bright red trunks and some kind of fancy belt decorated with large gold medallions that made him look cool and like an awesome winner. His gloves were open at the end so that his fingers showed, so he could grab hold of his opponent's nose and twist it off, no doubt. He was barefoot, and he looked fit and healthy and strong, and not like every bone in his body had been splintered, muscles slack, eyes shut for good. She sighed and tried not to think about Paulie Parker. Or his albino-tinted-white wife.

At the front desk, a young and extremely polite teenage girl with enough long and fluffy black hair to stuff a king-size pillow informed them that the person who had arranged the fight was back in the convention center overseeing the workmen who were taking down the cages. And that said supervisor was saddled with the unlikely name of Skippy Wainwright. So they hoofed their way through some long halls in search of Skippy, all of which were carpeted with lots of red swirls and dark green leafy patterns. It was warm as toast inside, so they shed their sock hats, scarves, and gloves, and parkas as they moved along the way and avoided all the folks who were checking out of their rooms, wheeled suitcases and nylon duffel bags in tow. Some of the hotel guests looked like how she assumed fans of brutal cage fighters would look, sporting unkempt graying beards and intricate blue and yellow and red tats in the inevitable redneck and rapper arm-sleeve, look-what-I-did-aren't-I-tough variety, as well as some painful-looking facial jewelry. She just didn't get it. Legit boxing wasn't her cup of tea, either. Maybe after she watched a bout or two of two buff guys going at it nearly naked, then she'd be utterly enthralled. After two seconds contemplating that scenario, she knew better. Nope, she was pretty sure that sort of thing was never gonna ring her bells. Sumo wrestling, either. Less buff that was, true, but still pointless in her book.

At the rear of the first floor, they followed a passageway to a large room where a steaming hot tub flooded ripples of warm water over some fancy fake gray rocks into a large indoor heated swimming pool. The room was lofty and spacious with foggy windows across the back and smelled cloyingly of chlorine and steam and stale complimentary popcorn. Outside, there was an outdoor pool covered with a green vinyl tarp barely visible under a foot or two of snow.

They passed a couple of young girls lying under some sunlamps. They smelled like coconut and Maui hotels. Bud grinned at them, and they responded with giggles, sitting up and giving him a better gander of their toned and scarcely covered adolescent bodies. She couldn't condemn them for their nearly naked state. Black bought her the tiniest little scrap of a yellow string bikini once and loved for her to wear it, at least until he took it off, which was usually a mere matter of seconds. But she wasn't complaining about that, either. Talk about ringing her bells. Thus was explained the giant diamond ring hidden on the sturdy chain around her neck, to be hastily slipped onto her left ring finger whenever Black was around and raising hell about it.

They took an enclosed, glass-windowed walkway to the convention center and immediately were inundated with the clang of hammers against steel and workmen shouting things like, *Got it, man* or *Hold it tight* or *Hand me that hammer, dumbass*. All of said ruckus echoed up high into the rafters of the nearly empty building. The convention center was one big room with one big cage made out of vinyl-covered chain-link fencing smack dab in the middle, fed by double runways on which the fighters no doubt made their spectacular entrances in hooded silk robes while clasping their hands over their heads. All of it was being dismantled, while other hired hands struggled to remove at least a hundred or so black folding chairs that surrounded it. Claire and Bud headed straight for the guy holding a clipboard and yelling nonstop at the other guys.

"Excuse me, sir," Claire said when they reached him, not at all sure he deserved that moniker, judging by the way he was hurling profanities hither and fro.

"Yeah? Now what? What the hell do you want? Can't you see I'm busy here?"

Claire gazed down at Mr. Skippy. He was a little guy, came to about her chin and real nervous acting despite his X-rated oratory skills. He moved from foot to foot while glaring at them, as if he couldn't stand still to save his life or had to go to the bathroom really, really bad. He was breathing hard from all his highly dramatic cussing and power trip, poor tiny little dwarf of a guy. Maybe she ought to get him in a headlock so he could calm down and control his breathing. She fought the urge, having learned to be rather calm and collected around imbecilic jerks since her recent sojourn in a three-week coma. Then again, she hadn't met Skippy Boy until now. He wore an old gray sweatshirt that said *Semper Fi* on the front. Yeah, right. He probably stole it from his hero older brother or his World War II great-grandpa. His denim jeans were well worn, too, and he sported a rather impressive sideways rainbow-shaped scar down his left cheek. Probably a broken beer bottle souvenir from his own fighting days or a girlfriend who didn't like vulgar words or his Marine gramps who wanted his sweatshirt back. He had long and kinky white-blond hair, really kinky, probably ten on the corkscrew scale, much like the clowns in Stephen King's scariest books or like her Aunt Helen's old-fashioned floor mop circa 1952. His face looked a bit battered and worse for the wear, as if it had been hit lots of times in unfriendly fashion. So did his nose.

She held up her shiny deputy badge and gave him a good look at it. "We're from the Canton County Sheriff's Department, sir. We have some questions to ask you."

That got his full-fledged, undying attention. He didn't curse anymore, either. He must have felt guilty since the first words out of his mouth were: "Hey, we got all the necessary permits for these fights. I got the papers right here. We got it right this time, so why are you hasslin' us like this?" He held up the clipboard and stabbed a disgruntled forefinger on the writing thereon.

"We're here about a homicide, sir. We don't really call it hassling. We prefer you didn't, either."

That threw him momentarily. "Here, at the Lake Inn? Somebody got killed in here? Wow, shit."

It seemed he was fairly articulate when he had to be. "No, we found a body out at Ha Ha Tonka State Park."

"What's with the suspense, lady? Tell me who it was."

Claire felt her teeth enjoying a cozy little clamp. Why did everybody they interviewed lately have to be such a damn smart-alecky jerk? It had to be the weather, days and days of freezing cold and annoying tons of snow. She and Bud were rather testy lately, too, and probably for the same reason. "I'm afraid the deceased was your winner here the other night. Guy by the name of Paulie Parker."

Skippy staggered backwards as if Bud had shoved him in the chest. Claire tried to determine if that was a theatrical Skippy kinda stunt or the real thing. He stared at them, and for once, and lucky for them, he appeared speechless. "No way. Not Paulie. I don't believe it. He's friggin' invincible."

"Believe it," said Bud, apparently not a sucker for the guy's charm, either. Claire could just tell, something about the total absence of Bud's usual charming smile perhaps. Then again, Skippy wasn't one of Bud's good-looking gal pals so that might explain his I-truly-despise-you-Skippy expression.

"No way," he repeated again, shaking around his mop of kinky platinum curls.

Claire decided to let the idea percolate until he got used to it. He stared at her face for a long moment as if waiting for her to tell him she was just kidding, *ha-ha, got you*, and then at Bud, who frowned and nodded impatiently, ready to get on with other things. Kansas City awaited. If Claire knew Bud, and she did, his first stop in KC was going to be his favorite barbeque joint on the planet. Fiorella's Jack Stack Barbeque was old and famous and located inside a really ancient building in Martin City, where customers had to walk through a virtual maze to be seated. It made Claire hungry just thinking about their smoked turkey and cheesy corn and baked beans. Apparently, Bud's encouragement got through to Skippy. He sank down in the closest folding chair, still hugging the clipboard. "That's just crazy, man. That kid's great. He was just a great fighter, man. I just can't believe this. Was it a head injury, or somethin'?"

"More like somethin'," Bud said, really cutting Skippy no slack now.

Claire took over. "Can you get us a list of all the cage fighters in this area, Mr. Wainwright? Names and addresses and family members."

"Yeah, sure, I can. I keep it up to date, too, because I'm the one who sets up the bouts around the lake. God, I still can't believe that Paulie's dead."

"He was murdered," she told him, watching his face closely for a guilty reaction. Despite his wont for dramatics, his initial astonished take looked real enough to her.

"No way, no way."

She nodded. "'Fraid so. You know anybody on the circuit who had a beef with the victim?"

"Well, most of them resented him winnin' everything all the time. He's the current champion, been the champ for over a year. Everybody's chasing his title."

"Not anymore," Bud said.

"It's so hard to believe. Give me a second, will you? Jeez, you two are cold. Don't you know that I'm gonna lose a lot of money if he's not around to bring in the fans anymore."

"Yeah, your concern is touching. Now back to my question. Anybody you know who might be interested in seeing Paulie Parker dead?"

"Well, I heard that he used to have some kinda deal going on over in St. Louis. You know, with some wiseguys over there. They got a couple of fighters on the circuit, too. But it was more than just the competition. Something to do with his wife. I dunno what. I keep my nose outta that sick shit."

Claire said, "His wife told us that he was born around here. Do you know where?"

"A lot of these guys grew up around here, you know, out in the hills and hollows where they really play rough. Lots of 'em out away from town. Lots of 'em are brothers or cousins, and stuff. You know, tag teams. Some of 'em are into wrestlin', too. Up there, they have the bare fists, no holds barred, you know, real nasty stuff. I've even heard that a couple of times guys got killed in the ring."

"Fighters died in the ring? Are you certain about that?"

"Well, I wasn't there but I wouldn't be surprised. They hold those kinda fights out in the boondocks, you know, in the middle of farm pastures and crap. But I've heard some of 'em were to the death, maybe not intentionally, but those guys just don't know when to stop. They raise their kids like little gladiators. Brag about it, too, say they're like those Spartan guys. You know, they teach 'em to be tough as nails and to never back down, no matter what. They beat 'em up if they won't fight."

Bud said, "The Spartans? Like in that movie *300*?"

"Yeah, that's exactly what I mean. Little kids used to fight out there, and I mean, five or six years old. And I hear they got knocked around pretty good, too. Of course, the circuit frowns on that now and makes sure the fighters know it. Probably doesn't go on anymore."

Claire had seen that movie about the Spartans, too, and read a book once about those male Greek idiots. Spartan warriors had been so intent on being the best fighters in the world that they abused and brutalized their little kids and made them into savage beasts. So, if that kind of thing was going on in her jurisdiction, she was going to ferret out every last one of them and make sure they regretted laying one finger on their children. "There are laws against abusing children. If you have knowledge of child abuse going on in this county or anywhere else, Mr. Wainwright, you had better tell us now or you're going to end up rotting in jail with the rest of them."

"Hey, don't bring this stuff down on me. I just hear the rumors. That's all I know about it. I'm bein' open and honest and cooperating, and now you're makin' threats on me."

"I'll ask you one more time, Skippy. Do you have knowledge of any child being put into a fight cage?"

"No. But it wouldn't hurt to check out the people that live out that way. I can point out the ones who come from that part of the county."

"You do that. And make it quick. Just circle their names, if you will."

"Okay, I got the list of those fighters right here. You can have this one. I'll print out another one for me."

"And you saw no openly antagonistic behavior toward Parker the night that the fight was held here?"

"No way. We don't allow it. Usually, they just doctor up their own injuries down in the triage unit and the fighters collect their winnings and go on their way. It's all very up and up, at least it is here at the Inn."

"It better be, or we'll shut this whole place down." That was Bud, stealing her thunder.

"It is, I swear to God. Everything's legit and by the letter of the law. We don't cheat nobody outta nothin'. And we sure don't never hurt any little kids. That's just sick."

"Yes, it is sick. Is there anything else you can tell us about Parker or anybody else on the circuit that we need to know?"

"I don't know them all that well. They all got issues, sure, with each other. This is a violent sport. Paulie won a lot of belts, won the whole thing last year, made lots of dough." He shrugged.

"Who was he here with on the night of the fight?"

"He was alone. He's usually alone. Wasn't never real friendly with the other guys, you know, not a jerk, or nothin'. He just did his own thing. A loner, I'd guess you'd say. Somebody said he liked to get home to his woman, was true blue to her, and all that crap. She's supposed to be a real looker, but she never came out to any of his bouts, at least not that I've ever seen. I heard she never showed up to support him anywheres, that she was kinda like one of those people who were afraid to come out of their house. You know, whatcha call it?"

"Agoraphobic?"

"Yeah, that's it. Don't know if that's true, though. Never laid eyes on the chick."

"Go ahead. Circle any of those guys you think might be abusing children. Make sure you give me their addresses, too. That's not going to go on around here. Trust me."

"Okay. I'm with you on that. Man, the Punisher's dead. Nobody's gonna believe it. That's gonna make some big waves around the circuit."

It was gonna make big waves in lots of places, Claire thought. Places she didn't particularly want to go but had to. Oh, well, that was the story of her life, now wasn't it?

Blood Brothers

Unfortunately for Punk and Bones, Pa woke up and remembered what they had done to him. So he beat them both black and blue with his fists for crowning him with that bucket, and then doctored them up and told them that he was as proud as a peacock about the way they took him on and knocked him out. He said they were the bravest of all the brothers, even if they were the youngest and the smallest. He took them into town and let them pick out new camouflage compound bows at the Walmart Superstore. He said that they were both bad, bad to the bone, and he was proud to call them his sons. So that's when Punk learned that strength and bullying and utter brutality meant success and admiration and reward. Afterward, he took that lesson to heart and followed it religiously. Bones already had done that, years ago, and he continued to excel, both in his father's eyes and inside the ring. They didn't plot to kill their father, either. After all, they were his favorites now.

By the time they reached their middle teens, they both were the undisputed champs of their division, usually number one and number two, both of them winning every match Pa set up for them. They put some of their opponents in the hospital with broken bones, especially Bones, who just loved to hear that sharp, brittle crack when a bone gave way. Also, and together as a tag team, they beat up their older brothers regularly and with a great deal of fatherly encouragement. Both learned to love the sound of shattering femurs and crackling phalanges under their hard blows or brutal foot stomps, that lovely loud pop that caused their opponents to scream and fall to the ground and writhe around before they gave up. They learned the names of all the human bones and where they were located and the best ways to break them. It had become their favorite thing, music to their ears, the feel of bones giving way under their fists, and it happened more often than not. That's when they began to call their obsession "bone music."

Once they even managed to break Pa's arm, and the bone in his wrist popped out through the skin on the back of his hand and made him pass out from the pain. That was the last time they ever got to enjoy a tag-team thrashing upon him. But it felt very good to hurt him so badly. Bones wanted to break his other arm, too. Truth was, Bones wanted to just go ahead and kill him, but Punk held him back because he was their pa, after all, and he still liked them the best.

After that day and when Pa came home from the emergency room, he seemed a little bit afraid of them. He started showering them with gifts and let them do pretty much whatever they wanted. He still beat their brothers some, but not them. He knew better. Yeah, things were pretty damn good for Punk and Bones, and they pretty much had free rein to do whatever the hell they wanted to whoever the hell they wanted to do it to. Life was good, and they didn't even have to kill their pa yet, either, which would give them a lot of explaining to do.

One particular day, in late November, they went hunting together for some wild turkeys to roast up for Sunday dinner. Their pa had acres of private land to hunt on, but there was one place on their property line that overlooked the widest part of the river and a spring-fed pond where turkeys came in to feed. So they both climbed high up in the tree stand that they'd built for bow hunting a couple of summers before. They got there at dawn and so it wasn't long before they dozed off, tired from their long walk and a full night of spying on a lady who lived down the road and liked to undress right in front of her bedroom window. Bones had seen her do it once before, so after that they often crept up the side of her house and watched her take off her clothes. She was really something, too. Older than they were, but she still looked good naked. Bones wanted to climb into her window and do her, but Punk wouldn't let him.

But something caused Punk to rouse up out of his light doze, and he realized that it was the musical sound of a girl's voice. Surprised that a woman was anywhere nearby, he sat up and looked around and then finally spotted her across the property line in their neighbor's big apple orchard. He could see her pretty well, and still hear her singing a song about flowers on the wall, or some such thing. So he focused his new rifle's high-powered scope right on her and got her in the crosshairs, curious as to what she looked like up close. He hadn't seen many girls his age anywhere. He and the brothers pretty much stayed on the farm or drove to the quick stop just down the road. She had her back to him while she was gathering up some apples and placing them in her long skirt. She was holding it up with both hands and making a cradle for the fruit. Her dress was white with little pink bouquets of flowers all over the fabric. He watched everything she did. He wasn't used to watching any real live girls around his own age, except for that naked lady they spied on. In fact, he hadn't been very close to any women at all. Pa wouldn't let any of the boys date girls. He said it would take their minds off winning fights and make them weak and lazy.

But Punk had seen a lot of them on the Direct TV satellite dish that Pa had ordered with their last winnings, and he liked the short little skirts they wore and the low tops that showed him their titties and got him all turned on down in his britches. And he also knew that this new girl was out there standing on his ma's family's property, where he had lived for a while when he was a little kid, at least until she died, anyway. He didn't remember much about those early years when he'd lived on the other side of that fence, but one thing for sure, he was very interested in that girl standing over there. He wondered what her name was and how old she was. She looked to be around his age, sixteen, maybe, like him. She had very white hair woven into one long braid that reached down all the way to her waist, and her dress was so long that it brushed the ground when she walked. He could see that she wore some kind of white socks and plain white Keds tennis shoes when she got on her tiptoes to pick an apple off a high branch.

Impatient, he wished she'd just turn around so he could see her face. He sure did want to see her up close, that was for damn sure. Then finally, she did turn slightly when she reached up for another apple. That's when his breath hitched a little inside his chest. God, she was just so pretty, as pretty as any of those Hollywood stars with all their makeup and sexy pouts. She had the palest skin he had ever seen, even whiter than his ma's had been, and his ma's had been the color of fresh milk. He did remember that a lot of people in his ma's family had pale skin and that same white-as-angels hair, and he adjusted his scope again, trying to see what color her eyes were. He found himself wanting to jump down off that blind and climb that barbed wire fence and run down the hill and look at her up close. Bones was still asleep, wasn't he? So why not?

Making certain that he was extra quiet and didn't make a sound, not wanting to share the girl with Bones, he climbed down to the ground, vaulted the fence, rifle still in his hand. He headed straight for the pretty girl with the flowers on her skirt, making noise when he got closer so that he wouldn't frighten her away. She didn't hear him until he was almost to her, and then she whirled around and looked really scared. She started backing away.

"Don't be afraid. I ain't gonna hurt you. I just saw you gatherin' up these here apples, and I thought you might let me have one. I love me them apples."

He grinned and tried to look harmless, but he was pretty big standing next to her and his face was pretty rough and busted up from his last fight so he wasn't sure how she'd take to him. She didn't say anything for a minute, just looked at his face. She also looked a little upset when she saw the long gun he was clutching in his fist. So he laid it down on the ground, all gentlelike, and said, real calmlike. "I ain't gonna hurt you, or nothin'. Truly, I'm not."

"Where did you come from?" she finally said.

"Up yonder, on the other side of that property line. My brother and me is huntin' turkeys up there in that blind."

"So you're one of *them*," she said, looking more interested.

"Yeah. I guess so."

"What's your name then?"

He told her, and then he said, "What's yours?"

She told him, and he said, "Wow, that's a right pretty name, sure is."

Then she smiled, and it sorta lit up her whole face and made her shine even more. She looked just like the floating angels in his ma's Bible, all white and sweet and soft. "You are really pretty, you know that? Like an angel come down from heaven."

She laughed a little, a real fine sound, and her super white skin got a little pink in the cheeks. But she looked pleased and no longer afraid of him. "Thank you." She lowered her long white lashes. She was pretty shy, really. "So are you."

"Men ain't pretty," he said, frowning and slightly offended at first, but not enough to leave her company and go back home. He liked this girl already. He had a feeling he was gonna like girls in general. They sure weren't like boys. Or that older woman Bones spied on. He looked down at the girl's pert little titties pushing out the front of her dress and how soft her lips looked. He wanted to lick her all over and see how she tasted. He bet she tasted like strawberry shortcake and whipped cream.

"Well, you are. You're the prettiest boy I've ever seen."

He frowned some more, thinking that made him sound weak and sort of stupid, maybe. Then she handed him a big juicy apple. He took a big bite. "Hey, this is real tasty. Real juicy and stuff. Sweet, too."

"How come you don't go to the high school down in town like we do?"

"Pa homeschools us. Wish we did, though. It gets lonely out there with just my brothers the only ones around."

"My girl cousins say that you and your brothers are all real handsome and stuff. You know, real hotties. They say that you all look so much alike that it's hard to tell you apart. Sometimes they watch you with binoculars when you guys are baling hay out in your field by the lake, you know, the one near that old collapsed mine shaft. You know, when you get all sweaty and dirty and take off your shirts."

"Really? No shit?" But he wondered why they wanted to watch sweaty guys get all dirty. He just didn't see it. But it made him want to take off his shirt and work up some sweat, just for her. Then he thought about her with her shirt off and getting all dirty with sweat dripping off her, and he suddenly got what she meant. He felt it down in his pants, too. Whoa, this girl was something else entirely. She almost made his mouth water.

She looked startled, and he figured that was because of his cuss word. "I'm sorry for talkin' like that to a lady like you. I'm not used to bein' around girls yet. Sorry."

Then she smiled up at him and her tongue swiped a wet path all around her pink lips, and he felt like his knees were gonna give way and go all weak and wobbly on him. That sure hadn't ever happened to him before. This here girl was a whole new ballgame.

"How'd you get those bruises and cuts on your face?" she asked him.

"We're cage fighters. All of us. Good ones, too. Especially me and Bones. We win every match."

"Bones? That's a funny name."

"He likes to break people's bones when he fights 'em."

"Why? That's gross."

"Yeah, I know. Don't know why. He just does. Makes him feel tough, I guess." He didn't want her to think he was gross, too, so he quickly said, "He likes it more than I do."

"You mean that it makes him feel, like, well, like he's invincible?"

A little embarrassed, he frowned. "What's 'invincible' mean?"

"That means that nobody can beat you."

"Well, that pretty much describes Bones, all right." He laughed. *Invincible,* he'd have to remember that word.

"What about you?"

"I'm gettin' better, but I don't like hittin' people as much as he does. Unless I don't like them, then it's fine, I guess."

"I think I'd like you a lot better than I'd like Bones."

Grinning, he sure hoped so. "That's good 'cause I already like you a lot."

She smiled up at him. "I like you, too, but I guess I gotta go back home now. Mama's expecting me to bring in these apples for some pies. You can take some of them home with you, too, if you want. We don't mind. We got a whole orchard full."

"You sure? Pa says you people don't like us hangin' around over on your property. We used to get whupped if he ever caught us crossing over on your land, even way back there in woods where the river runs."

"Well, you're different. I like you. You can come over here any time you want. I will even make you a pie, if you want me to."

That's when he felt another kind of thrill go through his loins, one he hadn't experienced much yet, except in his dreams. But it was her. She did it. She was just so darned pretty and nice and made pies. "I like you, too. A whole lot. I'd like an apple pie, especially if you make it for me."

"Then I will, and I'll bring it up here and give it to you. But now, I guess that I better get going, or Papa will come lookin' for me. I'm not so sure he'd want me out here alone with you. Maybe he'd be afraid you'd try to kiss me, or something."

They smiled at each other again, and he wondered if she meant that she wanted him to kiss her. He was sure all for that, if that's what she wanted, too. Then he said, "Hey, I know. Why don't you come up here around this time every day? That way, we can talk and get to know each other some more. And eat that pie you're gonna make for me."

She grinned really big, apparently liking the sound of that, too. "Maybe I will," she said with a little toss of her braid. "Bye, now."

"Bye."

Punk watched her go until she was out of sight, and then he reluctantly trudged back up the hill, vaunted over the fence, and climbed back up onto the tree blind. Bones was just then sitting up and yawning. "Where you been?"

"I just took a little walk, lookin' for turkey scratchin' and such."

"Well, get back up here or you'll scare them toms away. Pa'll make us eat bologna sandwiches again, if we don't bring in a big one."

So Punk settled back beside his brother with his rifle across his knees and watched the clearing below. But he was only thinking of the girl with the white hair and white skin and soft mouth. He liked her. A whole, whole lot. Maybe he even loved her already. Yeah, maybe he was in love, just like those bold and beautiful soap opera folks.

Chapter Seven

When Claire and Bud returned again to the sheriff's office, they got out together and slammed their doors shut with lots of feeling. The temperature was dropping; their breaths were pluming with renewed vigor in the cold air, white and smoky and wintry. They checked in with the sheriff, got what they needed for their out-of-town interviews, and then exited the building ten minutes later. They both stopped short when they saw Brianna Swensen standing across the lot, right beside Bud's Bronco. In her white furry parka, she looked as tall and willowy and blond and beautiful as ever. Bud just stood there, frozen in place, staring at his long-lost girlfriend.

After a long moment, Claire said the obvious. "There's Bri, Bud. You gonna talk to her?"

Bud didn't look so sure about that, or anything else. Claire felt for him. She didn't like surprises, either. "Want me to go talk to her?" she offered and hoped to hell he said no. She wasn't good at letting people down easy, or hard either, truth be told. And she liked Brianna a lot. Brianna had been a victim of violence, and it had just taken the poor girl a long time to come to terms with it. Bud just couldn't understand why that would be a reason to take off and leave him behind. And Brianna had hurt Bud deeply when she had done just that. Claire did not like anybody to hurt Bud, not ever, not for any reason, period, so she was on his side, no matter how their relationship turned out.

"No, but thanks for the offer. I need to talk to her, I guess. She and

Shaggy just sprung this on me, is all. Guess I'm sorta shell-shocked
to see her back and standin' over there, like nothin' ever happened."

"Listen, why don't you go on over there and talk to her?
Go someplace private. Let her explain things to you. Don't worry
about me. I'll call Black. He can pick me up or send somebody over
here to get me. Talk to her, Bud. Fix it, one way or the other. That's
what you always said you wanted. So here's your chance."

Bud was still staring at Brianna. She waited, staring back at him.
She had a worried look on her face but she still looked like some
heavenly creature who would model fluttery white wings in a
Victoria Secret's fashion extravaganza. "Thanks, Claire. I mean it.
I owe you."

"No problem. And no, you don't owe me." She stepped back
inside the door where it was warm and sheltered from the freezing
wind. As she dialed Black's private line, she watched Bud walk
slowly across the parking lot. He stopped a few yards away from
Brianna, as if afraid to get too close. His hands were stuffed in his
pockets. They talked a moment and then Claire breathed a heavy
sigh of relief when they both got into his Bronco and drove away.
They needed to hash it out. It was complicated. And they'd waited
way too long.

"Yeah, Claire? You okay?" said Black, instead of hello.

Black always expected the worst now, and rightfully so. Since he'd
hooked up with her, they'd had nothing but psychos and murderers
and monsters in their lives. Good thing it hadn't scared him off. At
least, not yet, anyway.

"Guess who's back in town?"

"Oh, God, who? Not some serial killer, I hope."

"Not this time. Brianna Swensen. Bud's talking to her right now."

"No kidding? Well, good. They need to talk it out. It's been a long
time since she left town."

"Hey, you busy?"

"I'm just finishing up with my last patient. Why?"

"How about picking me up at the office?"

"Nothing I'd like better."

"Well, hurry it up. I'm cold and tired and cranky."

"Terrific. I just love it when you're like that."

Claire had to laugh at his dry tone. Her foul moods weren't exactly fun to be around, and she knew it. She was trying her best to be less impatient lately; at least she was when she was around him.

"So why the cranky thing? If I might ask without fear of unpleasant repercussions?"

"I'll tell you when you get here. Just make it as quick as you can. If Charlie sees me hangin' around here, he might assign me more paperwork."

"You got it. Be watching for me."

He clicked off then, and she sat down in a chair in the lobby beside the front door and settled in for at least a thirty-minute wait. With snow and ice on the curves and hills around the lake, it might take him even longer than that. But that was okay. She had a lot of thinking to do. She spent some time studying the list of cage fighters, which had about fifty names on it. Once she zeroed in on the local guys that Skippy Boy had circled, and the other ones hailing from Missouri, she had whittled it down to about twenty, fifteen of them from the immediate lake area and the surrounding cities of Springfield, Columbia, and Sedalia. Five of the fighters were from Branson. Some of their fellow detectives could help interview most of them.

After she got back from her assignment in St. Louis, she was going to head for the boonies and any child abusers she might find out there. And they were going to pay if they had hurt one single hair on one single child's head, count on it. Exactly nine minutes after she'd hung up with Black, she heard the dull thumps of helicopter rotors and realized that it had to be Black in his chopper, making one of his grand yet rather embarrassing entrances. Jeez. All the sheriff's office personnel in the lobby were looking out the windows and then turning around and grinning at her. She walked out the front door and realized that he was putting down at the deserted end of the parking lot with a great deal of blowing snow and racket. A couple of patrol officers were outside, standing beside their car doors. They shaded their eyes and watched the copter land with Black's usual skillful precision.

One of them caught sight of her. "Wow, Morgan, so now you got yourself a personal helo to pick you up? Guess that matches that million-dollar ring you hide away inside your shirt."

That came from Josh Cutter, an old friend of hers, so she only smiled, but it was a tight smile. "Come on, guys. Cut it out or I won't invite you to my all-your-expenses-paid wedding in Hawaii."

"Yeah," called out his partner. "Oh, by the way, I forgot my flashlight so can I borrow your engagement ring?"

"Ha-ha," she called back over her shoulder. "You two are just a riot."

They laughed at her and shook their heads, but they were only teasing. She knew that, because she had gotten a lot of the same kind of good-natured ribbing every single day since she let it be known that she was Nicholas Black's main squeeze. So she made her way out to the helicopter, bending down low to avoid the wild wind thrown off the spinning blades, sliding the diamond back onto her left ring finger as she trudged along. She climbed in, and Black handed her a pair of aviator sunglasses and a headset. She quickly put them on and clicked her seat belt. Now that the sun was out and reflecting off the snow, the glare was almost blinding.

"Well, talk about embarrassing, Black. I meant for you to come get me in the Humvee."

"You said you were cold and in a hurry and in a foul mood. And I mean to please."

"Well, you do please."

"I know."

She laughed at that arrogant little bit of masculine self-confidence. "So, tell me, how would you like to go on a little weekend side trip to St. Louis?"

He glanced over at her as they lifted slowly off the ground. "Just the two of us? Well, hell, yeah. I'd like that a lot. Why do you ask?"

"I gotta do some interviews over there. Maybe we can squeeze in a little quickie romantic holiday, too, when I'm not on the clock. I've got to be there on Friday and Saturday and maybe Sunday, too, depending."

"If you're serious about that quickie, I'll make the time, although I don't usually do quickies. We can go right now. I'm gassed up and ready to roll. I'll call for clearance and a flight plan."

"Whoa, slow down. We've got to pack our bags, get our stuff. Take Jules over to Cedar Bend for the weekend."

"He's already there. I took him in with me this morning after you left with Bud. We can buy whatever clothes we need when we get there. I'll have Miki call for reservations at the Ritz-Carlton."

"A weekend's worth of clothes for both of us? That's gonna add up. Seems pretty extravagant to me."

Black merely laughed as if that was just-oh-so-silly. "Maybe we can visit a couple of bridal shops while we're there. You have a wedding gown to choose, remember?"

God, did he have a one-track mind, or what? She didn't answer, but she remembered, all right. She had a feeling his choice of wedding apparel wouldn't exactly jibe with her choice, especially the figures on the price tag. And she wanted to pay for it herself. She wanted to pay for the whole wedding herself, which Black was not going to like one little bit. But too bad. On the other hand, why get into all that right now? She had an ongoing investigation to think about, a bad one that needed her entire concentration.

The snowstorm had completely whirled off in its ferocity toward other unlucky climes, and the sun was brilliant and warm, so their flight east was uneventful. Claire kept her eyes focused on the ground far below. Everything looked like a winter painting, all white, all glistening. It seemed that the whole state of Missouri was smothered with a pristine and sparkling smooth white vanilla icing, everywhere, mounds and mounds, covering the trees and the roofs and the fields. At least it looked that way until the city of St. Louis came into view, and then the magical scene turned into dirty snow-banks along highways and honking traffic jams and crowds of bundled-up people scurrying about their business. They set down at Lambert International Airport, got a limo into downtown, and purchased tickets to the cage fights.

Black decided to stop at the Galleria Mall for their mini shopping spree, and they went into Macy's and bought all the clothes they needed for the weekend, more than they needed, in fact, but Black was nothing if not generous. They stopped at The Cheesecake Factory inside the mall for dinner and sat together at an intimate table for two that was set along the outside wall and had dinner. Claire finished her coconut shrimp and fries first and was studying the guys pictured in *Beat Down*, the cage-fighting magazine that she'd picked up at the airport bookstore. That's when Black performed his first wedding discussion maneuver.

"Well, while we're here, we might as well go upstairs to Nordstrom's. They've got a bridal shop. We need to get in gear with the wedding plans."

Claire looked up, the magazine still open in her hands. She attempted to be diplomatic. "I don't think we have time for that right now, Black. Let's wait awhile. I don't want to get my dress here, anyway."

Black seemed pleased that they were finally discussing it. Not that she'd put it off, or anything, but she had other important things to do, like solving her murder case. He said, "Okay, you're probably right. We'll go to New York and pick it out. I was thinking Vera Wang, maybe."

"Who's Vera Wang?"

"She's a designer up there. The two of you can talk about what you want, and then she'll sketch up a few ideas and let you take your pick. She's really good, a very famous lady, especially with wedding attire. I know her personally so I know she'll fit us into her schedule."

Wrong. "I don't want to talk to her. I want to do this myself. I have something in mind."

Black placed his coffee cup back down into the saucer. He looked tickled pink. "Really? I didn't think you'd want to mess with the details."

"Well, I do."

"Well, that's great. So, tell me about your ideas."

Claire felt as uncomfortable as hell. Why, she could not fathom. She just didn't like this conversation. She didn't want to talk about it. She didn't want Black to know what she was planning, but he looked like he was waiting on the edge of his seat, leaning forward even. Jeez. And she had been changing the subject off the wedding for the last few weeks. She couldn't keep that up much longer, or he was gonna go bananas and accuse her of dragging her feet, or something. She was, maybe a little, but he didn't have to know that.

"Okay, I'll tell you. It's no big deal. I thought maybe Bud could help me pick out what would look nice on me, and then Nancy Gill could sew the gown. She's really good at that kinda thing. I saw some of the fancy evening stuff she had made when we were down in New Orleans."

For a second or two, Black just stared at her. Then he frowned. "You want *Bud* to help design your dress? Bud Davis?"

Well, it was pretty damn obvious that Black didn't like her ideas. For some reason, that irked the absolute hell out of her. She felt resentment rising up inside her, fast, furious, and not much fun. "Well, now, if I recall, Black, you seemed to like that black gown he helped me pick out that one time. The one I wore to that stupid charity gala we went to out at that school. The one without a back on it. He's got good taste. You can't say you didn't like that dress."

"I liked what was in that dress, Claire. Just like I'm going to like what's in your wedding gown, whatever it looks like. But listen, we can go anywhere you want for your dress. Really, we can. Money is no object. We can fly to Paris, or Milan, or anywhere you want and you can have anything you want. Anything at all."

Grimacing, Claire slapped the fighter magazine shut. She kept her voice very low but she locked eyes with Black. "Well, money *is* an object for me. I do not make tons of money every day like you do. And this is *my* dress that *I'm* gonna wear, and *I'm* gonna do it the way *I* wanna do it." She stopped and took a calming breath that did not work at all. "And I'm not gonna take your bounty anymore, Black. I am not some poor little needy church mouse that you've got to support. I've got a job and I've worked hard every single day of my life. I've still got some pride left, believe it or not."

Fuming and fists clenched and breathing hard, she stared across the table at Black. He looked as if she had slapped him a stinging one across his face. She didn't think she'd ever seen such a stunned expression on him before. He blinked and gave a slight shake of his head, as if clearing his vision. "What the hell are you talking about? Church mouse? What's that supposed to mean?"

"Never you mind. Hey, you just finish up here while *I* pay the bill. I'm treating you for once, and with real money that I keep in my very own billfold, and everything."

"What the devil's the matter with you, Claire?"

Not liking his calm question or his calm manner or his calm little frown, Claire got up and stalked to the front desk and asked for the check. That's when she hoped she had enough cash to pay the bill because she didn't have any credit cards with her. Damn it. She should always carry a credit card. But hey, she had enough money, even if it pretty much cleaned out her very own billfold, though, but that was okay. Afterward, she headed for the ladies' room and stared at her angry reflection in one of the big ornate mirrors in a very fabulous bathroom.

That's when she settled back to earth and sensible thought. What in the devil was the matter with her? That had been Black's last question and certainly not out of line. She leaned over and splashed some cold water on her anger-flushed face and stood there and waited for her heartbeat to stop thudding. Good grief, he probably thought she was nuts. Maybe she was; she sure had acted like it. But there was just something about his attitude concerning Bud and Nancy and her desire to take care of buying her own gown that really, really rubbed her the wrong way. What did he think? That she and her friends were too damn *provincial* to know what looked good at his fancy socialite wedding? Was that it? Did he think he was better than they were because he had more money than he knew what to do with?

On the other hand, and in the rational part of her brain that wasn't working so well at the moment, she knew that Black wasn't the least bit like that. She also knew he hadn't meant to insult anybody. He just liked to give her things; strike that, he *loved* to give her things. And she usually loved to get things, well, at least some things. Their tastes weren't exactly like two peas in a pod. He liked ridiculously expensive and state-of-the-art and over-the-top everything. She liked comfortable and old and understated everything. But now she realized, all too well and in a way that made her squirm inside, that she'd thrown a stupid little hissy fit over nothing, and in a public place, too, and owed the poor guy sitting out there alone a very big apology. If he was still sitting out there and hadn't headed for the hills. She wouldn't blame him if he was long gone.

God, the aforementioned grovel was going to come out hard, too. Humble pie wasn't exactly her thing. So she hung around a little more, thinking she should comb her hair because it looked all wild and tangled from the rotors. But she didn't carry a comb or brush and she really didn't care how her hair looked. And so freakin' what? Mussed hair wasn't exactly a shotgun blast in the gut, was it? When a couple of older ladies came in, laughing and having a good old time, she bit the bullet and walked back outside, not exactly brimming over with joy at having to beg for forgiveness and admit to Black how highly ridiculous her behavior had been. But she was a big girl. She could do it, like it or not. And she didn't like it.

Chapter Eight

Nick Black still sat at their table, wondering what the crap had just gone down and not a little pissed off at being attacked in such a way and for no good reason. Claire's angry remarks hadn't made much sense to him and had come straight out of the blue. They had been having a perfectly nice dinner—talking, laughing, enjoying themselves, everything right as rain—only moments before she went off on him. Unfortunately, it had been the subject of their upcoming nuptials that sent her spinning off into that bizarre and resentful and ridiculous tirade. And that was not a good sign as far as future wedding bells were concerned.

So Black sat there alone and waited some more, impatient as hell, and still rather annoyed, too, but trying not to let it show. He kept one eye on the front door, in case Claire just up and took off and left him sitting there. She had been angry enough to do that, angrier than he'd seen her in months, in fact. They had been getting along better ever since they got back from New Orleans so this was unexpected, to say the least.

Fifteen minutes later, he watched her appear at the other end of the restaurant and approach the table again. She sat down across from him. He didn't say a word, just stared at her, waiting. This was her show. She was going to have to bring down the curtain. He sure as hell didn't know how it was supposed to end. She glanced around at the other customers, all chatting and eating and not having a silly fight, and she didn't say anything either. So they just sat there for several minutes and listened to the clink of cutlery and rattle of dishes and low hum of conversation. Finally, she looked directly at him.

"Okay, Black, listen up. I admit it. That whole thing was really stupid. Forget I said any of that stuff. I guess I'm just touchy today and took it out on you. I guess it's this case. Sorry I blew up in your face."

Black hadn't been expecting that. Usually, if they had a disagreement, both of them just ignored any kind of apology, got over it after a few hours, and carried on as if nothing had happened. He was the one who always wanted to talk about the problem. And he did this time, too. "Okay. And I'm sorry if I insulted you. Or if I insulted your friends. That wasn't my intention. You know that I think a lot of Bud and Nancy."

"I know. Okay, you finished here? Let's go."

"Wait just a minute, Claire. We need to discuss this for more than ten seconds, don't you think? Maybe there's some kind of underlying reason for what just happened."

"Like what?" She frowned and took a quick sip of water, and looked everywhere but at him. "You always think I've got an underlying reason for everything."

"Well, you usually do. And that last remark tells me that you're still a little ticked off."

She sighed audibly. "There's no underlying reason, Black. I apologized, didn't I? What else do you want? Want me to crawl around on the floor and beg?"

Black ignored that last remark. It just proved his point. "You know what that underlying reason sounded like to me? Like maybe you don't want to get married as much as you thought you did."

"Oh, God, please. If you start analyzing me right now, I'm really gonna flip out."

"I'm not going to analyze you. But I have noticed that you never seem to want to talk about the wedding. Which makes me think that you're either having second thoughts or maybe you already know that you don't want to go through with it. If you've changed your mind about getting married, it's okay. Just tell me."

Claire darted a look at him, as if startled by his last remark. "Is it really okay?"

Black grimaced. "Well, hell no."

After that, Claire glanced around, sighed again, and then looked back at him. "This isn't the place for this conversation."

"No, it isn't, and I won't push it, but let me say this one last thing. Starting now, you're in complete charge of the wedding. I don't care where it is or when it is or how it looks. You and Bud and Nancy can plan the whole thing, if you want, do it however you want, invite whoever you want. All I want is for you to be happy and want to get married, that's all I care about. But truthfully, right now, I'm not so sure that you want that at all."

Claire heaved in another sigh, even heavier this time, long, drawn out, and overly dramatic. "Look, would you just chill out about this? You're overreacting big-time. I jumped you for no particular reason. My bad. Probably because I'm really, really tired. I want to be with you. You know that." She didn't look at him. "We're together all the time as it is. We live together. It's like we're already married. I just don't get how all the fancy hoopla and a piece of paper matters."

"It matters to me."

"Okay, fine, let's just talk about it later. Like I said, I'm sorry. This whole thing is all my fault, and I know it. I do. I just thought I had a pretty good idea for the dress, that's all. You know, a surprise for you. Something that you'd especially like. I just wanted to do it my way. That's all this is. But fine, you and that Wang woman can do it. No problem. Now let's go. I already paid the bill. My treat."

Now that explanation was something that Black could live with. Truth be told, he was pretty much relieved. At least she wasn't breaking off the engagement. And she hadn't taken off the ring. It was right there on her finger. "Well, okay then. You know that I like surprises so I'll look forward to seeing the dress you pick out. And thanks for dinner. It was really good. Mind if I leave the tip?"

Claire laughed a little. She looked relieved that her apology was over and accepted. Black smiled, too, because it appeared that things were back to normal, just like that. And Claire was going to have the dress she wanted and however she wanted it, and he was fine with that. So it seemed *that Wang woman* wouldn't be designing anything for Claire, after all. That remark was just so Claire that he had to laugh a little to himself as he followed her out of the restaurant.

When they were back inside the car, their shopping bags stowed in the backseat, however, Black looked over at her and decided that maybe they weren't done with the subject, after all. Although Claire seemed comfortable enough to let the subject drop like a hot potato, the more he thought about it, the less well it sat with him. He needed a few more answers. "I know you don't want to talk about this anymore, and we don't have to run it into the ground. But I want to say something. You looked upset when I picked you up at the sheriff's office. What happened before I got there? Did something go wrong in your case? Or did somebody say something to you about my putting down the chopper in the parking lot?"

"Well, what'd you think? You landed a damn helicopter in the sheriff's parking lot. That doesn't go unnoticed, you know. I got some hassling, but I'm used to it by now."

"Well, I got permission from Charlie before I did it. And you don't act like you're used to the hassling." Pretty sure now that he knew what her problem really was, Black pulled out on Carondelet Boulevard and headed for the Ritz-Carlton. "The money comes with me, Claire. Can't help it."

"No kidding. I've got a small fortune worth of your gifts to prove it."

"I like to buy things for you."

Claire smiled. "Well, actually, if we're being completely truthful here, you like to buy them for you. The things you give me are things that you like or want me to have or to wear. But that's okay. They're usually pretty cool. I like them well enough. Especially that stuff from L.L. Bean."

"You're going to have to explain that a little more."

"Well, you know, all those designer things you buy me, scarves and handbags and coats and jewelry, all that crap. That's the kind of stuff you like, and you want me to like it, too."

"I admit that I want you to have the best. And you looked really good when you wore that Hermès scarf I brought you from Paris."

"Yeah, but that's because that's all I had on at the time. No wonder you liked it on me."

"Damn straight."

Claire laughed. "Okay. Like I said, I don't want to talk about this anymore. We've hashed it out, and things are good. At least for me. Drop it, or I'm checking into another room when we get to the hotel and spend some downtime with myself working on my case."

"Like hell you are."

"Don't you see, Black? I'm with you for *you*, not for your money. If you didn't have a cent to your name, it wouldn't make a bit of difference to me. I'd support you on my salary and we could live in my house. Just so you know."

Black rather liked the sound of that. She wasn't always one to gush about her personal feelings. He smiled over at her. "Well, okay then. That's good to know. But let's hope the destitute part doesn't happen."

After that, Black drove in silence the rest of the way, but something she had said was eating at him. He pulled into the front drive at the Ritz-Carlton, stopped behind a black Lincoln Town car unloading a ton of white Gucci luggage, turned off the key, and looked over at her. "I've got the Ritz-Carlton suite, and I've got a surprise for you. It's already all set up. I called them while you were . . . uh . . . paying the bill."

Claire smiled and shook her head. "Didn't we just get finished discussing this? See what I mean? You're doing what you want. You didn't confer with me on this stuff, now did you?"

"Okay, point taken. But you're going to like what I want for you this time, trust me."

"You are just so damn self-assured, aren't you?"

"It might even get you out of that . . . shall we say . . . *uptight* . . . mood of yours."

"I'm not uptight, damn it!"

"I rest my case."

"Well, it better be damn good after this lead up."

They sat there a moment, waiting for the valet to get to them. "Tell me about your case, Claire. Maybe that's what's got you so upset?"

"Probably, because it's ugly. Worst part? I just found out this afternoon that some of these cage fighters might be training little kids, you know, forcing them to fight each other in those stupid cages. And I'm talking five years old, Black. That just makes my skin crawl."

Black frowned. "That's against the law."

"I know, and just thinking about it makes me crazy. And now I've got to interview these loser fighters at the arena and spend the weekend here instead of going out in those hills and making sure that no child abuse is going on."

"If they're out there, you'll weed them out and put a stop to it. I have no doubt, whatsoever."

"It's just so sick. How could anybody do that to their own child?"

The valet showed up at Black's door a moment later, so they got out, gathered their shopping bags, checked in at the desk, and then headed for the elevator. The serious conversations were now over. Black planned to have a very enjoyable weekend, and he was going to make sure that Claire did, too.

When Claire opened her eyes the next morning, Black was long gone with no note in sight as to his whereabouts. Oh, well, he was probably out at the mall getting her another expensive scarf to slink around in. She was surprised, however, when she saw on the bedside clock that it was already nine o'clock. She had been more exhausted than she had even realized. Maybe that explained her silly miff from the night before.

But right now, she felt rested and relaxed and ready to go arrest some murderous cage fighters. She snuggled back into the soft and silky pillows, thinking about all the young belligerent men she was going to have to interrogate. More interesting, she was going to have to infiltrate Ivan Petrov's little enclave and push around his band of big bad guys. But hey, that was gonna be the fun part.

Not long afterward, she dozed but opened her eyes again when she heard the door in the living area open and close. Her 9mm and .38 snub were both loaded and under her pillow, thus close enough to grab, so if a weapon-wielding felon showed up on the threshold she could protect herself with the best of them. Not that she expected an attack, but one never knew in her line of work. A moment later, it was Black who appeared at the bedroom's French doors. He had on khakis and was wearing the dark blue denim shirt they'd bought at Macy's unbuttoned over a black insulated Henley shirt. He was carrying a rectangular black box. Oh, God, if that was a wedding dress, he was a dead man.

"I bought you a present. You know how I am. I liked it, so I wanted to force you to like it, too."

"Hey, don't be so sarcastic."

"Open it. I tried harder this time."

"What's that mean?"

"That means it's not a designer anything."

"It better not be my wedding dress. Just sayin'."

Black laid the gift down on the bed in front of her. "Quit being so picky and ungrateful. But you do look good with your hair all wild like that and wrapped up naked in that sheet."

"You flatterer, you." Claire sat cross-legged and pulled loose the white ribbons and then lifted the shiny black lid. Black tissue paper was folded inside, hiding the contents. She pulled it back, not sure what to expect. Then her eyes settled on what was inside. She instantly came up on her knees and grabbed it out of the box.

"Oh, my God, Black, you did *not* get this for me!"

Black was just sitting there on the edge of the bed, grinning and enjoying himself. "I looked for an Hermès scarf but didn't see one you wouldn't hate."

"Oh, man, this is so sweet. A Glock 19. I can't believe you actually went out and got me this." She looked up at him, truly thrilled with the new gun. "Oh, my God, I've wanted this ever since I lost the first one down in that swamp in Lafourche Parish. Oh, thank you, thank you. I love it, Black. I love it."

"You said I only bought you stuff that I liked, and after a bit of soul searching, I realized that was true. This is something you wanted, so now you've got it. Actually, I bought myself one, too."

"And you got me a leather belt holster to go with it. And a ton of ammunition."

"You like this gun better than your engagement ring, don't you? Admit it. You definitely weren't this excited when I gave you that ring."

"I was, too, but I can't protect myself with that ring. But this little baby, wow, Black, that's all I can say. Wow. You hit the jackpot this time."

"Yeah, I know. So show me how grateful you are."

So she did show him, and he liked it almost as much as she liked the gun.

Chapter Nine

Later, and after a leisurely breakfast with Claire still in one of the hotel's soft white monogrammed robes and Black now back in his robe as well, he said, "So you really like that Glock, huh?"

"Now you're just fishing for compliments."

"So I am."

"Okay. My, my, Black, you certainly have a way about you when it comes to buying a gal guns and ammunition."

"That's because I always try to think about what *you* like when I'm out shopping. For fear that, otherwise, you'll get mad, stalk off, and buy me dinner." He grinned, and yes, it was very smirkish, and then he picked up the *St. Louis Post-Dispatch* that came on their room service cart and opened it to the sports section.

Claire had to laugh at that little tidbit, because she deserved what he had said, but serious stuff was incoming now because she'd put off a very serious and case-related conversation for as long as she could. She was not looking forward to bringing it up, and he wouldn't like it, either, not even one little bit. In fact, his pleased-with-himself expression was going bye-bye-so-long in about three seconds. But, oh, well. "Okay, Black, brace yourself for something you're just gonna hate with a passion."

His wary eyes appeared over the top of the newspaper and were just so easy to read: *Oh, God, now what?* Which was the usual state of their lives of late, so she plunged in headfirst and willy-nilly, at that.

"Okay. This case I'm working on? You know, the dead and frozen cage fighter we found?"

"Yeah? What about it?"

Man, was he ever guarded now, hunkered down into dig in and defend, big-time. "Well, Bud and I uncovered an interesting connection right here in St. Louis. That's another reason I wanted you to come over here with me."

"Yeah? And?"

"Well, it's a little sticky, Black."

"I wouldn't expect anything less from you."

Claire inhaled deeply and let him have it. "Okay, it involves Ivan Petrov."

In the blink of an eye, Black's facial expression changed from guarded-as-hell to I-do-not-want-to-hear-another-word-about-this, and in a fraction of a nanosecond, too. He stared at her without speaking, and then he said, "Ivan Petrov runs a crime family here in the city. Drugs, prostitution, gambling, rackets, gun running. He's implicated with your victim?"

"Afraid so."

"Wonderful."

"Do you know him personally?" She hesitated, not sure how to put her next question. "Or does anyone in your family happen to know him?" God, that was so damn clumsy that she embarrassed herself, but it sounded a little bit diplomatic, even if it wasn't. What else could she say? Something like: *Tell me, sweet cakes, is your godfather brother, Jacques Montenegro, in criminal cahoots with this lowlife dirtbag?*

"By that, you mean my brother, I presume." He frowned and shook his head. Now he was dragging his feet, big-time. He hated it when they talked about his big brother aka New Orleans crime lord. "I believe they are acquainted. I doubt very much if Jacques does business with Petrov. Ivan's a very unstable and dangerous man. Jacques doesn't care for him personally."

Claire had a feeling that nobody on God's green earth cared for Ivan Petrov personally. "Well, I've gotta go interview him. In person. ASAP. I thought you might want to come along and be my backup since Bud's not here. You know, keep his goons from shooting me down."

"That is not funny. And you do not want to go anywhere near him, believe me, Claire."

Momentarily, Claire contemplated the reason why he thought she was being funny and couldn't think of anything. "Well, sorry, but I'm gonna have to. His ex-wife accused him of murdering her husband, and her husband happens to be my victim. Therefore, I'm on call to check him out. See if he's got an alibi for the window of opportunity."

"You do *not* want to do that, believe me, Claire," Black repeated firmly, his face utterly somber, his light blue eyes intense, as they usually were when discussing murderous mobsters.

Claire laughed off his concern. "What's he gonna do? Kill me?"

"Maybe. Don't joke around about this, please."

Claire sat up straighter. "Is he that dangerous?"

"What the hell do you think?"

"I think I don't have any choice. I need to know where he was when the murder went down and where his little army of villains happened to be hanging their black hats. I also understand that he has some guys in the cage fighting business. I need to question him about them, too. It's all connected."

"Tell me about this case, Claire. And don't leave anything out. This is not good. We are in dangerous territory now."

So she told him about Parker the Punisher, and his pale and fragile wife, Blythe, and the ugly circumstances of their love affair and their familial discord. And everything else they had come up with thus far.

"Oh, God, you have really stepped in it this time. Let me tell you again, it's not a good idea to mess around with the Petrov family. They're dirty."

"Oh, really? No kidding? Are they bad guys, or something, Black? Mobsters, maybe?"

"Like I just said, this is no joking matter. They are ruthless killers, the whole lot of them."

"This is police business. I've got to interview them, whether they're ruthless killers or not. In fact, I have interviewed lots of ruthless killers, including your brother. Blythe Parker believes they might have murdered her husband, and she seemed pretty damned sure they were capable of it. Charlie wants it checked out. I'm under orders here."

"Jacques is nothing like Ivan Petrov, damn it. He's trying to go legit. I told you that."

Uh-oh, he was offended. Understandable, of course. After all, Jacques was his only living family, and she had just insulted the hell out of him. "Sorry, Black, really I am, but they do have a couple of similarities, you have to admit."

Black leaned back in his chair and contemplated her for a moment. Then he stood up. "Stay right here. I've got to make a few phone calls."

"Who are you calling?" she called out to his back as he disappeared into the bedroom and shut the door.

Oh, well. She had a badge. Ivan Petrov would have to let her in. Trouble was, would he let her out?

Maybe ten minutes later, Black came back, still holding his smart phone.

"So, who'd you call?"

"I called Book. He needs to know about this."

John Booker was one of Black's best friends and his go-to private investigator. "Booker? Why?"

Black put his phone down on the table, hesitated for a second or two, but long enough to make Claire begin to feel nervous. He looked down at her, and yes, he did appear a trifle edgy himself. Then he said, "Let me tell you a story, Claire."

What the crap? Claire thought. Black was a lot of things but he wasn't usually a storyteller. He had never told her a single story that she could ever remember, not even at bedtime. In fact, he usually *was* the story at bedtime. But if he had a tale to tell this time, she had a feeling that it was going to be one heck of a doozy. Probably a tragedy, to boot. The Shakespearean kind of tragedy where everybody dies at the end.

"Oookay. I like stories. Never heard one of yours, though. Except when you told me you were in London when you weren't, and I didn't like that one at all. So go ahead, let me hear it."

Black sat down across from her at the table, and now seemed more relaxed than Claire now felt. Maybe the telling of stories mellowed out his Petrov anxieties. "Once upon a time, not so long ago, six years, to be exact, there was a really nice woman named Kate Reed. She lived in a cabin on a river called the Current. She adopted a little baby boy named Joey. One rather unpleasant morning a bunch of armed Russians from a Moscow crime family run by a guy named Kafelnikov barged into her house, shot dead her lawyer husband by the name of Michael Reed, and told her to hand over her baby or they'd kill her. Kate is a pretty remarkable woman, however, and managed to get away from them and flee into the woods with her child."

"Something tells me this tale doesn't exactly qualify for Dr. Seuss Day, does it?"

"Not in the least."

"I suppose it's got a big bad Russian wolf, too? If not a whole pack of them?" Claire said.

"Yeah, a pack pretty much nails down the parameters. The leader of that pack is Ivan Petrov's predecessor here in St. Louis, a real criminal psychopath who we'll just call Vince."

That little revelation brought her story enjoyment sliding down a notch or two or twenty. "This is not fiction, is it?"

"Not even close. Want to hear the ending?"

"I'm not so sure anymore."

"So, Kate Reed escaped the bad guys and fled into the woods with her baby. They pursued her and almost caught them, until she met up with a big tough guy who happened to live out there, and he decided to help her get away from the bad guys. He was on the run, too, you see, from military authorities. He helped Kate and the baby make it out of those woods alive, but guess what? That little baby boy? Joey? The child that Kate had recently adopted? Her lawyer husband, Michael, had arranged the adoption. Worse than that, Michael was unfaithful and had a girlfriend. So guess who Joey's father was?"

"Vince, the big bad wolf?"

"Nope, the baby's daddy was Kate's own sleazy excuse of a husband, Michael. And the mother was his girlfriend."

"You're telling me that he brought home his baby from an adulterous love affair for his wife to adopt? Without telling her? That's downright tacky. You better not ever try that."

Black gave a less than mirthful smile. "You just don't know. His lover's name was Anna. And not only was Anna married to Vince the Psycho, but she was also Vince's boss, Kafelnikov's only child. As it happened, Vince was out of the country when she delivered little Joey, over in Moscow reporting in to Anna's father. So Anna invented a story about Joey being kidnapped in order to get the child out of Vince's hands for fear he'd kill the baby if he found out she had gotten pregnant by another man. Vince was about the craziest son of a bitch who ever drew a breath, and he was obsessed with Anna. So there was no telling what he'd do. But Anna was sure he would kill all of them: Michael, Kate, her, and the baby."

"Good God, Black, are you kidding me? This sounds like the next installment in the *Godfather* franchise."

"I wish I was kidding. It's more like a Greek tragedy. Are you following me so far?"

"Sort of."

"So when they finally caught Kate and the baby and took them back to Anna to identify the child as her supposedly kidnapped son, Anna was horrified what her husband, Vince the Psycho, would do if he found out that little Joey wasn't his baby. So she told him that his thugs had brought back the wrong kid, that Kate Reed wasn't the kidnapper. That Joey wasn't hers. So they let Kate and the baby go."

"Great. So there is a happy ending."

"Not so much."

Claire frowned. "Okay, I think I've got the gist of it now. Anna didn't want Joey to grow up in the mob so she was unselfish and gave him up. Can't say I blame her. What I want to know is how Booker fits into all of this. Why did you call him?"

"Booker is that big tough guy in the woods who helped Kate escape. She ended up marrying him and he adopted little Joey. Therefore, he needs to know what's going down with Petrov, just in case any of this ancient history blows up. Anna is Ivan Petrov's cousin, but he doesn't know the truth about Joey, and Anna doesn't want him to, or he'll find the kid, kill Book and Kate, and drag that poor kid right back into that compound with the rest of the family. That is, if he doesn't just kill the boy outright."

Truly shocked, Claire could only stare at him. "Oh, my God. You live in a whole secret alternate gangster universe, don't you, Black?"

"No, I don't. I didn't have anything to do with any of this. But I know about it, and that's why we've got to tread very carefully right now. Petrov doesn't know anything about Joey, not where he is, not who he is, and especially not that the boy is his cousin Anna's baby and Kafelnikov's grandson. And Anna doesn't want anyone to know, not ever. He thinks Anna's son was taken in that kidnapping and was never found. He's got to keep on thinking that."

"But Current River's way south of the lake, down close to the Arkansas border, right? Why would Petrov connect any of this to me or to my investigation?"

"He probably wouldn't. I'm just saying we need to be cautious in what we do and what we say to him or anybody connected to him. Ivan Petrov was the one who murdered Vince on Kafelnikov's orders, slit his throat from ear to ear, right after they found out that he liked to slap Anna around and had allowed somebody to kidnap her baby. But Ivan Petrov answers to Kafelnikov in Moscow, no question about it, and if Kafelnikov ever finds out that Anna gave up his grandchild to Kate and Booker, he would kill them, and probably Anna, too, only daughter or not. So, that's why I don't want you going over there to see him. I don't want you anywhere near Ivan Petrov or his compound. He's too damn dangerous."

"But, Black, come on . . ."

"And you don't have to go in there, either. I have another way. A better way. I've met Ivan before, through Jacques, on one occasion, and in other situations. I can find out what you need to know. So I want you to tell me everything that this Blythe woman said to you and the questions you want asked."

Claire basically zeroed in on one particular sentence in that whole spiel. "You know him in *what* other situations? And they better be legal, Black."

"They are definitely legal. That's all you need to know."

"Sorry, Charlie, that just doesn't cut it. You tell me how you're involved with him, or you're out of the loop and out of this investigation. I'm sure I can get somebody down at St. Louis PD to go over there with me."

It was crystal clear that Black didn't like any of those pointed threats, but that was just too damn tough for words. He said, "Okay, this is breaking patient confidentiality but you're forcing my hand and I know I can trust you. I treat Anna Kafelnikov for depression. If she comes in to see me, she can tell us what we need to know. And if Ivan Petrov put out a contract on Paulie Parker, chances are that she'll know about it, too. As Kafelnikov's only child, she's on the family board of directors, so to speak. And that way, Ivan will never know that he's under investigation, which is safer for all of us."

"And how do you propose that we arrange this little private chat with Anna Kafelnikov, or whatever her name is?"

"Ivan's got fighters in the ring tonight. He should be there ringside. If he is, I'll go over and say hello to him and see if I can't get him to set up a therapy appointment for Anna. That's the way we do it. When I'm here in town, I call and ask him if she needs to see me. You and I can interview her in the office I use at Barnes Jewish Hospital, and in private. If we do it that way, Ivan will never know you're on to him. It'll be better this way, Claire. I promise you. Nobody will get hurt. Then if he's guilty, you can have a SWAT team go inside that compound and pick him up for you."

"I don't like it. In fact, I don't like any of this. Are you sure that's the only tie you've got with this guy Petrov?"

"How many times do I have to tell you that I'm not a part of my brother's organization?"

"Well, you've got to tell me again this time, if you want me to go along with your little plan."

"Okay, there was one time that I had to deal with those guys, and I swear to God it was innocent on my part. I met with Kafelnikov at his country estate outside Moscow. Petrov was at the meeting because he's the oldest son of Kafelnikov's sister and was acting then as Kafelnikov's right-hand man. All I did was carry what was pretty much a thanks-but-no-thanks answer from Jacques on Kafelnikov's proposal to bring some of their illegal weapons in through New Orleans. Jacques didn't want anything to do with them, but he didn't want to disrespect Kafelnikov, either. It's never healthy to do that. When I was there, I offered to treat Anna when her father told me she was suffering from depression over the abduction of her baby and then I gave him Jacques's message, and I was out of there. Like I've told you before. I don't get involved."

"And you don't call that involved? I thought we had an understanding about this stuff, Black. If you are some kind of courier for the mob, then we are done. I mean it. I am a law enforcement officer. I'm not going to look the other way on something like this."

"I went over there before I even met you. I was contemplating opening my Moscow clinic at the time and had a trip planned anyway. Jacques asked me to do him a favor. I haven't done another favor like that, before or since. Until now."

And was Claire ever glad to hear that. "That's a pretty convoluted bedtime story you just told me. A real Grimm's tale, all right."

"This kind of thing happens more than you might think. Once in the mob, you're trapped there, whether you like it, or not. That's one reason I never got in and changed my name to end any association with my brother's business."

"And you think Anna really will know if they hit Blythe Parker's husband?"

"She keeps her ears open. Ivan is Anna's first cousin, and she also knows Blythe well from when she was married to Ivan and lived in that compound. She'll know if anything went down in the family. I wouldn't be surprised if she helped Blythe get away from him, if she ever really did get away. The most important thing is that Booker's and Kate's names don't come up in all of this. It could put his whole family in jeopardy. It could mean that Joey's taken away from them. They couldn't handle that, Claire. Neither one of them. They love that boy as if he's their own."

Claire knew Booker pretty well by now, but she had never met his wife, Kate. But now she wanted to. The woman sounded like she had a lot of guts. Claire already liked her. "Okay, I guess. But if this Anna doesn't know anything, then I'm going to have to go see Petrov himself. I can't just ignore Charlie's direct orders."

"Do you really think Petrov is going to tell you anything, even if you do interview him in person? Well, I can tell you. He won't. But if we have to, we'll go see him together, but only if Anna doesn't come through for us. He thinks he owes me for making his cousin Anna feel better. He'll see you, but I don't want you to go inside his compound without me. Some people who go in there don't come out. I know that for a fact. We can plan to meet him right here at the hotel instead, where nobody will see us with him. All I ask is for you to talk to Anna before you approach him. It'll be better that way, believe me."

"Well, one thing's for certain, your little story makes it pretty easy to believe that Petrov and his pack of creeps are perfectly capable of beating a man to death with baseball bats."

"You bet they are. That's why I told you all this. And I've already talked to Jacques and Jose Rangos. They're making discreet inquiries within their circles. If anybody put out a hit on Paulie Parker, they'll probably be able to find out before we can."

Jose Rangos was another powerful Mafioso who hailed from Miami and with whom Black bore a closer acquaintance than Claire would have liked. She had met Rangos once and afterward ended up having a rather ugly scene with Black when she confronted him about some of his more dubious criminal associates. They had worked through it at that time, but only because Black had sworn that he was not involved with them, other than familial blood ties, which was also a GREAT BIG SECRET that they were all holding close to their proverbial, mobster-loving vests. But now, here they were again, the mob back in their faces and causing complications that Claire did not want or need.

"I don't like this any more than you do, Claire," Black said, obviously reading the absolutely disgusted expression on her face. "But let's just tiptoe through these interviews and get the hell out of here in one piece."

"Fine by me," she said and certainly meant it. *If* any of it worked. And it was a good thing Black had chosen that morning to give her a shiny new Glock 19, too. It appeared that around the Kafelnikov/Petrov families, she was going to need three weapons on her person in order to feel secure. Maybe she should stick a fancy Ritz-Carlton steak knife in her sock, too, just to be on the safe side.

Chapter Ten

Later that same evening, Nick Black followed Claire into one very rowdy, loud, and raucous Chaifetz Arena on Compton Avenue. He felt as if he were entering a Roman coliseum, with lots of thumbs just waiting to stab downward, gore galore, and hundreds of blood-thirsty fans shouting for no mercy. In other words, it was not his thing. He already knew it wouldn't be Claire's, either. She couldn't stand to watch legitimate boxing matches, which he did enjoy. This sport was just a little too savage, but apparently not to the excited people now crowded together in the seats.

Claire was busy searching the place for some guy named Sonny Randazzo, whom Black didn't really care to meet. In fact, he didn't care to meet anybody in attendance. But he didn't want Claire to meet them alone, either. He scanned the place for Ivan Petrov. Black didn't know Ivan well but had spoken with him before, on occasion, as distasteful as that had been. He was willing to do it again, for Claire, and for a couple of personal reasons, too.

Once they had threaded their way to their ringside seats, they sat down in the front row where they could watch the punching and kicking up close and personal and hear the dull thuds of fists and feet bruising muscle. That's when he found the object of his disgust. Ivan Petrov was sitting diagonally across from them, also in the front row, his usual entourage of enforcers and bodyguards surrounding him. If Black remembered correctly, they had two men inside their organization that competed in this sport. Hell, Petrov's minions probably fought each other on a daily basis just to see the blood spatter. They were well known for their violence, even against one another. Claire did not need to mess with these guys, not on her own anyway, so he was going to do it for her. And for John Booker and his family.

Claire was still looking for her own unfortunate prey without much luck. Black didn't envy the guy. Claire said he was obnoxious, and Claire usually didn't handle obnoxious with kid gloves. He leaned close to her ear and said over the crowd noise, "I see Petrov. I'm going over there and talk to him."

"Great. Let's go."

Black put his hand on her arm and stopped her. "You wait here. It will go better if I talk to him alone."

"Like I told you, Black, I've got a lot of questions to ask him. Parker's wife seemed pretty adamant when she accused him of murder."

"Yeah, and like I told you, Claire, a personal confrontation is the last thing you need at the moment. These guys are not to be taken lightly. They kill at the slightest provocation."

"Oh, yeah? They kill a police officer and they're dead meat."

"Which would also make you dead meat. Claire, listen to me. I am serious here. It will be better for your case if you don't go over there and get in their faces. Asking a bunch of questions about this kid's murder will only make them nervous. Please, let me handle this. I know a better way to get the information you need. Trust me, just this once."

Frowning, Claire's big blue eyes searched his face, definitely not wanting to relinquish control of her case, but finally and to his great relief, she said, "Okay. But if I see they're giving you grief, I'm coming over there."

"They aren't going to give me any grief. You, they'll give you plenty of it."

"Why doesn't that make me feel better?"

Black looked around, and lowered his voice. "Again. And like I told you before. I treat his cousin Anna, who he says he loves and respects—if he's even capable of those feelings. He thinks I make her a happier woman, which makes her father in Moscow a happier man, which makes Ivan more secure in his position. Kafelnikov dotes on his only daughter and will continue to do so unless he finds out she gave away his grandson to the Bookers. So just sit here and wait for me. I won't be long."

Claire did not look thrilled but she nodded. He got up and found Ivan Petrov's gaze was already latched on him, as well as the eyes of every other man in his group. Most of them, however, swiveled their attention unduly to Claire as Black walked around the cage toward them, something else that did not sit well with him. He steeled himself. He truly loathed this guy but was careful never to show it. He wouldn't show it this time, either. Ivan Petrov considered Black an equal, a loyal cohort who could keep his mouth shut. But Black wasn't. Not even close.

When he reached the roped-off area reserved for Petrov's thugs, Ivan stood up, smiled, and stretched out his hand. Black took it and hoped to God that there weren't any paparazzi in attendance. The last thing he needed was for a photo of him getting friendly with Petrov splashed all over the tabloids.

"Well, if it isn't Nicky Black in the flesh. Good to see you, man. Have a seat." The burly guy sitting beside Petrov got up and stood in the aisle.

Black realized that some of the wiseguys were still staring at Claire, who was staring back at them, and with a look that could kill a horse. In fact, she looked as if she was fantasizing about pulling out her new Glock 19 and throwing them all behind bars. Which she probably was.

"Is that Claire Morgan I see over there?" said Ivan in his slow, heavily accented Russian speech pattern, apparently nobody's fool, after all. "She here with you, Nicky?"

"That's right."

"I see her picture in the newspapers now and again. She's that hotshot detective, yes?"

"That's right."

The two guys sitting on the other side of Petrov were his personal bodyguards. They were twins and looked almost exactly alike. Ike and Mike Sharpe, if Black recalled. Their last name, however, was not the least bit descriptive. Neither of them had much of a brain in his head and both were as brutal as the day was long. They were the cage fighters owned by Ivan, if Black remembered correctly, and their scarred-up faces and smashed noses bore witness to their profession. One of them grinned up at him. "Man, they didn't make no cops like her when I lived at the lake. That babe over there? Hell, she can pat me down any time she wants and for as long as she wants. Wouldn't mind a body cavity search, neither."

The group of men around him all guffawed. Black set his jaw as they continued talking about Claire among themselves, mostly in explicit sexual and insulting language.

He said, "Claire Morgan and I are engaged to be married."

That cut off their sleazy repartee right away. Ivan studied Black's hard expression. "We meant no disrespect, Nicky, okay?" He glanced back over at Claire. "You really going to marry a cop? Yes, I can see her ring shining from here." He looked at Nick again. "No need for us to worry about that, yes, Nicky?"

"Yes, I am, and no, you don't."

Their mutual suspicious scrutiny continued for a few more seconds and then Ivan grinned. "Of course not. I did not think such. You better mind your manners, though, I think. You and Jacques both. Or that smokin' hot fiancée of yours over there just might take you down."

Black frowned, suddenly very annoyed with the way the conversation had been going. "I have no part in Jacques's business. Yours, either. What's more, I am beginning to feel disrespected by you, Ivan. I don't like that feeling. You understand me?"

Petrov's smile faded instantly. "No, no, no disrespect, no. So, hey now, let us quit all this kind of talk. How you been? It's been a long time, no."

"Good." *Yeah, right,* Black thought, *real good, that was rich, with Claire not long out of a coma, and all hell breaking loose no matter where they went.*

"What you doing here in my town? Didn't know you were into the fights, man."

Black sat down in the empty chair beside Petrov. "I've got a patient I'm going to see tomorrow at Barnes. I just wanted to let you know that I have enough time for a session with Anna, if she's interested."

"Oh, yes, of course. She's been down in the mouth some lately.

You know, it's still the kid, after all this time. She's never gonna get over losing that baby. And I'm still looking for him. And the sons of bitches who took him."

That didn't bode well. And now Ivan Petrov was all business. He loved his cousin Anna. In fact, he pretty much obsessed over her unhappiness. Only problem was, he still kept her as a virtual prisoner inside his compound and that was what was making her unhappy.

"Well, I've got some open time if you want to bring her over to Barnes tomorrow. How does around ten-thirty tomorrow morning sound? That should give us an hour or so to talk before I have to get back to the lake."

"I'm glad you came by. She always feels better after she sees you."

"That's good to hear." *And she feels better for a very good reason*, he thought.

"So you really getting married, huh? When's the big day?"

"We haven't set a date yet."

Petrov raised one eyebrow and lowered his voice. "Bet she's a real wildcat, eh, Nicky? If you know what I mean."

Unfortunately, Black did know what he meant. He frowned and restrained himself from punching the guy out. He didn't dignify Petrov's comment with an answer.

"Hey, don't take that wrong. That's just my way of sayin' best wishes."

"Yeah, well, thanks. Look, I've got to get back over there. The fight's about to start."

"Oh, Nicky, my man, I'd say you better get over there quick. Your cop just walked off with some other guy."

Turning to look at Claire, Black saw her disappear into the crowd with a man he had never seen before. Randazzo, he presumed. Damn it. Where was she going with him?

"Okay, tell Anna I'll look forward to seeing her tomorrow. If the time is inconvenient, please tell her to call and let me know. We can always reschedule."

"Better hurry. That guy looked like he could just eat her up."

Black had had it with the suggestive talk. "You are disrespecting me, Ivan. I don't like that. Nobody in my family will like that."

It was a veiled threat. Jacques Montenegro and Jose Rangos acting together would be a formidable enemy, and Petrov recognized his mistake at once. He sobered quickly. "I mean no disrespect to you or to Jacques. That's just the way I talk, man. I am foolish sometimes. I apologize."

"Well, I don't like the way you talk, man." Black was angry, and made sure Petrov knew it.

Petrov held up both palms, as if to ward him off. "I get it. I, too, would take your head off if you disrespected Anna or any of my women that way. I humbly apologize, Nicky."

"Okay. Just so you know."

"You bring Claire Morgan over to the compound someday. I know that Anna would love to meet her. My cousin thinks the world of you."

That'll be a cold day in hell, Black thought. "Maybe I'll do that."

"I plan to stay on the detective's good side. Don't want any trouble with the law."

Black nodded and bid Ivan a hasty good-bye and headed toward the spot where he'd last seen Claire. Where the hell was she? He finally caught a glimpse of her, wending her way through the crowd toward the locker rooms. Randazzo had no doubt agreed to allow her to interview his fighters. Black sat down beside her empty seat to wait for her. Across the way, Petrov gave him a two-finger salute. Then he said something to his motley crew that made them all laugh. God, Black hated that guy's guts. He hoped he never had to lay eyes on him again.

Blood Brothers

After that wonderful day in the apple orchard, Punk went to the deer stand every single day at the exact same time and waited for the pretty girl to show up again. She never did, but he didn't give up. He would see her again. She would come back. He knew she would.

In the meantime, he and Bones were getting really good with guns, now almost as good at shooting as they were with their fists. So one day when they were stalking rabbits out by the blacktop road at the edge of their pa's woods, they lay perfectly still on their stomachs in the bushes and waited for the dead leaves to rustle when a rabbit or squirrel moved through them. They had gotten very patient when stalking, could lie silently for hours, and all that, but at the moment, they were pretty bored.

Both of them froze in place when a jogger suddenly rounded the curve below them, running toward them at a slow and steady pace. It was unusual to see anybody running out this far from town, and they watched him for a minute without moving or saying anything. He had on Nike blue nylon running shorts and a sweat-drenched, sleeveless white T-shirt, and gray New Balance running shoes with a yellow stripe, and a red terrycloth band around his forehead. He had a bottle of water in a little holder attached to his waist.

"I can't believe that guy's running in this kinda heat," Punk whispered to his brother. "He's gotta be crazy."

Bones didn't breathe a word until the jogger got all the way past them, and then he muttered softly, "I'm gonna kill that guy. I need me some bones to break. It's been too long."

"What'd you mean? No way."

"Yep, that's what I wanna do. I'm gonna go out there and snap every bone in that man's body and then I'm gonna shoot him dead, right through his head."

"Don't be stupid, Bones. Pa's gonna get mad, and they'll put you in prison and you can't win no more fights if you're locked up inside there."

Bones turned his head and looked straight into Punk's eyes. He was grinning real big. "You think so? Well, who's gonna know but us? And who gives a shit what Pa thinks? He's so scared to damn death of us that he starts shakin' when he sees us comin'. Especially me. He thinks I'm nuts."

Before Punk could think that through, Bones jumped up and was out on the road, sprinting after the jogger. When he got close enough to his prey, he called out, "Hey, wait up a minute, mister."

The jogger jerked around, stopped, and leaned over, hands braced on both knees, panting hard. "Yeah? What?"

"Thought I'd kill you dead today, or somethin'. You know, just to pass the time. I'm downright bored. Rabbits ain't movin'. Too hot."

The jogger stood up and wiped sweat off his forehead with the back of his hand. He looked around, didn't see anybody. "What the hell are you talkin' about? That's not funny."

That's when Bones took his rifle by the barrel with both hands and swung the butt as hard as he could. The brutal blow struck the man in his left thigh. Punk could hear the bone snap from where he was still hidden in weeds, and then the man screamed so shrill and awful and loud that Punk cringed and looked away as Bones's victim collapsed on the pavement.

"Shut up, shut up!" Bones was screaming at the wailing, writhing jogger.

Punk looked around, but nobody was coming. The whole stretch of road was deserted, just like usual. Afraid to move, he stayed right where he was and watched Bones stuff his camo neck scarf in the man's mouth and then drag him down into the thick undergrowth in the shade of some big oak trees. Punk wasn't sure what he should do. He looked around some more, and then he slowly made his way through the weeds and bushes to where Bones had deposited his moaning victim. The man was holding his broken leg and trying to get up, but then suddenly, Bones raised up his weapon very high and brought the butt down hard right on the bridge of the man's nose. After that, the jogger didn't move a muscle. Blood pumped out of his nose and the gash above his eyes and ran down over his ears and made a red pool under his head.

"Bones, c'mon, stop this right now, you actin' like some kinda crazy person. Let's just get outta here before somebody shows up and sees us."

"No way, bro, too late. He's done seen me now. Want him to iden-tify us? Huh? That what you got in mind, smart guy?"

"I'm gettin' outta here. You do whatever you want with him."

"Okay, then. I'm gonna take my good sweet time and I'm gonna break every single bone in his body. Even those little bitty ones in his ears, you know that one that looks like an anvil. I forget what the others are called. I never gotta chance to do that before. You do-gooders always wanna drag me off and make me stop. You hear me, Punk? I'm gonna snap 'em and pop 'em and hear them crack and crunch and break him all apart. Just like we do to them chickens and rabbits and that deer we trapped in that mud pit. Maybe some of this guy's bones'll even come out of the skin. I like that, when I can see my handiwork. But not to worry, bro, then I'm gonna kill him the rest of the way and bury him out at that mine shaft where nobody ain't never gonna find him."

"Are you crazy, Bones? What the hell's the matter with you?"

"Maybe, but know what? I like bein' crazy. I like the way it feels on me." He stared at Punk, grinning in a way that Punk had never seen before, his eyes all glassy and dark and focused. "Remember, I'm the Bone Breaker, just like Pa named me. I'm supposed to break bones. I live for it, and know what? I love it. The more broken bones the merrier, that's my new motto."

Punk could only stare at him. "This's murder. You're gonna murder this guy."

"That's okay. Nobody's ever gonna know, and nobody's ever gonna find him. You know back there where the end of that shaft goes down forever. Nobody's ever gonna find him if I drop him down there, no way. I already got some stuff hid in those shafts for us to use."

"What stuff?"

"Bones and tools and stuff. You think this's the first man I went out and killed?"

Punk couldn't believe his ears. "I'm leavin' right now, you sicko. I'm not puttin' him anywhere. You're on your own with this guy. I ain't goin' to jail for nobody. Not even you, Bones."

"Yeah, go ahead, you little sissy punk. Who's always been there for you when you was gettin' your ass whupped on good, huh? Me, that's who. How many times have I showed up when you got yourself in a jam and needed somebody to come in and beat some guy bloody? Tell me that, you ungrateful little shit. You never were nothin' but a punkass coward."

Punk felt a hot streak of guilt then, and some anger, too, but he knew that was exactly what Bones wanted him to feel. Bones had tried to shame Punk before when he wanted him to do something that he didn't want to do by himself, but what Bones said was still true. If Bones wasn't there to help him from now on, he wasn't sure what he'd do. They were born together. How could he live without Bones around? So Punk just stood there and watched and said nothing else.

Then a look of triumph lit up his brother's face. Bones bent down and picked up a heavy rock and brought it down hard on the jogger's face. It hit him with the most horrible crunch, and Punk looked away. He couldn't stand this kinda stuff. This wasn't no kind of fair fight. This was just killing somebody because Bones wanted to. He said so.

"Just shut up, and quit whinin' like some damn little girl. Wow, did you hear the sound that rock made? Talk about awesome, man. Never heard nothin' quite like that."

"You broke all the bones in that guy's face, man. That's not right. Something's gotta be wrong with you."

Bones stood up and leaned over the unconscious jogger. "Look at him, just layin' there, all still and quiet and bloody and barely breathin'. He won't even feel it when I break the rest of his bones. I shouldn't've killed him so quick. There won't be no groans or moans or beggin' or nothin' fun like that."

"C'mon, let's just get outta here."

"I'm gonna break his fingers. All of 'em. One at a time. Just bend them back until they give."

"Let's go, Bones. You've done enough to him." Punk didn't wanna watch him do that, so he looked up at the tree limbs high above his head. But the fingers took awhile, and he heard each and every snap, and all too well. Ten little sharp cracks, and every one sounded downright awful to Punk. But the man didn't move. Maybe he was already dead and couldn't feel a thing. That was probably for the better if Bones really was going to break every bone in his body. He stood there, gazing into the distance, feeling slightly queasy, and tasting bile at the back of his throat as Bones whistled as he worked and methodically went about the business of breaking the bones in the guy's thighs and then in his lower legs and feet. Then he did his arms and then his shoulders and back. It was sickening, and the cracking, popping sounds were just horrible. Punk felt like he was going to puke.

"Know what, Punk. I've wanted to do this for the longest time," Bones said conversationally, now on his knees and panting a little from the exertion. He brought the rock down on the guy's kneecap. "It's my best fantasy, and lookee here, it's all come true. And I love it."

"You really are sick in the head, Bones. This ain't normal. I don't do stuff like this. Our brothers don't neither. You probably oughta go somewhere and see one of those head doctors."

"Yeah, I think I am crazy. Crazy as a loon, because I do really love this kinda work. I could do it all day every day!" Then he laughed out loud, a long, satisfied kind of gleeful happiness that echoed way up into the sky and that Punk had never heard before. "Wanna come see my secret burial grounds down on the riverbank? It's in that little quarry with the high rock cliffs all around it. Nobody's ever gonna find it. Wow, man, this's the start of something grand, ain't it? It can be our own little secret, our hobby when we're not fightin' in the cage. I feel like one of them gods of old, like I decide who lives and who dies. You can have that, too. Just come with me, Punk."

At that, Punk had heard all he could take. He just turned around and took off running through the woods, rifle clutched in his right fist, leaping over stumps and bushes, scared of his twin brother and sickened by what he saw and afraid that Bones would do it to him someday. He didn't look back, didn't want to see anything else, didn't want to see that crazy look on his crazy brother's face again, neither. He just wanted to get away from Bones forever and forget the fear in that poor jogger's eyes when he realized that Bones was going to smash in his face with that big rock. He wanted to forget this day and everything that had happened.

Punk didn't tell Pa or any of his other brothers anything about what Bones had done. But they all saw the TV news reports that search parties were out looking for that jogger who had simply disappeared into thin air. His name had been Tony Gabriel and he'd had a wife and three little kids, one boy and two girls. His wife was real pretty and blond and was crying really hard when she was on camera and talking about him not coming home that day. Man, it was a really hard thing to watch, and all that.

After that day, though, Punk kept his distance from Bones, too, and told him to stay away from him, and that he didn't want to hang around with him for a while, not until Bones got his head on straight. Instead, he spent his time alone, hunting squirrels and rabbits and waiting for the pretty girl in the pink-and-white dress to come back. She finally did, and he couldn't wait to climb over that fence and hightail it down there to talk to her again.

"Hello," she said, looking all soft and sweet, and this time wearing a pale blue dress that matched her very, very pale blue eyes.

"Hello. I've been waitin' for you every day for a month. Where you been at?"

"I was afraid I'd get in trouble. We aren't supposed to be alone with strange boys much. Especially the boys in your family."

"I ain't strange." *But Bones is,* he thought, *Bones is very, very strange.* He glanced up the hill at their property fence, just to make sure Bones wasn't creeping around and watching where Punk went and what he did. Bones liked to do that kinda thing, too. Both of them used to do it with their other brothers. Spy on them, and stuff.

"No, you are not. I like you. That's why I'm here again. And I brought you that pie I made."

"That's real nice of you. How about us takin' a walk over that-away?"

"Okay," she said.

Punk guided her along through some low-hanging branches of the apple trees where nobody could see them, even if they had binoculars, especially Bones. Hell, he was probably off killing somebody else, knowing him. Finally, they sat down together on a fallen log and smiled at each other.

"You ever kissed a girl?" she asked him suddenly, and then got all shy and blushing and wouldn't even look at him anymore.

"Uh-uh. You?"

"Me? Kissed a girl? I don't think so." She laughed and he did, too.

"Think I could kiss you a little bit? You know, let us see what it's like and if we like it and stuff?" Punk said, encouraged that she'd brought it up.

"I guess so. What do you do, just put your lips on mine and press down?"

Punk said, "Yeah, that's what they do on *The Bold and the Beautiful*."

"What's *The Bold and the Beautiful*?"

"It's a soap opera where there's lots of kissin' and sex and dumb people actin' silly. We watch it sometimes when we're eatin' lunch. They got a lot of money and free time to talk and not have to work, and stuff like that."

She laughed at that, but then she put her face up very close to his, and closed her eyes. Punk put his mouth on hers, real slow and easy-like. She tasted so sweet and her lips were so damn soft that he felt all giddy inside and wanted to lick her so bad he could hardly stop himself. He moved his lips around on hers the way he'd seen Brooke Logan do it with all the guys on that show, and he felt her slide her arms up around his neck. So he put his arms around her waist and pulled her in closer until she was clamped against his chest. It all felt pretty damned wonderful to him, and now he could see why they did it so much on all those TV shows.

Then she pulled back and kind of pushed him away, but not real hard.

"You like that?" he asked her, his voice downright husky now. It wasn't that way before he put his mouth on hers, but it sure was now.

"Yeah, I sure did. You taste pretty good."

He felt thrilled when she said that. "Want to do it some more?"

"Yeah. Sure."

So they did it lots more until they finally ended up down on the ground with him on top of her and trying to get inside her blouse like all those guys did to Brooke and the other ladies on that show. She stopped him from doing that, though, and right off the bat, too.

"Now you stop that right now, you hear me, or I'm goin' on home."

So he stopped that right now, but he sure didn't want to. He wanted to feel her body all over and see what it tasted like. "I think I know how to make love to you. How about us doing that someday? You know, when you're ready and want me to."

"Maybe. But Mama says I'm not supposed to let a boy touch me like that until I get married."

He thought about that for a little while. "I guess we could go ahead and get married if you want to. I think that sounds good. Then we could just do this all the time."

She giggled. "Now you're just bein' silly. Let's kiss some more. We're way too young to get married yet."

"Glad to oblige," he told her. "Can I lick you a little, too?"

"Do it, and I'll see if I like it, okay?"

So he licked her mouth and cheeks and swiped his tongue into her ear, and she shivered all over and said, "Yes, you can do that all you want to. It feels real good to me."

After that, they met nearly every day unless it was raining. He'd watch for her on rainy days, too, but she never came when it was bad weather outside. But on nice days she always walked up to the orchard, and they talked and kissed and licked each other, and then kissed some more, but that's all she'd let him do until they were old enough to get married. So right then and there, he decided that she was the girl for him, and that he was gonna marry this pretty girl who always smelled so good, and the sooner, the better.

Chapter Eleven

When Sonny Randazzo had asked her to follow him, Claire had glanced over at Black where he was reluctantly hobnobbing with his lowlife criminal acquaintances, and then she had followed the skeezy fight promoter through the crowds to the locker rooms. He had said that four of his fighters were ready to talk to her, and she figured Black wouldn't just up and take off without her. Not with Petrov and his goons around. She certainly wasn't going to go over there and get him. Not when he was getting cozy with a Mafioso and his minions in an arena full of screaming people. He had asked her not to, and now that Dazz had shown up, Claire had interviews to conduct.

Eventually they reached a black steel door where a huge guy with a broken-many-many-times nose, a bunch of white scars on his face, and a belligerent attitude stood guard. They stopped there beside him, awaiting admittance to the dressing rooms, and said idiot looked Claire up and down with enough lewdness to insult a skid row harlot. He had on a black plastic security nameplate that identified him as Roderick Lawson. "Got to frisk you if you goin' in there, sweet lips. How about leanin' up against that wall right there and spreading your legs real far apart? Don't you worry none, I'm a gonna make it fun for you."

Claire ground her teeth rather ruthlessly, but she remained decidedly polite. She lifted up her badge and held it in front of his squinty dark eyes. "Put your hands on the wall, asshole. And don't you worry none, I'm a *not* gonna make it fun for you."

"You a cop? Shit."

"Yeah, exactly. Now get up against that wall."

He did, and she patted him down and found a .38 revolver and a rather large bowie knife at the small of his back under his big triple-X T-shirt, the one with Mike Tyson's picture on the front, replete with the fancy facial tats. Actually, the knife was in a pretty cool tan suede fringed scabbard. Maybe she ought to confiscate it. "You got a license for this firearm, sir."

"Yes, ma'am. But it's at home."

"Well, you better run along home and get it. You'll get this back when I see it with my own two little official eyes. Knife, too. If I don't see it, I'll just have the St. Louis PD pay you a call. Got that, *sweet lips*?"

Sonny Randazzo said, "Now, let's all just try to get along. No need for all this nasty kinda talk."

"Get the hell out of here," Claire told the big guy. "You're not a good role model for the kids who fight here."

Huge Thug attempted a tough look. "You better watch yourself. Someday you gonna run up against the wrong fella."

"Oh, is that right? Well, tell me, are you the wrong fella?"

Then he had enough sense to drop his eyes and the bravado and slink off through the crowd. Claire took a minute to unload the guy's weapon and stick it in her waistband at the small of her back. She put the knife in her coat pocket. Extra lethal weapons always came in handy.

"Thanks for scarin' off our security guard."

"Maybe it's time to get a new security guard, Dazz. Maybe an off-duty police officer with some couth. Your guy's a real sleazebag who obviously gets off molesting women."

Inside the heavy steel door, there was a long white-tiled hallway and the distinct odor of rampaging-young-male-fighter testosterone. Randazzo turned to the left, and Claire followed him past three closed doors. The wide corridor also smelled like co-mingled sweat and damp showers and disinfectant and the aforementioned potent male hormone. When they reached a door that stood wide open, Randazzo walked right in. Claire followed him and found four young guys, just kids really, sitting there in various states of undress but all decent enough for her to interview without being charged for child molestation. They all stopped talking and stared at her as if she were an alien creature come to take them posthaste far beyond the Andromeda galaxy.

"Here they are, detective. Just don't stress 'em out. They all gotta fight later tonight so don't need to get 'em all upset and nervous."

"I need a private place to talk to them, and I want to see them one at a time. I don't do group sessions."

"You can use that office over there. I got DVDs of them in action, too, if you want to see them fightin'."

"Yeah, I do. Any chance I can take those DVDs home with me for a private viewing?"

"Sure thing. They're $9.99 each. We take credit cards, all of 'em."

"Then maybe I'll just borrow them for a spell. Or, if push comes to shove, I'll get you a nice little signed warrant. I'm not about to spend my own money to watch juveniles beat each other up for my perverse enjoyment. Can't imagine why."

"To each his own."

"Yeah. As long as you get your fifty percent cut, right?"

"Okay, okay, I know you don't like me much. You do what you gotta do. Just don't mess up my kids' heads. I'll get you the first one."

Claire walked inside the small adjoining office and glanced around. It had an old gray metal desk with nothing on it, except for three bent paper clips. There was one fluorescent light in the middle of the ceiling. It kept blinking and almost going out. Very similar in appearance to aforementioned midnight alien visitations. The boys were really gonna be spooked. She sat down behind the desk and took out her notepad and Precise pen. There was one scratched-up folding chair on the other side. There was nothing on the walls, unless you counted the black scuff marks and some rather inventive graffiti scribbled in red ink. Or maybe it was blood from uppercut wounds. No other furniture. No windows. Just a lovely little place to relax and meditate and sweat young fighters until they told her the whole truth, and nothing but the truth.

The first kid showed up about two minutes later. He stopped just inside the room and smiled shyly. He was naked except for a pair of rather oversized dark blue boxing trunks that hung to his knees. Barefoot and gaunt thin, but with hard, compact, well-developed muscles. Dark brown hair, cut short, with a deep widow's peak in the center of his forehead. He stood there like a figure on top of an ultra-featherweight boxing trophy until she broke the ice.

"Please come in and shut the door."

"Yes, ma'am." He quickly did what she asked but stood just inside the threshold. Obviously, this was a guy who needed step-by-step directions. She wondered if he required a Google map to find his way home.

"You can sit down now."

"Yes, ma'am."

"What's your name?"

"Doyle Carmichael, ma'am. Nice to meet you. I really do respect police officers. I think I'd like to be one someday. One just like you."

Oh, brother. Polite, clean-cut, as ingratiating as Eddie Haskell on that old TV show *Leave It to Beaver*, and she was pretty damn sure he was phony, phony, and even more phony. Probably as mean as a gar, too. "Tell me, Mr. Carmichael, are you really mean to most people, maybe even a big bully? Am I right, or am I wrong?"

His eyes reacted. Noticeably, too. Shock, maybe? But his sweet little smile did not. "Oh, no, ma'am. I ain't no big bully. I just like to make money so I can buy my mama nice things."

"Is that right? What kind of things?"

"Oh, just stuff she's always wanted down deep in her heart, ma'am."

Claire had a fairly good idea that Doyle was now envisioning getting Claire's head in a headlock and punching her in the face until it looked as raw and unappetizing as three-week-old ground beef. A kind of thrashing with which he was probably quite familiar. She had seen her share of psychopaths and she had a feeling this kid fit the bill. Too bad that Black wasn't there to give his professional opinion. She was curious to watch this kid's fight tapes and see how he performed inside the ring. See if he reminded her of Lucifer, or some other dastardly demon. Maybe he was for real, though, just taking good care of his mama like a good little son should. Yeah, right. This kid was messed up. She'd bet her gun on it. But not the shiny new Glock 19. She loved it too much. She should have loaded it and brought it along, too, but she had to sight it in first.

"That's just so nice of you, Doyle. Spending your hard-earned cash on your sweet mama. We need more kids like you in this world. What did you get her the last time you bought her something special?"

Carmichael's eyes narrowed a tad; his earnest smile did not waver. Yep, a baby psycho in the works, sans any conscience whatsoever. Take it to the bank.

"Why, ma'am, I got her a big white vase full of red roses. Dozen of 'em. She loves flowers. She grows them out in our yard. She's got, why, I bet, she's got a hundred of them pretty rosebushes that she tends."

"If she's got a hundred rosebushes in her yard, why do you need to buy her roses?"

Uh-oh, False Smiley wasn't adept enough yet to answer pointed, and yes, trick questions. He couldn't come up with a quick answer this time, but he'd get there eventually. But enough about his future criminal proclivities when she'd probably have to arrest him for serial murder. She was definitely going to remember his face, though, for when she scanned the Most Wanted websites.

"Okay, Mr. Carmichael, enough pleasantries, let's get down to brass tacks."

"Yes, ma'am. But just so you know, she ain't raisin' no *red* roses. They's all white and yellow."

Not exactly quick as lightning but a fairly viable answer. "Well, now, that explains everything, doesn't it?"

"Yes, ma'am." He grinned and looked sweeter than a mason jar full of golden honey.

"Did you fight at the Lake Inn the other night?"

"No, no, ma'am. Don't go down there no more. That place is scary weird, man."

"Scary weird?"

"That's right. Guys go missin' over there. Some guys call it the fight of no return. 'Cuz it is."

Okay, now they were getting somewhere. "Why don't you elaborate for me, sir?"

"So what's that supposed to mean?"

"Tell me more about those disappearances."

"Okay, first time I ever went down there? You know, the guy who won that night? He just flat out went missin'. Nobody ever saw him again. Just won that fight, collected the purse, left the building, and poof. He's probably rotting somewhere out in the deep woods."

"What was his name?"

"Morris Caplan, but everybody called him Moose."

"When did he go missing?"

"I guess it was about two years ago. He was good, too. Won ten or more matches. That's the last time I let Dazz set me up down there. That hotel is cursed."

"Anybody else go missing on the circuit?"

"Well, nobody's seen Paulie Parker since he won down there. That why you're here? He dead, or somethin'?"

"Do you know something about Parker that I need to know?" *Like when and how you beat him to death*, she thought.

"Nope, but I can read between the lines as good as the next one. He's dead, right?"

"Yes, he is."

"Bummer. I kinda liked him, even though he usually beat the crap outta me and never wanted to hang out and have a beer, or nothin'."

Claire asked him all the necessary questions, and then he left, still smiling, probably planning to surprise his mama with more roses. Black ones, perhaps.

Next up was Malachi Fitch aka Smooth Operator/Sex Addict/ Casanova in His Own Mind. He was big and strong with blue eyes and hair long enough and blond enough to give him free passage on a Viking ship. Oh, yeah, Malachi was a very handsome dude and spent most of the interview coming on to Claire. Claire had a feeling that whenever he had access to a mirror, he probably just stared wonderingly at himself and fluffed out his hair and congratulated his good genes. He also had a bright blue tattoo on his left forearm that said *Lick me. I Taste Good.* All written in fancy script inside a red heart. Cute as a button, yes, but a big-time whackadoodle.

His first words proved her initial assessment to be true. "How old are you, detective?"

"Too old for you, Malachi."

"Call me Mal. I like it better."

"You know what *mal* means in Spanish, kid?"

"No, what?"

"Bad."

"Good. I like that. I am bad. So bad that I'm good."

"Right."

"Know what? I like older women like you. They like me, too. I've had a lot of them, already. I think you'd like me, if you know what I mean."

"No, I don't know what you mean. Go ahead, tell me what you mean in clear and precise English. Remember, of course, that I am a police officer with the power to slap you in cuffs and lock you up. And yes, throw away the key forever."

"I do respect you. I like cops, and you are cop-alicious, to be sure, with that blond hair and those big blue eyes and that hot bod to die for. Those cuffs sound like a real turn-on. Been there, done that." He was too antsy to sit down, so he moseyed around the room, looking at things, which included the desk and the door and the trio of paper clips because there wasn't anything else to look at. Finally, he slouched down in the folding chair across from her. "I like to screw women, that's all I can tell you. And the ladies like it, too. So would you, trust me. I could show you the time of your life. What'd you say?"

"How old are you, Mr. Fitch? I can't really tell by your sopho-moric remarks."

He laughed. "Twenty-one. How old are you? Not that it matters. You are so damn hot that I'm breakin' out in a sweat just lookin' at ya."

"I do believe that you are being disrespectful to a police officer. Something about that last remark, I guess. I'm not sure why, but it sounded a little off to me."

"You're too cute to be a police officer. You oughta be a stripper down in Branson at the North Pole Bar, maybe. I'd come. I'd pay to see you naked. And man, the thought of you twistin' around on one of those poles in an itty bitty elf suit. I'm already reactin', if you know what I mean."

Unfortunately, she knew what he meant. "Didn't know they had strippers in Branson. It's a pretty clean-cut place down there with all those senior citizen tours and family Christmas shows. I'll have to alert my colleagues at Branson PD to pay the North Pole Bar an official visit."

"Come on, officer. They got strippers everywhere. You know that, don't ya? Man, I just can't quit thinkin' of you naked and all slicked up with baby oil. Whoa, momma."

"You're not very bright, are you?"

"Don't need bright to get what I want."

Claire only sighed. This boy was also headed for a jail cell. Probably one next door to Psycho Baby. Probably in the near future and for sexual assault. Time to nip his easily stimulated hormones in the bud. "These nasty sexual remarks make you look juvenile and foolish, childish even. You probably ought to edit what you say before it comes out of your mouth."

"Yes, ma'am. I'll remember that."

"How well are you acquainted with Paulie Parker, Mr. Fitch?"

"He beat me up twice. I tried to avoid matches against him after that. I like to win. And all my girlfriends don't like me to get my handsome face all bruised and cut up. They usually think black eyes are sexy, though. I got lots of girls, more'n you can shake a stick at. None a them complained about me sweet-talking them till you."

"Ever thought about thinking with your head, instead?"

Laughing, he said, "You're a firecracker, ain't ya? I like that in a woman."

"Sounds to me like you like anything in a woman."

"Pretty much."

"Where were you two nights ago?"

"Uh . . . oh, yeah, I was with a hooker down there in Lebanon, Missouri. I stopped at a big truck stop to gas up on the way over here. She was good, too. Well worth the money I had to spend."

"Okay, Malachi, spare me the sex talk. It's not working. Understand me? You're not my type. In fact, you're boring me."

"Your loss."

"Where are you from?"

"Up around Lake of the Ozarks."

Great, she had a jail cell with his name already on it. "Where at the lake?"

"We got a farm out north of Camdenton. You wanna come see me sometime? I got some big brothers around your age. They'd like to show you the ropes."

Okay, maybe this kid had been hit in the head too many times and couldn't discuss but one subject. She would just have to keep him focused. "Paulie Parker's from up around there, too. Did you know him before you started fighting?"

"Nah. Everybody up there stays to themselves. You know, sort of clannish."

"So you don't know the Parkers who live in that area?"

"Nope. We done here?"

First mention of the Parker family, and he was ready to forget coming on to her and fly the coop. Interesting. She had a feeling that the Parkers and the Fitches absolutely knew each other and not in a good way. "I'll tell you when we're done here, you got that, Mal?"

"Yes, ma'am." He kept his eyes steadfastly on Claire's mouth. What a creepy little boy. It appeared that Randazzo was rubbing off a little too much on his impressionable fighters.

She tried to discuss some of the other guys on the circuit. Malachi Fitch didn't seem interested in them. It appeared his sole purpose in life was sleeping with women or tossing out sexual innuendoes. And, yes, it was extremely tiresome. She took down his address and itinerary and told him that she and her partner might pay him a call. He said to ditch the partner and he'd show her a good time. Jeez. She wanted to belt the kid. She might have, if he had been older, and she hadn't been there on police business.

Number three's name was Frankie Velez. He was the Hispanic fighter to whom Shaggy wanted her to deliver his message. He was also the opponent who lost the fight to Paulie at the Lake Inn. But apparently he was ready to rumble some more. Frankie's bummed up face bore witness to his loss to Parker. He was big and muscular and pretty intimidating to look at until you saw his major tattoo. It said *I love my mama*. He appeared to be a lot more intelligent and articulate than Numbers One and Two, however.

"How old are you, Frankie?"

"Twenty."

"Been fighting long?"

"Two years."

"Like it?"

"Oh, yes, sir. I mean ma'am. I just love to fight. It's just something inside me that I was born with. Love it. I guess I don't have some kind of chemical inside me, or somethin', you know, that makes me feel pain, or somethin'. I just don't feel the blows rainin' down on me like most guys do. I get the bruises, though, but when I'm fightin' inside that ring, it's just the coolest thing in the whole USA. My brothers beat me up every single day of my life, but I never felt it much. They stopped when I got big enough for payback. But we're all still real close. The whole family is."

"Where are you from, Frankie?"

"Omaha, Nebraska, originally."

"Where do you live now?"

"In Lebanon."

"Lots of action over there?"

"Fightin', you mean? Oh, yeah. I pretty much dominate, though. I'm big. Tough, too." He proved it by flexing some serious biceps, which were indeed rather impressive for his age.

"Do you know Paulie Parker?"

"Yeah, I liked Paulie just fine. Too bad about him. You know who got him yet?"

"We're working on it. Do you know anybody that didn't get along with him?"

"Yeah, pretty much everybody, 'cause he always beat them. He got the best of me just the other night. But he did it fair and square. And you know what? He hung around that night after the fight to make sure I was all right before he headed home. Not many of the guys'd do that."

"Sounds like a pretty nice kid."

"Yeah, he was. He was just a lot better than the rest of us. More finesse. Just really tough and had a lot of heart. Know what I mean? Didn't ever say much, in or out of the ring, but he just took care of business, quick and efficientlike. He kinda exploded out at you all of a sudden before you could get your fists up. He'll be missed. He was my major competition. Poor guy."

"Know anything about the fighters operated by the Petrov family?"

Frankie became very wary, very quickly. He looked down at his hands. Then he looked up at her. "I'm afraid I don't know them at all, ma'am. I'm sure they had nothing to do with it, though."

"Do you know their names?"

"Yeah, sure do. Ike and Mike Sharpe. They're twins. Look just alike, well, almost. They're good with their fists. Not very bright, though."

"Do they win a lot?"

"Yes."

"How many times?"

Frankie hesitated. "More than they should. Some guys are afraid to beat them."

"And why is that?"

They stared at each other for a moment, which said a lot to her in a tacit kind of way. Then Frankie shrugged. "Can't really say."

And he didn't have to. Claire could read between the lines with the best of them. Who would want to beat a guy backed by a murderous, throat-slitting crime family, one known for putting out hits on people who annoyed them? Apparently, not too many fighters were that stupid. What Claire needed to do was talk to Petrov's fighters. Alone and somewhere outside of Ivan the Terrible's earshot. There wasn't a chance in hell that Frankie was going to tell her one single thing about them. He was a smart guy, smarter than the other two yokels she had just interviewed. Black would not like the idea of her interviewing the Sharpe brothers, not even a little bit, but she and Bud just might have to do it. Not that the Sharpes would ever tell them a single thing about the Petrov operation. They weren't that dumb, or they'd already be six feet under. Talking to them would be a dead end, no doubt about it. Then again, miracles happened.

"I've got a friend who watched you fight Parker the other night. Said you're really good, that you gave it your all. He's a fan."

"Well, ma'am, I really appreciate your telling me that. Tell him I said thanks for comin' over and watchin' me."

"I'll do that. Good luck, Mr. Velez."

After she terminated the conversation with Frankie, she called in Number Four, one Josiah Durning. It didn't take Claire long to realize that Durning was dumb, dumber, and even more than dumbest, all rolled up together in one big DUH. He was big, too, and red-headed and sturdy, probably two hundred forty or fifty pounds. He made the other three look like kindergarteners and also had a tendency to look highly confused after every question. But it looked like he had a couple of jailhouse tats on the backs of his hands. A swastika and a setting sun with red rays. Sort of Japanese flagish.

"Have you been incarcerated, Mr. Durning?"

"Yes, sir. Right here in St. Louis."

Sir? Everybody seemed to think she was a man, except for Mal Fitch, of course. He didn't understand the male concept. "Here?"

"Yes, sir."

"I'm a woman, Mr. Durning."

"Yes, sir."

Oookay. Maybe he couldn't see her all that well under the faulty fluorescent flickering light fixture. At least he wasn't coming on to her. That was a step in the right direction. But she might ought to check her appearance in the next handy mirror or try to soften her facial expression. She had on a baggy sweatshirt to hide her guns and no makeup, but come on. Black could tell that she was a woman.

"Why were you in jail?"

"They say I got anger issues."

"Do you?"

"Yes, ma'am." Well, good, her mealymouthed, soft new expression must have finally gotten through to the kid.

"And how does it manifest? How do you show it, I mean?"

"I break windows and punch walls and hurt people. Break bones, sometimes."

"Do you still have that problem?"

"Yes, ma'am."

"Is that why you fight in the cage?"

"Yes, ma'am. Folks say it keeps me outta trouble and lets me break the right bones."

"As opposed to the wrong bones?"

"Yes, ma'am."

"Does it?"

"Yes, ma'am. Unless somebody makes me crazy mad."

Well, that made sense in a crazy mad sort of way. "What's your ring name?"

"Cupcake."

"Why do they call you that? Because you're so sweet?" She smiled, lightened up on him a bit, tried to act like a girl some. Crazy mad was not a good thing, and she didn't particularly want to see it.

"No, it's 'cause I like cupcakes. The ones with red icing. I like sprinkles on top, too. Chocolate ones."

Okay, now she knew what to bake him for his birthday. She asked him some more questions, but didn't get any overly intelligent answers. Or even sort of intelligent answers. She took down his name, address, and schedule of bouts. She didn't think he had the intellect or attention span to kill somebody the way Paulie Parker had met his demise. But stranger things had happened. He could've been crazy mad at the time, for instance.

She and Bud would visit these guys in their own homes someday soon and see if something more enlightening revealed itself with the home fires burning in the background. She'd really like to meet Carmichael's roses-loving mom. But right now, Claire just needed to get out of that stifling little bare room and breathe some testosterone-free fresh air. She took the four DVDs and told Randazzo that she was good for the money and they'd settle up later, and then she escaped out into the noisy arena where the crowd was going ape over the bloodletting.

Right outside the black steel door, Claire searched around the arena for Black and found him sitting again in their rather expensive ringside seats. She headed that way, but stopped when her phone vibrated inside her pocket. Caller ID said Bud, so she punched on quickly.

"Hey, find out anything?"

Bud said, "Oh, yeah, and you're not gonna believe it, either. Know that guy I came to see, Shorty Dunlop? He wasn't here."

"Where is he?"

"Don't know yet. He up and took off without checking out. Nurse came in late one night on rounds, and he was gone."

"I take it they have surveillance tapes?"

"Yeah, and I checked them out first thing. And guess what? They showed a guy pushing Dunlop down the corridor in a wheelchair. Around one o'clock in the morning. I caught a glimpse of his face but it was fuzzy. Never seen him before."

"So nobody knows where Shorty is?"

"Nope."

"I think we better find out where all these guys live and pay them some official visits. Talk to their parents and/or wives. I'll try to get Dunlop's address from his manager. Where are you now?"

"Still at the motel. Incoming weather looks iffy for us to start back now."

"Black and I should be back home sometime tomorrow afternoon, if the weather holds out."

"Okay."

Claire paused. "Is Brianna still with you?"

"Yeah."

"You two good?"

"Yeah, real good. It's nice. See you tomorrow."

Claire smiled as they hung up. Well, at least one thing was going well. That was something to be happy about. She headed over to Black, but her mind was on tomorrow and what they'd find when they drove out beyond the lake to the boonies. Right now, however, she just wanted to grab Black and get the hell out of the fight zone, away from the sound of doubled fists pummeling bare flesh and grunts of pain and Roman-Coliseum-style-out-for-blood crowd noises.

Chapter Twelve

Around ten o'clock the next morning, Claire and Black were taking the Kings Highway down ramp off Highway 40 on their way to Barnes Jewish Hospital. They negotiated their car through the heavy traffic around the huge hospital complex, left the rental in a big parking garage at the Center for Advanced Medicine building, which everybody called CAM. Then, after a long stroll across a glassed skywalk over Euclid Street, they ended up inside a richly appointed office that Black used whenever he treated his head cases at the giant teaching hospital. There was a one-way observation window that looked into the next room, through which Claire could see several comfortable couches and chairs and tables with puzzles and Barbie dolls and blocks and Hot Wheels' cars on top of them.

"Do you use that room for therapy, Black?"

"Sometimes. Especially with the little guys. I usually let the parents observe from in here, unless the patient is over twelve. Teenage issues deal mainly with the parents, so the older kids want complete confidentiality about what they do and say."

"Do you treat a lot of little kids?"

"More than you would think."

"Well, that's sad."

"Yes, it is." Black hesitated, and then said, "I usually allow Joe McKay to watch from an observation room back home when I'm seeing Lizzie." He leaned back in the chair behind the desk and rocked a couple of times. Then he said, "Have you talked to McKay since he moved back to the lake?"

Surprised, Claire darted a quick look at him. "Joe's back at the lake? I haven't seen him or talked to him since we got back from New Orleans."

"Apparently, Lizzie is terrified of that old Victorian house he was restoring over in Springfield. He said she gets hysterical whenever she sees it and refuses to go inside. So he just closed it up and brought her back to the lake. They're living out on his farm again."

"Well, it's no wonder, poor baby. A real-life bogeyman kidnapped her out of that house. But it's a shame, really. Joe loves that place on Walnut Street. He had some big plans in the works for his bed-and-breakfast inn."

Black nodded and contemplated her for a moment. "Isn't Joe from out around where you said some of your fighters live?"

"Yes, he is. I hadn't thought of that."

"Maybe he knows some of them. Or their families. He might be able to fill you in on them before you and Bud go out there and look around."

"Yeah, I bet he can. I'll call him when we get back." She smiled, encouraged by the new lead. "So you don't mind me spending time alone with Joe, anymore? That's a first."

"Just so you wear that engagement ring on your finger and make sure he sees it. Then it won't bother me at all."

"That just sounds so unnecessarily possessive, Black. In your face, even." She held up her left hand. "This ring doesn't go in my nose, you know."

"But it's good enough right where it is to fend off interested men. Which means Joe McKay."

"I think you overrate my appeal. None of my suspects seem to find me as desirable as you do, unless it's that Fitch kid from last night. He thinks he's God's gift. One of those boys even thought I was a man. Kept calling me *sir*."

Black scoffed at that. "I find that hard to believe. And who the hell exactly is this Fitch kid?"

"One of the fighters I interviewed last night. His come-ons were so clumsy that I was more amused than insulted. You need to remember his name. He's probably one of your future patients."

"Maybe I should have a talk with him now."

Claire shook her head and then she laughed. "Or maybe you could challenge him to a duel. Come on, Black, give me a break here. You have nothing to worry about, and you know it. I'm a one-man woman."

Then Claire waited for him to bring up the wedding but he said nary a word. Well, goody. Maybe he had meant what he said about letting her plan the thing. But hey, she'd believe that when she saw it. Maybe she ought to just be flattered. She changed the subject. "So when is Anna Kafelnikov supposed to come in?"

"Ten minutes ago."

"You think she's skipping out on you?"

"No. Anna never misses a chance to get out of that compound."

So they waited some more, and then a little bit more, and then a whole lot more. "Well, looks like she fooled you this time, Black."

"She'll be here. Just be patient. She's usually late."

Fine, except that Claire wasn't patient and never had been. Bored to distraction while watching him scribble notes on some patient's file, she finally said, "So, what did you think of the fighters you watched last night?"

Black glanced up. "Not very much. You could take down most of them with one hand tied behind your back. Hell, you can almost take me down when we go at it."

Inordinately pleased, Claire tried not to show it. "Well, that is my ultimate goal, you know, to take you down. Hard, and make you beg for mercy."

"Hard is right. But hey, anytime, anyplace, baby. But if I win, I get the reward I want. And you know what that is."

Yeah, Claire knew exactly what that was, all right, and that certainly wouldn't be any hardship on her, either. In fact, she would look forward to it. *If* he won. On the other hand, he could be talking about freedom to discuss wedding plans all night long and all the next day, too. "You're on, buddy. Right here, right now. I dare you. Just come over here and see what you can do."

"Bring it. Give it your best." Black motioned her toward him using both hands.

Claire laughed at that, but their challenging words were cut short when Black's mysterious patient finally showed up. The woman walked right into the office from a back hallway that the doctors probably used so that their patients out in the waiting room didn't know they were goofing off or flirting with their nurses and/or dragging in to the office late with a hangover headache. Black stood up and gave the woman a quick hug. Then the Moscow crime boss's elusive daughter turned and looked directly at Claire.

"So you are Claire Morgan. Well, I can certainly see that you are every bit as lovely as Nicky described you."

Lovely? No way was she *lovely,* of all things, and Claire bet Black didn't use that word to describe her, either. If there was anything she wasn't, it was lovely. She glanced at him, and he was nodding and smiling, apparently as pleased as could be that Anna thought Claire looked lovely. Now that was truly annoying. Like she was one of his five-star hotels that someone was admiring and booking into. Truth, though? Anna was spot-on beautiful. Dark-lashed blue eyes, long and silky black hair, delicate and patrician features, very tall with that willowy thing going on. Yep, she'd do in a pinch to any man with eyes in his head. But alas, there was sadness about her face, too, and she wasn't trying to hide it. Not sure why, but Claire instantly felt sorry for her. She just looked so damn forlorn. Somehow she knew that the woman had suffered mightily, no question about it. She had given up her only child to Booker and Kate, and for the child's own good. Claire understood the terrible grief of losing a child. She related to Anna Kafelnikov on a very deep and personal level.

"Thank you, Ms. Kafelnikov. I really appreciate your coming."

"I'm Anna, Claire. And I'm always happy to see Nicky so I can escape that dismal armed camp I'm forced to live inside. This is just about the only privacy I ever have outside in the real world. Even now, there are two armed guards dogging my footsteps and watching my every move."

"I don't see how you can stand that."

"I don't have a choice."

"Please, Anna, sit down. Let me take your coat." That was Black, as polite as ever. The guy was just irresistible when he resorted to his Mr. Darcy-Jane Austin fancy good manners.

Anna slipped out of her long camel wool coat and matching leather gloves, and then she sat down in the armchair beside Claire's and crossed her long legs. She wore a black flannel maxi skirt with tall black leather boots and a belted pink sweater set that looked like the cashmere ones that Black kept buying for Claire in the hopes she'd ix-nay some of her favorite but ratty black T-shirts. Anna's hair was pulled back in a chic French twist without a strand out of place. She looked elegant and composed and yes, *lovely*, and she quickly settled into the same sad expression that Blythe Parker had worn. It looked like Missouri Mafia Molls were not exactly deliriously happy with their lot in life.

Black took his seat behind the desk again. "Claire is here on official business, Anna. She would like to ask you a few questions about Ivan. Are you okay with that?"

"Yes, I am. Of course." She placed her attention back on Claire. "Has he killed someone again?"

Well, that was unexpected and uttered as nonchalantly as hell. Jeez Louise. "I'm not sure. That's why you're here. You are acquainted with a woman named Blythe Parker, are you not?"

"Yes, I know her extremely well."

"When we interviewed her, she told us that Ivan Petrov was her ex-husband and that he had reason to commit the murder we are investigating. She had no proof to give us, but she seemed very sure that if he hadn't done it himself, then he had ordered it done."

"How is Blythe?"

"She looked fine when we saw her. Very pale and fragile and unhappy, but I think she is healthy, if that's what you're asking. She seemed devastated by her husband's death."

Anna sat straighter. "Paulie? They got Paulie?"

Oh, crap, Anna didn't know. "I'm sorry, Ms. Kafelnikov, I assumed you knew."

"No, I hadn't heard." She sighed, very heavily, very resignedly. "But I guess I'm not surprised. I knew Ivan was only waiting for the right opportunity." She stopped, and sighed again. "And please call me Anna. I am not particularly proud of my last name."

"All right."

Anna gave another morose little smile. "It's not easy being a member of a crime family. You are trapped inside a vicious cycle with people you love dearly but can't condone what they do. It's very hard to get out. It's like being trapped in a bad dream with no way to escape."

Claire dared a sidelong peek at Black, who sat stone-faced and said nothing. It suddenly occurred to her that Anna and Black had a lot in common. Maybe that's why he offered to treat Anna's depression and considered her such a good friend. Both were innocent people who'd done nothing wrong but had been caught up in the lawless acts of close family members. Except that Black had gotten out early and completely and had never really been involved. Anna had not been that lucky.

"Poor Paulie never had a chance after Blythe ran off with him. He was a marked man from that moment on. I tried to persuade my father to forbid Ivan to take revenge. I even traveled to Moscow to plead Blythe's case. But it didn't do much good. He wouldn't order Ivan to leave them be, and Ivan felt personally insulted by her rejection." She stopped, and shook her head. "Father did give Blythe permission to divorce Ivan, though, after I told him that I'd seen him slap her when he was drunk. My father cannot condone that kind of thing. He believes that a woman should be placed on a pedestal, especially one's wife. Despite all of that, Ivan still loves Blythe dearly. Still resents her divorcing him. Blythe was always his prize possession, as if she were some rare piece of art that he coveted and cherished and could finally own."

"So you think Ivan Petrov did kill Paulie Parker?"

"I wouldn't be at all surprised. How did he die?"

Claire hesitated and then said, "He was beaten to death."

Anna heaved in another deep inhalation and placed her gaze down on her lap. She didn't shed tears, but she looked very lonely sitting there, her hands clasped tightly together. Claire glanced back at Black, who still said nothing. This was her show, and Black was only there for moral support, as he liked to say when he was helping her on her cases. Which wasn't true at all, of course. Black just loved to jump right in the middle of her homicide investigations whenever she would let him, and with both feet, too. Hell, he ought to give up making money hand over fist and become a cop.

"Was Ivan gone for any length of time during the last three days?"

"No. In fact, he has been at home most of the time for the last two weeks. One of his little sons has been sick with the flu. But he has loyal lieutenants to do his killing for him. He doesn't dirty his own hands anymore. He had his apprenticeship down at that level in Russia, but he runs the show here. If he sanctioned the hit, he assigned it to his favorite hit men. If Paulie was beaten, it might have been Ivan's fighters who did it. Ike or Mike, either one, or both together. They're brutal, evil, disgusting excuses for human beings. I can't abide being in their presence, not even for one minute. I get up and leave the room if they walk in. But he loves them, almost as much as he loves his own sons. You do know, don't you, that Ivan got full custody of his and Blythe's two children. He did it mainly to punish Blythe for walking out on him, which you already know, I suspect. I help him take care of them, and he does adore them, but those two boys have a terrible future in store for them. At present, however, he's really into this cage fighting thing. He built a boxing ring in the compound. Since Blythe divorced him, that's all he thinks about anymore. He's obsessed with it."

"As I understand it, both Sharpe twins fought in Kansas City and then at Lake of the Ozarks. Did they return home after that?"

"No, they didn't. And they didn't send word back, either. Ivan was furious about it and sent some guys out to find them."

That info perked up Claire considerably. "Does that happen often? The two of them going out on their own like that without Ivan knowing where they are?"

Anna smiled. "No one dares to cross Ivan. He rules with an iron-clad fist. He gets off on it. Power. He's all about power. If he had specifically ordered them to be back at the compound at a certain time, they would have been there or suffered dire consequences. Apparently, he didn't expressly command them to get back quickly and was only annoyed they showed up later than he would have preferred. They said that they were out looking for Shorty Dunlop to dish out some payback. Apparently, Dunlop embarrassed one of them in the ring and they couldn't stand the humiliation."

"Did they say they found him?"

"No. They insinuated that they couldn't find him, but they are both liars. They could have found him and killed him. It wouldn't surprise me."

"Okay. Do any of your cousin's fighters have criminal records?"

Anna actually laughed at her question. "Of course. Everybody I know has a criminal record." She looked over at Black. "Except maybe for Nicky."

"Have you heard any talk about killing Paulie Parker lately? Anything that might incriminate Ivan Petrov?"

"No, but they probably wouldn't discuss that in front of me. But I have the run of the compound. Ivan loves me, believe it or not. He wouldn't ever dare hurt me, or my father would have him killed. But I listen. I like to know what's going on behind the scenes, in case my father should ever ask me, and I'm allowed to ask Ivan questions about his business. I didn't hear any talk of a contract hit or cars leaving in the middle of the night, late night phone calls, guns being taken out of the weapons room, nothing like that. I had thought that Ivan had pretty much given up after the last time they tried to get Paulie. I guess you know that Paulie used to be one of Ivan's fighters, before he took off with Blythe. That's how they met. Right there in the compound under Ivan's nose. Did you know that?"

"No, I didn't. We just started this investigation."

"I think Ivan secretly respected Paulie for continuing to fight professionally even when there was a hit out on him. Begrudgingly, for sure. Ivan always liked Paulie the best of all the fighters, even after the divorce when Blythe and Paulie got married. That's probably because Paulie usually beat up Ivan's top guys when they met inside the cage. Lately, he had seemed to lay off his obsession with killing Paulie, didn't talk about it much. Maybe he had gotten over Blythe and was thinking he could get Paulie to fight for him again. I don't know. It's hard to figure how Ivan's mind works. He's not right in the head anymore—maybe it is brain damage, maybe he was just born evil or learned it from my father. I keep thinking he'll mellow with age. Father has, to some extent, but it's not happening with Ivan. Not that I can see."

"When was the last time they went after Parker?"

"Last year, in October. They tried to force Blythe to come back home, even after the divorce was granted, because that's what Ivan really wants. He wants her back inside this compound with the rest of the family, but she ran off both Sharpes with a couple of shotgun blasts. Wounded one of them." She smiled, as if proud of the other woman's gumption. "I do love that girl. She's got more courage than I do. I tried to teach her how to adapt inside Ivan's world, but she hated it there. She said it felt like prison, and of course, it does feel that way, at least to the women living in there. Then she met Paulie, and the die was cast. I helped her escape with him. Ivan doesn't know that, of course."

"So Parker wasn't really part of the Petrov organization?"

"He was their winning fighter, but he wasn't one of Ivan's capos, nothing like that. Then after he met Blythe a few times, it was all over. Ivan had groomed him from his teenage years. He heard about him somewhere and recruited him to come to St. Louis and fight for him. I believe he was more upset at first about Paulie betraying him than about him stealing his wife. But that didn't last long. Ivan truly loves Blythe. He misses her like crazy. Still, to this day. Paulie made the family a lot of money back then, too. Mostly from Ivan's illegal betting on his fights, and such. Paulie's originally from over your way, you know."

"I know. Is there anything else that you can tell us that might help us find Parker's killer?"

"Actually, it's been relatively quiet at the compound of late."

"I may have to interview Ivan personally. Black doesn't think that's a good idea. What do you think?"

"I think he would be extremely polite, but only because of Nicky's . . . connections."

"Will he cooperate with me?"

"Not a chance in hell."

"Okay." Jeez again. Ivan sounded like a real monster, made her sorta want to meet him, just to look upon the face of evil. "Will you let us know if you hear anything pertinent to this case, Anna?"

"Of course. I can request an appointment with Nicky at any time. Ivan always agrees to that. He's afraid not to. My father dotes on me, and I suppose that's lucky for me, considering Ivan's temper."

Claire closed her notepad, and they chatted some more about the snowy weather and Claire's engagement ring, of course, and various and sundry other inane subjects. Anna seemed very fond of Black and almost as interested as Black was in their upcoming wedding, despite the lack of matrimonial details thus far. But after a few minutes, Anna turned to Black, her voice growing more eager. "Are they coming this time?"

"Yes, they are. They're late, in fact."

"Is Joey well?"

"Booker says he's doing fine, growing like a weed."

"And he is safe and happy?"

"Yes, but you can see that for yourself. There they are now."

Claire and Anna both turned to look through the observation window. John Booker was standing inside the room, dressed in tan Dockers and a black pullover sweater. He was with a pretty blonde, who was holding the hand of a sturdy little boy who looked a whole hell of a lot like Anna Kafelnikov, down to the black hair and blue eyes. Anna jumped up, smiled eagerly, and headed out of the room through the back door.

"This is the only time she ever gets to see her son," Black told Claire.

"At least she gets to see him," Claire said, but the words pretty much stuck in her throat.

Black reached over and put his hand on top of hers. He knew she was thinking about Zach. He always seemed to sense her suffering. "You okay?"

"Yeah." She tried to change the subject. She had to. "So Booker actually has a wife and son, a real family, and everything, huh? I was beginning to think he just materialized out of the woods all dressed in camouflage whenever you blew a dog whistle."

Black laughed and shook his head. "No, we usually just use our cellphones. The camo's pretty much on target, though. He likes to wear it most days. What can I say?"

Inside the next room, Anna appeared in the doorway. The little boy, Anna's biological child, saw her first and ran to her for a hug and kiss, and she sat down with him beside her, smiling and brushing a lock of dark hair off his forehead. Claire turned around and stared out the window at the people on the sidewalks far below. God, what she wouldn't give to cuddle her little baby, Zach, in her lap, hug him close to her like that, just one more time, or rock him to sleep or brush back his blond curls, or kiss his soft little cheek. But it was never going to happen, never, ever, and she knew it. He was dead and buried in the ground far away, and inside her heart, too. She didn't turn around again. She didn't watch the happy woman enjoy her beautiful child. She just stared out at the falling snow and was glad Black knew enough to let her deal with her most painful memories in her own way, thank God. She didn't turn around again until Booker and his wife entered the office behind her.

Within minutes, Claire knew that if anybody could tame a man as tough and independent as John Booker, it had to be Kate Booker. On first take, she appeared very pretty, very petite, very friendly, and very happy. Booker obviously adored her, which Claire found rather amusing. Touching even. So the mighty John Booker, as hard and intimidating as he appeared, had an Achilles heel. He looked at his wife in a way that left no question about his devotion. Black quickly introduced Kate and Claire, and then he and Booker huddled in the corner like two teenage girls, no doubt planning their next covert Psy-Ops mission.

Kate sat down beside Claire on the small tan-and-red plaid sofa. "It's very nice to meet you, Ms. Morgan. I never thought Nick would settle down, but I guess you accomplished the impossible."

But she was smiling, so Claire smiled back. "Yeah, he's a regular homebody now."

Kate smiled. "Well, I wouldn't go that far. He is known for his jet setting."

They smiled at each other again. Kate glanced into the next room, where Anna was helping Joey build a rather intricate airplane out of Legos. "I guess you know the backstory on all of this, right?"

"Not until yesterday. It sounds like you went through quite an ordeal."

"Yeah, it was pretty bad. But that's when I met John, so it was worth every terrifying moment. And it turned out well, thank God. Joey's our little blessed angel. We're so lucky to have him in our lives, safe now and secure. But poor Anna. She was so determined that he wouldn't grow up in the Kafelnikov family or in that awful criminal compound where she has to live."

"Does she get to see him often?"

"No, just once in a while, right here in Nick's office. But he loves her like his favorite aunt. And we're glad to let her get to know him. We owe her so much. She saved our lives when she denied to Vince that Joey was her son. Talk about a scary guy. She was forced to marry him, and she absolutely hated him. It was an attempt by her father to consolidate crime family loyalties, but it was nothing but hell on earth for her."

"You know, I didn't even know Booker was married until recently."

"Yeah, we both keep our private life private. If Ivan ever finds out what Anna did, he'll kill all of us."

"That's what Black said would happen. But would he really?"

"Yes, I believe he would." She stopped a moment. "The men they sent after me? They were some really bad guys. There was this one named Dmitri. He almost got Joey and me out there in the woods, and would've, too, if John hadn't saved my life. Truth, though? John scared the heck out of me, too, when I first saw him. He looked like a bearded mountain man, or a Sasquatch, maybe, or something utterly wild, but then I saw what he was under that tough façade. He is the kindest, gentlest man I know."

Kind and gentle? Booker? "Do you think they're still after you? After all this time?"

"Oh, yeah. We're very careful. Thank God that Nick gave John this job. I run a little bait shop and inner tube and canoe float business down on Current River, but it's not enough, especially in the winter. Nick pays John well—*very well*, I have to say—and it's made a huge difference for us. When John goes out on a call, he takes us with him most of the time, just to be on the safe side. We stay at a motel and enjoy the pool and room service while he's working. Nick pays for that, too, God bless him. Dmitri and his men attacked me the first time inside my own kitchen, and John's always afraid they'll find out about Joey and come down to the river after me again. I don't worry about that much anymore, but now I know how to handle weapons. John taught me well. We've got the whole place wired for security."

"Sounds like my place," Claire told her.

"Yeah, I've heard all about you. John speaks so highly of you.

Says you are one heck of a detective and gutsy as hell, as he puts it. And he doesn't give out that kind of praise to just anybody."

"Really? He says that? Well, he's not a bad investigator himself."

"No, he's not. Not at all. He's very good."

Claire felt completely at ease with Kate Booker, more so than she had with Anna. Kate was just a regular person like Claire was. Kate had come through some hard times but survived. Claire could relate. She was pretty sure they could become friends. "Tell me, Kate, do you have any cage fighting gyms down your way?"

"Not in Van Buren, but I think there's one in Poplar Bluff. Are you investigating a fighter?"

"Yeah. We found a body at the lake. I'm learning a lot about this cage thing going on now. Can't say I'm too impressed with it, though."

"I hate fighting and boxing. As far as that goes, I hate pro wrestling, too."

"Same here. Pretty brutal to have to watch."

"I'm glad I don't have to."

Claire nodded, but now she'd had enough idle chit chat. She was getting antsy to get back home and nail down who had killed Paulie Parker and why. She just hoped they didn't get snowed in. She was just raring to call Joe McKay and then pay some official visits to all the kids who got off punching each other in the face and see what kind of home life encouraged that kind of aggressive, mindless, and bloodthirsty behavior. She had a gut feeling that she wasn't going to like it very much but so what.

She didn't like a lot of things very much.

Blood Brothers

For the longest time, all Punk did was play with Banjo and win his bouts on Saturday night at the new fight place just down the road, but all he thought about was meeting up with his girl out in the apple orchard. He made sure that he prevailed in his fights because he wanted Pa to let him run free and not put him to work cleaning out the dog pens or hoeing the garden or cooking the meals. The losers had to do all the chores so it was in his best interest to win. So he went after his opponents long and hard as if they were wild and vicious animals and didn't stop until he beat them totally unconscious.

Sometimes Bones helped him when he needed it, but he usually didn't need it anymore. He tried to stay away from Bones as much as possible. Bones was doing his own thing, anyway, and Punk had seen blood on Bones's shirt and hands more than once when Bones came in from the woods that lined the blacktop road. Punk was afraid to ask what Bones had done to get so much blood all over him, so he just didn't ask. He didn't tell on him, either, because the truth was, Bones had always been his best friend and he'd always been there for him and he always would be. But people in town seemed to go missing now and again, and Punk knew it was Bones's way of keeping busy. He didn't know where he was burying the bodies, probably out in that mine shaft by the river, but he didn't even want to know for sure. He wanted no part of any of that.

Therefore, everything went along pretty well, nice and smooth, actually, until one day when one of his older brothers saw him walking with the girl over on her family's land. When he got home that day from his usual make-out session with her, his pa was waiting, holding his old bloodstained whip that he used to punish his boys. Punk was surprised. Pa usually acted a little afraid of him and Bones, but this time Bones wasn't around and Pa had been drinking too much whiskey again.

"Where you been at, boy?"

"Huntin'."

"You're lyin', Punk. Your brother saw you goin' off with that girl from across the fence. What're you thinkin'? Them people are our worst enemies in this world. And you know it."

"She ain't nobody's enemy. She's a real nice girl."

"Oh, is she now? Don't you know that if her pa sees you over there with her, he'll put a bullet in your head? We don't cotton to them people, and you better get it through your fool head. She ain't worth it."

Now that he was so much bigger than his pa, and stronger, and faster, he didn't really have to listen to his ugly rants anymore. "You can't tell me what to do no more. Got that, Pa? You ain't my boss no more. I'm gonna do what I wanna do, and there ain't nothin' you can do about it. You ain't Bones's boss no more, either."

"I'm your boss, as long as you live here in my house, you little shit."

Both furious, they glared at each other. Then Punk made a decision, right out of the blue. "Okay, then, I'll go. I'll go off with her and make me a life away from here. I don't need you. All you've ever done is hurt me and all the rest of the boys, too. We all should leave and fight for a livin' and let you rot here, all alone. Then you wouldn't have such a golden goose, now would ya?"

"Go ahead. But you'll be back. You'll come crawlin' back to your own kind and beg us to take you in. But we ain't gonna. You step foot off this land, and you'll never see any of us again. You'll never see me again. And you'll never see any of your brothers again, neither."

"That's just fine by me," Punk said, and he meant it, too.

"Well, you'll go with the clothes on your back. Get the hell outta here."

Punk walked away, but he didn't get far. Enraged by his defiance, Pa came running after him and hit him in the back with his shoulder. Punk stumbled forward hard and fell, slamming the top of his head straight into the dog pen. He went woozy for a second, and then Pa was flipping him over onto his back and slashing the whip down all over his face. Punk put up his arms to block the blows, trying to grab it and get back up to his feet.

Doubling his fists, Punk hit out as hard as he could, but his vision was blurry and his punches went nowhere. He fell to his knees when the whip cut into his left eyebrow and tried to stand up again, blood running down into his nose and mouth. But then, out of nowhere as always, Bones was there, pushing Pa off him and knocking him down on his back.

Cursing a blue streak, Pa came back up and swung a hard uppercut at Bones, but his twin easily dodged it. Punk staggered to his feet and hit Pa from behind, hard, right in the kidneys. That's when Bones grabbed up the pitchfork leaning against the hay bales. He lunged forward and rammed it as hard as he could into Pa's back, so hard that the prongs came out through his stomach. Blood slowly began to stain the front of Pa's denim overalls, and he just stood there, disbelievingly, staring into Punk's face until Bones jerked the pitchfork out. Pa fell to his knees and then forward on his face and lay still. Gasping, sweating with exertion, Punk and Bones stood there over him for a long moment. Then they stared at each other.

Suddenly Bones let out a delighted chortle. "Well, we finally did it, bro. We're free of that bastard now. No more whuppin's, no more chores, no more daddy dearest on our backs night and day. We shoulda done this when we was eight years old."

"You killed him," Punk muttered, still shocked to the core.

Bones picked up his pa's feet and started dragging him down toward the Rottweiler and pit bull pens. It left a long skinny red trail in the straw. He dropped him in front of the cage, where all the killer dogs were now snarling and gnashing their teeth at the smell of blood and at the sight of the man who had abused them.

"And you know what, Punk? That felt so damn good, it makes me want to do it again. I always wondered what killing Pa would feel like, and you know what? It felt real, real good. Better than anything I've ever done in my whole livelong life. Helluva lot better than killin' that jogger. You oughta try it. You want to kick him or stab him or something before I throw him to the dogs? They gotta get their revenge, too. Poor bastards."

Punk kept staring down at his pa. "He's not dead yet, Bones. Look, his eyes are movin'!"

"No problem. He will be soon enough."

Punk watched his twin pick up the heavy concrete block holding the dog pen's door shut. He raised it high over his head and brought it down on Pa's chest as hard as he could. He smiled the whole time, enjoying yet another cold-blooded act of murder.

"Stop it, Bones! He's our pa!"

But Bones was breaking his pa's fingers now, thrusting down the end of the pitchfork handle on them one at a time, making them pop just like he'd done with the guy on the road. Then while Punk watched, horrified, he picked up Pa's limp body and heaved it over the gate and into the jaws of the snapping, growling, biting, excited dogs. They attacked their tormentor's body like the monsters he'd made them into, snarling and tearing Pa's flesh clean away. They fought each other and barked and slowly tore him apart, until Punk turned away, staggered away a few steps and vomited in the hay.

"You are such a damn sissy, Punk. You hated him as much as I did. You wanted him dead since we was little kids. You told me so. Don't tell me you ain't glad I done killed him off. He was harder on you than on me. That's why I'm doin' this. I'm doin' it for you."

Punk backed slowly away from his twin brother. God, Bones had turned so damn evil. "I'm leavin' here. Don't you dare come after me, either, you hear what I'm a sayin', Bones? I'm done with you forevermore. You done gone bat crazy. You murdered your own pa, and you murdered that jogger, who never done nothin' to you. You just stay away from me. You hear me. I don't never wanna see your face again."

Then he burst through the barn doors and fled outside, but he could hear the faint growling and snapping of the dogs tearing at his pa's dead body, and the ring of Bones's laughter echoing behind him. He ran into the house, past his older brothers where they were watching a Rams football game and eating Funyuns and drinking beer. Upstairs, he hastily stuffed all his belongings in a duffel bag, and then he trudged across the field and toward the girl he loved more than anything else in the whole wide world. He never wanted to see anybody in his family ever again, especially Bones. Bones was terrible, sick inside his head. Somebody needed to put him in the nuthouse and never let him come out again.

The next day when his girl came out to the orchard to meet him, she found that Punk was already there, zipped up inside a flannel sleeping bag under the tree where they liked to kiss and touch each other. She woke him and then zipped herself inside with him, and they kissed and pressed up against each other and said how much they loved each other.

"Pa kicked me out," he finally told her, afraid to tell her more about what Bones had done.

"Oh, no. Why?"

"'Cause I've been meetin' up with you out here."

"Where you gonna go?"

"I thought I'd come over and live with you and your folks."

She looked terrified by that idea. But then she promised him that she'd ask her mama. After they made out for a while, she left and didn't come back until the next morning. Punk lay there the whole time, waiting, afraid that he'd never see her again. But when she came back to him, she was smiling and happy, and she told him that the patriarch of their family said that he could come live with them. Thrilled, he jumped up, and they walked hand in hand down through the apple orchard and into the little village where she lived with her own kind of people.

There was a group of men waiting for him, way down at the bottom end of the orchard path. They were all tall and burly and long-bearded and hard-looking, and just for a moment he felt frightened, as if he had made the wrong decision in coming down to meet them. He clutched his rifle tighter, readying it, not sure what was about to happen. Then the biggest man of the bunch, the one with the longest white beard and old wire-rimmed spectacles, stepped forward and stretched out his hand.

"Hello, boy. You are indeed very welcome to come back here and live amongst us."

After that, all of them took turns shaking his hand, and patting his back, as if real happy to see him. The old man in charge took him into a big white clapboard house on the main street of the little village, but everybody else stayed outside, even his girl. They went into a room that was big and warm with lots of uncomfortable furniture, but even so, that was sure a whole hell of a lot better than the old beat-up furniture at his pa's house.

"Please, sit down. We have need to talk."

"Yes, sir."

"Do you know who I am?"

"No, sir."

The man sighed, pulled at his long beard. "Well, I am your grandfather. Your mama's daddy."

Punk's jaw actually dropped. He shook his head. "No, I don't think so, sir."

"Yes, it's true. Your mama ran away and married your pa many years ago. Just like you want to run away with my youngest brother's child."

He stiffened, realizing right off what that meant. "That would make me and my girl, well, like cousins, or somethin'."

"I'm afraid so. And I'm so sorry. Marriage between first cousins is not allowed here in our family. You are family, too. You belong here with us. You are welcome to stay, and we will love you and try to make up for all the years you have been gone since your pa came and claimed you and took you away from us. But you can never marry Samuel's girl. It cannot be. It would be an abomination against God."

Punk could not believe his ears. He would not believe it. He might have to go along with what this old man said for a little while, but only so that he could be close to his true love. And he would marry her someday. Nobody could stop them. They would run away. He could make good money fighting. His older brothers already were making good money out on the circuit. Money his pa had always thrown away on booze and cigarettes and betting on their fights. But he'd play along with the old man who said he was his grandpa until it was time to take her away for good so they could get married.

"I understand, sir. I wanna be part of your family. I wanna live here with you. I'll work hard and try to earn my keep, I swear. I'll do whatever you say. I don't never wanna go back home. It's a terrible place over there."

The old man smiled and seemed very pleased. "Yes, I suspect you've had a hard time, have you not? But here in our village, you are my gift sent from our Heavenly Father. You don't know how much I miss your mama. She was my only child. She fled your pa and brought you here to live with us until you were near five years old, and then she died and your pa took you away to raise up with their other sons. She wanted to bring all of her sons here, but you were the only one she could take away. It was a terrible thing."

"I miss her, too. She was always good to me, but he wasn't. He's the meanest man I ever saw." Truth was, though, he barely remembered his mama's face anymore. And now his pa's body was a bloody torn-up mess branded into his mind forevermore. He tried not to think about it.

"Come, grandson, and I will show you to your room. We will talk more later, and I will introduce you to everyone in our village. We'll have a homecoming celebration for you. God was very good to us this day."

Yeah, right, Punk thought, *but only until he could grab his girl and get the hell out of this little dumb hick town filled with all these holy rollers.* But he followed his grandfather up the steps to the only private room that he'd ever had in his entire life, wondering what Bones was going to do with his pa's mutilated body. Maybe he was going to let the dogs eat him up like a canine garbage disposal. Truth was, he didn't give a shit what any of his brothers did anymore. He was never gonna see any of them ever again. Never.

Chapter Thirteen

Fortunately, good weather held the spitting snow at abeyance, and it was almost balmy at twenty-two degrees. Claire and Black made it back to the lake, safe and sound and relatively rested. Unfortunately, a new snowstorm had lingered over Kansas City, thereby snowing Bud and Brianna in for an extra day. Claire was pretty sure that Bud wasn't sobbing buckets over that delay, but he wouldn't admit it over the telephone. At least Bud and Bri had plenty of time alone to talk things out.

So Claire spent the next morning at the office, all by herself and writing up status reports. She also did all the research she could on various aspects of the case, including a background check on the not very Sharpe brothers. Some assault charges and public intoxication and disturbing the peace was all she had found thus far, but she intended to keep looking. Sheriff Ramsay was in Fort Lauderdale having a good old, sunny time at a beachfront law enforcement seminar so she didn't have to fill him in on the investigation unless he called and demanded it. He hadn't done that yet, so she turned off her computer and headed for the hills. She took her new Glock 19 9mm with her, intending to check it out and sight it in before she carried it in place of her old one. In this particular homicide case, she did not want to have her sights off even by one-sixteenth of an inch. Yes, the Petrovs made her a tad nervous, as did the poor battered and frozen body of Paulie Parker.

She didn't know the hill farms around the lake very well, at least not after she passed by the weird school called The Dome of the Cave

Academy for the Gifted, where she had investigated a really super
creepy case once upon a time. But she did know that Joe McKay
lived a bit farther along the same road, and Black had told her Joe
was back with Lizzie and living in his old farmhouse. So she turned
in his long graveled driveway and headed through the woods in
search of her friendly neighborhood psychic.

McKay's new Ford F150 white truck with an extended cab was
parked out front, and with Lizzie's car seat strapped in the backseat.
Gray smoke was curling lazily up from his brick chimney. He was
at home, and if it was warm inside that house, that's where Claire
wanted to be. The temperature had dropped again, now hovering
around sixteen degrees, and she was readily craving some warm sun
and wide sandy beaches. She got out and didn't make it to the front
door before it swung wide open. Joe McKay stood there in the
threshold, a big grin on his face. He had a gun in his hand, too, no
doubt still a little wary of uninvited guests after what had happened
to him the summer before when a bad guy had barged into his home,
shot dead his sweet little nanny, and kidnapped his little girl. Claire
swept that unwelcome memory out of her mind—that one, and about
a hundred others that were even worse.

"Oh, man, I must be asleep and dreamin'. I have fantasized for
weeks about you comin' out here to see me. Just walkin' up to my
door, slick as a whistle, strippin' down to the buff, and tellin' me how
much you love me and that Nick Black is now gone baby gone."

"Shut up, Joe. Sometimes you are just so lame."

"Come in, come in, stay for the rest of your life. I can't think of
anything I'd like better."

"I'm leaving, if you don't stop with the stupid."

Joe stood back and let her pass through the door and into his cozy
little home. The fire was going strong, flames jumping and darting,
logs crackling, and the living room was warm and welcoming. His
place was old-fashioned and homey with his mother's chintz-covered
pillows and rocking chairs and framed family portraits; Claire always
felt very comfortable there.

"Where's Lizzie?"

"She's spending a week over in Kentucky with my aunt and uncle.
I figured she could use a change of scenery with two people who

adore her. So we're all alone here, Claire, and we can get wild and kinky any time now. Just say the word, and I'm yours."

Claire ignored him. Outrageous was Joe McKay's middle name. She was used to his come-ons and ridiculous remarks. "How's she doing? Black told me that she's too scared to go into your house over on Walnut Street."

"Yeah, she can't seem to get over it this time. She's okay everywhere else we go, but that house really spooks the hell outta her."

"She was kidnapped by a psycho from there. I'd be scared, too."

"Yeah. Me, too. Hey, take a load off. How about some coffee? I've got some fresh bagels, but that's about it with the breakfast food. Except for Lizzie's Lucky Charms and Coco Puffs."

"Got cream cheese?"

"Yep. And it's not that low-calorie lite crap."

"Then I'll take one. Toasted."

Claire sat down at the large kitchen trestle table and watched him fix them breakfast. He looked good, still quite the hottie, with his rather long sun-bleached hair and five o'clock shadow and sexy charm. They had an interesting history together, but not a romantic one. He put down a plate of bagels and cream cheese, a tub of butter, and some home-canned peach preserves in front of her, and then handed her a mug of strong hot black coffee. Then he sat down across from her and stared unblinkingly at her left hand.

"I can't help but notice that great big, gigantic, huge rock weighin' down your ring finger. I guess it's a diamond. Didn't know they even made them that big. You forget to tell me something, darlin'?"

"Black asked me to marry him. I said yes."

Their eyes locked for a moment, and then he looked away. "Can't say I'm surprised. Or thrilled, either. Haven't seen the happy announcement in the papers, though."

"We're not announcing it. We get enough publicity without that, too."

"You sure you want to get married, Claire? I never figured you as the marrying kind."

"Well, I am. I guess."

Joe latched on to that quickly enough. "You guess? What the hell does that mean?"

"Well, you know me. I like my independence. I'm with Black anyway, and everybody knows it. I don't see why we need all the publicity a wedding's gonna saddle us with. It doesn't make it any better or worse. It just makes it legal."

McKay considered her for a rather long moment, and then he chuckled and shook his head. "If I were you, my unrequited future lover, I wouldn't use any of what you just said in the heartfelt wedding vows you recite to Nick at the altar. He might wonder if you have a few misgivings about the whole thing."

"He knows I don't have any misgivings, zero, nada, nil," she said firmly. But truth was, Black did think that, and she knew it. She guessed it was true, too, if she was being completely honest. But she wanted to be with him enough to marry him, if that's the way it had to be. And apparently, it was. It wasn't exactly a bad thing, after all, and it wasn't that she was dead set against a wedding. She was just a little nervous to take the plunge, that's all.

"So do you have your dress yet?"

Claire's frown was quick and massive. "I cannot believe that all you big, tough, grown men, and you a Marine, Joe, are so hung up on what I'm gonna wear to the wedding. What difference does it make, anyway? It's just a dress to put on when I walk down the aisle, and that's all it is. A bunch of fluff and lace and seed pearls."

"I wouldn't include that cynical little insight in your vows, either." McKay took a big bite of his bagel and eyed her askance while he chewed it. "Are you really gonna wear fluff and lace and seed pearls? You? Claire Morgan? That's a little hard to wrap my mind around. And I'm gettin' the distinct feeling that you are not exactly gung-ho about your upcoming nuptials."

"I am, too. I'm very gung-ho. I want to marry Black in the worst way. I just have my mind on other more important things right now."

"Okay. When's the worst day of my life gonna be? I don't want to miss it. Miss it in that I want to be a million miles down the road when you say I do. Besides that, I don't intend to give up on having you for myself until you actually tie the knot with Nick."

Claire sighed. He was just kidding, she knew that, but the subject was truly getting old. What did she have to do to discourage him? Tattoo Black's name on her forehead? "Okay, now you're coming off creepy, Joe, sleazy, even. And no, we haven't set the date yet."

"And again, I hear the heels of your Nike high-tops dragging a trail through the dirt."

"He said I could set the date, and I'm giving it a lot of thought."

"Well, that was his first mistake." He grinned, and looked like his cocky self when he did it. "What're you gonna do? Wait a decade or two, and then pick a day the poor guy can look forward to?"

"What's it to you, Joe? It's none of your business."

"Well, truth be told? I just think Nick deserves better than that outta you, although I envy him every single day of my life for landing you as his woman."

Claire laughed. "You make me sound like a big fat bass. And uncaring."

"Don't torture the poor besotted guy. I'm just sayin'. Hell, if it were me you said yes to, I'd hogtie you and carry you to the altar with my brute animal strength. Elopement, that's the only way to go. Get it done, get you bedded and pregnant and tied to me forever. Then reap the rewards."

"Yeah, and you're a Neanderthal chauvinist, too. But don't worry your little head about Black. He knows exactly how I feel about him, and he knows that we're gonna get married. He isn't insecure about me, believe it. In fact, I asked him to marry me. And, oh, yeah, he doesn't carry a big club to knock me over the head with, like you knuckle-dragging cavemen do."

"Well, good. I guess."

They laughed together a little and started eating their bagels, but Joe McKay was no fool. Between bites, he said, "Okay, what'd you need me for? Something for one of your cases, I take it? Otherwise there's not a bluebird's chance in hell that you'd come up here to my house in the dead of winter and sit down and slather up some breakfast bagels with me."

"Yeah, but don't say it that way. It makes me sound like a jerk."

"I'm happy to see you anywhere, anytime, that goes without sayin'. Even if you're just usin' me again." But he grinned and winked.

"Alrighty then. We found a victim frozen to the bottom of a cliff a few days ago. He turned out to be one of those cage fighters that are so popular now. My investigation led me up this way. I've heard a lot of these young fighters hail from around here. That true?"

"Yeah, I've heard that. What's this guy's name?"

"Paulie Parker. Wife's name is Blythe."

Joe put down his mug and leaned back. "I know him. I've seen her around, too, I think. Does she have real white skin and look like Casper the Ghost's skinny sister?"

"Yeah, pretty much, although that's not exactly the kindest way to put it."

"Parker's from a farm family who live out here. There's a whole clan of 'em up the road. And they are not to be trifled with. In fact, their property line backs up to mine. So does the Fitch property, and somebody else's by the name of Dale. All situated back behind my woods. There's a stream that runs back there, too, between all four properties. Forms a little lake, of sorts."

"Okay, I take it that you've trifled with the Parkers?"

"They have a kinda general store thing not too far up this road. Sells groceries and guns and ammunition and booze. They raise dogs and provide vet services and raise holy hell, now and again."

"Want to go up there with me, Joe? Nose around some? See what kinda dirt we can scrounge up on them?"

"Yeah. Like I want a hole in my head."

"Thanks for the enthusiasm."

"They're pretty much rednecks, I guess you'd say, and a little on the rough side of that spectrum. And I don't mean the Willie and Jace Robertson kind of rednecks, either."

"Who're Willie and Jace Robertson?"

"Hellooo? *Duck Dynasty*? Don't you have a TV? The Robertson family's got a reality show set down in Louisiana. Makes duck calls. Real good people. But listen up, Claire, the Parkers are the real thing and they can be dangerous. Especially if the Fitches are around."

"The Fitches?"

"That's the other family that lives up around there. They breed those fighters you're talkin' about, too. Those two families have got a real Hatfield and McCoy type of thing going on, one that you do not want to get involved in. I'm not kiddin' anymore, either. You need to stay clear of all that."

"Is there a Fitch out there who goes by the name Malachi? Mal, for short."

Joe shrugged. "Hell if I know. I don't know them all by name. There's lots of them. On both sides."

"Any of them have it in them to bludgeon somebody to death with a blunt instrument?"

"Yeah, each and every one, I'd say."

"You sound a little scared of them."

"I respect their proclivity to violence and the relish with which they indulge in it, true."

Sometimes, Joe actually shed his tough guy, bumpkin act and revealed his intellect and education. Not very often, true. In fact, it had taken her a long time to find out that he was college educated at UCLA and attained a high rank in the Marine Corps. He had a softie side to him, too, all right, especially when it came to his little daughter, Lizzie.

"I've gotta go up there today and check things out. See if Blythe has notified Paulie Parker's kinfolk about his demise. See if they know who might've done this to him. She thinks it was somebody in the Petrov organization."

"You don't mean those badass wiseguys out of East St. Louis?"

"Yeah, afraid so."

Joe sighed. "You just cannot keep your pretty little butt out of trouble, can you? It's a gift I guess."

"I just do my job. Law enforcement is dangerous work. We carry guns, and everything."

"Well, I can tell you one thing, and you can mark my words in red ink. The Parker clan is gonna think it was a Fitch who killed Paulie, and then they'll seek out one of them and kill him. Then the Fitches will retaliate and beat to death another Parker as payback."

Claire leveled shocked eyes on him. "No way."

"Oh, yeah. They're that dangerous, if you mess with them. Otherwise, they keep to themselves and cause no trouble. That feud runs hard and deep, I know that, but I don't know what caused it. They probably don't, either. I don't hang around up there and ask nosy

questions, believe me. You shouldn't, either, if you value your good
health and want to be a healthy physical presence at your own wedding."

"I'm getting similar warnings at every turn in this investigation.
Well, sorry, but I'm going up there, as soon as I finish another cup
of this delicious coffee."

"Are you armed?"

Claire smiled. "Well, what'd you think, Joe? And take a look at
this sweet little Glock 19 that Black got me." She slid the new nine
out of its holster attached to her belt and handed it over to him butt
first.

"Nice piece," he agreed, examining it carefully. "I've heard about
them, but I haven't shot one yet."

"Wanna help me sight it in?"

"Sure."

"You still have that shooting range set up out back?"

"Yeah. It's a little icy out there at the moment."

"Let's go. My snow boots have traction. Then you can decide if
you want to back me up when I ferret out the Parkers and the Fitches
and read them their rights."

"Over my dead body you're goin' in up there alone, so I guess I'll
have to tag along. At least, I know some of them a little. They are
the quintessential hillbillies. Distrustful, rowdy, dangerous, and unfriendly to strangers. Not to mention, deadly."

"Sounds like a fun bunch."

"Maybe to you."

"Well, if you ever hear a barrage of gunfire on your back forty,
come running. It'll probably be me taking down the Beverly Hillbillies."

"Don't worry. I'll keep my ears open."

But Claire had a feeling Joe was exaggerating a bit. After all, it
was the twenty-first century. Out back, the two of them took turns
shooting the 9mm for a while, and Claire was extremely pleased with
the heft and the way the new Glock handled. The trigger was a little
different than her other Glock, but it was a sweet little weapon, nevertheless. She loved it, but she wasn't giving up her other guns just
yet, either. Probably never, actually. She wondered if carrying three

guns would weigh her down too much. Sure would help boost her
self-confidence meter.

McKay insisted on taking his pickup truck, and it didn't take long
before he was driving up the twisting, turning, and heavily wooded
blacktop road, where all they saw were rusty mailboxes identifying
overgrown and snowy entrance tracks that seemed to lead out into
the middle of nowhere. If there was a feud, she wondered how they
ever ran into each other to start fights in such rural and isolated surroundings. Finally, and after quite a stomach-turning journey, they
rounded a sharp curve and came upon a rather large and rustic gaso-
line station/quick stop sitting on the right side of the road. It was
really just a large white house with a sign on top identifying it as
PARKER'S QUICK STOP. A hand-lettered sign taped on the front door
read: *NO DAMNED FITCHES ALLOWED.*

"Yeah, Joe. I'd say there's a feud, all right."

"Told ya."

McKay pulled up next to one of the pumps, and they both got out.
McKay said, "I'm gonna fill up here just so we'll get off on the right
foot with the proprietors."

"Scaredy cat."

"You'll see."

"I'm going on in, check things out."

"Don't start interrogating them until I get there, okay?"

"Sure. I'll buy us some hot chocolate and some Snickers bars
first."

"Just don't get in a fight with them until I get there."

"You and Black, I declare. You both act like I'm some kind of
bully or troublemaker."

"And your point is?"

"Shut up and pump your gas."

Claire left him doing just that and warily watching the front of
the store, as if goblins were going to fly out on brooms and dive-
bomb them. She couldn't help but notice several more signs around
the station, all warning off the elusive Fitches. She wondered if that
was even legal. She thought not. But she could think of more than a
few people that she would like to ban from her property.

Inside, the store looked a lot like the interior of a Cracker Barrel restaurant, except that the quaint gift shop had turned into a gun show. Of course, that was right up her alley so she browsed a time, but didn't see a single thing that she liked better than Black's prized gift, now snug in its bed on her right hip. The place also offered enough camouflage to clad the entire volunteer army, plus various and sundry hunters and fishermen. Yep, only Bass Pro Shop down in Springfield beat them in sheer quantity of hunting merchandise. There were also knives and army surplus and lots of insulated and thermal long underwear and fur-lined, ear-flapped, WWII era, leather bomber pilot hats for winter weather. She ought to buy one for Black as a joke. She laughed to herself to think of him sitting at his important conference table and wearing that kind of cap, maybe with the furry flaps down and snapped under his chin. Nope, not in a million years would he ever put something like that on his handsome head.

The other side of the big building held groceries like any quick stop anywhere that was worth its salt: chips, candy, gum, lots of beer, sodas, ice cream, bottled water, not to mention the doe urine, gun oil, snuff, and chewing tobacco. She didn't see much in the way of hairspray, combs, soap, perfume, body wash, or anything girly, not that she wanted any of it. There was also a little snack bar in the back with hot lamps blazing down on the food trays. She walked over and observed the goodies. There was fried chicken, fried fish, fried squirrel, fried potatoes, and fried pies for dessert. Smelled good, too. Maybe this place wasn't so bad, after all.

Only problem was, there didn't seem to be any people within a hundred miles of the place. So she just made herself at home, moseyed around, looking for bloody baseball bats or other deadly weapons used recently and didn't see a one. She made two supersized insulated cups of hot chocolate, sipped one as she picked up a couple of Snickers bars and walked over to the counter. She looked around again, noticing the myriad of surveillance cameras set up high in every corner and behind the counter. She placed her items on the counter, looked up at the camera, and pointed at her purchases. If that didn't work, maybe she'd shoot a few slugs up into the ceiling and see what happened. Hell, she wasn't a damned Fitch, was she? So what was the problem?

Turning around, she watched Joe approach the front door and

push it open. A rush of cold air came in with him and blew around the corncob pipes hanging on a rack beside the door. Joe came right up to her and said, "Where's the clerk?"

"You tell me. Shoplifters would have a heyday in here."

"Yeah, and they'd get their heads blown off by a Parker shotgun."

"Ssh, they might be listening and take offense."

"Maybe he's out back with the dogs."

Claire handed him his drink. "Well, let's go see, shall we? It'll give us a good excuse to case out the property."

"They've always been right here at the register when I've come in. This is pretty unusual."

So they moved cautiously to a swinging door that obviously led to some storage rooms, or maybe to an office in the back. Joe yelled, "Anybody here?"

No answer. Claire happily pulled her new weapon, and said, "C'mon, let's go. Something might be wrong. A robbery in progress, or something."

"Well, don't shoot anybody, or they'll think we're Fitches and all hell will break loose."

So they moved through the swinging door, Claire first, Joe right behind her. They found a storeroom in back with more camo and beer and ammunition. Surprise, surprise. There was a light coming from a door in the very back and they called out again and headed for it. They found a small and basically bare office with nobody in it, either. The back door was shut but not quite latched so they opened it and walked out into the rear parking lot. Across the way, they saw a long kennel-barn kind of building with lots of dog runs built along one side. Eight hundred and some odd dogs began to bark and howl.

"Well, they know we're here now," Claire said. She steeled herself, expecting to see somebody dressed like Grizzly Adams with a shotgun held braced against his shoulder walk out the kennel's door. Mountain men or rednecks, who could tell the difference?

Suddenly a tall man did thrust open that door. To her shock, he looked like a regular person, normal in every single way, truth be told. He had a curly mop of chin-length dark brown hair that made him look a lot like pictures of Achilles or other ancient Greek warriors and a dark green sweater that looked like it came from the Gap, and pressed gray Dockers. There was a neat mustache and beard trimmed close around his jaw with clean shaven cheeks, also in the Prometheus or Ulysses vein, big brown eyes with very dark lashes, nice even features, and a smile that he used to his advantage as he motioned them over. "Hey, Joe. Sorry I didn't hear ya'll. Got busy out here. Come on over."

"He doesn't look so bad if you like reading Homer," Claire said aside to Joe in a very low voice. "You had me expecting some kind of devil, or king cobra, or something equally poisonous."

"Give him time. Just don't mention the Fitches in his earshot."

Claire headed for the refreshingly clean-cut guy posthaste. She would give him time all right, time to tell her everything she needed to know about Paulie Parker and his possible Fitch enemies.

Chapter Fourteen

Up close, the Parker guy looked even better. Fairly hot, in a rugged hillbilly, Cabelis sorta way. She looked for cauliflower ears for proof of cage fighting adeptness but found his ears regularly shaped and clean of oil and grime. He was clean all over, actually. His nose was slightly crooked from a possible left jab, though. He kept his eyes on her the entire time they were walking over to him. Hmm. Now why would he do that? Checking her out for concealed weapons?

"Hi, Joe. Long time no see." Mr. Neat as a Pin glanced at Joe and then quickly returned his gaze to her. He must find her downright fascinatin' or want to sell her a fourth gun, probably at twenty percent off with a free box of ammo thrown in to sweeten the deal.

"Hey there, Patrick. How you doin'?"

"Who's your lady friend?"

Huh? She couldn't ever remember being called a *lady friend* before, thank goodness. That was almost as bad as *lovely*. Hillbillyese for girlfriend, maybe? Somehow that didn't compute. "My name is Claire Morgan, Mr. Parker. I'm a homicide detective from Canton County and I'd like to have a word with you."

If Parker was surprised to hear that, he sure didn't show it. So why wouldn't he show it? Hmm, again. That was the pertinent question, after all. He said, "Sure thing, detective. How you doin'?"

"Just great. And you?"

"Good enough, I guess. Come on now, let's go in my office and do some of that talkin'."

All eight hundred dogs were still barking. Well, maybe a dozen or so had lain off a bit and were just listening to the others. Their pleasant master ignored the racket. Maybe he was used to it. Maybe it was just background noise for him. Like static on the radio. She looked around his office. It was nice enough. Not as nice as that damn Dazz's, but nothing about this place had turned out to be what Claire had expected. Truth was, she had expected a log cabin with newspapers stuck in the cracks and cobwebs in the corners and ten or so deer heads displayed on the walls, and a bearskin rug on a dirt floor, certainly not a designer brown-and-rust chevron carpet and matching tan corduroy Stratoloungers.

"How you been, Joe?"

"Good. I've moved back down to the farm."

"How's that purty little girl of yours doin'?"

Parker was still looking at Claire while he carried on his conversation with Joe. Exclusively. She resisted the quite strong but rude impulse to manually turn his face toward Joe with her extended forefinger or perhaps the barrel of her new Glock. Joe was probably feeling insulted by now, too, being ignored the way he was. She was feeling insulted. What? Did she have a hot chocolate milk mustache on her upper lip that offended said hillbilly? Slightly curious, however, she set forth an inquiry into the matter. "Why are you rudely staring a hole through me, Mr. Parker?"

That didn't surprise him, either. Apparently, nothing surprised him. Lots of barking hounds didn't, either, but they were sure grating on Claire's nerves.

Parker presented with a big wide smile. "Well, ma'am, you're just so dang fun to look at."

Claire wasn't at all sure that was a compliment. Maybe he thought she was cute as a button or maybe he thought she looked like Chuckles the Clown. Hard to say. "Thanks, I think. But Joe's not all that ugly, you know, doesn't shave every day, or anything, but not that hard on the eyes. He's halfway fun looking a few days a week. You could glance at him now and again when he's talking to you. Just to be polite." She smiled so he would know she was just joking and wouldn't slap her with a police rudeness rap.

Patrick Parker laughed heartily, just so dang fun and good-natured, that it made her dang suspicious. Problem was, though, a brother who had received the news of his brother's recent and brutal demise, shouldn't be so danged happy. She had a bad feeling that he didn't know about it yet. Joe was laughing now, too, but it sounded forced and nervous. Joe McKay had a real wary thing going on about these Parker people, it seemed.

"Please, ma'am, sit yourself down. That's good quality hot chocolate you got there. I only buy the best."

"Yes, it is. I left some money on the counter. I'm not trying to filch it, or anything. I promise."

"Oh, I know." He was doing better about looking at Joe now. He had glanced at him once during that exchange. "Hey, it's my treat. It's cold out there, and gettin' colder by the minute, too."

"Thanks, that's very generous of you. I do love my hot chocolate."

All small talk died then, like a bum lightbulb. They all sat there, listening to the dogs yapping their heads off. Maybe the hounds were just hungry or wanted to be petted. That would take some time. Eight hundred heads to pat was a lot.

"You gotta lot of dogs out there," she finally said. "You sell them, or what?"

"Yeah, sixty-seven, to be exact. I'm the vet 'round here. Most of 'em are mine, though. My brothers and I hunt lots of deer and coon and such. And everything else, too. We got acres of some of the best huntin' land 'round. You're welcome to come up here anytime you want and shoot yourself a buck, both of you." He smiled, all ingratiating and sugary as sweet potato pie with maple syrup on top. He was being so saccharine that it was hard to ruffle his composure, it seemed. Claire wondered how many Fitches he had beaten, branded, or shot in his young and pleasant Dockers-wearing persona. "So, what's up, detective? What you wantin' with me?"

Claire heaved in a deep breath. "Do you have a brother by the name of Paulie Parker, by any chance, sir?"

"Yes, I do. In fact, he's a comin' up here later today, if you wanna talk to him. He's one helluva fighter, you know, out on the cage circuit. A real champ. We're as proud of him as we can be."

McKay and Claire exchanged a disturbed glance. Joe didn't say a word. *Uh-uh.* He wasn't going to make any such notification. It wasn't his place. It was hers. She wished that Bud was there so she could make him do it. It was his turn, anyway. "Mr. Parker, I'm sorry but I'm afraid I have some very bad news."

Patrick Parker stiffened all over, not exactly stupid, and knew all about bad news lead-ins, it seemed. Impressive muscles now tensed hard and waiting for the blow to the brain. "What's gone and happened to Paulie? He's okay, ain't he?"

"His body was found several nights ago. Murdered. I assumed his wife had informed you as to his death. I am truly sorry to have to shock you this way."

Patrick was shocked, all right. He looked as if he had grabbed a live wire and held on too long. Then his brown bearded jaw went slack, large and soulful Hershey's Chocolate bar eyes darkening into utter and sincere horror. He spoke through clenched white teeth. "The Fitches did it, didn't they? The dirty bastards. They been hatin' him ever since he started beatin' them up in the ring. Which one of 'em did it? Tell me! Tell me which one of them sons of bitches took him down!"

Claire suddenly wished Black had come along instead of Joe. He could calm down a crazy whack job in nothing flat, being a famous shrink, and all. He'd done it for her mood swings plenty of times. To her surprise, Joe stood up and placed his palm solicitously on the poor guy's shoulder. Parker was trembling now, all over, in the most pitiful, quietly enraged way. "Hey, man, I'm real sorry about your brother. I just found out today, too. We thought you already knew, we really did, or we wouldn't've ever just showed up out here and given you this sad news."

Okay, that sent Patrick into a calmer mode big-time and faster than Claire had expected. The guy acted like quicksilver ran through his veins. He was rather mercurial, to say the least. He slumped down in his chair, kind of like a blow-up figure with a pulled plug. His face looked absolutely stricken. "I just can't believe it. Paulie called me just the other night and told me he was gonna come out here and do some huntin' with us before he went out on the road again." He stopped. "Oh, God, I'm gonna have to tell my brothers when they get here."

"How many brothers do you have?"

"Lots of 'em, I guess. Paulie's in the middle somewhere. He was the best of us, too. We always liked him best."

Lots of 'em? He guessed? Nothing super creepy about that response, huh? He was so white faced and so openly struggling to control his rampaging emotions, however, that Claire almost felt sorry for him. Still, that answer had been straight out of bizarro world. She said, "Would you like a moment to gather your thoughts, sir? We can wait over there at the snack bar and give you a little time alone to pull yourself together."

"Yeah, yeah, I sure would. Thanks."

"Okay. Take as long as you like. We're gonna stick around."

Numb and mute now, he just nodded and stared off into space. He was taking it hard, all right.

Outside, Joe looked down at Claire. "I don't envy you and Bud having to tell people that somebody they love is dead."

"It's no fun, let me tell you."

"No. I just saw that."

They walked across the parking lot in silence. Claire stopped and looked across the way at a fence that stood about ten feet tall and was made out of corrugated metal and old boards. "I wonder what's inside that enclosure."

"Maybe he lives in there. I could just barely see a house and a barn standing way back off the road on that last curve we came around."

"You've never been inside that fence?"

"These people aren't my best buddies in the world, Claire. I barely know this guy. Just met him once or twice since I got back. I hardly know any of them, just from stoppin' occasionally at this place for gas and groceries. I don't know where the hell he lives. Maybe in that house way back there, who knows?"

"I'd sure like to get a peek inside that enclosure."

"Well, don't push it right now. The guy's suffered a loss. I know how that feels."

Claire looked quickly at him but McKay was smiling and looking pointedly at her diamond ring. He was talking about her engagement to Black. He just never gave it up. She ignored the insinuation.

Inside the quick stop, they moved at once to all the fried stuff.

Both of them were hungry, despite the bagels, so they filled up plates with crispy fried chicken and fries and other unhealthy selections and chowed down together at one of the small tables. It was all clean; spotless, in fact. Again, not the kind of place, she had been expecting. She had been expecting an outpost fort in the early French and Indian wars.

"So who are the bad guys, McKay? The Parkers or the Fitches?"

Joe finished chewing his bite of chicken, swallowed it, and said, "Depends on who you ask."

"This guy seems pretty normal, considering."

"We don't know him all that well yet."

"Have you met any of the Fitches?"

"I've been scared to."

Claire laughed, but softly, and both of them kept looking around for trouble. "I'm going to have to pay them a call one of these days. I don't have an official reason yet, other than checking out Malachi Fitch, who's a real piece of work, but I'd like to look them over and see if they're as civilized as Patrick Parker appears to be."

"I don't know them, but if the Fitches have any inkling that I'm friendly with the Parkers, they'll probably shoot me down on sight. Better wait and take Bud."

Before Claire could agree, three pickup trucks roared into the parking lot, skidding to dangerous stops on the graveled ice. Four guys piled out, all decked out in camouflage, all big and muscular with scary-looking expressions on their faces. They all had rifles in their hands, too. Bevy of brothers, by any chance? She hoped to hell not.

Claire stood up. She had a pretty good feeling what the guns were for. They came rushing in the door like a four-man battering ram. They looked angry and distraught and determined. But face to face, they weren't too bad looking, and looked a helluva lot like Patrick and Paulie. In fact, they looked exactly like Patrick and Paulie. Almost like a matched set of Parker sextuplets. Or identical clones developed by some evil woodsy witch doctor. They headed straight for the back door until Claire stepped out in front of them and halted their wrathful journey to kill or be killed.

"Excuse me, sirs."

"Who the hell are you? Get outta my way, girl," said one of them. Billy Goat Gruff voice, too.

"Get the hell outta my way," said number two, equally annoyed and even gruffer and goatier.

The other two stared at the badge she was now holding up and showed not a whit of gruff. A couple of them darted a sidelong look at Joe McKay, who had remained seated, out of regard for his own well-being, no doubt. Claire just tried to find something that differentiated them from one another, without much luck, since they all wore the same Mossy Oak pattern of camo, too. A lone gold tooth, chicken pox facial scar, black eye, anything would be helpful.

"You the cops?"

"Yes, I am. One of them, in any case. I'd like to talk to you. I assume you are some more Parker brothers."

"That's right. Where's Patrick?"

"He's out in the veterinarian office. Have you spoken to him recently?"

"He just called and said that them Fitches killed our bro, if that's what you talkin' 'bout."

"I'm Detective Claire Morgan, and I'm investigating your brother's homicide. I want you to know up front that I have no evidence that the Fitch family had anything at all to do with Paulie Parker's death."

"Bullshit, lady. They done it."

"I assume you have proof, if you're making that kind of accusation to a law enforcement officer."

"We don't need no stinkin' proof."

"That's from *Three Amigos*, if I recall." Not that movie quotes were her thing, but Bud knew everything about that movie and had quoted from it several times and just last week. "But alas, I'm afraid you do need stinkin' proof. Now please, sit down and calm yourselves. I have some questions to ask you."

"Don't have the time, lady."

"Don't call me lady. I am not usually a lady. But I am a homicide detective."

"You a lady, too, lady."

Oh, pul-ease, Claire thought. *Why in the world couldn't things ever just be simple?*

"Sit down. All of you. Now."

"Why?"

"Because I asked you to and you seem overly excited about killing members of the Fitch family."

The four brothers then started looking at each other wonderingly and scratching their Greek beards, as if they were mightily confused Athenians. The biggest one and the apparent leader noticed Joe. "Who's that?"

"That's my friend. Joe McKay."

"Yeah, Patrick knows him."

"Please, sit down, put down all those guns, and have a bite to eat. I'm sure Patrick will be out any moment now."

They considered all that, mumbled a short and whispered conversation amongst themselves, and then moved over to the snack bar and piled the rest of the fried chicken and fish on their plates. Okay, they didn't seem that overly distressed at Paulie's unfortunate circumstances anymore. Weirdos? You bet.

They huddled down together at a table meant for three smaller types and ate silently, their many rifles and shotguns propped in a nearby corner. None of them was crying or carrying on. That was peculiar, too, considering Patrick's reaction. Claire sat down beside Joe.

McKay said, "Thought for a moment that you were a goner."

"Yeah, you looked so worried that you continued to tear at that chicken leg with your teeth."

"This chicken is damn good. Nice and crispy."

"And you wonder why I'm with Black? He would've at least looked concerned for my well-being when confronted by four huge hooligans."

"I've seen you in action. You can handle them. Besides, I left my rifle in the truck."

"Maybe you oughta go get it."

"Really?"

"No, too late now. I was joking."

McKay took a drink of his icy Mountain Dew. "They don't seem overly grief stricken. Seems to me like they're more interested in killing 'em some Fitches than mourning their brother."

"Yeah. I noticed."

For some reason, Claire had lost her appetite. Adrenaline surging through one's bloodstream could do that to a gal, armed to the hilt or otherwise. But she had the energy and armament that she needed to take on the small herd of four large and heavily armed and mirror-image hillbillies. She looked up as Patrick Parker slammed through the swinging metal door. Oops, make that five large and heavily armed hillbillies.

All the Parkers jumped to their feet like marionettes attached to a single string. So did Claire. Joe took another sip of his Dew. He had been a Marine demolitions expert. He didn't get overly excited about much. He just came back later and blew the place to hell.

"Are you ready for that interview now, Patrick?" Claire smiled at the stiff-faced newcomer, but she kept her hand close to her Glock, glad she'd sighted it in at Joe's place.

Patrick's excited expression faded somewhat. He looked at his brothers, who were looking at Claire's gun hand. He took a moment to calm his engines. "Yes, ma'am. You met up wit' my bros, I guess?" Polite, so polite, all of a sudden.

"Not formally."

Joe laughed. Nobody else did.

Patrick said, "I've already told them the bad news."

"I gathered that by the firepower they brought along."

Patrick frowned darkly. The other pissed Parkers watched Claire's gun hand some more.

"Why don't you introduce us? Let things calm down a notch. We don't need anybody jumping to conclusions."

"Okay." He walked over to the table. "This here's Percy. He's the best shot of us all."

Percy Parker nodded politely, his ire receding admirably. He, too, had that same interesting short brown beard, brown eyes, longish brown hair, except his was pulled back in a curly ponytail. His eyes looked almost normal again, the pupils no longer spinning, which was always a good sign.

"How many brothers in your family?" Claire asked Patrick again, still suspicious about his last evasive answer.

The Parkers all looked around at each other, as if they weren't sure what to say. Then they all looked at Patrick, as if he would know. They all had the same expression on their faces. Claire wondered if they could even tell each other apart.

Patrick thought it through some more, and then he said, "Six, counting Paulie. Yeah, there are six of us, and that's all."

All the big, bearded, brown-eyed brothers began nodding, as if suddenly remembering that was the true number, too. Claire and McKay just stared at them, thinking them nuts, of course.

Patrick continued the intros. "This here is Phillip. He fries up the chicken."

"Hello, officer."

"Hello, Phillip. You're quite the cook."

"Thank you kindly."

"And this here one is Phineas. We call him Phin 'cause he likes to fish. And that one's number four, Petey."

Petey just looked at her and grunted. Claire assumed he had no mentionable talents.

Okay, first off, it appeared that their mama had enjoyed a true love affair with the letter P. That was a given. Good thing the poor woman didn't have any more sons. There weren't all that many male P names left. At least, Claire couldn't think of any. Except Pancho, maybe. Or Paco.

"I'm very sorry for your loss. It's a terrible thing to lose a brother."

"The Fitches did it." That was Phin, speaking for all of them, no doubt.

"Mind if we push the tables together so that we can all sit down and talk about this in a civilized manner?"

The nodding of various heads gave her the go-ahead. Joe did the honors with a lot of scraping and heaving while everybody else watched. They all sat down and stared at each other. Claire got out her notepad and pen. "Okay, first thing, maybe you should tell me a little bit about all these accusations you were throwing around concerning the Fitch family. I take it that you've got a beef with those guys?"

"They is our mortal enemies," said Percy aka best shot.

"And the reason for that is?"

"They just always has been," said Phillip aka Colonel Sanders.

"Which one of you fellows would like to explain the genesis of this feud, if it is a feud."

"They kilt one of my great-granddaddy's cousins, and then they stole some of our hill pastures back in the thirties."

"So it goes back a good long while."

"Yes, ma'am."

They were awfully polite all of a sudden, which made Claire think maybe they were playing her until she drove off with Joe, none the wiser. Then they would go find and annihilate a serious amount of Fitches. She would have to put the FEAR OF THE LAW in them and make it stick.

"Tell me, boys, do you murder Fitches often? Or vice versa?"

Joe smothered another laugh, but not very well. Claire would never, ever bring him on an investigation with her again, no matter how helpful he could be. But the Parkers were smiling slightly, too, under their chicken-greasy mustaches.

Patrick seemed to take the helm then, so to speak. That was probably a good thing. He was the articulate one. "No, detective. We ain't murderin' them. Ever. Unless they murder us first."

"I see." *And then I arrest you, each and every one,* Claire thought. "You do know that all these threats are gonna come back and bite you, if even one Fitch reports any assaults."

"We're calm now. It was just a real hard thing to process." There you go. Patrick was waxing articulate.

"Do you think everyone is calm enough now not to commit murder the minute my back is turned?"

"Yes, ma'am."

"Well, now that's settled. And you're saying that Paulie's wife, Blythe, did not call you and tell you what happened?"

"No, ma'am, but she wouldn't. She hates us all. Says we're cretins."

Okay, now that was a woman getting it out in the open with no concern for hurt feelings. "So I assume that means that you guys don't get along well with Blythe Parker."

"No, we like her just fine. She's real good to Paulie."

Maybe they just didn't know what the word *cretins* meant. Yes, that was entirely possible. Maybe they thought it meant sweet or talented or brainy people. "Do you have other relatives that we should notify?"

"No, ma'am. It's just us boys now."

"Are you fellas married?"

"No, ma'am."

"None of you are married?"

"No. We all live together up at the old house place."

Supersonic creepy? It did seem to be. "Where exactly is that?"

Patrick sort of swung his arm toward the secret enclosure and related to her some rather roundabout, confusing directions, but it didn't sound far from where they now sat. "Okay, let's just forget about the Fitches for a minute. Has anybody else ever made threats against Paulie? Or has he had an altercation with anyone that you know of? Perhaps his fellow fighters?"

"We don't go down to town much to see him. He brings us videos of his fights and shows off his medals and trophy belts now and again."

"Has he ever mentioned anybody that he didn't like or that he had a problem with?"

"No, ma'am. He was the most popular of us all."

"Popular in what way?"

"Well, people liked him the best."

"Why?"

"Dunno."

Man, this was not going well. She wondered if Patrick was now holed up inside his head, just waiting for her to leave, or if he and his band of brothers were merely mighty unpopular dudes on the hill farm circuit.

"Tell me about his relationship with his wife's family."

They all looked around at each other, and got all quiet again. Then Patrick said, real slow and careful-like, "We don't know nothin' 'bout her family."

"Okay, so this was not a close family relationship then?"

"Are they all albinos like her?" That was Phin, definitely not the brightest bulb in the pack but no doubt hell to pay when catching bass and crappie.

"I can't really say. Now, when was the last time you saw Paulie?"

"Last week, right 'fore he went up to KC. He came out here and spent the night with us up at the house."

"Did he seem strange or act any differently while he was with you?"

"No, he was the same old crazy Paulie."

"Crazy?"

"He liked to have fun, stuff like that."

"Did he seem worried or nervous?"

"Nope." Patrick looked at the others, all of whom had now settled down into near catatonic states. Initial adrenaline levels were washing out now, to be sure. Still, the collective lack of grief for their recently dead but fun-loving brother bothered Claire a bit. Go figure.

"Do you know a fighter by the name of Shorty Dunlop?"

"No." They all concurred with a rather somnolent lack of human expression.

"Do you know of any reason why anybody would've helped him leave a hospital up in Kansas City before the doctors released him?"

Slow shaking of shaggy heads. "Did your brother bring that guy up here and hide him out at your place?"

Percy answered for everyone. "No way. We'd a seen 'im by now."

After that obtuse response, Claire blew out a frustrated breath. She stared at Percy for a moment. Wow. Just wow. Then she asked, "What's out back inside that enclosure?"

Patrick looked surprised at the question, which was why she asked it. "Just a junkyard with old cars, and stuff. Goes way far back on our property. They made us put up that fence 'cause they called it an eyesore. You wanna go out there and have a look-see around?"

Since he offered, she didn't expect there was much to see. "Maybe one of these days. I'll be around again. Not to worry."

Claire hesitated. Their lack of emotion concerning Paulie's death was puzzling and bothering her big-time. She didn't want to appear rude. She already had, not to mention threatening to jail them if they didn't settle down, which wasn't exactly not rude. All right, when in doubt, don't mince words. "I'm sorry, but it doesn't seem like any of you are very upset by your brother's death."

Petey took offense and instantly became verbose. "We just real bad upset. Enough to kill us some Fitches first off. But that's done over with now. Once we stack our guns in the corner, we done over it. Done for the day."

Man alive. These guys were not exactly dripping with smarts. "Well, I hope so. That's against the law, you know. Murdering your neighbors, and such as that."

McKay was frowning now. He hadn't been on many police calls out in the hills, obviously. But neither had she. But he was keeping his mouth shut and not laughing, which was a good thing and unusual for him.

"We ain't gonna go out killin' nobody. I promise. Cross my heart."

Petey's solemn oath was just so reassuring. Kind of. After all, he had crossed his heart, even made the sign with his forefinger.

"What do you guys do for a living?"

"I run this store, and they take care of the farm and the cattle. And we fight sometimes for the cash prizes."

"You do all right here, I guess?"

"Yes, ma'am. We do really good."

"What do the Fitches do for a living?"

"They get drunk and cause trouble and go to church like they ain't as bad as us. Fight and stuff. That's why nobody wants them around. They're real bad, all of 'em. Not very popular, no."

Sounded like everybody within fifty miles was highly unpopular. "Where do they live?"

"Their farm butts up close to ours. They try to rustle our cattle, but we keep a close watch and make sure the barbed wire fences are in good repair."

Now Claire felt as if she had been thrown into an episode of *Rawhide*, that old Clint Eastwood television show where he looked down and scuffed the toe of his boot in the prairie dirt. All these guys needed were some cowboy hats, spurs, lassos, and a hangin' tree. "Well, having rustlers in the neighborhood is always irksome."

"Are you gonna investigate the Fitches? Then you'll see. They got something to do with this, you'll see."

"I probably will give them a call, if it becomes warranted. I do have your word, right, that none of you will go out there and make accusations and stir up trouble, right?"

They all nodded and maintained similar serious expressions on their similar serious faces.

"You do understand that we are investigating this murder, and I do promise to keep you apprised of our progress."

"How'd those Fitches kill him?" That was Phillip, now with tears filling his eyes.

Claire didn't want to tell him. It came out reluctantly. "Let me remind you again that I have no proof linking the Fitches to your brother's murder. But to answer your question, Paulie Parker was beaten to death."

That caused the brothers to jerk looks at one another with lots of nodding heads and I-told-you-so expressions.

Patrick was still the major spokesman. "That pretty much wraps it up, now don't it? They love beatin' on people with baseball bats. Carry big clubs around everywhere."

Well, that was truly interesting, and probably a good reason to visit some unpleasant Fitches. "Have any of you been attacked by them with a baseball bat?"

They all nodded in tandem.

"Does that indicate that you fight with them a lot?"

"Yes, ma'am. We been fightin' with 'em since we was little bitty kids. Our pa and their pa used to make us fight each other."

Now it was Claire's turn to flinch. Okay, now they were getting somewhere. "Then I need to talk to your pa."

"He's dead, been gone for a long time now. Ma, even before that."

"How old were you when they made you fight?"

"Five years old, sometimes six. They started us out early so we'd be real good by middle school."

"This still going on around here?"

"Not at our place anymore. We ain't got no kids amongst us."

"What about the Fitch family?"

"Probably not. We heard their men put a stop to the fights. But they still is nuts, the whole lot of 'em."

"That's against the law, you know. Kids fighting each other."

"We figured it was, but nobody ever came around to make 'em stop fightin' us."

"Well, spread the word. I'm around now, and I'm gonna stop it. Understand me, guys? That's child abuse and there are laws against child abuse. If the Fitches are still doing it, I'm gonna arrest them."

The Parker brothers all broke out in ecstatic smiles, happy as proverbial clams to hear such glad tidings.

"I guess that's all I need right now. I may be back as the investigation proceeds. You might want to get in touch with Blythe Parker and find out about Paulie's funeral arrangements."

"Yeah, we wanna plant 'im up in our cemetery."

Claire and McKay stood up. "You do have hunting licenses for all those weapons over there in the corner, right?"

"Oh, yes, ma'am. I sell 'em right here, and I get 'em for the boys every year."

"Good. Well, thank you for your cooperation. I'll be in touch."

Claire gave Patrick her card, figuring he'd share it, if necessary, and she and McKay walked outside, relieved as all get out. "Well, you weren't much help in there, Joe."

"I never interfere in police business. I never take on four or five big guys at once either."

"So I noticed."

"Hey, I don't have one of those shiny badges that lets me do whatever I want, like you do." They got inside his truck, and he leaned on the steering wheel and looked over at her. "But, if any of them had laid a finger on you, my dear detective, I would've taken care of it." He pulled back his jacket and let her see the .45 handgun stuck in his back waistband. "And yes, officer, I do have a conceal-carry license. Just so you know."

"Well, that makes me feel a little better, sort of. In an after-the-fact kinda way."

McKay nodded, and they headed back toward town. Claire sat silently as he concentrated on maneuvering the car around all the curves and icy patches on the hills and dales and wondered how everything fit together. She was picking up pieces of the puzzle right and left. Problem was, none of them were connected up into a nice clear 3-D picture of the perpetrator. Not yet, anyway. Well, maybe

Bud had come up with a doozy of a lead in Kansas City. She hoped to hell that he had good news. She was still sitting on empty.

Blood Brothers

As it turned out, Punk moved into his maternal grandfather's house, where he was treated like an absolute king. Or maybe more like a prince. Yeah, all he needed was a gold crown with big rubies and emeralds on it. As patriarch of the family, his grandfather was highly revered and therefore so was his grandson, whether he deserved it or not. And living within walking distance of his true love was just about everything he had ever dreamed of. He got to see her every day, and they would steal off and kiss and touch and whisper how much they loved each other. And they were very careful not to be found out. Grandfather considered what they were doing to be the great and terrible sin of all unholy sins, but it wasn't. It was just the opposite. She was heaven-sent, just for him, and he knew it.

Despite himself, he did begin to miss Brother Bones after a while and wished he could see him sometimes. But that was out of the question, at least for now. Little Banjo had found her way through the fence and tracked Punk all the way to his new house, and Punk had been so glad to see her. He had been worried that nobody was taking care of her. Sometimes, he thought about his other brothers, too, but not as often as he wondered about Bones. Bones was his twin, after all. And he was curious about what happened to all the dead bodies and what his older brothers had said about their pa being dead and gone forever. They might like it, or maybe not. He wasn't sure what they'd think. Bones probably put his corpses in the hog pen and let the sows eat them up. But Punk didn't really care. With his true love nearby, he soon forgot all that stuff and finally didn't really care about anything or anybody else. He had stopped his fighting, stopped getting so angry so quickly, stopped hunting, stopped worrying about his twin killing people. He didn't care about anything but his girlfriend. So he set about learning her family's ways and their strict religious rules and was getting ready to be baptized into his mother's family, so he could be a true believer.

Even better, the two of them had found a really cool place where they could be all alone. She would steal like a phantom out of her upstairs bedroom and climb down the big rose trellis and find her way through the woods to the back acres that edged the neighbor's farm and the river that led to the lake. He would pretend he was napping or studying his new religious books, and when Grandfather was asleep or counseling his flock, Punk would go out behind the big house and run through the woods until he found the little ramshackle cabin that they had made into their warm and cozy love nest. It was high on the hill near a big limestone cave that they liked to explore with flashlights and a picnic basket. Sometimes they made love inside the cavern depths in the cool, damp quiet, snuggling inside his sleeping bag together with her vanilla candle flickering on a low rocky ledge.

One day he found that she was already at the cabin waiting for him, and she threw open the door and then she was in his arms and he spun around with her, his heart thundering with desire. He took her down quickly to the soft blue blanket that she had spread out on the floor. They stripped off each other's clothes as fast as they could and then lay tightly together, naked and turned on. He loved the pure white skin of her body, so pale against his own dark tan. Then they made sweet love, slowly and gently, and it was as good and fine as it always had been, even better, because it had been three whole days since they'd last met. He needed her so much, all the time. She was like the weed that his pa used to smoke in order to get high. She was Punk's illegal drug and always would be.

Afterward, she snuggled in closer against him and kissed him on his chest. "Your grandfather told my papa that we can't ever be together. I heard him. His word is law hereabouts. Papa will never let me marry you. What are we going to do? I want to marry you."

"We're just gonna run away, that's what we're gonna do. It's time now. I can get me a job. I can find us a good place to live at. I can fight some more. I'm good at it, and stuff. I can win us lots of money in that cage. I got some brothers already doin' it. Good money, too, real good."

"No, no, please don't. I hate all that fightin' that goes on over at your place. Sometimes in the summertime, we can hear the cheering and see the car lights on Saturday nights. I don't want you to get yourself beat up. I don't wanna see you come home all bruised up and sore and bleeding, like you was the day I met up with you. I can't bear to think of you getting hurt."

"Nah, I'm gonna be all right, I promise. But let's just do it. Now. We gotta get our things together, tonight, and then we gotta just get outta here for good—"

When the door was suddenly thrown open, they both jerked up-right and she screamed in horror. There stood his grandfather and her father, and many of the other men who were the church elders. The men all stared down in disgust at their nakedness, their faces hard and cold and unforgiving.

"For shame, for shame, you Jezebel. And you, my only grandson! You have ruined this poor girl that you profess to love." Grandfather's voice started out harsh, and then began to tremble with his burgeon-ing rage. "You cover yourself, girl, and get yourself home with your father. You are doin' the devil's handiwork out here with this sinner."

Punk's true love burst into tears and quickly tried to pull her dress over her head, only to be jerked up roughly by her father and dragged out of the shack, struggling and screaming her lover's name. Punk tried to get up and stop them, but a couple of the men grabbed him and tried to tie his hands behind his back. He struggled desperately and then fought like a demon, harder than he had ever fought in his life, landing powerful blows, knocking them down, breaking their bones, and this time without Bones coming to his rescue. Enraged, he put three of them on the floor, before one of them grabbed a piece of firewood and clubbed him senseless.

When Punk awoke again, he was back inside his bedroom in his grandfather's house. Rousing up, his head was thudding hard and steadily and he felt dizzy and sick to his stomach. Then he realized that his right wrist was handcuffed to the bed, and his grandfather sat in the spindle rocking chair beside the window. The old man stood up but he didn't approach the bed. "You have greatly dishonored me and that poor innocent young girl. You will have to repent and ask God's mercy and forgiveness."

"Where is she? What'd you do to her? Is she okay? You better not of hurt her, I'm warnin' you."

"It doesn't concern you where she is or what's been done to her. She has already repented and asked forgiveness for her sins. She is being dealt with."

"She's not sinful, you old bastard. She's perfect and beautiful and she's mine. We're gettin' married and you cain't stop us. No matter what it takes, we're gonna get married."

"No, you are not. Thanks to your reckless behavior, she is to be married to the man her father has chosen for her, something decided long before you came here and led her to ruin. Despite her deflowering and wanton behavior, her chosen husband has agreed to marry her."

"No! No! I won't let her do that! She won't do that to me!"

"She will do it, and she will do it tomorrow morning at the church across the way. You may watch out your window and see that her disgrace will be corrected and forgiven by her loving family. Then you will leave this place and never come back. You will forget she exists and never try to speak to her again. I never want to see you after this day."

Sick at heart, horrified at what he'd been told, Punk stared at him, mute and destroyed. He felt as if he were dying inside. He could not let that wedding happen. He could not let them take her away from him, no matter what he had to do. He would kill them. That's what he would do. He would kill them all, every single one of them, before he would let them take her away from him.

When the morning light finally grayed the sky and dawn crept up over the trees that crowned the hills, he pulled the long chain that tethered him to the bed so that he could stand at the window and watch for her. He had already tried to get out the door but it was bolted tight from the outside. The windows were, too, and very high, with a sheer drop to the ground. He had given up hope. There was nothing else he could do. Then he saw three people walking down the deserted dirt street toward the little church. His true love and her father, and another man, a very old man with a white beard, who looked old enough to be her grandfather. She had her head down and her hands held prayerfully together. He could see the bruises on her face. He pounded on the glass, hysterical, screaming her name, but she couldn't hear him, couldn't see him, didn't even know he was there. Horrified that the wedding was really going to happen and there wasn't anything he could do to stop it, he pulled the chain over to the door and beat his fists on it, kicking it and screaming for them to let him out. Nothing happened. Not a sound, no one came, and he finally sank down onto the carpet in a distraught heap and wept hard and anguished tears of helplessness.

Hours passed, and he just lay there, alone and miserable. Then the night came and went. It wasn't until the next morning that he heard the door open, and the man who stood guard outside his door stepped inside. The older guy still had bruises on his face and a black eye from when Punk had struck him in the shack. He was holding a breakfast tray in one hand, and a sturdy wood club in the other.

"Be calm, sonny," he said warily. "Don't make any sudden moves. You understand me? I don't want to hurt you."

"I am calm. There's nothing more I can do. It's over. She's married to that old man. I saw it happen through my window."

"Good, good. Now you—"

Punk darted at him so quickly that the man couldn't react. Punk hit him hard in the left ear, and the brutal punch put the man down on his side. The tray and dishes and silverware went flying to the carpet, tinkling and breaking and clanking against the floor. The guy came back up, almost at once, club back up and ready to defend himself. But then Punk heard feet pounding up the steps. He turned to the door and saw that it was Bones! Come to help him, just like in the old days! Bones jumped on the guy from behind and tackled him to the floor, then climbed on top and held his arms down with his knees. He grabbed the club off the floor and beat the guy in the face, hitting him over and over, his facial bones crunching like the sound of a car's wheels on gravel, until there wasn't any face there anymore, just raw red meat and broken teeth and blood drenching everything.

"Well, he ain't gonna bother you no more, bro," Bones said, panting hard from the effort of such a brutal kill. His shirt and pants were covered with blood, and he licked some of it off his skinned-up knuckles. "Tastes good, but not as good as Pa's did. Pa's tasted as sweet as sorghum to come out of such a bastard." He grinned at Punk. "I got here in the nick of time, didn't I, Punk? Just like always, huh?"

"C'mon, Bones, help me break this chain. We gotta go get my girl and get her outta here. They made her marry this guy she didn't even know. This old man, lots older than Pa."

"We'll get him and break 'im up good, but first we gonna get that old geezer downstairs. He's the one that started all this shit, right? We gotta kill him first."

"Yeah, we gotta kill my grandfather, but how did you even know all this stuff was goin' on? How did you even know I was locked in up in this here room?"

Bones finally broke the chain and freed Punk. "I been watchin' and listenin' and creepin' around this stupid little place. Cain't rightly see why you ever came over here. These loons are religious fanatics, cain't you see that? I just wanted to know what you was up to over here with that silly little girl. So here I am, at your service, ready to save your ass, so you best be grateful."

"What's going on up here?" came a deep voice from out in the hallway.

Then his grandfather was standing in the doorway, his wrinkled face shocked when he saw all the blood on the floor and bed and the maimed and beaten body lying motionlessly on the carpet. Punk and Bones just stared at him for a few seconds. Then Bones was on him like a bat outta hell, knocking the old man back out into the hallway where his grandfather started shouting hysterically for help. Bones took the wooden club and hit him hard in the Adam's apple, and his yelling stopped abruptly with the terrible pop of neck bones bursting apart. Then he was sitting on his knees beside the old man's body, slamming down the club on one bone after another and shivering all over with delight at each loud crack he heard. Punk stood there and watched, but he was pleased this time. That old guy ought to suffer and die. He shouldn't ever have messed with Punk and his girl and their true love.

After a time, Punk said, "Now hurry it up, Bones. He's dead, ain't he? Quit breakin' him up. Let's get his money out of that drawer in his office and get her and get the hell outta here before they ring the alarm bell."

Downstairs, they broke into the top desk drawer and found great bundles of green bills, all rolled up and bound with rubber bands. That was going to be a very nice nest egg for him and his true love, and Bones, too, now that he was back in the picture and had saved Punk's ass. They found the house where her new husband had taken her captive, and they crept inside the front door and up the steps. The newlywed couple was in the master bedroom, and he was raping her. When they burst in, she screamed her head off, and the old man jumped off her, but only to meet Bones's heavy club right in his face. He groaned and fell back on the bed, and they both started beating the hell out of him with their fists and clubs. His bones were snapping and crackling like a hot fire, just like the flames of rage burning inside them. Blood was spattering everywhere, all over them and his true love's naked body and the bed and the walls and the floor and the ceiling. She kept pressing herself back away from the gore and violence, and screaming and screaming, shrill, horrible shrieks of shock and horror, until the brothers finally stopped and tried to catch their breath. Then Punk heard people shouting outside the house. He got up off his knees and looked around. His girl was cowering in the bed, hiding under the covers, and Bones was long gone. Then before he could think to run, too, yelling, angry men burst into the room and subdued him, and he could only stare at his blood-spattered, trembling true love peeking out from under the bloody sheets as they dragged him out of the room and away from her forevermore.

Chapter Fifteen

After Claire picked up her Ford Explorer at Joe McKay's farm, thanked him, and bid him good-bye, she headed back to the office to see if Bud had made it home from Kansas City. He hadn't. At that point, she began to wonder if he was ever going to come back. Brianna was that beautiful and had that kind of magnetic effect on Bud. Since it had started sleeting rather hard again, she sat down at her desk and fired up her computer. She first pulled up the county database, and it didn't take her long to find a long list of Parker and Fitch rap sheets. Wow, these guys flaunted each and every law on the books, all right.

Yes, this job was going to take her some research time, but she had plenty of that, since Bud was off enjoying himself somewhere and Black had flown back down to New Orleans for an emergency meeting with his Hotel Crescent staff while the weather supposedly held, and hopefully would not be partying it up somewhere on Bourbon Street with his old friend, Jack Holliday, and/or Black's godfather brother. He hadn't called in, which he usually had done by now, but that was a good thing, since she'd spent the morning with Joe McKay. He probably wouldn't like that, even though he had suggested it himself. So maybe he didn't need to know.

Pouring herself a cup of extremely strong black coffee in the department's snack room, she settled in for a long winter's night of the Parker-Fitch hillbilly feud. It was not a good thing, not by any stretch of the imagination. The first arrests had been noted in the 1920s, believe it or not, and okay, that was hard for her to believe. Hell, the two families had tangled and their wounds had festered for almost a hundred years now. Good grief. Some people were just so ignorant and apparently bred with a slightly unforgiving bent, to boot.

She pulled up the report on Arrest Number One, as opposed to Arrest Number Six Hundred and One. She read through it quickly. Well, it appeared the initial altercation had been fought over a woman. Surprise, surprise. Men, for pity sake. Can't live with them and can't keep them from beating each other to bloody pulps. From what she could ascertain, a long-ago Grand Poo-bah of the Parker tribe obviously had an itch he couldn't scratch all wrapped up in a giant hankering for the young fiancée of the Grand Poo-bah of the Fitch idiots. They had fought over it for decades like the insane people they probably were. Parker had killed the Fitch with a bowie knife plunged straight into the heart, no less, and said fair maiden had thrown herself off a nearby cliff onto the rocks below. Shakespeare would've loved these people, oh, yeah. This tragedy was just made for Bard Will's whilsts, and thous and Falstaffs and lengthy soliloquies. However, the most sought-after lady's headfirst plunge off a cliff sounded pretty damn familiar to Claire's current case, so maybe history was repeating itself. Maybe there was a star-crossed romance going on up in them thar hills that ended in Paulie Parker being turned into a bruised up and broken, grape-hued Popsicle stick. But if that was the case, how did ghostly-hued and avian-looking Blythe the White fit into this ugly little screenplay? And where was Blythe anyway? Had she come in to identify the body or was she still staring out that high window for her lost love and looking all pasty and forlorn?

A quick call to Buckeye Boyd indicated that it was a big "no, ma'am" on the identifying the body question and that somebody needed to get the hell down to the morgue and claim the poor guy's pummeled body posthaste or even faster than that. Claire told Buck that she'd look into it and tried to call Blythe Parker, but could not get an answer, so she left her number and settled back to read more of the entertaining arrest records, which included lots of fisticuffs and broken noses, mostly on the police officers sent to run them in, which didn't bode all that well for Bud and her. It didn't take her long to brand said families as Crazy Lunatics of the Highest Hillbilly

Order. Lots of phrases came to mind: "like father, like son," or "sins of the fathers," or characters like Romeo and Juliet, or Hamlet, Scarface, and the obvious Hatfields versus McCoys. And various and sundry other skid row hard luck stories that were better left forgotten.

On the other hand, there was lots of fighting going on and all down through the ages, too. Fistfighting, cage fighting, martial-arts fighting, sibling fighting, dogfighting, cockfighting, child abuse, spousal abuse, elder abuse, animal abuse, and just plain want-to-hit-you-in-the-face-because-I'm-drunk-and-you're-handy abuse. And that brought her up to drunkenness, assaulting a police officer, evading arrest, fleeing the scene of a crime, battery, assault, assault with a deadly weapon, vice, prostitution, illegal distillery, and theft, robbery, armed robbery, and murder.

Fortunately, most of that occurred before 1990. She zeroed in on the recent charges, of which there were also plenty. Wow, maybe she and Bud ought to just set fire to the whole kit and caboodle of said whacked-out-of-their-gourds Old MacDonalds, and be done with it, already. That might save future Canton County detectives a whole heck of a lot of grief in the upcoming decades.

Interestingly, she found that a call had come in about three weeks ago about an altercation at the Parker Quick Stop. Apparently, some customer had called in and reported that the Parker brothers were having a fistfight in the driveway of the very restaurant where she and Joe had enjoyed the excellent crispy fried chicken and titillating Parker repartee. According to the unidentified 911 caller, they all were going at each other in a serious assault worthy sort of way, with their fists and weighted saps, a fight that quickly turned into an all-out brawl. By the time, the patrol officers arrived, however, all was over and nobody knew anything about anything. But the reason the caller gave for the altercation was rudeness. *Rudeness?* Lord have mercy. Apparently, one of the Parkers had asked another one rather impolitely to exit the family establishment and had quickly been knocked into next week. Hmm. Not a brotherly thing, that, nope, not by a long shot.

Staring at the screen, she thought about it for a little while. So the Parker family wasn't quite so full of brotherly love, after all. Maybe the Fitches were gonna get a pass this time. Which would probably be the first time since the early days of Elvis, when their mutual hatred was young and just getting up to a nice strong boil. Now what would make one of the Parker siblings get so bent out of shape that he would attack Brother O' Mine? A woman, no doubt, oh, yeah. Why was it always a woman? Again, the you-can't-live-with-them analogy filled her mind. She was glad that Black only beat up people when he had a good reason, and it was a rare occurrence, even then. Ditto with her.

Then Claire wondered if Blythe had something going on in her past that they just hadn't turned up yet, but that might be a trigger to all this infighting and violence. It was worth investigating. Yep, another call on said albino sparrow was definitely in the cards. And they might want to ask her what the hell was the delay on dealing with her poor dead husband's cadaver, too. But in a nice way, of course. Bud probably would have to do that. Claire was becoming annoyed with the whole double dose of nutty as a fruitcake.

Deciding that there was no better time than the present, she Googled the name Blythe Petrov Parker and seconds later, the page displayed the top sites for dirt on the aforementioned lady. Claire picked one that bragged about giving all background information. She got the address of the ultra-modern house overlooking cliff and lake vistas. She got the spouse's name as Ivan Petrov followed by Paul Parker. But the one fact that really stood out in bright and blinking black cursor was in the maiden name slot. Because, *ta-da*, it said FITCH. Wow, and more wow, a dozen wows echoing into oblivion. So then, was that the Fitch connection to Ivan Petrov and Anna Kafelnikov? Something else she was going to have to delve into and clear up ASAP, accentuating the *S*. But man, oh, man, this case was gonna be a doozy and a wild ride of epic proportions. Well, good. That's the way she liked it, got her engines revving, and all that.

"So, why the cat-ate-the-canary look on your face?"

Still smiling over her uber interesting discoveries, Claire looked up and saw that Bud was standing before her, holding two large cups full of Starbucks coffee. He set hers down on the desk in front of her. "Got you a caramel latte. Don't say I never gave you anything."

"Hey, thanks, just what I needed. Sugar and caffeine. When did you get back?"

"Just now."

"So, how is Brianna doing?"

Bud pulled off his brown sock hat and shrugged out of the heavy fur-lined brown parka that matched hers and hooked it on the coat rack. He shook his head and glanced around at the nearly deserted detective bureau, and then he lowered his voice. "Man alive, Claire, it was as if all that bad stuff hadn't happened and she hadn't been gone at all. We just talked and laughed and had a good time. A real good time. That long drive up and back gave us an opportunity to be together alone, hash things out, you know."

"Gettin' snowed in probably helped, too."

"Oh, yeah." Bud wiggled his eyebrows. "Heaven-sent weather just for me. I love winter."

Claire laughed at him. He was as euphoric as a Disney character, and most likely that would be Goofy. "Well, good deal. That's really good news, Bud. I know you've missed her."

"She's not staying. Not this time. But she's thinking about moving back here." He sat down and grinned at her across their bumped-up-together desks. He did have a nice grin, and his face was all wind burned and his cheeks were ruddy pink from the cold air outside. "I think she will. I hope she will."

"Me, too. Great. You guys are good together."

"Yeah, we are, aren't we?" More wide grins and aren't-I-somethin' expressions.

Claire had a feeling that his dreamy expression wasn't going anywhere for a while. The guy was smitten, yet again, with the leggy and sexy Swede. But time to get his attention off Bri's good bone structure and smokin' bod and back on the case. "So, what did you find out up there?"

"I traced the car license of the guy who took Shorty out of the hospital. The security cameras caught it. It went back to a non-chain local car rental agency at the airport, which said that it was rented to a guy named Fitch, no first name given. Paid cash. Is that one of those fighters you talked to the other night?"

Claire sighed. "Well, I met a rather horny kid by the name of

Malachi Fitch over at the fight arena in St. Louis, but I doubt it was him. He was too interested in bagging every woman he laid eyes on to bother with getting anybody out of the hospital. But it could've been, I guess. He had time to do it before he got to St. Louis. And I haven't had the pleasure of meeting any other Fitches yet. But I'm more than eager to. I did confront a whole passel of Parkers today, though. You'd love them, believe me, as in love to arrest them, I mean. Ever heard of Hatfields and McCoys?"

"That mini-series with Kevin Costner and Bill Paxton? Yeah, that was good. I sided with the Hatfields. What about you?"

"I rarely take sides in hillbilly feuds. I arrest everyone I can."

"Yeah, I know." Bud took a swig from his Starbucks cup. "So? These two families don't get along, I take it?"

Claire tossed the printout she'd made of the less-than-neighbor-friendly rap sheets onto the desk in front of him. "Take a look at this stuff, and then you tell me."

While he thumbed through it, Claire explained everything that she'd done since he'd been off with Bri having a good old time. His dreamy I'm-in-love-with-a-beautiful-girl expression died away, and pretty much right off the bat, at that. "This sounds like it's gonna get complicated."

"Oh, yeah. That's the understatement of the year, Bud."

"I was hoping we could wrap it up quickly. Brianna invited me down to Miami for a long weekend."

"Well, you can kiss that good-bye for a while. I just gave up a trip to the Big Easy with Black, so I know how you feel. It's a bummer."

"Okay. What's up next?"

"I believe a visit to the fabled Fitch family is in order. By the sound of my research, it'll take some time to meet them all. It appears they have their own little village up there. Fitches galore, I tell you. Fitches comin' outta the woodwork, it appears."

Bud grinned. "Okay. You want to go on out there tonight?"

"No way in hell will I approach the Fitch reservation in the dark. First thing in the morning okay with you?"

"Yeah, I'll pick you up. Where you stayin' tonight?"

"At my place. As I said, Black's off somewhere, most likely

listening to blues and drinking beer down at Pat O'Brien's with some of his old Tulane college buddies."

"Hope he's got frequent flier miles. Didn't he just get back from takin' Harve out to LA?"

"He has his own jet, remember?"

"Oh, yeah." Bud laughed. "How could I forget? How long's he gone for, this time?"

"Who knows? The Saints are headed to the Superbowl this year so I may not see him again until February."

"That'll be the day."

Claire nodded, but he was probably right. If Black was going to stay awhile in New Orleans, it would probably be because he was browsing bridal shops and catering services and ladies named Wang, despite his vow to let her handle everything wedding related. So, after she had run the entire case for Bud, she made the horrendous drive through a renewed storm of sleet and ice to her little snug cabin on the lake and spent a pretty damn lonely time there with her trusty poodle, Jules Verne, before Black called in to check on her.

"So, Black, how's it going? Miss me?"

"You bet. How about you?"

"It's lonely here in this hot tub. Nobody for me to rub my naked body up against."

"Well, I'm glad to hear you're alone in that tub, but please don't say things like that when I'm six hundred miles south of you. God, Claire, you make me want to forget blizzard conditions and fly home. I didn't used to need anybody like this. You've made me too damn vulnerable."

Actually, Claire rather liked the sound of that. It certainly had become a vice versa kinda thing. "Oh, yeah, that overwhelming vulnerability of yours. It sticks out all over you."

"It's true. When you came into my life, all hostile and beautiful and started accusing me of violence and murder, I knew you were the one. I knew I had to fight my way into your hard heart and drag you back to my hotel, kicking and screaming."

"Then you're way weird. That still holds."

"Maybe. Turned out all right, didn't it?"

"You bet it did. But know what I think, Black? I think I was just a challenge for you. The only woman you ever met who didn't drop to her knees and beg you to love them. Admit it."

"Such a challenge that I had to beg you to marry me until you finally said yes. And now I'm pretty much having to drag you to the altar, and yes, again it's kicking and screaming and badmouthing Vera Wang. This kicking and screaming stuff seems to be a big part of your personality. Are you really in the hot tub? Naked?"

"Yes, and all this kinda talk is turning me on, so please stop it."

"Me, too. Damn it. You should have come down here with me. It's a pleasant sixty-five degrees. I'm sitting out on our bedroom balcony listening to the fountains down in the courtyard."

"Next time. When are you coming home?"

"As soon as I can. We've got some zoning problems at the hotel. Juan and Maria send their best. They miss you. I do, too."

"Well, I sure do wish I was there. It's down to ten degrees here and sleeting. Can you hear the ice pellets hitting the glass?" She held the phone out next to the window.

"Let me send the plane for you."

"Right, if the pilot wants to commit suicide. I'm not kidding you about the sleet. Can't leave here, anyway, unfortunately. Still working that case of the busted up fighter."

Black hesitated. "Is anything wrong? You haven't talked to Petrov, have you?"

"No, but this case is turning into a real headache."

"How so?"

"Just lots of strands to follow. Very complicated. But we're making some progress."

"Is your head really bothering you?"

"Yeah. It's pretty much pounding out a kettledrum ditty at the moment. I need to go to bed and sleep it off."

"Did you take the meds I left for you? Are you having dizzy spells or a racing pulse?"

As it happened, the racing pulse thing only came up when he was around, but he worried incessantly about her ever since she survived that blasted coma. "Just the headaches. I've already taken some pills and hope they'll knock me out until morning."

"For God's sake, Claire, don't take those pills when you're in the hot tub. That's dangerous."

"I know. I'm nice and relaxed now so I'm getting out as soon as we hang up and going straight up to bed. Jules Verne is already up there waiting for me to snuggle."

"Are you really naked?"

"Come on, Black. What are *you* wearing?"

"I've still got on my business suit but I loosened my tie. Tell me what you intend to do as soon as I get home."

"I am not gonna do this over the phone with you, Black. Come on. Seriously? Get real. We were adults the last time I looked, right?"

"Sometimes you have to make do. Why don't you go put on some of that lingerie I brought home from LA?"

Claire smiled at that idea. "I don't know why you buy that stupid slinky stuff. You just rip it off in about ten seconds and then I have to throw it away. It's a waste of good money."

"But it's worth it. Now humor me for once. What are you wearing to bed?"

"Okay, ready, lover boy? Listen to this, baby. I'm gonna get out of this hot tub, dry off, and go upstairs to the loft. Then I'm gonna put on one of your big old comfortable Saints jerseys to remember you by and pull on some long thermal underwear and flannel pants to keep me warm in this stupid freezing weather and then my thickest wool electric socks. I might even put on a hoodie, if the furnace starts acting up again. Turned on yet, honey?"

"Of course. I like to take that kind of stuff off you, too, you know. Just so you're somewhere underneath, that's all I care about."

Claire shook her head. Black didn't usually talk about that kinda stuff. He must really miss her this time. "Just stop already with all this sexy talk. If you want to be with me, get yourself home and let's get it on."

"You are so right. Maybe I'll cut this trip short and come back tomorrow, weather permitting. Or drive up there. As soon as we hang up, I'll call the guy who takes care of the heat at Cedar Bend and have him come out there tomorrow and put in a new furnace. Are you drying yourself off yet?"

"Would you just cut it out, Black? I'm hanging up now. I'm tired.

This is a tough case, and I've got a long day tomorrow. And you're making things worse. I'm lonely enough without all this romantic angst of yours."

"Okay, I'll call and let you know when I'm landing. Duck and weave and be careful, and give Jules Verne a hug from me. He misses me, doesn't he?"

"Oh, yeah. He's whining for you right now, in between his snores."

Black laughed, and they hung up. Claire sank back down in the warm bubbly water and looked around. The house was pretty damn lonely and quiet without her honeybun there to keep her warm. Oh, well, maybe that was a good thing. She could get some much needed sleep for a change. She had a bad feeling that tomorrow was probably gonna be a fireworks and bottle rockets and pull-out-the-new-Glock-and-start-shootin' day, at least if everything she'd heard about the Fitches was true. But maybe some excitement was just what she needed. It was definitely way too boring around the house with Black out of town.

Chapter Sixteen

The next day when Claire and Bud were on their way out to the Fitch farm, Sheriff Ramsay called and ordered them to put a hold on that interview and instead check out Blythe Fitch Petrov Parker. So they took an abrupt U-turn and headed back to Blythe's home high on its fabulous overlook, fighting spitting snow the entire way. But hey, maybe the sheriff's concern was a good thing. Maybe Blythe could give them some pertinent dope on her birth family during their second visit. Apparently, she still had not shown up to identify the body of her husband and was not answering her telephone. Neither of which were good signs, of course. So away they went to find one shrinking pale violet and make sure she was still in one piece and planning a funeral. Problem was, however, when they got there, she wasn't in one piece and she wasn't planning a funeral.

"Oh, my God, look at that."

Claire stared down at what Bud was talking about. They had reached the fancy and ultra-tall front door and found it standing wide open with snow blowing inside and making a nice little icy mini drift on the polished wood floor. Also inside, a trail of smeared bloodstains and bloody footprints led up the wide spiral staircase. Weapons out and in hand and very on edge and ready for trouble, they followed the blood spoor, not exactly thrilled to find out what they would discover at the end of that scarlet path. The tracks led them upstairs and down a hallway to a master bedroom with an out-of-this-world view from a giant wall of undraped windows and a gory crime scene that was pretty much out-of-this-world, too.

Blythe Parker was not to be seen but they did find a big canopy bed with a pale blue-and-white comforter, not to mention the huge bloodstain about the size of an inflated eighteen-wheeler truck tire right smack dab in the middle of it. More red smears led off the bed and across the pricey blue-and-tan Persian carpet to a pair of French doors that opened onto a Juliet balcony. Almost afraid to look down at the ground below, Claire stepped out to the edge and peered over the railing. Mrs. Parker was down there, all right. Tossed off the balcony like a bag of rags. She had apparently landed in some bushes and bounced off onto the snow. More blood was staining the pristine white ground into a sort of Florida-pink flamingo color, and most of it had come from a gaping and horrendous neck wound, easily apparent and horrific-looking, even from up so high. She had been slit from ear to ear, no doubt about it. Most likely, the jugular had been cut last and thus spewed out blood all over her body and the surrounding snow.

"Oh, God," Bud said. "Look at her. I think she's a chunk of ice, just like her husband was."

"Yeah," Claire said. "She is. Definitely. This looks like payback, don't you think? Or maybe just finishing up the job."

"Could be. Or revenge."

"A popular Parker, a winning fighter, goes down. His Fitch wife goes down a couple of days later. Score: Parker, one. Fitch, one."

Bud looked disgusted. "What the hell's the matter with these people?"

"Family feuds are senseless. Sins of the fathers, blah, blah, blah. Hillbilly justice, stupid but effective."

"Bet they also beat the hell out of her like they did to her husband."

"Probably, if it was the same people, and yeah, I think she went fast." Claire took out her phone and called it in. She talked to Sheriff Ramsay a moment, and then she hung up and turned back to Bud. "I'm surprised she didn't wound one of them. Anna Kafelnikov said she once scared off some of her ex-husband's thugs with a shotgun."

Bud said, "It could've been Petrov. He's into cutting throats. Or maybe he sent his goons up here to bring her back to the big boss where she belonged. She resisted, and they cut her and threw her over that railing."

"From what I've heard about Ivan Petrov, nobody would have the guts to kill anybody without his direct order to do so. He might've gotten sick of trying to get her to come back home and just offed her to be rid of the headache. You know, to teach her a lesson. Maybe he was the one who came up here, one last time, and tried to reason with her."

"If that's the case, he might've murdered her husband, too. Had some fun beatin' him to a pulp first. It's not inconceivable."

"I suspect he would've wanted to do the deed himself. His cousin, Anna, she also said he hadn't left the compound around the time of Paulie's murder. But this means we're probably gonna have to go over there again and talk to Petrov. Black is not going to be thrilled."

"We'll just take him along to smooth the ruffled feathers you will no doubt run your dainty little fingers through, thereby annoying the guy beyond any vestige of self-control."

Claire gave a slight smile, but her eyes were on the poor woman sprawled out below them. She was hard to distinguish from the snowy ground and looked even more white than she had when she was alive, if that were even possible. "Come on, Bud. Let's go down and check her out before Buck and his guys show up."

They got protective gloves out of the car, and Claire grabbed her camera. There were no footprints in the snow. The perpetrators hadn't gone out and checked to make sure she was dead. Apparently, they knew how to cut a woman's throat where she would bleed out in a hurry. Lots of practice at it, that was her guess. Throwing her out the window was just an afterthought or an act of rage.

They made their way around the side of the house and approached the body. They kept as close as possible to the bricked flowerbeds lining the wall so as not to corrupt the scene. Once they got next to the woman, they found Blythe lying there, her strange eyes wide open and staring up at the sky. The iris of her right eye glowed with a surreal and whitish blue color. The left one still had the garish green contact in place. The other contact was frozen to the side of her nose. Yes, Blythe Parker was an albino, all right. A beautiful, graceful, ethereal, and very dead albino.

Bud moved closer. "Look at that white satin nightgown. You know who she looks like, Claire? Veronica Lake. You know who that is, don't you? She's that movie star from the thirties who wore her hair in that blond pageboy kinda thing. 'Member her? Kim Basinger dressed up like her in *L.A. Confidential*."

"Yeah, she does. White satin. No whiter than her skin, though." The victim had landed on her back, right knee up, left leg straight. One arm was bent, too, with the hand behind the head, the elbow sticking straight up out of the deep snow and frozen in that position, the other arm extended toward the bent leg. It looked like a sun-bathing pose, sort of. As if it were a nice warm day, and Blythe was floating on a raft out on the lake. But dead and frozen stiff. "The front door was not broken into. She must have let him in. Or he had a key. Or knew where it was hidden. Do you think she knew her killer? Maybe had a lover on the side?"

Bud shook his head. He blew into his gloved hands, and his breath turned vaporous in the frigid air. "She seemed pretty hung up on her husband. She was definitely devastated when we told her he had been murdered, no doubt in my mind about that."

"I think she knew the perp but didn't expect him to kill her. Maybe it was a member of her own family." Claire stared down at the woman covered in a thin layer of ice, one that made her look shrink-wrapped in glass. "Why would they want her dead, though? For marrying a Parker?"

"Who knows? Maybe her family's anger and resentment's been festering since she hooked up with the enemy. I haven't met any Fitches yet so I don't know how crazy they are," Bud said. "But my initial take is that they are crazy as loons, one and all, and need to be committed."

"The Parkers intimated as much. But they're not exactly the defi-nition of well-adjusted themselves, and they hate anybody born with a Fitch last name, bar none. They had a 'No Damned Fitches Allowed' sign on their front door, for God's sake."

"This is just so way eighteenth century. I bet they use pitchforks and six shooters to whack each other. And the women probably wear pantaloons and bonnets."

Claire looked at him. "Pantaloons, Bud?"

"Yeah. So?"

"Whatever. Okay, I read the rap sheets, pages and pages of them.

Not that many murders until now. Enough, but not as frequent as all their other crimes." Claire looked at Bud. "How long you think she's been dead?"

"A couple of days, I guess. It's hard to tell when the body's frozen. Buck can tell us."

"What's your gut telling you that this's all about?"

"I think this looks more like the St. Louis mob's handiwork than some hillbilly beef goin' on out in the boonies."

Claire sighed. "Me, too. Which is not good, not good at all."

"Cheer up. Maybe they left some evidence behind, just for us so we could nab them and get in outta this Antarctic cold. Maybe we can nail them in nothin' flat and I can go to Miami with Brianna."

"Dream on, and nary a chance in hell. You can quote me on that."

So they began to look around, but found nothing outside that would help them. The driveway was cleared and hard frozen so there were no tire tracks and covering rapidly now with a new layer of snow. Back inside, they had shoe prints, but it didn't look like anything else in the house had been touched. Not ever, in fact. Undoubtedly, it was the cleanest, most orderly, and downright austere home that Claire had ever seen in her life. Black's places weren't even this clean, and he always had a ton of housekeepers. Maybe albinos were allergic to dust particles. Maybe Blythe also had seventy or so housemaids who were all on vacation when the crime was committed. Maybe she simply had a very real and lifelong affection for Mr. Clean and all his products.

The closet was full of lots of white clothes, or at least the "Hers" closet was. Guess she liked to look rather invisible in her clothing, too. She seemed the type to want to look invisible. Expensive clothing, lots of cashmere and suede and flannel. Mostly pants and sweaters and long skirts and tall boots. They finally found the room that was obviously Paulie's refuge from the Comet and Scrubbing Bubbles and Spic and Span. It was the only normal room in the house. It had a desk that, oooh, actually had stuff scattered around on it. Fighting magazines, western novels, and a few classics, mostly *Leatherstocking Tales*. There were pictures on the walls, mainly Paulie's own fighting posters, and glass cases holding his awards and certificates and championship belts and newspaper and magazine covers. He had a red sweater hanging over the back of his swivel desk chair, as if he had gotten hot and whipped it off. She felt like she almost knew him, being in that room. Could almost smell his aftershave. She had a feeling he had been a good guy, but a good guy caught up in one hell of a family feud, one hell of a profession, and one hell of a wife's ex-husband. She felt very sorry for the man, and she'd never even met him when he was alive.

Buck and Shaggy and the rest of the gang showed up within the first thirty minutes and got right down to work. *But they weren't gonna find anything,* she thought. Just a very bloody and white and icy woman, who probably did not deserve to be murdered and thrown out that second-story window. So it was up to Bud and her, and one thing for sure, they were up to the task. No matter what it took; no matter how long it took. And the first thing it was going to take was a trip to the Fitch farm. Claire could not wait. Now she was getting angry.

Blood Brothers

When Punk awoke from that last brutal blow to his head, he found himself inside a stark white room with thick padded walls and floor and ceiling. His arms, legs, and torso were secured with wide blue nylon straps to an iron hospital bed. Even so, his first lucid thoughts were of his own true love. At least, though, and no matter how bad things were, she was no longer married to that old man. She was a widow now, and Bones had escaped and was free as a bird. And that meant that Bones would come to Punk's rescue again, just like he always did. All Punk had to do was be very patient and wait for his twin to show up and get him out of this place. It looked like a hospital, probably a mental institution. Good, at least they hadn't put him in jail. Bones could get him out of a nuthouse in nothing flat, no question about it.

But Bones didn't come for him. Punk tried to stay hopeful as the days lengthened into months, but still nobody came to see him, much less to rescue him. Not even his own true love. Her father was probably holding her captive again, of course, locking her up so she couldn't get to him. Now, though, she had nobody to help her out unless Bones had stepped in and done it for Punk. Where was Bones, anyway? Why wasn't Bones helping him get out of this stupid hospital? Why hadn't he even come to see him? Or written him a letter?

There were many doctors and nurses and a whole lot of security around the locked ward in which Punk was imprisoned. He found out from one friendly orderly, a black guy named Marcus, that he was in the State Hospital for the Insane and that it was located in Fulton, Missouri. That put him pretty far from home. Maybe Bones didn't know where he was, maybe that was it. Punk was forced to have daily sessions with all the staff doctors, one-on-one, private talks that were a real waste of time. They shot him up with drugs and always kept him restrained in wheel chairs or to beds with tough leather cuffs on his wrists and ankles. What did they think, anyway? That he was Dracula, or a zombie, or something? And after a while, it was a good thing that they did keep him cuffed because he wanted to kill all of them about as much as he had ever wanted anything in his life. He wanted to crush their bones into powder.

One doctor was in charge of things, well, at least Punk thought so. Punk was forced to talk to him every single morning, over and over and over. It always turned out the same way, the same questions about Bones and his own true love, and killing his pa, and his pa liking to beat him up, all that kinda stuff, the same old, same old crap. It was no different one particular day as he sat down in the doctor's office, clanking his chains and shuffling his feet. He sighed, and spent his time fantasizing about beating to death the prissy little pipsqueak doctor with his black-framed glasses and red-and-gray, old-man-plaid, button-down collar shirt, and navy cardigan sweater.

"Good morning," the doctor said in his usual bright and cheerful and careful and annoying voice. "And how are we feeling today?"

"We are feeling fine."

"You say *we*. Who are you talking about?"

"You said *we* first. Who were you talkin' about?"

"True. Very perceptive." The doctor steepled his fingers and rocked back in his chair, as if they had made an important break-through. "So, is Bones here with you today?"

Punk looked around the empty office. He shook his head. These endless stupid questions were really getting on his nerves. "Don't see him anywhere, but I sure wish he was. Maybe he could get me outta here and away from you and these chains."

"Is he your best friend?"

"No, sir. He is my twin brother. I done told you that every single day since you locked me up in here. Aren't you listenin' to me, at all?"

"Are you aware that your older brothers deny that you ever had a twin brother named Bones?"

Punk stared hard at him. Now both those things were great big stupid lies, but he'd heard the doctor say them before, and nearly every day, too. "If they did say that, they're just tryin' to protect him. They probably think you're gonna lock him up inside this place like you did me. Hell, they probably think you're gonna lock *them* up. Like I told you a million times, he's the one who killed Pa, not me, and he killed some other people, too. He's probably hidin' out some-where over there on the farm."

"They said that Bones is a figment of your imagination and always has been since you were a small child. They say they went along with it so you wouldn't have one of your temper tantrums and attack them with a hammer."

Punk threw his head back and laughed out loud. "Well, then they're all lyin'. Find our birth certificates, why don't you? That'll show you that I'm tellin' you the truth. What is this, anyway? What're you tryin' to get me to say?"

"Please, now, remain calm. I'm not trying to upset you. As a matter of fact, we've been searching for your birth certificate, but there isn't one to be found. It appears that you and your brothers were born at home and never were legally registered by the state of Missouri. Therefore, there is no legal documentation for your birth."

Frowning, Punk tried to think what kind of joke they were playing on him. "They're lying to you, I tell you. Lots of people have seen

Bones. He fought people in the cage, just like Pa made us all do every Saturday night. The guys he put face down in the dirt sure do remember him. Ask 'em."

"Well, to date, we haven't found a single person who admits to ever having seen this twin brother you talk about. This Bones person. No one has a picture of him. No one has ever spoken to him or seen him or even known about him. How do you explain that?"

Then they stared at each other. Just like every day, always the same questions, the same answers, the same dumb idiots. Punk didn't know what the hell to say this time, either. They didn't know what they were talking about. Or it must be a trick, a shrink's trick to make him say things that would keep him locked up in the looney bin and far away from his true love. Finally, he said, "Well, I'll just say it again. I don't understand any of that. Bones is my twin brother. He's tougher than anybody and he always helps me when I get in trouble. You must be askin' the wrong folks. Or they're still scared to cross him. Look for the ones with the broken bones and fear on their faces."

The doctor gave Punk his usual kindly, you-poor-crazy-nut smile. "I know all this must seem very confusing to you. Would you like for me to tell you what I suspect has happened to you?"

Sure, spill it out again, I've only heard it a million times, Punk thought. Then he stared at the doctor, trying to remain patient, but always expecting some kind of double cross or a new untried psychiatrist tactic to throw him off. He didn't trust doctors, none of them. Especially the ones he had met in this place. He had never even seen a head doctor until they locked him in and chained him up and ogled at him like he was some kind of wild animal in the zoo.

"We've talked to you a lot since you came here. Not just me, but everyone on our psychiatric staff. We've come to the conclusion that you have Dissociative Syndrome. Split personality is the layman's term, and that's probably what you've heard of."

Actually, Punk had never heard of either of those things. This guy was a real kook, way out in left field. He was the one that needed to be in handcuffs. "What the hell does that mean?"

"Simply put, it means that you probably experienced some kind of terrible trauma at some point in your young life, so horrible that your mind just could not handle it. Therefore, it created another stronger personality to handle the most stressful situations that would otherwise cause you to shut down. We have come to believe it was as if two different people lived inside you, two distinct personalities, but you only related to the one you identify as Punk. Although you obviously were aware of the Bones personality as well and what that second personality said and did, we don't think you metamorphosed into him. We believe that you always remained identified with the persona that you refer to as Punk, which allowed you to stand by and watch as if another person, all the deeds you perpetrated when you became Bones, but without realizing you were actually committing them."

Punk did not move a muscle. This guy was so far out in left field that it was pitiful. "I see you're still spouting the same old crap, right? You can't really believe all that crazy stuff. Bones is as real as I am."

"We don't use that word here."

"What word? Crap?"

"No. Crazy. The patients here are ill, not crazy."

"Well, I'm not talkin' about them, I'm talkin' about you. Anyways, you oughta wake up and smell the coffee. Everybody in this place is pretty much bonkers, and you know it, too."

"Please, listen to me. You have a serious mental disorder brought on by severe childhood abuse. Please understand that we're all working very hard to help you resolve this issue. If you will allow yourself to relax and cooperate with our diagnosis and treatment, then you will be fine one day and you'll be able to go home and lead a pleasant and productive life with your brothers."

Listening to all that, yet again, Punk mainly latched on to the going home part. "What kind of therapy? What are you gonna do to me? You gonna cut up my brain and make me dumb like I saw once in that movie about flying over the cuckoo's nest."

"No, no, not to worry. We'll just continue with your sessions where you'll be encouraged to chat with us about your past and what you went through with your father. We want to try to figure out what initiated this fantasy figure that you've created inside your mind.

Once we figure out what specifically caused this mental aberration, then we'll talk through it with you."

This doctor dude was so weirded out nuts that it was downright hard to watch, Punk thought, disgusted. Bones was every bit as real as he was. Nothing they could say would ever make him think otherwise. Just ask all the boys he beat up all those years. Just ask anybody who watched all those Saturday night fights. Nobody up around home gave out information to the cops, and didn't trust them doctors, either. Maybe that's why nobody copped to knowing Bones. It had to be something like that. But, maybe, if Punk just played along with this guy, see if he could get the shrinks to take off the chains, then he could escape and go back home and find his girl. He heaved in one deep breath. "Okay, but I'm tired of being locked up like this. Can't you let me go around here some without all these restraints? I won't hurt nobody. I swear to God, I won't. I don't even want to, not anymore."

"In time that will happen. Once you convince us by your good behavior and willing cooperation that you never intend to hurt anyone else, ever again. You beat several men to death on the day they brought you here. Do you remember anything about that?"

"Bones did it. Not me. Why won't you believe me?"

"You see, here again you have returned to that story, and rather convincingly, I must say. But as I said, there is no one named Bones in your life. He does not exist, and you need to accept that. He is nothing but a strong character in your imagination. One that is very real to you and that protects you and handles all the stressful events that you are forced to face. Your brothers have all told us that you've been volatile and unpredictable since you were a small boy."

"What's 'volatile'?"

"In this context, it means high-strung, easily angered, aggressive, and prone to physical altercations."

"That's Bones to a T, I'm telling you. Not me. It's not *me*! Why don't you just believe what I say? I'm tellin' you the truth. Why wouldn't I? I wanna get outta here! My brothers are the ones who're lying."

The shrink just looked sad. He shook his head. "Okay, I think that's enough for today. You're becoming agitated again. How about we make us a little deal, okay? If you are quiet and behave well and cause no more trouble for the nurses and orderlies, we'll take off the restraints and let you mingle with the other patients in the common room. How does that sound?"

Now the guy was talking. "That would be good. I won't make no problems at all, I swear it."

"Then I guess you may go back to your room now and think about all the things we have discussed, and we'll chat again tomorrow. Same time, same place."

"Yes, doctor," he said meekly. What a laugh. He couldn't wait to fool this little sissy guy and head back home. He and Bones had some serious work to do.

Chapter Seventeen

Man, alive, Black was gonna be so royally pissed off, it wasn't even funny, Claire thought, frowning at the mere idea of what he was going to say about what she was getting ready to do. But then again, he was still way down yonder in New Orleans waiting for the skies to clear, and totally unavailable to warn her off and/or accompany her to St. Louis to step into Ivan Petrov's creepy and highly dangerous compound. Unfortunately, Charlie had ordered Bud and her to again postpone their planned trip to Fitch Hillbilly Hollow and to instead pay an up close and personal visit to a certain East St. Louis criminal don. They were almost there now, using Bud's GPS to find the place. It was fairly isolated, too, especially being located so close to a large metropolitan area, but they finally found it, way out in some snowy woods in the middle of nowhere.

There were two armed guards at the front gate, and Claire stared at them as Bud rolled the Bronco to a stop. She wondered if Black had been right, and if they were going to be swallowed up in said Russian Thugland, as surely as if plunging headfirst into a deep space black hole. He had certainly overreacted the first time he thought she was going to visit Petrov, acted as if it equated with entering a Moscow-run portal to hell. Right now, they were on the verge of walking straight into Petrov's compound and checking out all the bad things, and yes, they certainly did have their hands full, oh, yeah. Murderous Mafioso, or not, however, surely this guy wouldn't dare lay a finger on them. He better not. Charlie would have every cop in both Missouri and Illinois on his back, if he did.

Of course, they'd both still be in corpse mode, and Black would be pissed about that, too.

"Yes, sir, may I help you?" the polite lowlife guard said to Bud, no doubt pretending he was a regular, normal human being. Then he leaned down farther and examined Claire's face, where she sat watching the action from the passenger's seat. "Oh, hello there, Detective Morgan. How you doin'?"

"Have we met, sir?" Claire asked him pointedly. She'd never seen the guy before in her life. He was clean cut for a henchman, not as heavily muscled as most of them. He sported a little goatee and mustache that reminded her of the Three Musketeers but he had no detectable French accent. Nope, his accent was American with a Russian lilt that she could just barely pick up. He wore wraparound black sunglasses and a long black trench coat that helped with his menacing image thing.

"No, but I saw you at the fight arena with Nicky Black. Congrats on the upcoming wedding."

Claire frowned, somehow feeling dirty. "Thank you. We're here on official police business to see Mr. Ivan Petrov. Is he at home?"

"Yes, ma'am. Let me call up to the main house and get permission for you to enter the compound."

"Very courteous guy," Bud said, pressing a button and rolling up his window. "He probably smiles when he knifes people, too. And what is this, anyway, the White House?"

"More like the Kremlin. I did hear that people who go inside this compound don't come out. At least, not alive."

Bud jerked his face toward her. "*Now* you tell me that?"

"Well, Charlie knows where we are. If they try anything funny with us, they won't get away with it. And I did put in a cautionary call to the East St. Louis PD to apprise them when and where we were going in. I'm supposed to call them once we're safely out."

"Oh, wow, Claire, that makes me feel so much better. Who told you all that?"

"A little birdie."

"A Black birdie, maybe? Hope he doesn't know what he's talking about."

"Alas, but he usually does."

The guard was tapping a bent knuckle on the window. "He said to come on up. Just follow the road until you hit the end of the line."

"Thanks," Bud said, and then accelerated through the gate, which closed behind them in a rather final way. "I don't think I like the sound of that. End of the line—that sounds like a premonition to me."

"We're gonna be fine." She hoped.

The parking lot was just up around the first curve. There were several more beefy men standing out there waiting for them. All were wearing heavy winter overcoats, scary black ones like the other guy's that hung past the knee, probably with M60 machine guns hidden under them, loaded for bear. They also had on mafia-inspired fedoras and black leather military boots with their pants tucked in. Probably hobnailed, too. "Looks like we're gonna be outnumbered, Bud."

"Great. I can't tell you what a good time I'm havin'. Yeah, and just when Bri gets back, too."

"Okay, let's go see what's so scary about our deceivingly chummy Moscow buds."

A rather hefty and pockmarked and swarthy Slavic giant examined their badges, even turning them over and looking at the backs, no doubt looking for Toys "R" Us tags, before he motioned them to follow him. He wasn't particularly chatty. Or friendly. In fact, he said nothing. Maybe he couldn't speak English. Maybe he couldn't speak any language and just grunted and gestured his way through life. They trailed him up a wood ramp to an extremely modern structure that appeared to be the main house. Another hood stood guard at the front door. His big gun was readily apparent, in his big hand, even. He checked their badges, too. Jeez, there probably weren't this many checkpoints at Fort Knox.

Ushered into a surprisingly spacious living room, all burgundy and black decor, and maybe about the size of a basketball court and a half, they found the King of Red Square sitting in court beside a huge walk-in stacked stone fireplace with a giant moose head above the mantel. All the furniture was black leather with lots of studs and rough wood with my-owner's-one-tough-mother appeal. Oh, yeah, everything looked mucho manly, in an elegant East European sort of way. Maybe Ivan needed tough surroundings to help him scare his visitors to death. It was working.

"Ah, there you are, my dear, the future Mrs. Nicholas Black. Please, do come in, come in. I've been absolutely dying to meet the woman who slipped that ring through Nicky's nose. Nobody thought it could be done. Me, included."

Nice. Not. Okay, true, that little spurt of nasty certainly rubbed Claire the wrong way. What a creep. Everything about the man, the giant room, the deep voice, and the roaring fire, all of it made her want to rub him the wrong way, too. Rub him out, maybe. She fought the extremely strong urge overtaking her, the one that compelled her to sprint the rest of the way to the smug Russian and make his nose bleed. Instead, she remembered her mission and stopped in front of the supposedly scary-as-hell Mafioso, and said, "Thank you for seeing us, sir. We do need to ask you a few questions. It won't take long. This is Bud Davis, my partner, and my name is Claire Morgan."

"Oh, yes, ma'am, we're all at your service. Any friend of Nicky's is a friend of mine."

Then Ivan Petrov finished his annoying name-dropping and looked her up and down as if she didn't have on a bulky parka and a sock hat that made her hair stick out with static, and all of which pretty much hid anything that he might be interested in insulting. Lascivious? You bet. Why, she wasn't quite sure. Her insulated down parka and jeans and makeup-less face didn't exactly excite strip club ogling. No way could he tell what was underneath all those layers; she could look like a geriatric bag lady, for all he knew. To her sensibilities that branded the remarks as simply hateful and meant to provoke wrath.

So, okay. Who gave a hot damn what a deadly imbecile thought? He hadn't gotten her goat yet, if that was his plan. But he had one hand on its bleating neck with malice aforethought in his head. Bud was frowning, also understanding the tacky innuendo and not liking it any more than she did. But he didn't punch out their host, either. They both remained the picture of official restraint. She shuddered to think what Black would've done to him, but the mental picture did have a certain happy appeal for her.

"This concerns your ex-wife, Mr. Petrov," she told him, still calm, watching his face for a revealing reaction to the subject.

His face registered on cue. Open and easy to read. Surprise, shock even. He got that under control quickly enough. "Blythe, you mean? You probably want to talk to her current husband, not me. We were divorced several years ago."

"Well, yes, but thing is, sir, we recently found that little text message you sent to her cell phone on occasion. You know, the one that said, 'I'm gonna kill you, bitch, if you don't come home.'"

Curtains down on incriminating expressions, just like that. He'd had some practice evading answers in police interviews, all right. "I really have no idea what you're talking about. But please, where are my manners? Please, sit down and make yourselves comfortable. Let me get you something to drink. Shall I call someone to take your coats and hats?"

"No, thank you. We're fine." They took seats across from the chair aka throne on which he sat. However, he immediately stood up, and moved to where he could warm his back at the huge grate with its leaping, crackling flames. He looked extremely relaxed now. As if he had them where he wanted them, and was oh, so pleased with himself. Claire fought her desire to pull her weapon and blast him a good one right through the chest. All humanity would be better off.

After a moment, Petrov pondered aloud. "That message sounds like a terrible thing to say to anyone. I assure you that I would never say such a thing to my ex-wife. Blythe is much too fragile and easily upset to frighten like that." He smiled, easy and self-assured, and now really hunkered down into his lies.

"Then I guess you didn't slit her throat and toss her out her bedroom window, either. Right?"

Okay, he wasn't smiling anymore. He looked stunned. Then he looked disbelieving. Then he looked stricken. Then he looked like he was crying on the inside. Then he really was crying on the outside, real live godfather tears running down his cheeks. Whoa, Nelly, he wasn't holding anything back, either. He was in full-fledged grief mode. Bud looked over at her as their tough-guy host hid his face in his hands and sobbed out loud. "No, no, no," he kept saying.

Well, well, what'd you know, the guy had a heart in there somewhere, after all. And Anna had been on target about him still loving Blythe Parker. But now, he had resurfaced again, super creep once more, coming out of his two-minute mourning period just like that, and now onto fierce, stampeding mad-elephant anger mode, which was definitely a transition worth watching.

"Who? Goddamn it, who killed her? Tell me!" Abruptly, he went silent, then let out a pitiful little sob muffled behind his hand, then mopped the tears off his face with a white handkerchief that he pulled out of the inside pocket of his dark brown suede smoking jacket. "You tell me, girl, you tell me right now who dared put his hands on her."

Girl? Alrighty now, enough is enough. "Or what, Mr. Petrov? I am an officer of the law, and I expect you to remember that and address me with respect. You got that, sir? Now compose yourself, because I want to ask you some questions we need answered for our homicide investigation. Are you ready to proceed? Or do you need time to get control of your emotions?"

He didn't need time. And he didn't like her anymore, and didn't think Black was so lucky to hook up with her, either, she supposed. He glared at her, and she took it in stride. Not exactly something she wasn't expecting. Lots of people glared at her. Even Black, now and again. She was used to it.

Bud chose that moment to enter their polite back and forth. He said, "You need to sit down, Mr. Petrov, or we're gonna think you're tryin' to hide something."

Then Petrov shared his glare with Bud. Apparently not used to people answering back without being shot in the temple right where they stood. She wondered if he had one of those devious trapdoors under their chairs, like in all those 007 movies when the villain pulled a lever and his victims plummeted into a pool of sharks or a vat of acid. They waited for the plunge or attack by summoned thugs, both of them matching the guy stare for rude stare.

Surprisingly, Petrov didn't pull the lever. "I'm sorry, detectives. I'm just in shock, I guess." He sank down into a different big wing-back chair covered with fabric that had designs of German castles standing majestically on high cliffs, or maybe they were Russian strongholds. He shook his head. "I never stopped loving her, even when she ran off with that fighter. I always wanted her to come back home and live here with Anna and me and the boys. I could've protected her from this. Better than Paulie ever could." He leaned his head back against the cushions and shut his eyes and sighed, really pitiful now. So tired of murder and dead wives and getting blamed for everything.

Okay, that was all very interesting. Fearing he'd dropped off to sleep, however, she raised her voice. "Protect her from whom, Mr. Petrov?"

He jerked up to sitting, faster than a blink, accent growing thicker now. "From her crazy family, that's who. The Fitches. Those goddamn crazy sons of bitches. They're all nuts, insane, all of them, every single one, down to the smallest child. That's why she fled her parents in the first place and came to St. Louis to be my wife. She knew I could protect her, that's the reason she married me. And I did. As long as she lived in this compound, they couldn't get within an inch of her. Then she up and ran off with Paulie. I tried everything to get her to come back, but she could be so stubborn, and she thought she was in love with that bastard. And now, she's dead. Just like I told her she would end up."

Claire and Bud sat there and listened to all that and studied his very emotionally charged face. Nothing about this interview was going as she had envisioned. Black had talked as if this guy was Attila the Hun, for God's sake, and now Petrov was acting like Little Orphan Annie at Daddy Warbucks's funeral. But Black the Shrink was not usually this much off with his take on other people's character traits. If he said that Ivan Petrov was a scary, maniacal killer, then he was one. But he was also doing a pretty good job of acting like a sad and distraught former husband who still loved his wife. Maybe he could be both, which was a more likely scenario. Still, she didn't feel sorry for him. She wasn't so sure he hadn't ordered the hit on Blythe, either, and/or cut her throat himself with his own special finesse and the sharpest, one-swipe blade in the world. Maybe he was putting on an Oscar-worthy performance. Maybe he had been president of drama club at Moscow Senior High School.

"Let me make sure that I understand you, Mr. Petrov. Are you telling us that Blythe Parker is a member of the Fitch family?"

"Yes. You mean, you didn't know that?"

They did, of course. But milking him for additional information was not above her pay grade. "Are you talking about the Fitch family who live out north of Lake of the Ozarks?"

"Yes, they've got a regular little town out there. All the family lives together in a fenced in and guarded property that's been in the Fitch family for decades."

Ivan Petrov had uttered all of that with a high degree of contempt, which was a bit like the pot calling the kettle black, in Claire's biased opinion. Guarded, fenced mob compound equaled guarded, fenced regular little town in her playbook. Poor frail Blythe just couldn't win for losing. "What can you tell me about the Fitch family, Mr. Petrov? It's important that we know what we're dealing with here."

He put his hands, palms up, in the air with an expansive gesture of how-the-hell-should-I-know. "They're all just crazy. And I really mean *crazy*. Inbred, if you ask me. Except for Blythe. She's different. She's incredible, beautiful, fragile, ethereal." He paused, trying to think up more adjectives that meant the same thing. Yeah, he did like his synonyms. Claire might've thrown in Snow White, but she waited politely and didn't interrupt. "Especially those crazy brothers and cousins of hers. They are completely obsessive about protecting her virtue. You'll see what I mean when you meet them. It's a real strange place up there."

It seemed rather *X-Files* to Claire, too, as did this interview, but it also seemed that everybody was awfully obsessive about one highly beloved albino lady. Excessively so, in her studied opinion. Why they were, though, was the pertinent question. "You've been out there? On the Fitch property?"

"Once, but only once. That's about all anybody can take. Poor little Blythe had to grow up there. She had to escape like some kind of trapped animal who had to bite off her foot to set herself free."

Cute analogy, Claire thought, *but also here came the old pot and kettle scenario again.* Petrov was kidding himself if he didn't see that he had imprisoned her every bit as much as her folks had. And now was imprisoning his cousin, Anna, the very same way.

"And if they'd found her, they would've dragged her back, hogtied and under house arrest." Petrov gave a bitter laugh. "She had lots of guts to thwart the old man."

Claire wondered how he had met up with the Fitch clan. Probably some kind of crooked business deal that might bear looking into, too. It wouldn't surprise her. The whole case was getting pretty messed up, but it looked like their visit to the Fitch farm, or 'Salem's Lot, or whatever the hell it was, was certainly now in the cards. Tarot cards, probably.

"We'll be going out there for a death notification. Right now, however, we need to ask you where you've been for the last forty-eight hours, or so. Just to rule you out, you understand."

"I've been here in the compound. Any one of my men can alibi me. Or Anna. That's my cousin, who also lives here with me. We've been spending a lot of time together the last few days. We usually take our meals together with my sons since Blythe walked out on me. Nicky sees her as his patient at times. He might've even mentioned that to you."

"No, he did not," Claire lied with blatant nonchalance. "Then we will need to talk with this Anna. You understand, don't you, that we'll have to see her alone."

"Did she suffer? Blythe's such a fragile little thing. Did you know her before you found her dead?"

"We interviewed her about the death of her husband, Paulie Parker. Were you aware that he was beaten to death a few days ago?"

"I heard that he was murdered." Ivan didn't seem nearly as upset about that death. Concern for Paulie ran off him pretty much like water off the proverbial duck's back. "Have you found his killer?"

"Not yet. You have any ideas?"

They locked eyes, but he didn't give anything else away. He had sobbed away his initial raw and heartfelt emotions and now it appeared that he had none left, meaning a heart, of course.

"Also, we'd like to speak with your two fighters. Ike and Mike Sharpe. Are they available?"

"No, I'm afraid not. They're on vacation."

"Where?"

"Europe."

"For how long?"

"They're tired. I wanted them to get away and recharge for the championships being held later this year in Houston."

"What about a phone number where they can be reached?"

"They're staying at a cabin high in the mountains. I haven't been able to get hold of them for several days. No phone reception there."

Somehow Claire thought he was being disingenuous. "What about Anna? I guess we'll need to see her before we go."

"Fetch Anna," he called out to somebody standing guard nearby, somebody with two Canton County detectives in their gun sights, no doubt.

Claire turned around in time to see a big guy saunter off down an outer hallway. She wondered how many other Petrov lieutenants were hiding behind the draperies. "Do you know why anyone would want to hurt Blythe, Mr. Petrov?"

"I know that you probably think it was me. But I never wanted to hurt her. I just wanted her to come home to me and the boys, to get over whatever it was she saw in Parker and come to her senses. I loved that woman. I still love her. I could've protected her from her family. She still would've been alive behind these gates."

Bud said, "So she had no enemies that you know of?"

"Are you serious, man? Blythe? She was an angel. She looked like an angel, and she was one. She made me a better man when she married me."

If he was a better man now, Claire would have hated to see what he'd been before the nuptials, since he was presently a cold-blooded killer, drug dealer, and probably arms dealer, too. Not to mention all-around jerk of the universe and smart aleck. Maybe he meant that Blythe made him attend mass with her or go to confession now and then.

"Can I have her body?"

Okay, that just sounded just so damn creepy. Visions of Hitch-cock's *Psycho* cellar came to mind, swinging bare lightbulb, and all.

"I'll have to check on that, sir. Usually, the body is released to next of kin."

"If you let those damn albino Fitches have her, they'll bury her inside that farm, if they even bury her at all. Being buried in that hellhole is the last thing she'd ever have wanted."

"We'll have to get back to you on that. Perhaps she left some in-structions with her lawyers."

Anna walked into the room behind them, and Ivan jumped up,

Mr. Gentleman to the core, all of a sudden. She had a feeling this guy had as many personalities as that mentally tortured girl in *Sybil*.

"Anna, dear, this is Claire Morgan and Bud Davis. They're detectives from over at Lake of the Ozarks. Our darling Blythe is gone. They found her body. She was murdered."

Anna indeed looked horrified at that news, but she hid it quickly. She glanced at them and nodded, doing a pretty good acting job herself. Man, they ought to hand out Oscars at the Petrov compound. "How awful. I am so sorry, Ivan. Blythe was an exceptional woman."

Ivan grabbed his cousin bodily and held her tightly, obviously needing somebody to cling to. Claire was just glad it didn't have to be her. Anna was watching them over his shoulder, her fine blue eyes saying: *What the hell are you doing here? Didn't you hear what Nicky said about us? Get out, flee while you still can, you silly goose!*

A bit disconcerting? You bet.

Finally, Anna disentangled herself from her emotional and bloodthirsty killer cousin and turned to them. "How do you do, officers? I'm Anna Kafelnikov. I understand that you wish to speak to me. Is it about our poor Blythe?"

"Yes, we'll need to talk to you in private, if that's all right."

Anna looked at Ivan, ostensibly for permission. He nodded, and then she said, "I was just getting ready to take a walk in the gardens. Perhaps you would like to accompany me."

Since the temperature was in the teens outside, Claire was fairly certain that Anna was telling them that the entire house was bugged to the rafters, or there were hidden cameras or peepholes in the woodwork. "That would be fine, ma'am. Please lead the way."

Outside, they moved into a garden of sorts, one now heavily coated with snow and ice, but the paths were cleared and safe enough for some very cold and unpleasant strolling about. As they walked along together, their breaths smoky in the crisp wintry air, the sun sparkled against all the snowdrifts and ice encasing the tree limbs in a blinding display of natural beauty that made Claire long for her sunglasses. Anna kept up the pretense a bit longer, probably unsure about Bud's allegiances. So Claire did, too. Maybe Petrov wired Anna for interviews like this. Black would probably think so. Black also probably thought Petrov was Satan, by the description he had given her. So far, Petrov wasn't any better or worse than any other godfather she'd met up with. But she'd only seen his polite side, so there you go.

"Was Ivan Petrov here in the compound the last three days, Ms. Kafelnikov?"

"Yes, he was. At least, I saw him every day. If poor Blythe was killed at the lake, I doubt very much that he had time to make the trip so far away and come back in time for dinner every night. We usually take every meal as a family, and dinner is at four. He didn't miss any lunch or dinner for the last fortnight."

That was an antiquated way of saying two weeks, Claire recalled. "And his men? Did you notice any of them being absent long enough to make a couple of folks turn up dead at Lake of the Ozarks?"

"They come and go at will. There's no way that I can keep track of all of them, even if I wanted to."

"Do you know anyone who might want both Paulie Parker and his wife dead?"

They stopped beside a frozen pond that nearly blinded them with its icy glare. "I do know that Blythe had a, well, I guess you'd say an unorthodox type of family. There was a lot of ill will among them. She never really explained it all to me, but I did understand that they were a rough bunch and that she was afraid of them. She endured a rough life, in general."

"Was her family rougher on her, than others that you might know of?"

That was a veiled reference to Ivan and his cretins, albeit a clumsy one, and one which Anna picked up on right away. "Probably, yes."

Hell, that was pretty damn rough, Claire would say. At least, according to Black's opinion of their weepy host. "Is there anything else that you might be able to tell us, ma'am?"

More veiled references, not exquisitely done. Claire searched the other woman's face.

Anna said, "Not at this time, but I'm going to give this a lot of thought and if I think of anything at all, I will try to get word to you."

Good enough. She was probably wired, or Petrov had sensors out in the garden or listening devices on the roof. Jeez. No wonder Blythe and Anna wanted out of the compound. But for an afternoon spent in a mob crib, hobnobbing with dastardly criminals, they were still pretty much in the dark. Now everybody was pointing fingers at the Fitches, who, by all accounts, were a bunch of morons and idiots and inbred cousins, but probably morons and idiots and inbred cousins with lots of sharp knives and loaded guns and witch-burning pyres. Which was not all that different than most of their cases of late. She bid Anna good-bye and left the compound with Bud, not feeling good about anything, especially about the idea of telling Black she had visited the monster in his lair after she had promised him she wouldn't. Oh, well, he'd just have to bite the bullet and get over it, just like he always had to do since meeting up with her.

Chapter Eighteen

Fortunately for Claire, Black didn't call her until his plane had landed in Camdenton and he was in the chopper and almost home to Cedar Bend Lodge. She had been back from St. Louis for about an hour, and now sat in Black's private indoor heated lap pool on the bottom floor of the hotel, the one with the huge plate-glass windows overlooking the lake and marina and heliport. She decided it wiser to tell him over the phone, considering how intense he got when discussing Ivan Petrov's villainous attributes.

Black said, "Hey, I'm almost home. Ten minutes at the most. Be ready for me."

Oh, she was ready for him, all right. Ready for an argument like no other in human history. "Good deal. How're all things on Governor Nicholls Street?"

"All good. Nice weather. How's your case coming along?"

"Okay." Claire took a deep breath, and then another more bracing one. She could already hear the thump of rotors in the distance. Hell, she was more reluctant to tell Black this little bit o' bad news than she had been about entering Petrov's den of iniquity. She dove in and hoped for the best. "Well, just so you know. Bud and I had to go over to the Petrov compound earlier today and interview Ivan and Anna."

Silence. Heavy, pissed-off, angry, irked, I'm-gonna-throttle-you-with-my-bare-hands silence. She'd heard that from him before. Once, maybe. Then Black said, "Did I not ask you not to go in there alone, Claire? Did you not promise me that you wouldn't?"

"You did, but can't say I remember promising you anything.

Maybe intimating it slightly, but listen up, though. I wasn't alone. I was with Bud, and Charlie told me that we had to go inside and sweat him. Charlie's my boss. He trumps you on this one, Black. Sorry. That's just the way it is."

"Good God, Claire, what the hell's the matter with you?"

"Let's talk about it later, when you get here, okay? Call me then, after you get over it."

Claire clicked off, and immediately headed off down the pool in another hard lap in the nice warm water. The heat coming off the pool and hot tub fogged up the windows pretty good, but it felt lovely to unwind and work out her muscles, even if Black was as mad as a swatted hornet. The snow drifts made it a little difficult for her habitual daily run but the swimming was sweet, and done inside, and as warm as summer sun. She came back to where the hot tub gushed over into the lap pool and sat on the bottom step, where she was mostly submerged in the water, and watched the heliport out on the point.

This little delay in their unhappy conversation would get Black used to being mad at her and ready to calm himself down like a good shrink should. The helo appeared from out over the lake in about two minutes and she watched it set down on the cleared landing pad. Then she watched Black jump out and head up the marina toward the hotel. Uh-oh, he was trudging. He always trudged when he was ticked off at her, and there was no loose-limbed and relaxed stride in sight, which was his usual way of getting from here to there.

Black headed straight for the door that led to his private penthouse elevator, and she waited, curious about how long it would take him to call and want to resume their oncoming huge fight. It didn't take him long. Her phone rang, and she punched on. "Hi, sweetheart, I'm so glad you're home. I just missed you so much," she gushed sweetly.

"Where the hell are you?"

"Down in the lap pool. Come swim with me. Loosen up a little. You know, veg out, get it on with me in the hot tub ASAP."

"I'll be down in a minute."

It was more like twenty minutes, but that was okay. More time for him to cool off. She got all sixty of her daily laps in before he showed up. He finally made his appearance, already in his swim trunks and long black terry-cloth robe. He trudged toward her, and he was still not happy. She just waited, calm thus far. Let him make the first move. He was the one who was uptight, not her. His first move was just to get in the pool and start his own series of laps. That went on for a great long while until she got tired of the silent treatment and got out and wrapped up in her matching terry-cloth robe and headed for the door. She stopped with her hand on the lever and reconsidered the wisdom of that move. Okay, maybe he had a right to be upset. She had promised, sort of. Not on her life, or anything, and she had left herself a caveat, which he probably just didn't catch. So she returned to the pool and waded down the steps and waited for him to work off his miff. It took at least twenty more laps. Then he sat down across from her, panting a bit and still frowning in an openly annoyed fashion. He looked good, though, with his black hair all wet and slicked back and those intense blue eyes.

"Okay, I know you're ticked off," she started out, but didn't get far with that line of meeting him halfway.

"Ticked off doesn't even touch what I'm feeling right now. Don't you ever listen to a word I say, Claire?"

"Look, I'll give you some anger, okay, but don't think I'm gonna sit here and let you jump me for doing my job."

"Do I ever?"

"Yeah. You do. You're doing it right now."

"No, I'm not. But this is something I happen to know about. Did you just casually stroll in there and confront Ivan about Paulie Parker's murder? Good God, Claire."

"No, I did not. Actually, if you must know, I strolled right in and confronted him about Blythe Parker's murder."

That got him good. "Blythe is dead? When? How?"

"You see, you need to learn all the facts before you start getting all hot under the collar and jumping me."

"When? How?"

"Yesterday. At her house. With a slit throat and lots of broken bones and a headfirst dive out her bedroom window."

"Oh, my God. How'd he take it?"

"Not good. He loved her true, trust me on that. If he was pretending about his feelings, he can land a role in the next Tom Cruise picture."

"He didn't do it. Like I told you, he was obsessed with that woman. Totally obsessed with her. Pathologically obsessed."

"I gathered that by his flood of wet-to-the-touch tears. And just so you'll calm down, after a tacky comment or two, he was as polite as polite could be. A real gent. He must think the world of you."

"He'd kill me as soon as look at me."

"Didn't get that vibe, but he was obviously trying for nice."

"You did a very stupid and dangerous thing today."

"That happens when you're a homicide detective."

"Tell me about it."

"And I resent the word *stupid*. We were acting under direct orders."

"The direct orders were stupid."

Okay, and there lies the rub. And right where it always had been. Her job was a thorn stuck so deeply into his protective instincts that he couldn't begin to pull it out. Trouble was, she wasn't sure she wanted him to pull it out. Claire frowned. She didn't even like her own damn analogy. Crap. She didn't want there to be thorns in their relationship, but there were, and she couldn't get them out, either.

"What?" he asked.

"I don't know, Black. I'm just sorry that my job makes you crazy. That's all. It's usually the only thing we ever fight about."

He sighed and let go of some of the anger. "It's not your job, Claire. You love it. I know that. I only get crazy when you put yourself in unnecessary danger, like you did today."

"It *is* my job. You know it is."

"I'm not asking you to give up your job, damn it. I just wish you'd go private so you can pick your cases."

Well, that was a relief, because she wasn't going to give it up, not any time soon. "How would you like it if I insisted you give up your job and do something else?"

Big frown. "I wouldn't like it, but my job isn't dangerous."

"Your little covert trips with your buddies never present any danger? That's what you're saying? Seriously?"

"Okay, I get your point."

"Alrighty then. I rest my case."

They stared at each other, and then he said, and yes, rather begrudgingly, "I missed you. It's good to be home."

"I missed you, too."

Black reached out his hand toward her with his fingers spread apart. That was what he did when he wanted to make love to her. And any time he did that and she threaded her fingers through his, pleasure came a-calling, and plenty of it, and plenty fast.

"C'mere, Claire."

"No problem."

She entwined her fingers with his, and he squeezed them and pulled her toward him. They smiled at each other, and then she sat down on his lap, and that was that. At least it would be until tomorrow, when she told him that she and Bud were paying an official visit to a fenced-off farm containing a bunch of crazy hillbilly nut jobs by the name of Fitch.

Early the next morning, Claire and Bud headed out to hillbilly heaven, neither one particularly craving the opportunity to hobnob with aforementioned Fitches, about whom they'd heard nothing good in the slightest. Surprisingly, however, Black didn't seem to mind her going out there, at least not with the same outrage he did when she visited Ivan Petrov. He just told her to be careful and wear her GPS tracking device so he could find her when she inevitably got herself into trouble. Not *if* she got into trouble, mind you, but *when* she got into trouble. Oh, he of little faith.

When they had finally circumnavigated the belly-tightening road curves long enough to reach the entrance to the Fitch property, they stopped out on the blacktop road and stared at the big sign over a substantial-looking locked iron gate. FITCHVILLE, it read. Oh, brother. Maybe she ought to name her cabin, CLAIREVILLE, and put up a big sign designating it as such. She laughed to herself at that visualization. Maybe even BLACK AND CLAIREVILLE.

Bud stared up at the sign and the smaller one underneath it which read: NO ADMITTANCE POSTED PROPERTY. He said, "I thought you were kidding about that being the name of this place."

"I *was* kidding."

"They've got a button there. Ready to go inside and meet the famous Fitches?"

"No, let's drive up the road a ways and see how far their barbed wire fence goes. I've got a feeling they've got their own tiny kingdom inside that row fence. Maybe even a castle with a moat and knights and a dragon, or two."

"I could go with the dragon possibility."

Bud drove on, but Claire turned out to be right about the size of the farm/cult/commune. The fence along the thickly wooded property snaked along the tarmac for at least three miles. When the fence finally took a right-angled turn and snaked up a hill through some even heavier woods, they pulled over and climbed out. Claire picked up her binoculars off the backseat, and her Moss high-powered rifle with its super-duper nightscope.

"Okay, let's take a little hike up this way. See if we can get a look-see at what we're dealing with. And yes, I'm feeling a little insecure about walking blindly into this place. The heralded tales of woe concerning Fitch people are large and rampant and off-putting."

"Tell me about it."

The snow was deep and untouched, and they left a wide and wallowing trail behind them, Bud in the lead, Claire right behind him. But the crisp winter air was as refreshing and bracing and cold as Hudson Bay ice fishing. So was the wind, which was picking up. Back at her cabin, Claire had never seen the lake so frigid and clogged with ice. The mother of all winters had indeed paid them a call this year.

After ten minutes of slogging their way up a steep incline, Bud decided the trek was ridiculous and unnecessary. "Come on, Claire. This is pointless. Look up there, it goes on forever."

"I wonder how the Fitch family got their mitts on all this land. Good grief, nobody owns farms this big anymore."

"I'm freezing. I'm not dressed for fighting my way through deep snow drifts."

"Here, let me forge the trail for a while. You're from Atlanta."

"Can you honestly say that you're not cold? No, you cannot. Your face is red and your lips are chapped already. Let's go back to the Bronco, warm up the heater, and then hold our interviews in some nice warm Fitch farmhouse."

"Aha. Pay dirt. At last. Just when I was losing you to the call of luxurious heat and warmth."

Scrabbling her way up to a sheer rock outcropping that jutted out at the top of the rise, she beheld her first panoramic view of the shallow snow-covered valley stretching out below them. It looked like Fitchville was indeed a tiny little self-proclaimed town. In fact, it looked like something old-timey settlers on their way to California might have built when they got tired of jouncing along the Oregon Trail in those springless covered wagons. She had the urge to look for those self-same covered wagons, but she nixed that when she saw some cars parked around. Mostly pickup trucks and four wheelers painted with brown and green camouflage. She sat down on the rocks and put the binoculars to her eyes. Close up, the place looked even more like a scene out of *Unforgiven*. There had to be a saloon down there with girls dressed like Madonna in her cone bra heyday.

"See any dadgummed Fitches?" Bud said, and then he laughed at his own joke.

Claire laughed, too. "This is so way freaky that I can barely believe it. Look at those log cabins. All of them have wood smoke coming out of the chimneys. What year is this again? 1850?"

"Yeah, and I bet they're warm as toast down there. We could be, too, Claire. Wouldn't that be better'n wadin' through snow up to your waist?"

"Can it, already, Bud. I'm gonna buy you six pairs of thermal underwear, just to keep you quiet on days like today."

"I've got some of that stuff on, damn it. Two layers. Not helping, I'd know."

"You act like it never got cold in Georgia."

"Not this cold, thank God. Only Alaska's this cold. Port Barrow, maybe."

"You shoulda brought along Bri. She gets you hot in no time flat."

"You got that right."

"Look, here comes somebody. Fast, too. Wow, they are barreling down that gravel road into Fitchville like there's no tomorrow."

"The pickup? Looks like it's got a bunch of guys in the back."

About that time, they heard the shots going off and saw the people on the little antiquated main street below scattering in every direction. The truck was heading straight into Fitchville, and still shooting up the place, like Frank and Jesse James at their worst.

"Oh, my God, Claire, they're shooting at those people."

Claire needed no further encouragement. She jumped up. They took off at a run and both made the return trip to their vehicle in record time, which amounted to slipping and sliding their way down through the deep walls of snow they'd made as they'd fought their way up. But at least it worked up a sweat and got them warm. They jumped into the SUV. Bud skidded out and did a truly impressive sliding turn on the tarmac, and they were on their way. Claire used the time to pull out her new Glock and check the magazine.

When they got back to the gate, it had been rammed down and was lying flat on the ground, no doubt by the assailants in the camouflaged truck. Bud didn't slow down and they both were jounced and thrown up against their seat belts as they roared over the metal gate. It took several minutes to reach the interior valley, even at Bud's bone-jarring rate of speed. When they got into eyeshot of the village, the pickup truck was long gone but the little village was teeming with lots of terrified people. Fearful Fitches, no doubt. Not long after, a man ran out in front of their vehicle and held a shotgun trained on their windshield. That slowed Bud down in nothing flat. He stopped his vehicle on a dime and Claire held her badge up against the windshield. The other guy lowered his gun and looked contrite as they climbed out.

"Sheriff deputies! Canton County! What just happened here?" she cried out, not in the mood for idle pleasantries.

The man was nonresponsive. He was dressed in jeans and a rather fluorescent pumpkin-orange parka, no hat. He had a buzz cut and wore a dark cropped beard that followed his jaw but no mustache. "Nothing," he said, and straight-faced, at that.

"Like hell. We just saw you fired upon by a truck full of armed men."

"I really don't know what you're talking about, ma'am."

Claire looked at Bud. He was frowning. Massively. "What? You always carry a shotgun and point it at visitors. Just sayin' hello, or what?"

"Yes, ma'am. I always do."

"Well, hell," said Bud. "Then you're under arrest for threatening a police officer."

"I didn't threaten anybody. What's your business here? This is private land."

Bud took a step toward him, apparently his hands much too cold to be patient and understanding. Claire spoke again before he could warm them up by slugging the guy in the stomach. "Look, we're here on official business. Who's in charge of this—place?"

"We got a mayor at Fitchville. I guess you mean him."

"Hope he didn't get shot a while ago by those nonexistent assailants in the nonexistent truck."

"We take care of our own. How'd you get through that gate without bein' escorted in?"

"The phantom truck paved the way for us. The gate was lying on the ground so we took that as an open invitation." That came from Claire, slightly annoyed with the guy herself. "Okay, you listen to me. Take us right now to your leader. Or I'm calling dispatch and getting a dozen patrol cars out here to shut this place down." It did occur to her that she sounded like an alien new to earth and wanting to talk to the president, which wasn't such an alien idea, as she looked at the Fitch person standing in front of her. Suddenly, she began to believe the tales of Fitches marrying Fitches and begetting little stupider Fitches.

"You have a nerve," Fitch said.

"You just don't know," Claire said.

"And you are getting on my nerves," Bud said.

Claire smiled a little at that, but the guy turned and headed off at a dead run down the gravel road and back into the fold as if he could lose them if he hurried real fast. What the hell? So they got into the car and followed him at a snail's pace, but at least it was warm and out of the wind. Clouds had come in now, covering up the sun, and painting everything a nice pearly gray, as if they lived on the hilly slopes of Seattle. They looked around the little private township, disbelieving anything so quaint could exist in the twenty-first century.

"You ever see that movie *The Village*, Claire? Made by that M. Night somebody, you know, the one who did *The Sixth Sense*?"

"Nope."

"We've crashed that set."

"Right, Bud."

"Looks like a helluva way to live. Glad I wasn't born here."

"Do you think this is a cult, or something? Look at that woman over there. Under that long coat? I can see a long gingham skirt. And that's a damn sunbonnet on her head, for God's sake. In January? And she's wearing a shawl like the Amish wear over the coat."

Bud scoffed. "These guys aren't Amish. Amish people wear black and white. Our friendly guide's got on jeans and wearing neon orange. And what the hell? Everybody's going on about their business like a bunch of hillbilly yahoos didn't just ride through and shoot up the place."

"Maybe it's their idea of fun. You know how cool it is to ride around in the back of pickups raising hell, don't you? Maybe it's the way folks hereabouts blow off steam. Nobody looks any worse for the wear. Stable and general store, business as usual."

"This is even worse than I thought it would be. How do we get ourselves into this kinda stuff? Doesn't anybody just shoot the windows out of their neighbor's garage or just break and enter, anymore? Why's it always have to be bizarre in our jurisdiction?"

"Wish I knew, yep, sure wish I knew, Buddy boy."

They stopped when the guy sprinting like a gazelle through the snow skidded to a slushy stop in front of a large white house on the main road. He came up to Claire's window, panting, and huffing clouds of labored breaths into the frosty air. "Get out, and I'll see if he'll see you. He's a busy man."

"Yeah, I'll bet," she replied, but she got out and waited while he climbed the steps and went inside a front door with a large stained-glass window with angels floating on clouds and playing harps. It was extremely quiet, except for a whole bunch of dogs barking somewhere off in the distance, out somewhere behind the house, maybe. Sounded like a huge kennel full, in fact. She hoped the frenzied canines were in secured pens and wouldn't be sicced on them with a tear-to-itty-bitty-pieces command. Tag that as just more lovely gifts off the Fitchville Unwelcome Wagon.

Bud made his way through the slush and around the car. "Well, now I know how Clint Eastwood felt in that movie when he stopped being a gunslinger and started farming."

"What's with you and the movie trivia lately? You know I don't watch movies." Claire pointed down the street. "Look, there *is* a general store. That's what the sign says. Fitchville general store. And over there. My God, there's a saloon, too. Maybe this is a movie set. Maybe Clint or a John Wayne impersonator will show up any minute now and draw on us."

Actually, the street was fairly empty now. The snow was coming down steadily. Bud stamped his feet and clapped his gloved hands together.

"Good grief, Bud, I'm gonna buy you a hand warmer."

"Well, hurry up and do it. Maybe the general store over there's got some."

"Mr. Fitch will see you now."

Mr. Neat Beard/Shotgun Happy was back and motioning them into the inner sanctum. Claire climbed the steps, unable to imagine what awaited her inside. What awaited her inside, however, was just a plain entry hall with lots of Amish style, uncomfortable-looking furniture sitting around, but it was warm, gloriously so, at least seventy-five-degree warm.

"This way, please."

The guy was really polite all of a sudden. Butler extraordinaire, in fact. They tried to wipe the snow off their boots on the homemade rag rug just inside the threshold, and then they tramped after him down the austere hallway. He opened a door and stood back, courteously pointing his shotgun at the floor instead of Claire's head. Claire entered first because Bud was always a gentleman and then found herself in a large bare room with dozens of people sitting around the perimeter in a circle of folding chairs positioned with their backs against the walls. A big guy with lots of bushy white hair sat in the chair of honor, aka The Oracle of Fitchville, she supposed. He motioned them toward him. Claire took off her sock hat and gloves and unzipped her coat on the way over. She still had her weapon in her hand, and there it was going to stay. Just until she decided how many standard deviations these folks had gone down the normal scale of IQ scores.

"Hello there, officers. Welcome to Fitchville," said the mighty white patriarch. In fact, he was almost as white as Blythe Parker, as were quite a few others lurking in the shadows. Shoulda called the place "Albinoville" she guessed. But alas, that would be politically incorrect, and very much so.

"Thank you," she said. "And who might you be?"

"Harold Fitch, at your service. I see you've already met my cousin's son, Bad Fitch."

Okay, now their trip inside the newest episode of *Supernatural*, which happened to be the one and only TV program that Claire always put in the DVR, was truly complete. She turned to the guy with the shotgun. "Your name is Bad? For real? Bad?"

"That's right. Badadiah. I earned it, too."

Claire wondered if he earned it from kicking dogs or eating raw hamburger meat or shooting people through windshields with sawed-off shotguns. Harold was the one who picked the right answer. "He's the best sheriff we ever did see in this town. He can put somebody down, break a bone in twain with just one punch."

"Gee, I'm impressed. Remind me not to fight with him without firing my weapon into him first."

Albino Harry threw back his hoary head and laughed all the way down into his gut. Claire wondered if that hurt his lungs. She had certainly never laughed that hard, and she had seen some pretty funny things, too.

"He just can hit really hard with his fists. Nobody wants to take him on. Used to fight some but not many have bested him."

"Well, bully for him. Now, how about you telling me who that was that attacked your little burg about ten minutes ago? I'd like to arrest them pronto, if you don't mind."

"I have no idea what you're talking about."

Claire and Bud exchanged one big-time and tired-of-this-Fitch-crap skeptical look. Bud said, "You know the ones we're talkin' about, don't you? You know, the ones making all those loud gun bangs and roaring right past this house in a speeding pickup truck."

Harold looked nonplussed. Maybe he just had a ten-second memory span. Maybe he was a narcoleptic. The old man glanced around at his silent crowd of followers sitting with their backs to the walls. "Did anybody hear any truck go by here? Anyone?"

At that point, anyone could hear a pin drop. Okay, they were of one mind. One mind that said: *Follow my lead, my pretties. Act ignorant. Do not talk to those with shiny badges. Here, my flock of sheep, drink this Kool-aid and kill yourselves. Amen.*

"I guess you wouldn't mind us searching all your buildings then? Just to make sure those nonexistent bullets didn't hit some nonexistent body and make them bleed to nonexistent death."

"I sense your anger, miss."

Got a real genius by the coattails here, no doubt about it. "Mr. Fitch, we saw that truck. We saw the men in the back of that truck. We saw the bullets flying and people running. Both of us. With our own four, well-trained official eyes, and a very good pair of high-powered binoculars."

"Hmm. Well, I guess we couldn't hear any of that inside here. This building is very well insulated. All our structures are. It gets cold out here in the winter months."

Bud said, "They better be insulated, with those shoot-'em-up guys on the loose out on Main Street."

"Do the men that you didn't happen to see in that truck happen to be upstanding citizens of your little personal domain, by any chance, Mr. Fitch?"

"Could be. We all carry guns. You know for hunting, and we're careful to protect our womenfolk."

"'Womenfolk'?" said Bud. "Did you really just say womenfolk?"

"Yes, we value our wives and mothers and daughters."

Claire said, "Either you tell me the truth about who those men were, or we are taking you, and Mr. Bad over there, down to a real sheriff's office for a real under oath discussion with our real sheriff."

Frowns, frowns, and more frowns. Furrowed frowns. Disbelieving frowns. Confused frowns, and lots of them. "Well, now, deputy, it could've been some of those Parkers from just up the road. They like to mess with us now and again. We've learned to tolerate them. We're peaceful folk out here."

"Mess with you with weapons blasting?"

"They never hit anybody. They can't shoot worth a plug nickel.

They like to think they're scaring us, but we just take their shenanigans in stride. They're rather harmless and godless men."

"Anybody ever die taking it in stride, sir?"

"Oh, no. It's just the Parkers displaying their high spirits. They only do it when they're drunk. We pretty much ignore them."

Claire was pretty tired by now of this ridiculous excuse of a conversation. "We'd like to talk to you, sir. In private, please."

"I have no secrets from the town elders."

Oh, for pity sakes, Claire thought. "It would be better without the town elders looking on. Trust me on that."

"We have no secrets here."

"Yeah, I'll bet."

Claire looked at Bud. He looked confounded; maybe even a little unsure if they really weren't in a time travel movie, or *Hell on Wheels*, maybe, since this seemed to be quote-a-movie-a-day week. "All right, Mr. Fitch. Question number one: Are you acquainted with a woman by the name of Blythe Parker?"

The quiet got quieter. Not a peep. Not a foot moving into a more comfortable position from those sitting around in those hard chairs, nothing. Finally, Harold said, "Blythe is my granddaughter. Why do you bring tidings of her?"

Tidings? Jeez. Maybe she should take him in, just to show him off to the guys at the office. As a sort of bizarre throwback to the distant antebellum past. Black would have a field day analyzing this kook. Probably could even get a new bestseller out of it. "I'm afraid my tidings are not good tidings. Mrs. Parker was found dead at her home."

Okay, now the dead silence was broken with some heartfelt gasps and shuffling of high-button shoes. Maybe even a stifled cry, or two. "Was she ill?" her grandpa asked, not looking particularly troubled by the dire news.

"No, but she had lots of broken bones and a slit throat." Claire cast a sidelong, and yes, suspicious look at Bad Fitch, who now looked nonresponsive to all stimuli. Inbreeding might indeed have gained a foothold in this little community of theirs. "Her husband was found dead several days earlier at Ha Ha Tonka State Park."

This time there was no reaction. Yeah, almost as if everybody there already knew and approved of Paulie Parker's early demise. She wouldn't doubt that. Nope, she wouldn't doubt anything about this place or the people in it, no matter how absurd or utterly asinine. "Somebody will have to come into town and claim Blythe Parker's remains once the medical examiner releases the body," she told them en masse.

"She cannot be buried here at Fitchville. She married that Parker fellow willingly and against my wishes so she will never be welcomed back." A chorus of masculine amens followed. The womenfolk were biting their tongues, no doubt.

"Are you telling us that you will not claim your own grand-daughter's body?"

"That's right. It's unfortunate but we must abide by our covenant."

"Maybe you ought to provide us with a copy of that covenant, sir." It was probably written in blood—womenfolk's blood, no doubt.

"As you wish, but I doubt that you'll find it informative. It only contains the tenets we Fitches live by."

Good grief, no telling what that was comprised of, judging by their mere fifteen minute but eye-opening acquaintance. But she had made the notification and gotten a look at Blythe's wacko relatives, and that was what she came for. "Do you mind if we take a look around your town before we leave? Just to make sure no bullet-ridden bodies are lying about groaning and bleeding to death while you have your meeting of elders?"

"Canton County authorities are welcome here anytime. It was my sincere pleasure to meet you, Detective Morgan."

Well, now. "I don't recall telling you my name, Mr. Fitch."

He hesitated, but not for long. "I've seen your photograph in the newspapers. I read several editions every day. By those articles, you appear to be very good at your job. I am honored to make your acquaintance. But you will find nothing untoward hereabouts."

Nothing toward, either, Claire decided. But okay, fine, but that honor of meeting her might not last too long because there was definitely something rotten in the state of Fitchville, and she had a feeling it encompassed everybody in the room.

"Oh, by the way, sir, we understand somebody who hails from Fitchville was in Kansas City several days ago and took off with a hospital patient who hadn't been released. Know anything about that?"

More silence. "Yes, I think you are probably referring to Malachi. I believe the two of you have already met. Is that true?"

"Yes, sir. Is he here now?"

"The boy's upstairs with his friend. I believe he is the one for whom you're looking."

Bud and Claire glanced at each other. "Is his name Shorty Dunlop by any chance?"

"Yes, I believe it is."

"Then we'd like to speak to both of them."

"By all means. We have nothing to hide here."

Claire wasn't falling for that little tidbit of innocence, not in the least. But Bad led them up the steps to a second floor and also mightily austere hallway and knocked on a door. Malachi Fitch opened it, looked surprised to see Claire, and then looked her up and down with his usual impertinence. So now they had a Bad Fitch and a Mal Fitch. She wondered if they had a couple of guys stashed somewhere named Nasty and Horrible.

She looked at the kid. "Well, now, hello, there, Mal. How you doin'?"

"You said you was gonna come see me, but I didn't believe you. Couldn't help yourself, huh, gorgeous?"

"This is my partner, Bud Davis. Mind if we come in and talk to you?"

"Sure thing. I knew I'd get you in my bedroom, sooner or later."

Claire ignored that. This kid was so getting on her nerves. Bad took off, probably not wanting to miss prayer meeting. But they did find Shorty Dunlop, and with sound body. He was reclining in one of the twin beds, looking as if he was just as fine as fine could get. He didn't look all that short to her, either. Five-ten, probably.

"Shorty Dunlop, I presume?"

"Yes, ma'am."

"We thought you were missing. So we're glad to see you alive and well."

"I'm just hidin' out from the Sharpes. They put word out that they was gonna get me for beatin' Ike and takin' all the winnings."

"That would be Ike Sharpe who fights for Ivan Petrov."

Both young men looked like they didn't want to talk about Ivan Petrov. She didn't blame them. Even Black thought he was demon worthy material. But Anna had said the same thing, that the Sharpes had been out looking for Dunlop. So that much lined up as a true statement. Where the Sharpes were now was the big question, because Claire certainly didn't buy the on-top-of-the-Matterhorn-without-phone-service story.

Malachi said, "I got him outta that hospital because he's my best buddy. He'll be safe here in Paw Paw Harold's house. Anywhere else, they would've found him and beaten the holy hell out of him."

"So, this kind of thing has happened before."

"Oh, yeah, fighters disappear sometimes."

"Are you saying that these guys kill their opponents?"

"I don't know, but we didn't want to take that chance. Not while Shorty's on crutches, and stuff. They don't fight clean. They gang up on you. Pretty cowardly, really."

"You've seen them do this?"

"No, but that's just the way they are."

"No proof? No eye witness? No 911 calls?"

"No, that wouldn't be good for your health." Malachi was really serious now. No talk of women, even, and that was saying something where he was concerned. "You do know who Mr. Petrov is, don't you, detective?"

"I've heard the name."

"We stay clear of him and his guys."

"Okay. At least, we found you, Mr. Dunlop. I guess neither of you heard a truck go by out front with guns blasting every which way, did you?"

Both shook their heads and looked angelic. After that, Bud and Claire told them to stay put and not to go out looking for trouble and then they took their leave.

Outside in the fresh air again, Claire said, "Something is terribly wrong in Fitchville."

Bud glanced around and then turned to Claire. "You think?"

"Well, at least, we've solved the Shorty disappearance. Too bad that's all we've solved." Claire looked around the little town, now absent of anybody at all. Streets cleared, everybody tucked away doing God's work, or Paw Paw Harold's, she guessed. "Know what, Bud? Suddenly, all those whacked-out, Fitch-hatin' Parkers are lookin' a whole lot higher on my normal human being meter."

Bud said, "I know, let's poke around here some and make sure there aren't any dead bodies lying about. Then you can introduce me to the other side of this equation. Maybe we'll find out if the Parkers have a camo-covered pickup and half a dozen or so high-power rifles and men out gunnin' with them."

"You mind reader, you. Let's be off."

Blood Brothers

It took months for Punk to fool the hovering shrinks into thinking he was accepting their cockamamie story about Bones not being real. But after that he was free to roam around the halls and watch and listen and figure out the best way to escape. Without much luck. The place was worse than a prison with all the locked barred doors and big orderlies watching his every move. And he'd heard that they called it a place for the criminally insane. Come on. He was not criminally insane. But his time would come eventually and he could get out and find his girlfriend.

Punk especially liked to sit around in the common room where patients could play cards or checkers or just talk to each other. Most of them stayed off by themselves or wandered around or stared out the windows, and such as that. He usually found a table in a quiet corner where he could see everybody and watch for an orderly to accidentally leave a door unlocked. He was particularly interested in one patient, though; fascinated, really. That guy also kept to himself and didn't say a lot. But he smiled often enough, and seemed friendly, when and if he ever did talk to somebody else. A couple of times

Punk locked eyes with that guy and smiled, all friendly like. Maybe they could be friends. Allies, who could help each other escape.

One day when they were all just sitting around, taking their meds from the male nurse and chilling out, he started watching that interesting guy again. The nurse had injected someone near where the other guy was sitting, and the injected boy had gone absolutely berserk in the common room and shouted that some imaginary bird called a phoenix was pecking his eyes out, when the truth was that he was scratching his own eyes out. During the tussle with the orderlies, the guy with whom Punk would like to be friends bent down and picked up the hypodermic needle that the nurse had dropped in the struggle. He hid it quickly under his shirt and glanced around. When he saw that Punk had seen him steal it, the other man winked and held his forefinger up to his lips, trying to tell Punk to be quiet, that it was their secret. Punk looked away, but he was highly curious as to what that guy was planning to do with that needle. So he decided to figure out what room the guy was in and check him out. Maybe he was the criminally insane one and was gonna kill an orderly with that needle, stick it in his eye or his ear, or something. Maybe that could be Punk's way to get out of this stupid place.

But he didn't have to go searching. The guy with the needle found him after he was moved out of the restraint ward into a regular room. The first night the other guy appeared there, well after lights out, and just as Punk was almost asleep. At first, he was scared and put up his doubled fists, ready to knock whoever it was flat on his back.

"Hey, buddy, I'm not here to cause you no trouble. You're that fighter kid that the orderlies are always talkin' about, aren't you? They say you gotta honey of an uppercut. That true?"

"What'd you care?" he whispered back, looking at the door. If anybody found another patient in his room so late, they were both going straight back into restraints.

"I just wanna talk. I thought maybe we could be friends. Everybody else around here is really stupid or nuttier than a can of cashews, but not you. I've been watching you. You seem okay. We can team up. You know, take care of each other. Watch each other's backs. Be friends."

Punk contemplated the other man. "Okay, I guess. But don't try anything with that needle you stole or I'll beat you till you're dead. Don't think I won't, either."

His new friend laughed softly, as if happy about that threat. "I like you. You're a tough guy. I like tough guys."

"That's right, I am, so don't go messin' with me. What'd you really want? Why'd you risk gettin' in trouble by comin' in here?"

"I'm getting out of here one of these days, and I'll take you along, if you can keep your mouth shut."

Punk lowered his voice, but he was getting excited. "I can keep my mouth shut. How you plannin' to do it?"

"Don't know yet. But I'll find me a way to get what I want. I always do."

"What you gonna do with that needle? Kill somebody?"

"No. I got me the most beautiful girl in the whole wide world, and I wanted to tattoo her name on me so I can show it to her when I get outta here, and then she'll know that I'll never, ever forget her. I already done it. Wanna see?"

"Sure. Show me."

They moved stealthily over to the window where an outside flood-light was slanting little horizon stripes through the open mini blinds. The other guy lifted up his T-shirt and proudly displayed his artwork. Punk stared down at the big letters scratched right across the guy's chest, just above his nipples. He could make out an A and an N. "What's that say?"

"Annie. That's my girl's name. She's out there somewhere, just waiting for me to come get her so we can be together forever."

"Hey, man, those cuts are still bleedin'. When did you cut it?"

"Tonight. It hurt like hell but she's worth it. I'd do anything for her, anything at all. I can't wait to see her and take her away with me."

"Can I lick it?"

The guy looked surprised for a moment. "Sure, I guess, if you want to. Kinda strange thing to do, though. Why do you want to?"

"Nothin' strange about it. Dogs do it all the time. Their saliva has medicinal purposes, you know. I had a dog once, name of Banjo. I really miss her, but she's probably dead by now. Pa used to beat our dogs until my brother Bones killed him. I hated him. We all hated him."

"Hey, I killed my pa, too. Hated his guts. Want me to lie down on the bed so you can lick my wounds?"

"Yeah. It'll make you feel good, as much as me. You'll see. I like people to lick me a lot. Bones used to do it for me sometimes. My girl did, too."

Once the guy had his shirt off, Punk started swiping his tongue over the little bleeding scratches. It tasted good to him. He liked the taste of blood. He used to get to taste it every time somebody bloodied his nose. "I used to do this to my twin brother when he got cut up in the ring. He said it felt good."

"It does feel good. I like it, too."

"Those damn doctors are tryin' to tell me that Bones don't exist. That I been makin' him up. That I got a split personality, or some such thing. Hogwash."

"Yeah, those doctors are stupid fools. Don't believe anything they tell you. They think they're smarter than we are, but they're not. If you know that you've got a twin brother, then you do. Believe me. I know these things."

"I know, too." He licked each scratch one more time, and then he said, "There, all better now. That oughta help you heal up real quick."

"I'm glad to know that, about that licking stuff. It'll come in handy, I bet."

"Yeah, and it helps you know what the person you're lickin' is feelin'. You know helps you sense stuff. Dogs' senses are a lot more powerful and developed than yours and mine."

They were quiet for a moment, listening while two orderlies passed Punk's door out in the hallway. Then Punk said, "Why're you locked in here?"

"I just wanted to be with my Annie, that's all. Hey, I know, how about letting me carve her name in your chest, too?"

"What? Screw you. No way."

"It's magic. If you do it, then I'll end up with her someday. Hey, I'll do it for you. Don't you have a girl you want to get outta here and hook up with?"

"Yeah. People are tryin' to keep us apart. But I'm gonna find her and take her away. Just like you gonna do with your Annie."

"You got that right. I've gotta go get her as soon as I get out. So?

What'd you say? Can I put her name on you? I'll let you put your
girl's name on me. We'll put her name on our backs. Then the magic'll
work double-time."

"I dunno. That sounds pretty dumb to me. You really believe in
that stuff?"

"Yes, my momma told me. She knows stuff like that. That's why
I love her so much."

"I dunno. Sounds like it'd hurt real bad."

"Yeah, it does, but only for a little while. They're just scratches,
is all. Then after we get all healed up, we'll do your girl's name on
both of us. It'll make us blood brothers and best friends. And I tell
you somethin' else, we need friends in here. You can't trust nobody
here but me. I been here a long time now."

"Okay, I guess. Why not? What's your name, anyways?"

"Thomas. Thomas Landers. Nice to meet you. What's yours?"

"Punk. But the doctors think I'm Bones, too."

Thomas Landers laughed softly. "Cool name, kid. So, you ready
to do it now? I brought the needle in here, in case you said yes."

"Shit, yeah. Let's get this over and make us blood brothers before
we get caught."

So Punk lay down on his bed and watched Thomas scratch the
letters of *Annie* into his chest. It hardly hurt at all. After all the cuts
and bruises and beatings he'd endured in the cages, it was nothing,
nothing at all. And he was glad he had a friend who was gonna stick
by him, like Bones always had. He was real happy to know Thomas.
Together, they just might bust out of this place and find their girlfriends.

After that night, they were true blood brothers. You for me and
me for you. That's what Thomas told him they had to say. Slowly, as
time passed, Punk began to love Thomas like a brother. Thomas told
really cool stories about cutting off people's heads and traveling
around with them in his old trailer house, and all kinds of kinky, fun
stuff.

And he was just plumb crazy about that Annie girl. Just like Punk
felt about his own girl. In time, they carved his girl's name on their
backs, but this time, they got caught before they were done. The doctors put them in restraints again and stuck them both back in isola-

tion and chained them to their beds, but that was okay. The magic spell was gonna work and they would be free soon to find their girls and live with them happily ever after. That's what Thomas always said, that he and Annie would live happily ever after, and travel around with his mother inside their trailer forever. That's what Punk wanted, too, but he didn't know where his girl was. He hoped she was somewhere out there waiting for him. It had been a very long time since he'd seen her.

After a lot of time and more therapy sessions, he and Thomas were allowed to mingle again. Thomas was as happy as usual and still tryin' to find a way to escape. They were glad to see each other, and found a moment to duck into a storage closet and lick each other's faces and necks. It made them feel better and closer, like real true brothers. It was almost like havin' Bones back with him.

One day Thomas was called into a therapy room with a different doctor, a new one that Punk had never seen before, which was very unusual. Punk waited on pins and needles, wondering if Thomas was going to get transferred to another hospital, or maybe even set free to find his Annie. That would be great, but he would miss the hell out of him. Thomas was the only friend that he had in the whole nuthouse.

When Thomas finally came back, he was grinning from ear to ear. He joined Punk at their table in the corner. "What's goin' on, Thomas? Why'd you see that new doc?"

Thomas didn't say anything at first, just held out his fist. Then he slowly opened his curled fingers, and Punk saw that a door key was lying in his palm. "We got our way outta here, Punk, my boy."

"Where'd you get that?"

"That new doctor I just saw. He said I needed to escape, that he had something he wanted me to do, and he just handed this key over to me and told me how to use it to get outta here. He said that Annie sent him, and that she wanted to see me." Thomas grinned then, real happy about it.

"No shit. Why's he doin' that for you, anyways?"

"He says he knows where Annie is. He says he's gonna take me to her. He says she's sick and needs me to take care of her."

"Can I go?"

"Sure, you can. But you can't come with us to see Annie. Once we get outta here, you're on your own, okay? Doc said so."

"Okay. No problem. I wanna find my true love, and that's all."

And that really was fine by him. Finally, finally, he could go back and find his girl and rescue her from whoever was keeping her away. He was thrilled to high heaven, and just like he thought, Thomas Landers had come through for him. The magic had worked, just like Thomas said it would. That guy was the smartest guy that he'd ever met. He hoped they met again someday. Maybe Thomas and Annie and Punk and his girlfriend could all go out together and have some fun. Or ride around all over the country in Thomas's trailer with his mother. Wow, that would be just awesome.

Chapter Nineteen

After nosing around a little longer and finding all the little denizens of Fitchville snug as bugs inside their matching log cabins, Claire and Bud drove back out of the place, glad to get away from *WEIRDVILLE* and wishing that they had a whole passel of search warrants to serve on its people, one after a-freakin'-nother. But they had no real cause, not one that a judge would listen to, anyway, so they left the men and their well-protected and gingham-loving womenfolk to their old-timey fantasy land and headed back to Parker's Quick Stop to gauge the other end of the Crazy vs. Crazy Teeter-Totter Feud. Maybe they were just a tad bit less disciplined about telling tales on each other. What's more, Claire wanted to find out what was inside that suspicious walled-off enclosure behind the store, which could very well be a mud-spattered, camouflaged pickup truck with a bent-up front fender and empty shell casings still rolling around in the bed.

This time when they pulled into the parking lot at the Parker place, there were cars and pickup trucks galore. Busy, busy, busy. All the trucks were painted with camouflage, too. Wonder why? Sure wouldn't disguise you on the highway but in the woods perhaps? That was a different story. Several men were filling their gas tanks, but nobody even glanced in their direction. Looked like everybody got the memo, all right. Or maybe they still relied on smoke signals.

While Bud filled his tank, Claire walked inside, feeling hungry all of a sudden. Maybe because the smell of fried catfish and fries and fried peach and apple pies again filled the air and made her mouth salivate. Ah, the smell of smoky saturated grease. Yummy. All the Parker brothers were lounging around the food court, probably inventing a new reality game called *Shoot at the Neighbors and Watch Them Run*. She walked over to say hello. None of them stood up or even looked at her. Ah-ha. Guilty consciences, one and all. Their fearless leader was forking fried fish onto some bearded ruffian's white Styrofoam plate. She waited for him to get finished.

"Hello, Patrick. How's it goin'?"

"Just fine, detective. What can I get you for?"

"Maybe some truthful answers for a change. How's that sound?"

"I thought I already did that."

"You been driving through any keep-out gates lately? Shootin' up the neighbors? Piddlin' little felonies like that?"

He laughed, no doubt because Claire was such a back-slapping hilarious comedienne. "Please answer my questions, sir."

"I got no idea what you're talkin' about."

"Why doesn't that surprise me?"

"I don't get it."

"I think you do, but hey, we'll play that game all the way until I land on Finish and have the evidence I need to arrest you and your brothers, down to the very last P."

Patrick just looked so extremely puzzled. "Somebody accusin' us of something illegal?"

"Oh, no, that would probably violate the Fitch-Parker feud's ancient code, now wouldn't it?"

"What code's that, ma'am? I'm afraid I don't get any of this, Detective Morgan. You sure I can't dish up you and your partner something good to eat. On me. Catfish is caught fresh. Phin had him a real good day down on the river. Tastes as good as it gets."

"Sure. And then you can take us out back and show us what's inside that big secret enclosure you got back there. Any problem with that?"

"You got a warrant, ma'am?"

"Do I need one, sir?"

Hesitation, and then an interruption by a new diner who wanted three pieces of catfish and then "slap on a couple of them thar hushpuppies while you're at it." Then Patrick said, "No, you don't. 'Course not. I'll be glad to show you around the place. Anywhere you wanna go, just name it. We're real proud of this here store and the dog kennels and our house, too. Sit down over there with your partner. I'll bring you both big plates full of food."

Okay, now they were getting somewhere. And Claire was hungry, but she watched Patrick Parker with eagle eyes and made sure he didn't slip a roofie in her Pepsi or arsenic in her ketchup. Bud joined her and gave hearty thumbs-up about the chow and the permission to search the place. However, they both agreed that they weren't going to find anything with a carte blanche tour offered up as if the guy had nothing to hide. Still, she was more than interested in turning over every rock in the whole joint, even the pebbles.

After that, they ate, and the food was really good, too. Maybe Claire would take some home for supper, or maybe to Harve, since he was back home and she wanted to stop by there and see what he knew about the hillbilly feud still going full bore over the river and through the woods of rural Canton County. As hush-hush as the two families kept the fighting and their reluctance to tattle on each other, she doubted if many people knew about the sicko shenanigans going on in the area. Yep, no *po*-lice allowed. Leave the killin' and deadly stuff to their respective papa bear patriarchs.

"God, this's good catfish. It'll even give Harve's a run for his money. And nobody fixes crappie as good as he does. 'Cept Buck, maybe."

Claire watched Bud filch a piece of catfish off her plate and stuff it into his mouth, but she was used to him stealing her food, so she placed her gaze back on the pack of Parkers. They were all staring at her now, all five, as if they'd never seen a woman eat fish before. In fact, however, it occurred to her that she hadn't seen many so-called womenfolk inside their establishment, either. Maybe all women had learned a long time ago to avoid this part of the state and its hillbilly chauvinists. She vowed to look up sexual assaults and rapes and domestic violence committed in the area as soon as she got home. Or, maybe they were looking at Bud, maybe they wanted to adopt him into their all-male and brotherly lineup. She laughed to herself.

"What's so funny?" Bud asked her, his mouth full of hush puppy.

"Nothing. Just had a funny thought. How much of that are you gonna eat? Good grief, you're gonna make yourself sick, Bud."

"Are you kiddin' me? I'm eatin' all of it. Want the rest of yours?"

Claire shook her head, slid her plate over to him, and took a drink of her Pepsi. Her phone rang, and she pulled it out. It was Black.

"Hi, honey," she said brightly.

"What's wrong?"

"Why do you ask?"

"Because something's always wrong at your end of the line."

"You exaggerate. But not this time. I'm just eating fried fish and enjoying the company of a whole heck of a lot of Parker brothers."

"What?"

"You know, the Parker brothers."

"The guys that make board games?"

"No, the ones who drive around in pickups full of armed ruffians and shoot at other people's womenfolk."

Silence. "Are you and Bud all right?"

"Yeah, I'm just kidding around. Where's your sense of humor? How are you?"

"Past experience tells me that you're not kidding."

"What's up with you?"

"I'm still in Jeff City, but I'm coming home now."

"Good. You're quite the travelin' man lately. When?"

"Tonight. Be at Cedar Bend, okay? I miss you."

"Okay, no problem. What time?"

"Eight at the latest. You sure everything's all right? You're safe, if only for the moment, right?"

"Yep, right as rain. See you later."

They hung up just as Bud took his last bite. She hoped he didn't lick the crumbs off the Styrofoam container like he usually did when it held chocolate cake with fudge icing. That was truly embarrassing, especially out in public. Thankfully, he remembered his manners. "That Nick?"

"Yep, he's coming home from Jeff City." She looked at him. "So how are you and Brianna doing by now?"

"Things are just fine. I'm glad she came to see me."

Their lovelorn conversation ended there when Patrick Parker came a calling at their table. "Okay, how'd it taste, guys? Good?"

"Some of the best fish I ever ate," Bud gushed, washing it all down with a gulp of Coke.

"Phillip's got the gift," said Patrick. "We all love his food."

Enough with the polite how-de-dos. "You ready to show us all your secret places where you've probably stashed your illegal weapons and drugs?"

Patrick laughed heartily. "You are just so danged suspicious, detective. But I'm gonna alleviate your fears and show you that I'm strictly legit, and so are all my brothers. Ready?"

"You bet."

Patrick then smiled warmly at her, legit personified. Yeah, right. Time would tell, as per usual in her cases.

Outside, the snow was still coming down and their breath was still frosty and hung around a few seconds as if loathe to dissipate. They followed Parker across the back lot to the heavily fortified gate they'd seen on their last visit. He unlocked it with a key on the chain hanging from his belt, and stood back while they walked through in front of him. Inside, it was a junkyard, okay. Car after wrecked car as far as she could see.

"We make us a lot of money back here, off used parts. Very lucrative little sideline."

"What? No junkyard dog?"

"No need. Nothin' back here that anybody wants that bad."

True, oh, yes, it certainly was. "Mind if we look around for ourselves? Snoop like us coppers just love to do?"

"Sure, but I better tag along. Wouldn't want you to cut yourself on any sharp pieces of metal, or nothin'."

Like your skinning knife in my back? Claire deduced.

Bud said, "Where do you guys get all these wrecks?"

"Insurance companies, mostly. They call up and we go get 'em with the wrecker and haul 'em out here."

There was a fairly large green-and-white house trailer sitting out in the middle of the enclosure. "That your place?" Claire said.

"Yeah, I gotta stay close to the store. Pretty isolated out here in the sticks. Wouldn't want vandals comin' by, breakin' the windows, such as that."

Meaning the Fitches, no doubt. Trading insults and break-ins, tit for tat. "Mind if we take a look inside that trailer?"

"Not at all. Be my guests."

They walked to it, climbed up some concrete blocks acting as steps and wandered around inside. It was nice, actually. A double wide that had clean, fairly new furniture, nice carpeting, and a super heater that was working quite well. Much nicer than Claire had expected. Patrick obviously noted her surprised expression.

"What? You expect me to live in a dump?"

"Truthfully, I'd never considered where you might live."

"Yeah, nice place you got here," said Bud, trying to save her bacon. Yet again.

"You're welcome here any time, detective. Just come on out. You don't even gotta call. I'd love to have you out here. We can drink some beer, watch a movie, maybe, have some laughs, whatever you wanna do."

At first take, Claire wasn't quite sure that was a proposition, but pretty damn sure it was. Maybe she should wear Black's ring on her finger, after all. Yeah, a flirtation with a hillbilly junkyard dealer who was probably neck-deep into a myriad of hillbilly crimes was right up there atop her wow-me scale. Not that he was bad looking or ignorant, or uncouth, or anything.

On the other hand, Bud took offense. "Hey, don't come on to my partner that way, or I'll bust your chops. Show some respect, got it?"

Aw, Bud—Claire's hero and champion. What a guy. What a partner. Why, she'd hang her fluttery scarf on his jousting lance, if he was a knight and she was a lady with a pointy silk hat.

But then, uh-oh, Patrick took offense. He said, "I wasn't talkin' to her. I was talkin' to you, Bud. Didn't mean no disrespect. Just thought you might like to hang out, do some huntin', or something."

Claire wanted very much to laugh out loud but didn't dare. Bud's face was already red enough. Instead, she turned away and moved back through the house trailer. They tossed the place pretty good, but in a neat and orderly and polite way, looking for weapons or drug paraphernalia, but with no luck whatsoever. Either Patrick was superbly clean, or he was tidy and had a hidden safe where he stowed his illegal stuff.

Outside again, she listened to Bud and Patrick discussing at length deer hunting stands and doe urine properties. Hell, they seemed to be hitting it off extremely well, so she took the time to wander off by herself and do some snooping. That's when she rounded the front of a smashed-to-bits Dodge van and found a nice little fight ring cage with floodlights and everything. Aha.

"That's where me and my brothers spar. Paulie built it for us."

The voice was right behind her now, and she tried not to jump at the unexpected sound. She turned quickly and found one of the Parkers standing right behind her. She thought it was Percy, but they all looked alike to her so she wasn't sure. He had seemed to materialize out of thin air, which creeped her out a bit. He smiled, as if he knew he had her spooked and thought it was funny.

She shook off her initial nerves, and said, "You're Percy, right? The good shot."

"Yep, that's me. I'm a very good shot. Can shoot the eye out of a gnat."

"A gnat, you say. Well, that's a pretty damn good shot, all right. But tell me, Percy, you sure there's no betting or illegal fighting going on back here? Maybe fights featuring little kids. I would frown upon that. I would lock you up and throw away the key and there wouldn't be any more shooting of gnats where you're concerned."

"What'd you take me for, detective?"

That was a good question, and a hard one to answer. She ignored it. "Any fights coming up in the near future? Maybe Bud and I could come up and watch. You know, just drop in without calling. Enjoy the festivities?"

"No, we're still mourning Paulie."

Their gazes locked, but funniest thing, she didn't see any woeful expression on his face or in his eyes or anywhere else on his person. "Are you aware that Paulie's wife, Blythe, was found murdered at their home?"

Again, no reaction in his eyes. No shock, no sorrow, no nothing. "Oh, no," he said with a flat voice inflection. "How awful. That poor, poor lady. It's just ain't safe to walk around anymore, is it?"

Claire had a feeling Percy was not a Blythe Parker fan. After all she was a Fitch slash Mortal Enemy. She decided to pursue that line of questioning. "Are you aware that Blythe grew up in Fitchville?"

"Never thought much 'bout it. She did have all that white skin and hair, though, like the lot of them."

"Hard not to notice that about her," offered Bud who had just walked up.

"Weird family. You met 'em yet?" That was Patrick, now joining the party and taking over the false statements for Percy and getting pretty damn inquisitive himself.

"Yeah, we met them today, as a matter of fact. Paid them a visit right after somebody drove through their gate and shot up the place."

"That's awful." Percy was back, and with a great deal of downright dishonesty.

"Yeah, we saw it with our own eyes. Apparently, none of the Fitches noticed the attack. Funniest thing."

"They like to take care of things, you know, in their own way. That's what I heard tell, anyways."

"Like you Parkers do?"

Patrick smiled. "Oh, we are law-abidin' citizens. We call the police whenever the Fitches come around. Check your records, Claire."

Claire? This guy was getting on her nerves. Now the Fitches seemed to be winning her Most Polite Hillbilly blue ribbons. She frowned at him. Bud sensed her agitation verging on loathing and took over.

"Well, I guess we've seen everything here that we need to see. Thank you both, for allowing us entry without the bother of obtaining a warrant. Like you said, nothing's out of order."

"Okay, Bud. I mean it, any time you get the itch to kill you a buck, you just come on up. We got lots of good places and lots of stands all ready. You can take your pick."

"I just might do that, Patrick. Thanks for the tour and the fish dinner."

"Well, I can tell you one thing," Claire said to Bud, once they were back inside the Bronco. "Brianna better watch her step with you and

Patrick. I thought the two of you might start sharing more than deer stands."

"What's that supposed to mean?"

"You're getting awfully friendly with our suspects, aren't you?"

"Ha-ha. Maybe I'm just being official. Maybe you should check your own attitude. It's pretty obvious that you don't like that guy."

"Liking him has nothing to do with it. He's hiding stuff. I think he was driving that pickup truck today, and I'm going to prove it."

"Yeah, and as long as the Fitches don't prosecute, we have no case, anyway." He started the motor. "You catch more flies with honey, and all that crap."

"I don't waste honey on guys like him."

"Okay. Way I see it? We don't know any more about any of these people than we did yesterday. Charlie's gonna be pissed."

"Yeah, he sure is. Let's head down to the morgue and see what Buck's got on Blythe Parker's body."

"Okay, let's go. Nothin' else to do."

Chapter Twenty

Their visit to the morgue didn't show up much that they didn't already know. Blythe Parker, throat slit, wide and deep, the rest of her beaten brutally by somebody who didn't do things halfway. Claire drove home alone, but she dropped in first at Harve Lester's house. Now back from Los Angeles, her retired LAPD partner was watching a Rams football game on his gigantic television set. Rolling ahead of her in his motorized wheelchair, he took the fried fish dinner she had brought him and got them both a cold beer out of the fridge. Then they sat down and watched some of the game together.

"So, how are the Rams doin'?"

"Gettin' beat right now. But they'll come back in the second half. Just like always."

Claire watched him feast on the fish, very glad to see him home and well. They didn't hang around as much, now that Black was in her life. She missed being with him, too. They needed to go fishing or duck hunting. "Hey, Harve. You know anything about a feud going on out on those hill farms north of the lake? Between two families named the Parkers and the Fitches?"

Harve swallowed the bite he was chewing, and then he said, "Oh, yeah, that's the stuff folklore is made of. All of them are crazy sons of bitches, if you ask me."

"So you do know them?"

"My pop used to go up there on plumbing calls. He had some stories that you would not believe."

"Oh, I'd believe them. You bet I'd believe them. Bud and I were up there today. That's where we got that fish."

Harve stopped in the process of poking a French fry into his mouth. "Maybe I shouldn't eat it then. Those guys are more than suspect."

Claire laughed at that. "Bud and I ate it, and we're still alive, at least so far we are. The poison could be slow acting."

Harve didn't laugh. "You better be careful up there in those parts. Those guys are some very, shall we say, *eccentric* people, and that is putting it mildly."

"That's one word you can use. I prefer *bizarre* and *scrambled brains*."

"That works for me, too."

Claire sighed, feeling tired of it, all of a sudden. "Yeah, I'd say. It's like driving your car down into a different century, especially when you enter the gate at Fitchville."

"So they still have that little village thing up there?"

"'Fraid so. Looks almost like some kinda cult. That what you think it is?"

"Hell if I know. Pop just told me they had a little self-contained village. One that the state doesn't recognize. They pay their taxes and all that so nobody cares what they do back in there."

"Oh, yeah? A village run by a big bearded prophet that looks like Rasputin?"

Harve shrugged. "Pop always said their women needed to get the hell out of there and get themselves a decent life. He was always proactive when it came to women's lib and equal rights."

"They wear long gingham dresses, Harve. Pastel ones. Even now, in this weather. Can you believe that?"

"Oh, yeah. The elders out there arrange marriages, too. I hear there's a lot of inbreeding, if you know what I mean. And old men with fourteen-year-old brides. That's sick. Don't know if they're still doin' it."

"Oh, I know exactly what you mean about inbreeding. Lots of amorous first cousins, just a feeling I got."

"Or brothers and sisters. Wouldn't put it past them."

"Jeez, Harve. Please, you're making me sick. Not to mention, all that is against the law."

"It's the way they believe."

"It's the way they're brainwashed. I just might oughta raid that place and have a gumption seminar with those poor women."

"They won't testify against their men."

"Yeah, that's the way it usually is. What about cage fighting? Your pop ever mention that?"

"Yep, raised the daughters docile, and the sons brutal. Trainin' them young for marriage, I guess. Parker family, too. Rivals in the cage, big-time. Pop said they started kids out early."

"And if I find out that's going on, those guys up there are toast."

"Good. They could be on the up and up now, who knows? Laws have certainly tightened up on that sort of thing."

Halftime came along, and they sat there together and talked about other things. Harve was doing really well, and Claire was happy to see him and catch up on his life. After about an hour, she took her leave and headed home to her place just down the road. It still looked warm and inviting, even sans the presence of a big handsome doctor, which was a downer, to be sure. But there did happen to be a strange boat tied up at her dock, one she'd never seen before. Not to mention the even stranger stranger sitting on her front porch waiting for her— in some very frigid weather, at that.

Instead of driving into the garage, she stopped out front and got out of the Explorer. "Well, well, if it isn't Mr. Badidiah Fitch himself, or should I just say Bad? Trespassing on my property and giving me one helluva good reason to throw him in jail."

"Hello, detective. Thought I'd drop by and say hello. See how you're doing."

Claire glanced around. "So where are all your old-timey cohorts? I thought the Fitches traveled in covered wagons."

He laughed and shook his head. "I like you, detective. You've got a sense of humor, if not a lot of smarts. I like that in a woman."

"I'm sure you do. Guess you wish I was standing out here shivering in a gingham frock, too, huh?"

"Not so much, but I'm not into women's fashion. You look pretty damn hot in those jeans, though."

"Maybe that's because you've never seen a woman in jeans before. What do you want, Fitch? I'm busy."

"Just came by to say hello."

"Hello. Now, good-bye. Get off my property and don't come back. Fitches don't agree with me. Just haven't got the 'no damned Fitches' sign up yet."

"No can do. Mayor Fitch wants me to bring you back to the village."

"Well, you can tell Paw Paw Harold that I don't take orders from him."

Bad stomped his feet and clapped his hands together, acting almost as if it were winter dusk and ten below. "Oh, come on now. It's just a friendly visit. Surely you know how to be friendly? Once or twice in your lifetime, at least."

"Never had any lessons in friendly. So, now what? You gonna pull out that shotgun that you like to brandish about and scare me silly again?"

"Don't think so. How about you asking me to come inside? It's pretty damn cold out here. You sure took your time getting home tonight."

Who the Sam Hill did this moron think he was? Wow. But she was curious. What did he really want with her? Or did Big Daddy want something? Or any run-of-the-mill Fitch? "I think it might be better if we had our chat down at the sheriff's office. You call up and make an appointment, got that? How did you find my place, anyway?"

"I read about it in the papers when you got your badge jerked for sleeping with the enemy. Also known as your prime suspect at the time and/or Nick Black."

Claire just stared at him. Then she said, "Get out."

"No offense meant. There were pictures in the paper, you know, and the mayor knows who Harve Lester is and where he lives. So, here I am. Ready, willing, and able to escort you personally back up to our farm. We'll go by boat. Lake happens to inlet on our property."

Claire considered him for a moment. He was such a colossal jerk, smug, arrogant, stupid, hick to the max. But he was intriguing, too, and suddenly using better English. She was pretty sure he hadn't come hither to off her or force her to marry an old bearded Fitch. She'd like to see him try. She clomped up on the porch and punched in the code on the security system. "Please do come in, Mr. Fitch. But you can't stay long. Just long enough to tell me why you are protecting those mortal enemy Parker thugs who shot up your little old wild West world today."

He laughed, and it actually sounded genuine. Maybe he did like her. Well, yippee-ki-oh, but she didn't like him one bit and he certainly wasn't going to like her for much longer, either.

"You are very entertaining, you know that, Claire?"

"Oh, yeah, I am, and plenty of times, too. Usually when I laugh and throw away the key. And don't call me Claire."

But he climbed the steps and walked inside and looked around. "Nice place."

Claire took off her coat and gloves and hat and pulled out her Glock 19. He looked down at it. "Awesome weapon. Wish I had one. Will you let me shoot it sometime?"

"Will you be my target sometime?"

He grinned.

Claire frowned. "I do have the funniest feeling that you'll see me shoot it at you before you'll ever get your hands on it."

"You are just so damn hostile that it turns me on a bit." He unzipped his orange parka. "Mind if I sit down? Got any coffee? Or better yet, hot chocolate? Some of those little marshmallows on top would be good, too."

This guy was something else, reminding her a little bit of Joe McKay, but he had to be there for a reason, and Claire really, really wanted to know what it really was. She watched him take off his coat and sprawl down in Black's big brown corduroy easy chair beside the fireplace. And, no, Black would not like that. She walked into the kitchen, picked up the remote and hit the fire logs, and then spun the little coffee cup holder and chose him the ultra-strong French blend that Black liked to drink. She put a mug on the Keurig, put in the cup, and pressed the button. Bad was now standing in front of the fire, warming his backside. At least, he was out of Black's favorite chair. "Here's some coffee," she told him, putting it down on the counter. "I'm not bringing it to you. Guess I'm not as subservient as the Fitch womenfolk. I hate servitude and chauvinistic men."

Bad Fitch crossed the room and sat down on a bar stool. "I don't like my women subservient. I like 'em like you."

"Could've fooled me. Hey, do the gals out there wash your feet, too?"

Laughing, he picked up the mug and took a small sip. "Um, um, good. I do like my coffee strong, just like my women."

Claire gazed at him. "Know what, Mr. Fitch. I could care less how you like your women, if you've ever even had a woman, or anything else about you, actually. Understand that now? Tell me why you came here and then get the hell out. I have better things to do."

"I think I'm in love with you."

"Okay, that does it. Get the hell out of here."

"Sorry. Just joshing with you. I'll be good."

She doubted he had that capability. There was just something about him that gave her the Norman Bates willies. In fact, he sorta looked like the psycho in the original *Psycho* film. Maybe he was the murderer. Maybe he was the one who liked to break the bones of helpless people. "Tell me true, Mr. Fitch, did you murder Paulie and Blythe Parker?"

He didn't laugh at that, but he didn't take the question seriously, either. "Now you are hurtin' my feelings. You're a hard woman to reach out to. I'm just tryin' to touch your sensitive side here."

Claire sighed. Enough, already. Her life was just unacceptable, of late. The Fitches and Parkers were definitely getting to her and not in a good way. She needed Black to examine her head and make her unconscious with a magic pill, or anything similar. "Either you tell me why you are here and what you want, and right now, or I'm going to escort you out with my weapon stuck up against your jugular and then call for a patrol car to pick you up and hold you in the psych ward for seventy-two hours. Do you understand me, Mr. Fitch?"

"No need to be rude."

Claire pulled out her phone. She punched in the number for dispatch. She had truly had it with this guy.

"Wait, I'll tell you the truth. Hang it up. Please. I swear I'm on the level now."

"I am not kidding around, Mr. Fitch. I do not like your showing up here like this. Don't ever do it again. Are we clear?"

"Yes, ma'am."

Claire told the dispatch operator that she'd call her back, and then she put the phone down on the counter and waited. Fitch didn't say anything, but he reached for something in his pocket. She had her weapon in her hand again before he could blink.

"I'm not goin' for a gun. Good God, you are a jumpy woman."

"Not jumpy, just careful. Whatever you're taking out of that pocket, you better do it nice and slow."

So, very nice and slow, he brought out a badge and laid it on the counter.

Claire stared at it a moment, and yes, she was extremely shocked to see such. "You're undercover?"

"Yes, ma'am."

"Who the hell are you?"

"My real name is Kevin McGowen, and I work for the ATF. There's the badge right there."

"Then how the devil are you passing yourself off as a bona fide Fitch?"

"My great-great-grandmother was a Fitch who had the good sense to leave the fold, thank God. Those guys out there are lunatics."

"Yeah? And they fell for that lame story?"

"They aren't particularly brilliant. I'm sure you've noticed that."

"I've noticed, all right, all those first cousins getting hitched, I suspect."

"That really happens."

Claire picked up the badge and examined it. She even turned it over and looked for the tag. "Well, that's gross and unnatural. Tell me what you're looking for up there, Agent McGowen."

"We think they're running guns into Mexico. I'm trying my best to take them down. All of 'em."

"How long have you been under out there?"

"Goin' on eight months. And it's no party living there, believe me. Pretty much sucks."

"Is it a cult?"

"Maybe, sort of, I guess, but all family. I've earned the mayor's trust, and he made me his bodyguard. That puts me in a good position to know what's going down."

"So, McGowen, I guess you don't mind if I check you out, do you? You know, see if you're lying through your teeth. Stuff like that. Those badges aren't exactly hard to come by if you're a thief."

"Be my guest."

So he sipped more coffee, and she called Bud, told him the guy's rather flimsy story, and had him do a background search, and for him to also contact McGowen's superiors at ATF for verification. Until then, she kept her weapon in her hand. "So why won't they identify the Parkers as the ones who attacked them?"

"They don't ever involve the authorities. When this kinda stuff happens, they retaliate. It's like a stupid dance. Back and forth, back and forth. People die so it's no joke."

"So their little ho-down two-step includes murder?"

"Not since I've been there. But he has other guys for that kind of thing. He calls them Helpmeets. I do know that the whole clan shunned his granddaughter. Your victim, Blythe, actually. They all act as if she never existed. It's crazy. I can't imagine how she ever got out of there in one piece. The women are veritable captives."

"No kidding," Claire said. She punched on quickly when Bud called back. "Yeah, Bud? So is this guy for real, or not?"

"Yes, he is. They got all bent out of shape when they thought we had blown his cover."

"Okay. Tell the guys over at ATF that he's still secure. Thanks, Bud. See you in the morning."

McGowen was smiling. "Believe me, now?"

"I guess I have to. You did fool us out there, I'll give you that much."

"I do have Fitch blood, but I'm not exactly proud of it. How about going out with me when I get outta that hellhole?"

"I'm engaged."

"I don't see a ring. Trust me, I looked."

Claire had not been come on to this many times since, well, never, actually. Most men were usually scared of all her weapons and her I-don't-like-you-even-a-little expression. Most of the ones who did hit on her, however, had only been trying to schmooze her into going easy on them. Fat chance, that. Either that, or the guys she ran into were turned on by severe windburn and frowns and chapped lips and incarceration threats. "Look, McGowen. I am working a double homicide investigation. Can you help me, or not?"

"I can keep my eyes and ears open and poke around some. Blythe's mother is out there. A couple of her sisters, too. And a bunch of her brothers."

"Is the big guy ruthless enough to order his own granddaughter beaten to death?"

"I'd say so. He's in total control out there. Nobody crosses him, and I mean nobody."

"Did he really send you down here to get me?"

"Yeah, but I'll tell him I couldn't find you. He trusts me now."

"He wants to get me out there and beat me to death, I take it?"

He shrugged. "Maybe. He didn't really say why he wanted you brought in, and I didn't ask. Not healthy to question that guy. He might just want to talk to you in private. Without all his followers listening. He keeps lots of secrets from them. From me, too. I have to watch my step."

"Sounds dangerous. Maybe I ought to go out and hear what he has to say."

"Think again. That would not be a good idea. You might end up dead before I could stop it."

"I am armed, you know. Highly trained, too."

"So are they. To the teeth, and with some heavy duty armament. I'm just waiting for them to make a deal with the Mexican cartel. It's been slow in coming. That's who we think they're dealing with."

"Are you kidding me?"

"They are not who they seem."

Her phone rang again. Black, this time. "Where the devil are you?" he said first off. "It's nine o'clock at night. You're an hour late. I've been waiting on dinner."

"I'm at my place. I've got a suspicious undercover ATF Fitch here with me, trying to convince me that he's for real. I'll be there in a little while. Don't wait up."

"Well, make it quick. I'm hungry, and I am waiting up."

They hung up.

"That your guy? Nick Black?"

"You seem to know an awful lot about me."

"I looked you up in our database before I came down here." He grinned.

"Well, one thing I can say for you, McGowen. You make a very good dumb-as-a-stump hick."

"Thank you. It comes natural."

They smiled a little. Claire's was reluctant. "You better get back up there before Big Daddy gets suspicious."

"Yeah, you're right."

"Is he gonna believe your story?"

"Yeah, unless he had me followed. He has everybody followed who leaves that compound, but I'm usually the follower."

"You are playing some dangerous games, McGowen."

"Tell me about it. So, just a warning. You stay away from there and let me do my job. I'll see if I can't get something that will help your case. But you stay away or you'll screw up my investigation. We got a deal?"

"Sure. Then again I'm not making any promises. If I need to come out there, I'm coming. Got that? But do tell me one thing. Have you ever seen them put little kids in a fighting cage?"

"Nope. The kids pretty much stay behind the women's skirts. They're all afraid of Harold. He's hard on them if they get in his way. You know, the old children-should-not-be-seen-or-heard-or-anything-else philosophy."

"Just do me a favor. Bring that psycho bully down. Put him on his knees. You know, the old cut-off-the-head-and-Fitchville-will-die scenario."

"Precisely," McGowen agreed.

"Okay, keep me posted. Check in when you can and let me know what's going on." She gave him her cell phone number.

McGowen said, "Oh, one more thing."

"Yeah?"

"Somebody's pickin' off people up there."

"Pickin' them off, as in murdering them?"

"That's right."

"And you didn't think to mention that before now?"

He ignored that. "They think it's Bones Fitch. They signed him into a mental hospital a time back and now he has supposedly escaped. They think he's out for revenge."

"Do you think it's him?"

"I don't know. But this guy likes to ambush people when they're alone out in the fields or orchards, and then he abducts them and beats them to death. Or just makes them disappear forever."

"Sounds familiar. How many?"

"Five. So far. Since they say he got out."

"Do they think he also got to Blythe and Paulie?"

He nodded. "They're searching for him. They think he's holed up somewhere in the hills and woods at the back of their property or their neighbor's property. You know, they suspect he's got some kind of a killing lair somewhere. He's sort of a survivalist type, apparently, and can make his tracks disappear."

"A killing lair, you say?"

"That's right. So be careful if you plan any surveillance anywhere up around there. They say he moves stealthily and just pops up out of nowhere and puts you down before you can blink. He used to be a top-notch cage fighter, probably still is."

Claire sighed. "Well, now, didn't everybody up there? But, hey, thanks for the warning. We'll be careful."

"Good. I gotta go now. He'll be waiting up for me to bring you in."

"You be careful. I've never seen so many nutcases in my life."

McGowen grinned. "Not to worry. I'm good at my job. You've seen me in action."

"You better be good at it."

After he took his leave, Claire called Black back and asked him if he would come over for the night, that the hot tub was just bubbling up with the need to entertain them. He said no problem, keep the motor running, he was on his way. She got undressed, kept her weapons handy, and slid down into the warm water, more than eager to see him, too. It was winter, and said hot tub was their best friend. She had had her fill of Fitches and Parkers and undercover agents and Russian mobsters and pretty much everyone and everything else in her life right now. Black was the only one who could take her mind off the dark and dreary so she wished he would hurry it up and get there already. Time to relax and have some fun, and it couldn't come soon enough.

Blood Brothers

The night they were supposed to escape from the psychiatric hospital finally came. Thomas Landers took the key the doctor had given him and told Punk that he would come back for him as soon as he found the doctor and made sure that the coast was clear. But he didn't come back for him. Neither one of them returned to help Punk get out. The bastards double-crossed him. He waited and waited, hoping that he was wrong, but he wasn't. The doctor had never intended to take him along. Thomas had lied through his teeth, and then they were gone.

For hours, Punk lay in his bed, filled up with white-hot anger, rage that was almost uncontrollable. He stayed alone in his room all night and thought about how he would hunt down the two of them and wring the life out of them with his bare hands. In the following days, he tried to hide his fury but couldn't, and it erupted sometimes in the common room and then the doctors ordered him into restraints again. Then one day, he overheard the nurses talking about how Thomas and his doctor friend were both dead, one shot and one drowned in some river. He felt no pity, only pleasure that they got what they deserved for leaving him behind.

That's when his anger began to fade, and he started making new plans. He would escape by himself. If Thomas could do it, then he could, too. He would just wait and wait and be patient until the perfect moment came along and then he would do whatever it took to be free. Months passed before the opportunity presented itself. It happened about a month after the Christmas holidays, when a blizzard was burying the hospital grounds in snow and wind-whipped sleet. The staff was shorthanded because most of the nurses and orderlies couldn't make it to work because of the icy roads. There was only one orderly left overnight to man Punk's floor, so Punk jumped at his chance. He pretended to be ill and collapsed in the hallway right outside the room where the orderly was sitting at his desk. When the guy rushed out, Punk came at him so quick and hard with his right fist that the man went down, breathing shallowly and bleeding from the mouth. The corridor was quiet, all the other patients asleep, and Punk dragged the man out of sight, stripped him down, donned the white scrubs and snow boots, and bundled up in the hooded coat that hung on a hook behind the door. Then he took the guy's gloves and money and ID badge and keys, unlocked the door that led to the main hospital corridor and stealthily made his way down through a dark and empty fire escape to a ground floor exit.

Outside, the wind was billowing stinging sleet right at his face. He pulled his hood tighter and ducked his head against the swirling ice and headed straight for the parking lot, pressing the button on the key fob over and over until he finally saw interior lights come on in a late model white Jeep. He made his way through the deep snow, swept off the windshield as best he could, and then climbed inside, and drove slowly and carefully until he left the hospital road and turned onto the outside city street.

Nobody was around anywhere, everything dark and deserted at such a late hour and in such terrible weather conditions. He had no trouble with the ice, just a slight sideways slide of his wheels once in a while, but the Jeep handled well once he put it in four-wheel drive. He could not believe he was actually free, that nobody was chasing him down yet. The weather had brought everything in the city of Fulton to a standstill, except for him. It was very late by the time he found the interstate and drove on it west, headed back home, turning finally off onto the partially cleared state roads, which were lined with lots of jackknifed semis and cars stuck in ditches. The windshield wipers beat a hard cadence against the driving snow, but he drove the Jeep steadily along. Nobody stopped him, not even at car crashes, where Missouri Highway patrolmen just motioned him past them with their flashlights. It took him nearly all night but he finally reached the narrow gravel road that led up through the woods to the back of his pa's farm.

When at last the old family farmhouse came into sight, he parked outside, very eager to see Bones again. Once inside the house, he stopped in his tracks and stared down at the corpse lying on the living room floor. It looked like the body had been dead for a long time. Shocked, Punk put his hand over his nose and mouth to block the putrid smell. The telephone was on the floor, too, the cord jerked from the wall. Frowning, he studied the dead man. It wasn't Bones, thank God. It looked like it was his oldest brother, maybe. The arms and legs were fixed in death at impossible angles, probably most of the bones broken. That's when he knew that Bones had killed their own brother, just like he had killed their own pa.

"Well, hello there, Punk."

Bones's voice came out of nowhere, and Punk spun around and saw his twin brother standing halfway up the stairs. He was grinning down at him.

"You did this," Punk accused him, his voice hoarse with disbelief.

"Yeah, I sure did. So what?"

"So he's our own blood. Why'd you do it? What'd he do to you?"

"He was upset that I killed Pa and took over out here. He was gettin' ready to call the cops. I had to do it. I was protectin' you, too, bro. We both would've ended up in jail."

"Why didn't you drag him outta here? When did you kill him, anyways? Looks like he's been laying right there for a long time."

"That's right. I did him about the time you went sniffin' after that damn pasty-assed girl next door. Smell don't bother me none, and it keeps our other brothers scared shitless. They all moved out of here right after I did him. They got them a big house trailer just down the road, but don't you worry none, they aren't gonna say nothin' about me killin' him or I'll kill them, too. They aren't gonna say nothin' about nothin' unless I tell 'em to. I got 'em lyin' about us to those damn doctors that keep comin' around, asking nosy questions about you and me."

Punk was still thinking about his girl. "She's not a damn pasty-assed girl. You take that back."

"I ain't takin' nothin' back. And that's what you say now. Wait'll you hear what she's been up to since you been locked up inside that hospital."

Anger gushed through him. "Okay, Bones, what's that supposed to mean?"

"Wanna know what I saw after they took you away that day?"

"You stayed around and spied on them?"

"That's right. I sure did. I saw everything, too."

"How is she then? Is she all right? Tell me where she is. I gotta go see her. It's been a long time. She's gonna be worried 'bout me."

Bones laughed. "Better sit down, bro. You ain't gonna like this. No way in hell are you gonna like this."

"Just tell me where she is, damn it!"

Punk watched Bones sprawl down on the couch, very near their rotting brother. The smell was stomach turning, probably left over from the body fluids soaked down into the carpet. Punk gagged a bit and then covered his nose and mouth again.

"I creeped around her house some, Punk, that's how I got the scoop."

On edge and shaking with anger, Punk waited. He knew good and well that the more he begged and demanded Bones to tell him, the longer Bones would make him wait. Bones was just ornery that way. "Never you mind then. Keep it to yourself. I'll just go over there and find her for myself."

"Wouldn't advise that, Punk. They already got it out on the tube that you escaped from the crazy house. Heard it on my police band radio about an hour ago. They found that orderly you beat up and now everybody's lookin' for you. Our pretty face will be plastered all over the news by sunup. Good thing I've been hiding out at the mine shaft, or they'd of picked me up already."

Punk just stood there and tried to think what he should do. He felt like throttling Bones, and that would be good enough for the jerk. He hadn't changed at all.

Bones was still grinning, all relaxed and comfortable. "Okay, if you gotta know so quick, she done went and got hitched again."

"No, she did not. You're lyin', Bones."

"Oh, yeah, she sure did, too. And get this, Punk. She lived over there in St. Louis with that new husband of hers for a time and then she just up and ran off and shacked up with one of our own brothers."

Punk felt unable to breathe. Like his world had come to an end. "No, she did not. You're lying to me, Bones. She'd never do that. Never, ever. She'd wait for me. She always said she only wanted me."

"Ain't lyin', bro, cross my heart and hope to die. But I got some good news for you, too. Our dear brother who is now screwin' your own little true love is gonna be fightin' tonight down at the Lake Inn. We can get him there, easy as pie. You know, wait 'til after the fight, when he's tired and won't have much left in him. He's pretty good now, but not against the both of us, and I'll help you put 'im down. Never liked that kid, anyways, and I haven't got to break all that many bones since you left. Had to lay low and such." Bones laughed and started cracking his knuckles because he'd always liked the sound of that, too.

"You been stayin' here? With that?" Punk looked down at what used to be his older brother.

"Nah, not so much in here. I've been livin' out at my new hideout in the mine shaft mostly. Especially since the snow started up. Got it fixed up pretty good, too, nice and warm. Nobody can find us out there."

"Okay, c'mon, let's get outta here. We gotta make us some plans."

Chapter Twenty-one

Before noon the next day, Claire and Bud were back out in boondock paradise checking out some of the less crazy neighbors of the two feuding clans. She had a bad feeling that every single person with a functioning brain stem residing in the immediate feud vicinity hated all Fitchvillers and Parkervites worse than the proverbial poison dart, each and every single one. Thus, they would probably unload upon inquiring detectives any ill will and incriminating details about their nutty neighbors with gleeful alacrity. So they drove past Fitchville's newly repaired and reinforced entrance gate and passed the place where they had first trekked through the deep snow and spied on the quaint quasi-village/hillbilly cult. They passed a trailer park that sat across the road, but it looked deserted so they decided to have patrol cars canvas that area while they concentrated on the neighbor whose property abutted the two feuding families. When they found a road leading off to the left, they followed it and found the gravel in fairly good repair and partially scraped of snow. So they bounced and jounced along, Bud telling her about his latest romantic phone call from Brianna. At least they did until they heard a barrage of gunfire coming from the direction in which they were headed.

Bud cut his love story short and accelerated until they swung around a thick stand of pine trees and a large two-story, white clapboard farmhouse came into sight at the end of the road. They slowed to a stop and peered out over the seemingly innocent-looking place, until they heard more gunshots coming from somewhere behind the house and then echoing down through the woods. Drawing their weapons, they got out together and stealthily made their way up the snow-slick front yard, where they found a couple of vans parked out front and a few more shots ringing out in the cold and crisp air, definitely emanating from out back. Claire gripped her new 9mm a little tighter and took the right side of the house, while Bud crept around the other side. She inched slowly up to the rear corner, where she could just glimpse the woman standing out in the backyard.

Fortunately, she was facing away from Claire. Unfortunately, she was holding a huge .357 magnum in both hands, and keeping a steady bead on the six people stretched out at her feet, spread-eagled belly down in the snow. The woman suddenly cried out in a loud voice that brooked no funny business, "Hear me good, people! Do not move a muscle or I'll shoot you. And don't think I won't. Do exactly what I say or you are gonna be dead."

Okay, that was enough for Claire. She stepped out behind the woman, her own weapon out front and aimed dead-center on the woman's back. "Drop it, lady! Now! Drop your gun!"

The woman froze where she stood, and then slowly turned her head around until she could see Claire. Then before Claire could blink, the other woman spun and crouched low, her giant weapon focused on Claire's chest. "Don't think so. I don't disarm for anybody. So you drop it, lady, or I'll shoot you. You hear me? I am a very good shot, and this gun will blow a hole the size of Montana through your lungs."

Okay, now. Claire stared at the woman, but she kept her weapon right where it was. She wasn't known for disarming herself, either. The woman holding the gun on her was tall and striking, gorgeous, really, and young, probably in her thirties, long silky black hair pulled back in a ponytail. Her cheeks were pink from the cold, but her eyes were green, sorta like pure Chinese jade green, unwavering, unafraid, and definitely harboring nothing but business. Claire decided to go official.

"I am a police officer. I said drop that gun!" Claire kept her own weapon on target and unwavering.

Luckily, Bud decided to show up, and not a minute too soon, either. The situation was sticky, to be sure, and Claire was very glad she had brought him along to have her back. Standing against a .357

was never a good thing. Bud moved out of his cover at the other end of the house, weapon extended and pointed at Vivid Green Eyes. "No, *you* drop that gun, lady, just like my partner said, and nobody'll get hurt," That was growled in Bud's most intimidating voice, and Claire welcomed the gruff menace as a step in the right direction.

Then, before Bud or Claire could move, all the women lying on the ground lurched up onto their knees, almost in tandem, with six guns held in expert two-handed grips and all aimed directly at Bud, followed by a whole lot of unsettling sounds, like safeties going off and rounds being chambered.

"Oh, crap," said Bud, and for very good reason.

Exactly, thought Claire. "We are Canton County Sheriff detectives," she said with more calm than she was actually feeling at the moment. "Now all of you relinquish your weapons. We have backup on the way." That wasn't true, of course, but maybe they'd believe it. Claire waited a few seconds for them to obey her command, but to no avail. Looked like an eight-woman, one-man standoff, all right, which was always a pretty dicey affair, especially since there were just two of them on her side.

Finally, the lady with the .357 magnum said, "Okay, and I am FBI. I will, if you will."

What the hell? Claire didn't think so. She wasn't born yesterday, after all. "You first. I always try to be polite. And do make it quick. A gun that big pointed straight at my heart makes me feel downright insecure."

At that, the self-proclaimed Fed gave a slight smile. Then she spread her fingers wide apart and let the gun dangle by the trigger guard on her right forefinger. She squatted down slowly and gently laid her weapon on the snow and then raised both arms out to her sides. Immediately after that, the half dozen ladies on their knees did exactly the same thing in exactly the same manner, and with impressive syncopated movements, at that, almost like an Olympic water aerobics team without the bathing caps and water. Then to Claire's utter surprise, they all looked around at each other and started clapping their hands and laughing as if they were having the time of their lives.

"Great show, Laurie!" one called out to Madame .357.

"Wow. I wasn't expecting that," cried another delighted female.

"That's the best exercise we've done so far! It seemed so real. Especially the expression on that cute guy's face when we all drew on him."

Claire watched that cute guy's face color to the exact shade of a sugar beet. He said with a more pleasant inflection, "Well, I hope all those weapons aren't loaded."

"Oh, they are loaded all right," said Laurie, the alleged FBI agent. Then she looked at Claire, who still had not holstered her Glock and didn't plan to do so any time soon. "You got a badge, detective? Or is this some kind of shakedown?"

Claire pulled the chain with her badge out from the neck of her parka and showed it around. The FBI lady examined it, close up and suspiciouslike. "Alrighty then. I'm satisfied. I'm Special Agent Laurie Dale, glad to meet you." With a wide smile, she jerked off her right glove and stuck out her hand, all friendlylike.

Claire holstered her weapon and took the other woman's hand. Laurie Dale gripped it nice and tight, and said, "These are my students. We're the Ozarks Chapter of the Pack Those Pistols Gun Club. The ladies here are all participating in my carry-conceal class. We were reenacting a hostage crisis of sorts when you showed up. We got a bit of a bonus lesson today, right, girls?"

The girls all nodded and started rising to their feet, excited and talking together and seemed very happy nobody got shot. Actually, Claire was pretty happy about that herself. For, truth was, it could've been a bloodbath.

Claire said, "You're really FBI?"

"Yeah, assigned out here at the farm for the moment."

"You have time to sit down and talk to us? We need to ask you some questions about your neighbors."

"Those crazy ass Fitches? Or those idiot Parker boys? I'm not surprised you're on to them. Just a sec, and we'll go inside and have a nice little chat." She turned back to her waiting students. "Well, ladies, I guess that's gonna have to be it for today. You got a little taste of the real thing, quite a surprise for all of us, I'd say. Hope you learned something from these two detectives. See you next week.

Same time, same place. Bring plenty of ammo. We're gonna do some target shooting."

The chattering girls holstered their guns and proceeded around the side of the house to their cars, and Laurie Dale led Claire and Bud up onto the screened-in back porch and then through a door and into a nice big warm country kitchen, replete with the delicious smell of homemade chocolate fudge cake in the air.

"Have a seat. How about some cake and coffee? I've also got chocolate chip cookies. I baked a big batch this morning for the club."

"Thanks," said Claire.

"I'll take both," said Bud, trying not to drool.

While Claire and Bud shrugged out of their heavy winter parkas, Special Agent Dale poured them both big white mugs full of steaming hot coffee and then put down a platter full of homemade cookies in front of them. She cut them both a piece of the most fantastic looking cake, three tall layers, with fudge icing and miniature chocolate chips on top, and sliced strawberries all around the edge of the cake stand. Claire's mouth actually started watering. That's what she got for skipping breakfast. She put the first bite in her mouth as Laurie leaned against the bar and gazed at them. "So, you two are goin' after all my yahoo neighbors, huh?"

"That's right. We're working a double homicide case. One of the Parker boys and his wife were both murdered recently."

"Yeah, I heard about that. One is the body they found over in Ha Ha Tonka, right?"

Claire nodded, and Bud concentrated on eating his cookies.

"Well, I'm out here surveying my property lines, too, so join the club. And I'm filming any movements from about a dozen different game cameras I've got strapped to the trees out there. My SAC is interested in what they're up to over there. Want my take? They're all a bunch of mental patients running wild when they should be locked away somewhere."

"So, you really are a Fed?" Bud asked, swallowing a bite of a rather large chocolate chip cookie, one about the size of a saucer, in fact. Claire took another bite of the cake, too, and almost shut her eyes in ecstasy. Laurie Dale was one helluva a cook. She ought to open a bakery, no doubt about it, maybe one with a gun range out behind it.

"That's right. Out of our Springfield office. Love this assignment, though. Gives me more time to spend out here in the boonies with my husband, Scott. This is his farm, been in his family for years so they've dealt with those ignorant Fitches and Parkers for decades. Scott's an attorney, and a damn good one. They all know he'll sue if they ever step one foot on our land or cause us a spot of trouble. So they behave themselves where we're concerned. But they go at each other nonstop. You'd think we lived in the hills of Kentucky during the Civil War."

"What are you looking for with those cameras?"

"You name it. Gun running, prostitution, child abuse, illegal imprisonment, and that means those poor women born into Harold Fitch's realm. He does like to degrade them. I'm surprised they don't try to run away every single night of the year, and/or kill themselves. I sure couldn't hack that kind of sexist treatment. There'd be a bunch of dead male chauvinists lying around all over that damn valley." She paused long enough to take a drink of her coffee. "What about you? Any luck yet?"

"Well, we're working both cases. The guy at Ha Ha Tonka. Paulie Parker. And we recently found his wife, Blythe, too, murdered in their home. Both beaten to death with blunt instruments. Her throat was slit. His wasn't. We believe she was born a Fitch. You ever heard of either of them?"

"Nope. Scott and I don't exactly swap recipes with those weirdos. They stay on their side of the fences, and we stay on ours. The surveillance thing is relatively recent. Chatter is that they are working on a deal with some organized crime elements, but I haven't been able to prove it yet."

"Could be the Petrovs out of East St. Louis. They've got ties to Blythe. Both of our vics died brutal deaths. Have you ever heard of a Parker marrying a Fitch?"

"I'd say not. That certainly doesn't happen every day. Maybe never before those two hooked up."

Claire took another bite of the cake, couldn't help herself. She wasn't going to leave a crumb on the plate, and Bud wasn't gonna get any of hers this time, either. "You know anything about the ATF having a man in deep cover over there in Fitchville?"

Laurie shook her head. "Nope. That's news to me."

"We didn't, either, until he paid me a call at my place last night, showed me his badge, and told us to back off and let him do his job before we got him killed."

"Well, that's interesting, I must say. Agency cooperation at its worst. Too bad nobody tells anybody anything. It's a miracle we all don't end up shooting each other. Like this morning, for an example. I almost shot you. We need to coordinate, and do it all the time. But that double murder you're working on doesn't surprise me. It's a regular Hatfield and McCoy war going on up here, with our property stuck right smack dab in the middle of it."

"Have any of them attempted to harass you or your husband?"

"No, like I said, they respect Scott and his ability to sue their pants off in court. They do not want their backward lifestyles plastered all over the newspapers. That goes double for the Fitches. It would be harder to make their women wear gingham and walk three steps behind their men, if the media ever got hold of it and it hit the air-waves. As far as the Parkers go, they pretty much keep to themselves. A brutal bunch of guys, not too smart, either. I heard they had a father who abused them. But the Fitch men don't spare the rod, either." Laurie sat down on the high stool beside Claire. "But I can tell you one thing, there's lots of shooting going on over there, at all hours, both sides, too. Most of it comes from an area that our land doesn't abut. I think they've been holding illegal fights for money out there, too, and for years. Can't prove it, though. Ever heard of a guy named Punk Fitch? Story is that he's got a twin brother who's even worse than he is. Real badasses, both of them, and they like to work together when they beat the crap out of people. I've got a feeling they're in the middle of lots of the illegal stuff going on around here."

"Yeah, actually, I have heard of him."

"Well, we're pretty sure now that he's been beating people to death around here for years. We do know that he was placed in the Fulton State Hospital for the Criminally Insane, but he recently escaped.

That probably means he's slinking somewhere around here as we speak."

"Have you seen this Punk guy on any of your surveillance? Or his brother?"

"Not yet. I have a feeling that they know we're watching. And somebody's been sneaking up outside camera range and putting our equipment out of commission. Nothing we can prove, of course. Don't have enough yet on either family for a warrant to go in and search. They are careful, and sometimes they are smarter than they look."

Claire said, "We don't have much, either, not yet. We were hoping you could help us out, living next door to them like this."

"My advice? Go over to Fulton. Check out the doctors who treated that guy. Hear what they have to say about him. They might know something that'll help you. He was in there quite a long time before he escaped, I think. They've got to know what makes him tick, or not tick, I might ought to say. Stories I've heard, his brain ought to be sitting in some lab, next to Hitler's, maybe, on the most defective specimens' shelf."

"Sounds like a plan. We'll look further into that guy. Any chance you can make us copies of those tapes if you catch anybody skulking around?"

"Sure. Could take me a day or so, though. I doubt if you'll see anything you haven't already seen. They are very careful and they post guards around here and there, guards with binoculars and high-powered rifles with nightscopes. Not sure that's to keep intruders out, or the women in."

Bud said, "Yeah, I hear you on that one. We saw those women for ourselves the other day."

After they finished their cake and coffee and warmed up some, they got up and thanked Laurie Dale for her help, and then she walked them through her big comfortable farmhouse to the front door. It was beautifully decorated but in a cozy way that made a person want to settle in and stay a spell. As they were leaving, Laurie looked at Claire. "Hey, detective, how about joining our little gun club? We've got some nice women involved, and I've made some good friends. We have lots of fun when we meet up here or down at the lake. You can handle that Glock with the best of them, from what I observed when you got the drop on me and had me in your sights. That hasn't happened all that often in my career so I'm sure glad you were friendly."

Claire smiled. "Yeah, and same back at you. Maybe I will. I'll think about it and let you know."

Laurie pulled a white card out of the pocket of her red sweater. "Here you go. Now you know where to find me. Good luck with your investigation. Let me know if I can help you. Any time, night or day. Just ask. Truth? It's pretty boring tromping around out there in the snow watching those backwoods creeps do their thing."

After they said their good-byes, and very much encouraged, Claire and Bud climbed back into Bud's Bronco and returned to town. But Claire had already decided a little trip to a state mental institution was definitely in order, and who better to arrange that little excursion than her own personal and famous shrink of all shrinks, the one and only Dr. Nicholas Black. He could probably open any doors over in Fulton as easy as one, two, three. Even the padlocked ones. And those just happened to be the very ones she wanted to go inside and take a look around.

Chapter Twenty-two

The State Hospital in Fulton, Missouri, had opened its doors in 1851 and was purported to be the oldest public mental health facility west of the Mississippi River. Tidbits obtained by Google, each and every one. And it looked to Claire like it certainly lived up to its ancient billing. The state highways and byways were nice and clear after a day or two of extremely cold sunshine and zero precipitation. Black elected to drive his big shiny Humvee that she found so super awesome, probably chosen over the helicopter, because it would take them longer to get there and back, and thereby keep Claire far away from the super-crazy people he knew she was investigating of late. He didn't tell her that, of course, but she knew him well and could read between his motives even better.

Black also called ahead to the mental asylum so as to make an emergency appointment with his fellow headshrinker of the ultra, ultra, bark-at-the-moon crazies of Missouri society. His colleague there happened to have the unfortunate moniker of one Dr. Henry LeCorps, which Claire decided was one of the most terrible names any doctor could ever possess, right in line behind Dr. Will Killyou.

"How well do you know this LeCorps guy?" she asked Black, when they stopped in the wide, green-tiled corridor outside said doctor's office in Biggs Forensic Center, which turned out to be the maximum security unit where the worst of the worst dangerous and psychotic maniac killers were kept in their nice soft padded cells, no doubt.

"Pretty well. Hank's an old friend. So don't make fun of his last name. He's sensitive about its connotation."

Claire laughed softly. "You think? Well, I'd say he should be. It's a tad off-putting for new patients, I suspect."

"Just don't taunt him about it, Claire."

"As if I'm that rude. Really, Black. You offend me."

Black ignored her sarcasm, opened the door, and then stood back politely for her to enter first, quite the gent whenever he wanted to be, which was most of the time. Not that she usually wanted him to have to open every damn door for her, but it was sweet and rather retro on his part, and she liked it, as well as just about everything else about him, too. Inside the waiting room, she found a combination secretary/clinical nurse/warden manning a rather old white metal desk to match the rather old rest of the building. Black had told her that they were trying to get state money designated to overhaul the hospital, mainly because they were still using old kitchen appliances that had been taken off decommissioned Korean War battleships, or from some other equally ridiculous and embarrassing place. But, oh, well, it all did seem a little worse for the wear while trying valiantly to hold up, and that was the truth.

The nurse said hello and good morning and please wait and good to see you again, Dr. Black, and the doctor will be with you shortly and take any seat you wish. Blah, blah, blah, and more blah, just like all physicians' receptionists everywhere, almost to the letter, at that, and all said while the phone was ringing and waiting for her to pick up the receiver and say all the same things again. They ought to just make a recording, and be done with it. Just press the button when they see somebody approaching, play their little spiel, and smile ingratiatingly.

So, they sat down in the seats of their choosing and waited for almost twenty long and endless minutes. Black took the time to be his usual calm and relaxed self while reading through a patient's file that he'd brought along on his iPad because he probably knew how long shrinks like him make people like her wait, being a crack and often sought-after one himself, and who also probably made people wait too long. After about twelve and one-half minutes, Claire began twiddling her thumbs and started to get all antsy and annoyed and wanting to flash her badge and make threats.

So she got up, paced to the windows, and stared out over the rather lovely grounds and thought about Laurie Dale, FBI Lady/Cake Maker Extraordinaire, and how they'd almost had the shoot-out at the O. K. Corral in her backyard with her and her trigger-happy gun club. What a headline that would've made: CANTON COUNTY DETECTIVES ANNIHILATE ALL-WOMAN GUN CLUB. Or, even worse, ALL-WOMAN GUN CLUB ANNIHILATES HAPLESS DETECTIVES or the most horrific of all, EIGHT DEAD IN SNOW FOR NO APPARENT REASON. Thank God, none of that had happened. Because, truth be told, Claire rather liked Laurie Dale. Now that was a lady who could handle a .357 Magnum with the best of them. Even Dirty Harry would be jealous if he weren't fictional, and she did it all the while looking as cool as a cucumber, too. Maybe Claire would join up with that club and play some war games, especially if they agreed to name it something less cheesy and ridiculous. Perhaps The Gun Club, for instance.

The door beside her suddenly opened and out walked the specified handler of the really, really bloodthirsty head cases captured anywhere in the wilds of the great state of Missouri. Which had once included one Thomas Landers, a psychopath who had displayed a neat bullet hole in his forehead the last time Claire had seen his scary face bathed in some equally eerie blue blinking light. But that nightmare was over now, and a hearty thank-you to Black for that rather excellent sharpshooting and deader-than-dead-man ending. But she didn't want to think about that right now, or any other time ever in her entire future life, either. Never would be too soon, in fact.

Black was up on his feet now, as athletic and agile as he was on the tennis court or golf course, no doubt, hand outstretched, that famous dimpled and killer smile on his face. He glad-handed his old colleague with lots of goodwill and happy feelings. "Hey, Hank. Good to see you. Thanks for seeing us so quickly."

Henry LeCorps looked and dressed a lot like some nerdy professor who played bridge with a bunch of women on Tuesdays and taught some dumb university course like Greek Literature and Its Effect on Hedonistic Values of the Renaissance Female, or something even worse. Little tiny guy, with a narrow blond mustache and wavy blond hair, black-rimmed glasses, navy argyle sweater vest with a yellow-and-blue pastel plaid shirt underneath, soft hands, soft face, soft everything. He was now smiling up at Black, way up, since Black was six-four and LeCorps was five-four, if that. "My pleasure, of course. It's good to see you, too. What's it been now? A couple of years, at least."

"Yeah, about that. Please allow me to introduce my fiancée, Claire Morgan. She's the detective I was telling you about on the telephone."

LeCorps turned to her and observed her in such a professionally interested way that it made Claire wonder exactly what Black had been telling the guy about her on the telephone. Probably just about anything LeCorps heard about her life would necessitate an emergency clinical evaluation and immediate enforced hospitalization, straitjacket buckled tight.

"So you are *the* Claire Morgan. Well, I can see now what all the stir is about."

After that, Claire had an almost irrepressible desire to insult him soundly about his last name. If Bud had been there instead of Black, and if Dr. Corpse hadn't been Black's old bud, she might have dressed him down a tad. However, she was no doubt overreacting again to her infamy and controlled herself and was nothing if not polite.

"How do you do, doctor? I'm not sure what you mean by *stir*, but I guess you're going to tell me, right?"

LeCorps smiled and studied her face very closely some more, just like every stupid shrink she had ever been forced to go see, except for Black, who usually just wanted to kiss her and smooch a little when he stared at her like that. Okay, he'd wanted to analyze her, too, a couple of times, but not lately.

"Oh, my dear, I fear that I have offended you. But please don't take my words in the wrong way. It's just that you were all that Thomas Landers would ever talk about in our sessions, and then after spending a lot of time in Landers's company, Mr. Fitch did so as well. They were very good friends for a while when they were here together. Actually, they were inseparable during their free socialization time in the common room. But, please, come into my office so we can sit down and talk privately."

Yeah, a Landers and Fitch duet was a match made in hell, all right. One was already there. One down and one to go, if all went according to plan.

But in they went and found the proverbial couch on which to have one's head examined. Actually, it was a tufted red leather chaise longue with a matching doctor's easy chair right beside it. Thank God, Black was forward thinking and avoided couches in his practice. She had reclined on more psychiatrists' sofas than she liked to think about in her rather horror-filled past.

They all sat down around his desk, and LeCorps studied Claire some more, enough, in fact, to set her teeth on edge. "I take it that you haven't located Mr. Fitch yet," he finally said. "We were all so shocked when he managed to escape the way he did."

"No, we haven't. But I do have a court order right here that would allow us to look into his files as documenting his stay here at this hospital."

"Of course. It's highly irregular, of course, but as I'm sure you know, Mr. Fitch is extremely dangerous. Even more so than was Thomas Landers, in my professional opinion. In fact, I believe he's the most dangerous psychopath that I have ever encountered in my practice of thirty-two years."

Claire and Black exchanged a skeptical look at that one. "That is surprising," Claire said to him. "Even worse than Thomas Landers, you say?" Who had been an insane, bloodthirsty, raving maniac, plus some.

"I understand why you would be surprised. Nick told me some of the background concerning your association with Mr. Landers, and of course, I already knew a lot of what had transpired from Thomas's own words and actions during our sessions. I am so sorry that you had to go through so much at his hands, detective."

Well, that makes two of us, Claire thought. But she did not want to talk about that. "Why do you think Fitch is more dangerous than Landers and the others?"

"For one thing, Thomas Landers was really only interested in you. He would only harm people who he felt were keeping him away from you or that you cared about or who would help you get away from him or who he needed to kill in order to get to you. You see, it was all about you, every single facet of his life. Fitch, on the other hand, he kills at will because he likes it. He likes to kill just about anything breathing, but he especially loves killing people, and anyone will do. Man, woman, or child. Apparently, he's been trained from childhood to hammer a person with his fists with no regard for their pain or horror or terror. He has zero empathy, absolutely none. He could care less if he hurts someone, or if he subjects them to inhuman amounts of pain and suffering. He came from a highly dysfunctional family, you understand."

No kidding, Einstein, thought Claire. "Yes, sir, I've met a few Fitches in person, which is a few too many."

"His father was so brutal to him and his brothers that it's a wonder any of them turned out to be normal functioning members of society."

"Yes, I gathered that, too. And I don't think any of them are normally functioning human beings, none that I've met, anyway." Both shrinks nodded sagely, all of them in agreement on that account, despite her lack of shrink licensure. But back to business. She needed to pick this nerd's brain, and time was a-wasting. "I have been told that he has a twin brother, one who is even more screwed up than he is. That they had a good old time together, sort of swimming through life, side by side, like a man-eating shark tag team, and did so enjoy their time beating up anybody who even looked at them sideways, especially true of the other twin. You know anything about any of that?"

LeCorps considered her for a moment. "Well, I'm afraid you didn't get quite the correct information."

"How do you mean?"

"I mean that after several years sitting here in this office and listening to detailed stories about his twin brother, of whom he appeared to be extremely fond but also frightened, we finally deduced that his twin was a mere figment of his fractured mind."

Black said, "Are you saying that Fitch has DID?"

"What's that mean?" Claire said, always annoyed by tossed-around psychiatry jargon. "Are you talking about a split personality?"

"Exactly, Detective Morgan. We finally diagnosed him with Dissociative Identity Disorder. Some call it Multiple Personality Disorder. He's probably somewhere on the schizophrenic spectrum, as well. He truly believes that it was his brother performing the heinous acts that he himself perpetrated, but in truth it was him while he was entrenched in his other evil personality. He considered himself an innocent victim who could not control his twin brother's terrible deeds. We believe that he was so brutalized when he was a small child that he psychologically hibernated, so to speak. His true personality went deep inside his psyche and let his stronger alter ego come out to handle whatever horrible things that were being done to him at the moment."

Claire considered that diagnosis while LeCorps and Black commenced with a lot of shrink mumbo jumbo with big terms and nary the word *crazy* ever uttered. But crazy this guy was, and it appeared he just loved to use his fists when he killed people. And he was on the loose at the moment in her neck of the woods with nobody hot on his bloodstained trail, free as a bird to pummel to pulp whomever he chose in whatever manner he chose. And according to LeCorps, he always chose an ending that equated with dead, baby, dead.

"Doctor, could you tell me more about him? I need to know everything I can in order to track him down."

So the doctor did so, and it was all quite chilling and grotesque, of course. Just like most psychotic serial killers that she had run into. "Did the family commit him? Or was it the court system?"

"Well, actually, he killed his grandfather, and also a man who married some girl with whom he was infatuated. Both of them with his bare hands and some kind of club. The coroner said that Fitch beat his girlfriend's new husband to death, still whaling on him until he could barely lift his arms to strike him anymore. They had to knock him unconscious to stop him. Both victims died, of course. Fitch was still in his teens. That's when the family decided he was way too dangerous to be allowed to roam free and his temper much too volatile to remain living at their farm with the rest of the family. So they brought him over here to us, tied up nice and tight in the back of a pickup truck. After that, he vowed he was going to get out and kill them all. One by one and in the worst possible manner."

Well, well, what'd you know. Claire found that more than interesting since she had checked the background of all Fitch and Parker crimes in Canton County and had seen no mention of any such crime. She told the shrink as much.

"They probably didn't report it to the police. They keep to themselves. I believe the victim was one of their own. I doubt very much if they ever report any kind of crime occurring on their property. In our sessions, Fitch talked a lot about the fights they liked to sponsor out around where he was born, and how he was the best of the best. Truth? He just loves to fight and hit other human beings until they stop moving. Anywhere, any time, anybody, and that was exactly the way he put it. He said it gave him great pleasure, as nothing else could. Although he was transferring much of that onto his fictitious brother that he referred to as Bones."

Great news, just what she wanted to hear when she went out looking for him again. "And he vowed to kill the members of his own family?" It appeared that he had already started out upon that deadly murder quest. Blythe Parker was a Fitch, and one that was easy to get at, all frail and alone in that big empty house of hers. Easy pickings for a homicidal maniac on the loose.

Black was still asking doctor-specific questions. "Did Fitch ever transform into his alter ego in your sessions?"

"No, but he did it with some of the other patients, especially after Landers managed to get away from here. We caught his violence on camera several times in the common room. It was a textbook transition. Fitch always seemed rather subdued and quiet when in his day-to-day reality, the one in which he wanted us to call him Punk Fitch. But when he became Bones Fitch, and as I said, that's the name he called his imaginary brother, he became angry and irate and loud and brutal and looking for a fight. He did manage at one time to beat another patient seriously enough that he had to be hospitalized in the intensive care unit for a week. That's when we realized just how dangerous he was and the kind of brutality of which he was capable."

Wonderful, just great, now she'd probably have to strap all three guns on her person, Claire thought. "And you are absolutely certain there is not another brother, a twin called Bones?"

"Yes, absolutely convinced. We did in-depth family histories with the people who brought him here, members of the Fitch family. They

all knew that he was convinced he had a twin brother, but they swore
to a person that he did not. They said his fantasy about having a twin
called Bones started very young, at which time Fitch made up several
imaginary playmates, but he was especially adamant about the brother
named Bones. We got the same information from the family in which
he grew to manhood. All of it was well documented by every doctor
on our staff who worked with him."

"Let me get this straight. Now you are telling me that this guy's
not really a Fitch?"

"No, I'm not saying that. Mr. Fitch is a Fitch on his mother's side.
She was a Fitch. His father was a Parker."

"I see." Claire thought about that a moment. "That's surprising.
Considering how the two families loathe each other."

"Yes. The mother was shunned for a time, until her family took
pity on her and allowed her to return to the fold. Apparently, her husband was rather brutal, to both her and the boys, so after our patient
was born, she took him and went back home to live. When he was
about five, she died, and his father took him back to live at the Parker
household. That's when we believe his personality split into the
Bones and Punk personalities."

"So what was this guy's real name? The name on his birth certificate?"

"His birth name is Preston Parker, but he wanted everybody to
call him Punk Fitch when he moved back in with his mother's family,
which he did in order to be with the girl he loved at the time. When
he was in residence here, he would become angry if we called him
Preston Parker, and insisted that we call him Punk Fitch. So we did
so, in order to keep him calm and cooperative. I believe, however,
that the dominant personality is Bones."

Good grief, was this guy a whack job of epic proportions, or
what? "So he *is* one of the Parker brothers who still live out there in
the hills?"

"Yes, but when we tried to interview them, they wouldn't claim
kin to him, either. They said he wasn't their brother, and never had
been. We couldn't get them to admit it. Personally, I believe that they
are so afraid of him that they didn't want to tell us anything. I think

they feared that if he ever got out, he'd go after them if they told us anything about him. Therefore, they completely denied his existence. This is a very strange case, believe me."

Claire glanced at Black. He was wearing a massive frown, one of professional bent. When he looked like that, it meant that said subject was big-time weirded out up to the rafters. "Surely there were school records that verified Preston Parker's existence. School pictures that we could obtain? Surely you have pictures of this Punk/Bones guy while he was under your care?"

"All the Parker children were homeschooled. No school records could be found. No medical records to speak of. A few hospital visits for the father and a couple of the boys, but the admission information given was vague. But yes, we do have a picture of him when he was admitted here." He opened the manila file in front of him and slid a photograph across the desk to her.

Claire picked it up and stared at it. It was a close-up of a young man who looked a whole hell of a lot like Paulie Parker. Problem was, though, he also looked a whole helluva lot like a younger version of Patrick. And Percy. And Phin. And Petey. And Chef Phillip. The guy in the picture even looked a slight bit like the randy little Malachi Fitch. Yep, they all looked so much alike that they could be quintuplets or sextuplets, especially now that they were all older and bearded and dressed exactly alike in green and brown camouflage. Oh, fabulous. And inbreeding raises its ugly head. One of them was a psycho who was killing people right and left. All she had to do was figure out which one it was. Maybe she'd just arrest them all, and wait for the full moon to see who howled.

Claire sighed, not exactly thrilled at the road she could see stretching out ahead of her. "So he was a Parker as a child, and it was a Parker father who beat him when he was small. Do I have that much right?"

"From what we can ascertain. We interviewed everyone in both families who would agree to talk to us. That's the way we understood it. But some of the stories they told didn't always make sense to us or go along with what the Punk Fitch personality told us."

"No kidding," Claire said. "Think any of it is true?"

At that juncture, Black decided to jump into the fray. "Are there other credible extenuating factors from his childhood that indicate he was DID that far back?"

"Yes. Punk told us that he was often placed into dog pens and metal cages for punishment and for long periods of time, and without food or water, but that apparently caused him to bear a strong love of canines. He admitted that he adopted their habits and that he enjoyed licking other people and himself the way dogs do. He told us that it gave him insight into their souls and what they were thinking. Especially if he managed to insert his tongue into their mouth or ears."

Well, yuck, yuck, and more yuck. "Well, that's just about as gross as gross can get, Dr. LeCorps." Man, she just could not get that name to roll easily off her tongue. Same went for cadaver and decapitation.

"Yes, it is. But it was something he felt he had to do upon meeting someone new. Sometimes he was strong enough to physically force himself on his victims. Not so with Thomas Landers. Landers liked the licking. Punk apparently taught Landers how to lick the face and neck for sexual gratification, and Landers took to the whole process at once. It was a very clinically significant development in their relationship. You can see why, I'm sure."

And Claire was beginning to see why, all right. They were after a super psycho/pervert/dog licker, to be sure, but that wasn't exactly news to her. She had seen Paulie Parker's frozen body and the bloody brutality of Blythe Parker's murder, too. Bones Fitch/Punk Fitch/Preston Parker/Nut Job was indeed a whacko of the highest order, all right, and he was running all over the place and probably licking God knew what as they spoke. Great. As far as Claire was concerned, he could be anybody in either one of the Fitch or Parker clans. And the Petrovs, too, with their murderous proclivities, as far as that went. Maybe she should arrest the whole lot of them, all three families en masse, and make the world a safer place in which to grow and prosper and stay alive. Meanwhile, she would take a copy of Dr. LeCorps's file home with her and read about crazy people until she went crazy herself. Which wouldn't take long, not the way things were going.

Blood Brothers

Making a plan to kill their betraying brother didn't take very long at all. Punk and Bones had always liked keeping things simple, which was just easier, and all. So they decided to hide out in the hotel's parking lot on the night of his fight and wait for Punk's true love's new love to come outside. He had the last fight, the showcase one, and most everybody was gone before he had showered and finished up in the locker room. When he finally did show up, he was all alone and the parking lot was nearly empty. So as soon as he put his gym bag down so he could unlock his car door, they attacked him from behind with baseball bats and knocked him down with double blows. Then Bones hit him again and cracked his right kneecap before Punk could get the duct tape over his mouth. He screamed in agony, and they dragged him behind some trashcans, but nobody heard, or came outside, or anything, which was very lucky for them.

Then they tied him up and threw him in the back and took off in the orderly's Jeep and headed for a nice deserted place in which to take their time breaking him up. It was snowing hard again but they were used to that and the new Jeep was well equipped for bad weather. The roads were nearly deserted so late, and they turned onto a cleared road that led up into a big state park. Punk stopped the Jeep, and Bones got out and unhooked the chain across the entrance. Then they drove inside, found a good spot, and then got out and left the car lights on. They dragged their moaning, groaning brother to a high cliff that overlooked the lake. It was pitch dark, still snowing, but the white snow reflected the headlights and made things nice and bright, as they flipped a rope over a tree limb and strung him up to a tree by his wrists. They stood under him, both holding the old aluminum baseball bats that the three of them had played with as children.

Bones said, "You wanna go first? Since he's screwin' your girl?"

Growling with rage at the mental picture that brought up inside his mind, Punk swung the bat against their victim's spine. He didn't hear any vertebra snap so he hit him again, harder this time. Bones laughed at the way Punk was yelling and cussing at their trussed-up brother. "Now that's what I'm talkin' about! You miss that while you was locked up, Punk? You glad you're back here with me, the way it oughta be?"

"Just hurry it up and hit him. We gotta get rid of him and make my girl a free woman again, now that I'm back and ready to get married. Nobody's gonna stop me now from havin' her. Nobody."

"Sounds good to me. You're finally showin' me some guts. Don't know why you want that lily-white tail, anyways. She sure don't do it for me."

"Nothin' does it for you except breakin' people's bones. Go ahead, it's your turn. Hurry up. Somebody might see the car lights."

Punk stood back and watched Bones raise the bat over his head and bring it down hard on the man's collarbone. It snapped, but their brother probably didn't feel anything anymore, not now that his spine was splintered all apart. But the furious revenge was still burning hot inside Punk, a hard red rage that he'd locked up so long, just at the thought of other men sleeping and having sex with his girl. Now he was wreaking his vengeance, and he was gonna enjoy it.

So he took his turns with passionate eagerness, beating one brother alongside his other brother, glad for Bones's help. Maybe he didn't swing his Louisville Slugger with the same kind of maniacal glee that Bones did, but he bet he was getting a lot more satisfaction. It felt good to be free from those stupid doctors. It felt good to kill somebody, somebody who had touched his woman's pure white skin while he'd been gone.

After almost an hour, the blizzard intensified so much that they could barely see where to aim their blows. They couldn't hear the bones pop anymore, either, and they were cold down to their marrow. So they cut the broken corpse down off the tree limb and heaved him as far as they could off the cliff and into the water below. Nobody was gonna find what was left of him until the snow melted and the park opened in the spring, if even then, after the animals had gotten to him and dragged his broken bones to hell and back, which was just good enough for him.

Both of them were highly satisfied with their night's work, and they took off back home to the warmth of Bones's little cozy digs in the mine shaft, wanting to get toasty again and rest awhile before they went in search of his true love and brought her back with them. When they did find her, Punk was just going to have to give her the bad news about her dead lover boy and maybe even punish her a little bit, just for being so dadburned disloyal, and then he'd take her far away and marry her, once and for all, and they'd be happy again, like it had always meant to be. Yeah, finally, finally, his life was looking up. Things were gonna be good from now on. All he had to do was wait a teensy bit longer, and she would be his alone.

Unfortunately, it took them several days to figure out exactly where she lived but they finally found the house. The place was pretty isolated, high up in a fancy subdivision with big houses bought by lots of rich folks. He wondered how they had even afforded it, but then again, her dead lover had been a damn good fighter. Not as good as he and Bones were, but he probably made plenty good money.

They drove up to her place in the middle of the night. All was quiet, and that evening the snow had finally stopped falling. The entrance road was cleared, but Punk stopped the car a good distance from the house. "We better walk in from here, Bones. She might call the cops if she sees us comin'."

"Let's just do it. You gonna break her arm for messin' around with those other guys while you was sick and in the hospital?"

"I wasn't sick, and you know it. And no. I love her. Can't you get that through your thick head. I love her. She's mine. Live with it."

Bones looked surprised and then his face crinkled all up, and he started crying real tears, and everything. "You act like you like her more'n you do me."

"Don't be stupid. I just like her different, is all. Now after we get inside, you wait downstairs 'cause I bet she's upstairs where that light's burnin'. I want to handle this alone. Understand that, Bones. You wait here, if you can't do what I say. This here is an important night in my life and I don't want you messin' it up."

"I can do what you say, and you know it. But if you do break her arm, I wanna see it."

"I'm not gonna break nothin' on her, you idiot."

"Don't call me that. I'm not no idiot."

After that, they didn't say anything else to each other, both still a little bit mad. They snuck around and found the backdoor up on a high deck. It was locked up tight, but they just kicked it in, simple as pie. So she knew they were coming when they ran through the rooms to the front of the big house, and Punk started up the steps to get her. The chandelier in the front hall flared on all of a sudden, and he finally saw his true love again. She was standing at the top of the stairs, wearing a white satin nightgown, and she was holding it together at the throat with both hands. She was barefoot. His heart trembled and almost went still with his need and his love and his pleasure.

"*You*," she said, obviously shocked to see him.

"Yes, it's me, all right. I've come to take you home with me."

Then she got a frightened look on her beautiful face. "You killed him, didn't you? You killed my husband."

"Oh, yeah, we sure did. What did you expect me to do? You shouldn't've ever been sleepin' with him. You're mine. You know that. You said you were. I'm gonna have to punish you for screwin' him and that other guy, too, I guess. I was all locked up and waitin' for you, and look what you were doin' behind my back."

After he said that, she whirled around and ran for the bedroom. He was on her in seconds, and he could hear Bones laughing at the bottom of the steps. She was still as light and delicate as he remembered, and he clamped his arms around her from the back and held her arms down at her sides as she struggled frantically against his tight hold.

"Let me go! I hate you, I hate you, you killed him! I loved him! I hate you!"

Pure fury, unlike anything he had ever felt in his entire life, gushed up into his blood, the rush of adrenaline and pain and hurt at her cruel words. He let go of her, spun her back around to face him, and hit her in the face with his fist as hard as he could. Blood spurted from her nose, and she fell down and didn't move at all. He jerked her back up again and hit her in the head again and then he threw her bodily onto the bed. He was panting, breathless with anger and exertion and disappointment, but then he realized that she was already dead. He had killed her. He had hit her too hard. Her beautiful pale eyes were open and staring at the ceiling. Sobbing at what he'd done, he fell on top of her and cradled her bleeding head in his arms.

"Oh, no, oh, no, you can't die, I love you, I love you," he kept whispering as he pressed her head into his chest, but she never moved again. He began to lick her cool white skin, his tongue moving over every inch of her body. God, why had he killed her so fast? Why? Now he couldn't ever marry her or take her away or have sex with her, ever again, or nothing.

"Well, that didn't last long," Bones's voice said from the doorway. "I thought you wanted to keep her around forever."

"I did, I did. But she said she hated me, and I got awful mad. And now, look what I did to her. I killed her. Why did I do that?"

Punk fell face-first down onto the soft and silky comforter and wept heartbrokenly into the pillows, holding her limp body tightly up against him. Bones stood watching him, leaning his shoulder up against the doorjamb and not saying anything. Finally, Punk pushed her dead body aside and got off the bed. "C'mon, Bones," he said, walking across the room. "Let's get outta here."

Bones halted him with a hand on his arm. "Can I slit her throat or break some of her bones before we go? She's dead. She's not gonna feel nothin'. I haven't had any fun like that in ages. Come on, Punk. Please. She deserves it, and you know it."

Squeezing his eyes shut, Punk felt slightly ill, still shocked at what he'd done. He hadn't even given her a chance to change her mind and love him again. What was the matter with him? "I guess so. Like you say, she's not gonna feel nothin' now, that's for damn sure. I'll wait in the car. And clean up after yourself this time, will ya? I gotta think about all this. I feel sick. I shouldn't've done this. I've gone and done something real stupid."

Before Punk reached the top of the stairs, he heard the muffled sound of a bone cracking. He stopped there, mourned his true love for a moment longer, as the muted sounds of her bones crunching continued, and then he walked down the steps and ran down the driveway to the car. All he wanted to do now was go back home with Bones and mourn the greatest loss in his life. He sat there for a long time, waiting for Bones to get done with his fun and watching the big white snowflakes spiraling softly down to the ground. He just felt so lonely without his true love. He was gonna miss her so much. Damn her, anyway, for making him kill her so fast.

Chapter Twenty-three

During the drive home from Fulton, Claire sat quietly and listened to Black telling her how careful she needed to be. Then she went to the office and ran the case for Sheriff Charlie Ramsay, who also ended up telling her how careful she should be. After that, Claire joined Bud to decide if another visit to Fitchville and its bizarre and murderous and sexist inhabitants was in the cards. Luckily, Bud didn't mention any extra safety precautions she should take, not one time. Surveillance was what they talked about, deciding it was indeed necessary and from several different vantage points, so they took two cars and headed out. Bud elected to conceal himself and his Bronco in a hidden grove where he could watch the comings and goings at the main Fitchville gate, with the heater on full blast, no doubt.

Claire drove on to Laurie Dale's house, where she and her new and sharpshooting FBI special agent friend climbed atop Laurie's two rather sweet and brand-new snowmobiles and headed up the Dale property line that edged Fitchville environs. Claire stopped her vehicle at the same spot from where she and Bud had watched the Parker brothers attack the compound in their pickup truck the day they had met their first Fitchvillers.

"How about you staying on watch here, Laurie, while I go on up farther along the property line and see if I can catch sight of tracks or campfire smoke, something like that. If it is Bones or Punk Fitch, or Preston Parker, or whatever his name is, who is camping out around here somewhere, I want to get him before he kills one of us and/or somebody else."

"Okay. I've got on my extra-duty thermal underwear." Laurie looked up at the clouds darkening the sky on the horizon above the trees and gauged the weather with a practiced eye. "It's gonna start snowing soon. Mark my words."

"Yeah, I saw the forecast. I'll be back after I scope out the cliff up there. It shouldn't take me all that long."

"Okay. Take your time. I'll check the game cameras while you're gone. Good luck."

Claire proceeded up the fence row, enjoying a day out in the crisp cold weather for a change. It felt good to ride on a fast snowmobile and enjoy the fresh air, but the sun was not out and it was gradually growing colder. Black was busy with staff meetings and conference calls all day long at Cedar Bend Lodge, and she did not envy him those boring hours going over a bunch of boring reports with a bunch of boring people. She hated meetings. They were just a useless waste of time. Good thing that Charlie didn't like them, either, and usually cut departmental powwows short because he got impatient with everybody after about ten minutes.

Laurie Dale's farm was quite large with vast tracts of woods and pastures and even a small lake fed by a river that ran behind her property, one that also touched on Joe McKay's land, as well as that of the two quarreling clans. Claire drove the snowmobile to the extreme far end of the Dale property where the fence row took a sharp right turn and headed away from the Fitches' property and back across Laurie's land until it reached some of the Parkers' acreage on the opposite side. If she remembered correctly, Joe McKay had told her that the Fitch orchards also touched a portion of Parker lands that lay well behind Laurie's place. Yep, one big unhappy, un-neighborly family, to be sure. She stopped there in a dense glade of snow-laden cedar trees and thoughtfully contemplated the woods across the small, swift river, a short trek through which would apparently bring one out into the open fields surrounding Joe McKay's farmhouse.

Then she peered out over the adjoining Fitch and Parker properties. It looked rather vast, too, lots of hills and rocky ridges, which were probably pockmarked with caves, not to mention the enormous sinkholes prevalent in the area. The whole of Canton County was riddled with immense networks of caves and grottoes and old and abandoned lead mines. She had once worked another case where she'd crawled through some dark and creepy caves and tunnels, a horrible case she would not soon forget. But it was completely conceivable that Bones Fitch had holed up inside a similar kind of hideout. So all she had to do was figure out where it was, find it, and then arrest him before he beat and licked her to death. No problem, piece of cake.

Climbing to the top of the highest outcropping of rocks that she could find, she positioned the tripod of her high-powered rifle securely in the snow, a gun that was affixed with the most excellent nightscope when needed, and surveyed the vast panoramic valley spread out below her. There were many rolling hills of woods and pastures along the highways of middle Missouri, some stretching into the distance as far as the eye could see. Yes, it was indeed a perfect place for a man on the run to hole up, especially if he was a survivalist. Their work was cut out for them, all right.

Next she checked the skyline for any gray wisps of smoke rising up off any evil psycho's campfire. But no dice there. Besides, there were plenty of places where she would never see it, anyway. As it gradually grew dark around her, Claire kept searching, determined to find Bones Fitch, slowly moving the scope over every inch of the surrounding landscape, back and forth, bringing the distance up close and in focus. It seemed a bit disingenuous to her that the Fitches could not find this guy, especially if he was really a former adopted son and was wandering around on their own property. On the other hand, the acres farthest away from the paved county road did consist mainly of heavy woods and dense undergrowth and rocky ridges that would be hard to search for any moving target, and one who possessed those crack survivalist skills. They might have to resort to a search warrant and about a hundred police academy recruits if they didn't find the guy soon. Maybe McGowen and his ATF friends could help out with that a bit. If McGowen was still alive, which was iffy, providing if all the scary stories she'd heard thus far were true.

Claire wondered then if the Fitch brood was really looking for their prodigal insane sonny boy or if they were helping him kill recalcitrant people or rebellious women on their little sicko reservation. When her phone rang, it was Black again, no doubt worrying himself silly some more, so she picked up in a hurry.

"What are you doing?" he asked.

"I'm lying on my stomach in frozen snow and ice in falling winter darkness and trying to pick out in the far distance a homicidal maniac who we think is sneaking around and killing his family members. As you well know."

"Same old, huh?"

Claire laughed softly to herself. Black was just so on target with that one. "Yeah, pretty much, smart guy. And I'm gonna have to turn off the phone soon because I'm up high on a granite cliff and it might echo and alert aforementioned killer that I am hot on his trail and getting hotter by the minute."

"Like I said, same old stuff. So, when will you be home for dinner, sweetheart?"

"I won't be home for dinner. We've got nightscopes and rifles and video cams, and apparently nighttime is when the action usually goes down. In the dead of night, the operative word being *dead*."

"I take it that you're not in mortal danger, though, right? Bud's still out there with you, I assume. I shouldn't already be on my way up there with an M16 and a posse, should I?"

"Not to worry. Bud's here, and so is my new FBI friend. I am as safe as safe can be, and we have no warrant to go anywhere on the Fitch or Parker properties, which handcuffs us big-time because that's where the guy is preying on his victims with occasional murderous side trips elsewhere."

"Well, that's the best news I've heard all day. At least, the safe as safe can be part."

"I'll be home later. Where will you be?"

"Cedar Bend. Let's spend the night here."

"You got it. Jules is there with you?"

"Yeah, don't worry about him. Are you warm enough? Don't want you to come down with pneumonia right before the wedding."

Claire smiled. Not subtle, that. He had an innate ability to work wedding references into every conversation. "I have on at least ten layers and my electric socks, both on my feet and inside my shirt. I will be hale and hearty for our upcoming wedding day."

"Want some company?"

"Nope. No need to come save me tonight. I am safe and secure and having a ball. In other words, I'm cold and miserable and want to come home and be with you in the worst way imaginable."

"Well, I like most of that. Don't be too late, dear. You know how I worry about you and all those killers you hang around with."

They hung up a few minutes later, and she switched off her phone. She looked back and could not see Laurie's stake-out spot, but she didn't expect to. Laurie was good at her job. She knew exactly what she was doing. As dusk disappeared and all became black and impenetrable, she found that her night vision scope was absolutely top of the line. She gripped the rifle with her gloved hands and continued to scan the outlying back acres of all four properties for any signs of movement, but didn't see anything at all, not even a rabbit or squirrel. Even they had the sense to go home to their nests. She kept herself aware, however, because there were other varmints in the area, too, bobcats, for instance, known for attacking lone joggers now and then. Not to mention, fox, deer, raccoon, and maybe even a bear or two, if she was her usual really unlucky self and it was nixing hibernation and wandering afar from its den. Maybe even a wild dog or two. Or Patrick Parker's eight hundred hounds out for a group walk.

After about two hours of nothing but blowing tree limbs and whistling wind, she climbed back on the snowmobile, switched on the headlamps, and headed back down the hill again following Laurie's back fence row, but this time the one that separated the Dale property from the Parker land. Yep, Laurie Dale had two sides of psychos to contend with, all right. So did Claire. She certainly hoped side three was Joe McKay's domain because Laurie and her husband needed a normal neighbor who carried and used guns. She wondered if Bones Fitch was spending a lot of time on the Dale and Parker and McKay back acres, which were awfully damned isolated and desolate, instead of his own homestead and that was why he had been so successful at evading capture. The night was really getting cold now, and the snow slanted down through the beams of the headlamps, big and beautiful and wet. She had dressed appropriately so she was still warm enough, except that her nose and cheeks felt slightly frozen.

When she got to the far end of the Dale property, she took cover once more and focused her nightscope over on the Parkers' dark and quiet farmland. It was pitch black now that she had stopped. If this guy really was a Parker brother, he would know their land like the back of his hand, too. It wouldn't hurt to watch how the bearded brothers were passing the time. They were as nuts as the Fitches. And any one of them could be Bones Fitch. Maybe she'd get lucky, for once, and spot the guy.

So she lay down on her stomach and adjusted the barrel of the rifle on the tripod again. Below her, there was a lot of Parker property, but most of it was covered in evergreen trees and the snow was coming down so hard now that the visibility had dwindled almost to nil. She stayed where she was a while, thinking it made sense that somebody in the two clans would use this isolated no-man's land to do their retaliations and murder hunts. The Parkers hadn't shown a lot of brilliance, anyway, not ever, in fact, especially when knocking down the Fitchville gate and driving recklessly into the compound with guns blazing. It had occurred to her before that it was surprising that the Fitches hadn't retaliated right then and there. They had all been armed to the hilt, wearing gun belts Cowboy style. Even McGowen looked like Wyatt Earp in an orange coat. Maybe they knew that Bones would take care of it for them. And hey, maybe that's who the Parkers were looking for.

"Don't you move."

Claire went rigid at the low whisper coming from behind her and did not move. Maybe that was because she felt a gun barrel pressed against the back of her head.

"Put your hands straight out to your sides on the snow. Don't move. You have any other weapons on you?"

"No," she lied, glad she could.

"Put your arms behind your back. Don't try anything, either."

Claire did not want to do that, uh-uh. "You don't have to tie me up. I'm not going anywhere. You got me cold."

Her assailant only laughed. He flipped her over like she weighed nothing and started frisking her underneath her parka so she took that opportunity to ball up her fist and slug it as hard as she could into his Adam's apple. That did the trick, and right off the bat, too. He fell over sideways, clutching his throat, coughing and choking, and she scrambled up, drew out her Glock and nosed it tightly against his chest. "Now, don't *you* move, buddy."

He didn't but he was in a world of hurt. Apparently, her fist had been dead on and more than effective. She put the flashlight on his face and jerked off his ski mask. "Well, hello there, Percy Parker. Trespassing on Laurie Dale's land and attacking her guests? That it? Nothing else to do tonight?"

It took him awhile to get out any words, but he finally said, "I didn't know it was you. I promise."

"Yeah, right. Turn over so that I can cuff you. You aren't very good at capturing people, are you?"

"I thought you was one of them coming to get us. They are crazy and they hate us and they try to kill us every chance they get. You don't believe us, but it's true."

"Yeah, I know. And you hate them. And on and on and on, ad infinitum. What were you gonna do to me after you tied me up, huh? Kill me? Take me home to the boys as a souvenir?"

"No, I was just gonna scare you some. You was spyin' on us. You think we killed our own brother? That it? You think we killed his wife? That's just not us. That's them. That's what they do. You guys just never catch 'em at it. They're too clever."

Clever was a word Claire would never use to describe Fitches. Probably Percy was the only one who ever had. Now the snow was intensifying, it was hard to see, even after she switched on her headlamps again. The wind was picking up, practically howling around the rocky outcroppings and sounding a lot like wicked banshees. Her own breath was coming out hard. "Maybe you come up here from time to time and pick off some Fitches yourself. I hear they're disappearing right and left off their place."

"No way. I just came out here to protect my brothers, that's all. I swear. Just to see who was creeping around and tryin' to kill us. I'm on guard duty tonight."

Claire peered down into his face, where he lay handcuffed and on his back in driving snow. He had regained his innocent *who me?* expression again. The one that she was pretty damn sure was contrived. This guy was not so innocent, she felt it. He knew how to sneak up behind her and take her by surprise. Unfortunately for him, that was as far as his assault skills went. "Where were you going to take me?"

"Nowhere. I just didn't want you to hit me or shoot me, but you did anyways."

Claire frowned. "Just sit there and shut up."

Taking out her phone, she dialed up Bud. The line buzzed with static and cut out now, but he answered quickly and said, "You ready to hang it up for tonight? I am. The snow's really comin' down now. Bet you're freezin'."

"Yeah, but I've got a prisoner that you need to take back and book into jail."

"No, no, please don't," whined Percy. "I need to stay up here and guard the house so my brothers can get some sleep. We're all in danger. You just don't know how much or who's after us."

"Yeah, I do. Now quit whining. Patrick can come bail you out tomorrow."

"I don't want him to. I wanna go home now before he finds out I'm in trouble."

"Well, you're outta luck, kid."

"Who's that? You okay?" Bud asked.

"Percy Parker. You know, he's the Parker who can shoot the best. Can you take him in for me? I want to stay out here a while longer. Maybe I'll catch me some more guys. I have a feeling they're lurking behind every tree now."

"What's the charge?"

"Assaulting a police officer with a weapon good enough?"

"You okay?" he asked again.

"Yeah, he's not very good at it."

Percy Parker now appeared to be sulking, even while the sleet hit him in the eyes. "If you take me in, my brothers are gonna be worried about what happened to me. You just don't understand the truth about stuff."

"Just take it like a man, Percy, okay?"

"You just don't understand."

"Then explain it to me."

"I can't."

"Why not?"

"I just can't. But you are makin' a big mistake. I'm not the one."

"All I know is that you're the one who held a gun on me tonight. That's enough for me."

After that, Percy just sat silently in the snow and looked bummed out about going to jail.

Within fifteen minutes, Laurie Dale had found them and was escorting Parker back to her farmhouse to be placed into Bud's custody for a ride into town. Claire took over down the trail at Laurie's vantage point, one that had the bird's eye view of the village of Fitchville, but couldn't see it all that well with the snow and sleet falling so heavily. She moved laterally up the fence row, ready to call it a day. About fifteen yards up, she saw that the fence had been knocked down. It hadn't been down the last time she saw it, so she hunkered down and looked around and then moved cautiously to where it was lying on the ground. Then she looked at the thick pine trees all around her. Unfortunately, at that point, she was also looking at about five men who materialized like phantoms out of the snow-driven curtain, all holding very large shotguns and rifles that were pointed directly at her.

"Hello, detective. Nice to see you again." Big Harold Fitch in the flesh with lots of little armed Fitches all around him.

Claire focused her rifle square on his chest. It seemed like the thing to do. "Yeah, nice. So move along now. I'm working. You are trespassing on Dale property."

"Put down the gun. We will kill you. Don't think we won't."

"Oh, I don't think you won't, but I do think you won't get away with it. My partner knows where I am, and so do a lot of other people around here. Including the FBI. And you guys aren't exactly ghosts, you actually leave your tracks in the snow. Tracks that they can follow home and arrest you, one and all. By the way, which one of you is Bones Fitch? You can tell me, really."

"It's gonna snow all night," answered a new voice. One Claire immediately recognized as belonging to one undercover ATF officer by the name of Kevin McGowen. "You should've minded your own business. Now we've got to take you out."

At that point, Claire was hoping to high heaven that he was playing his role of fellow Fitch murderer and cohort and that he was just joshing her, and didn't really mean all those deadly threats, although he sure did sound like he meant them. These undercover guys, what was a girl to do? "You will never get away with this. Killing a police officer. That's not so smart, not that anybody ever accused you of being smart. In fact, it's gonna blow up in your face any minute now."

"Well, you won't be around to worry about it," said Harold Fitch. "Kill her, Badidiah."

Damn. They weren't ones to mess around and shoot the bull with their victim like was done on most TV crime shows. Hell, two minutes hadn't even passed and they were ready to pull the trigger. She had to make a move, right now, or die.

McGowen aka Badidiah said, "She's right. Let me take her out to the killin' field and do her there. We're too close to the Dale farmhouse. They'll hear the shot and come running. Our tracks won't be covered up yet, not for a couple of hours."

Claire sincerely hoped he was buying her time. Very sincerely. Meanwhile, she was deciding who to shoot first. Big Harold won that lottery.

"Just get rid of her," Big Harold said suddenly, and then McGowen jerked his shotgun at her head and so quickly that she couldn't even get her rifle around to shoot him. The end of the butt cracked up against the side of her skull just behind her ear, and she went down hard in the snow, dizzy and disoriented, but still slightly conscious. The last thing she remembered was McGowen jerking her up by the front of her jacket and then heaving her bodily over his shoulder.

Chapter Twenty-four

When Claire forced her eyes open again, she was lying on her back in front of a roaring fireplace. She could feel heat from the crackling and popping logs warming one side of her face and body. She no longer wore her heavy parka and insulated fleece jacket. The fleece had been folded and placed under her head for a pillow. She put her fingertips to the throbbing lump behind her ear and realized her sock hat and gloves had also been removed. Then she saw McGowen. He was sitting in a rickety old rocking chair beside her, creaking back and forth and smiling down at her. He said, "Well, you really stepped in it this time, detective. I'll give you that much."

Realizing her danger, she jerked up to sitting position, and then groaned when a white arrow of pain shot through her head and hit her agony receptors head on.

McGowen was still calm and conversational. "I found this cabin way back in the woods behind Fitchville. Nobody knows it's here. The ATF contact radio's out here. I guess you've got a headache?"

"Oh, yeah, I sure do. Thank you so much for clubbing me like that."

"Had to, but I picked my spot and didn't hit you hard."

"Felt plenty hard to me."

"Better call your partner and tell him that you're okay."

"Oh, you think so?"

"Yeah, he'll be worried and come looking for you."

"Maybe I want him to come looking for me. Maybe you want me

to do that so you can take your time killing me without a SWAT team busting down the door."

"I'm not gonna hurt you, Claire. If I was, you'd be dead and buried by now. Problem is, now I've got to keep you out here and out of my way until I can arrange for your partner or somebody you trust to come in and take you out. Unless you think you can make it out on your own without your weapons. Otherwise, Big Harold's gonna see right through me and then you're gonna end up dead, and so am I."

Claire wasn't so sure she could or wanted to believe a single word he said. She slid her hand under her left arm in search of the Glock 19. It was still snug in its holster. The .38 was in its little bed, too. She could feel the heft of it on her ankle. He had not disarmed her. He had not taken her cell phone off her belt, either. She turned it on. McGowen didn't try to grab it, just sat and rocked and watched her check herself and her weapons out. He wasn't wearing a gun belt, not that she could see, which was good.

"I've got a little confession to make," he told her.

"What now? You're just kidding, ha-ha, and I have two minutes to live?"

He laughed, very softly, his black eyes glittering in the dim firelight. "You don't take prisoners, do you?"

"Wish I could say the same for you."

"You're not my prisoner. But I'll tell you one thing, you are way too reckless. You gotta get that in hand or you're gonna end up six feet under."

"Thanks for the tip. Well, go ahead. Hit me with the big confession. I can take it, I hope."

"Okay. I'm not really with the ATF."

Oh, God, that was not exactly something Claire wanted to hear. "No? So you've been lying to me. You are a bad guy, after all. With orders to kill me?"

"Well, I've never really thought of it in black and white. Everything's gray in my world."

"Yeah, I can see that. Hitting a police officer in the head and dragging her out here in the woods seems pretty black to me."

"For your own protection. Harold found out about the real ATF agent right off the bat. The real Badidiah Fitch. Then he was very dead and very quickly. That's how much they like undercover cops. Now I'm impersonating him to keep the ATF off their backs until they can clean out this place."

Bigger question was: *Why wasn't she dead yet?* She glanced around, wondering if McGowen had any kind of ulterior motive for keeping her alive. Then she thought: *What the hell?* She pulled out her Glock and pointed it at McGowen's face.

The fake agent/fake best buddy didn't move a muscle to stop her. "No need for that, detective. I haven't been ordered to kill you, at least not by the guy I really answer to. So you can rest assured that you're safe with me. I want you to get out of here in one piece, and the sooner, the better."

"Yeah, I'm just so ready to rest assured, since you're so honest and straightforward all the time. How about I just call in that SWAT team to get me outta here? They can take down the Fitches while they're at it. You, too, depending on who you answer to. And by the way, are you Bones Fitch, by any chance?"

"You are just so suspicious." McGowen kept up the smiling. "I'm not going to hurt you. Don't want to. I like you, detective. Like I said, if I wanted to do that, you would no longer be breathing."

"So what's your real name? And who do you answer to?"

McGowen stood up. "So, how about a cup of coffee? Might help clear your head. Warm you up some, too."

"Wow, you're quite the gent when you're not bludgeoning me in the head with your gun butt. But, hey, sure, I'll take some. Got cream?"

McGowen laughed. Claire didn't. She did not trust him, not one whit. He turned around and that's when she saw the Beretta that he had stuck into his back waistband. He leaned over and picked up a pot that was suspended over the fire and filled up an old tin cup like Gold Rush prospectors used to drink out of. He handed it over, handle toward her.

Claire took it in her left hand; she kept her weapon in her right hand and pointed at him. Just in case. She took a sip. The coffee tasted pretty damn good. Nice and hot and strong and highly caffeinated. No arsenic aftertaste, which was always a good indication. "So, okay, you gonna tell me your real name, or not?"

McGowen sat back down in the rocker and thought about it. She drank the coffee, hoping it would stop the thudding in her head.

"Well, I guess it won't hurt to tell you. Won't matter much, one way or another. My name is Misha Chicherin. Nice to meet you."

Then Claire figured out the whole thing. Without the slightest doubt, she knew exactly who he was. "Okay, I get it now. The Petrov organization, right? Please say no."

"That's right. And Ivan told me in no uncertain terms that nothing better happen to you, or there's gonna be hell to pay. In other words, I'll die a very painful death at his hands. Orders came down loud and clear that I'm not to kill you, no matter how much you provoke me. And you are an annoying lady. But intriguing, too. You'd be a valuable asset for us. You interested?"

"Yeah, I'd like that like a hole in the head. Well, what do you know? Ivan Petrov is my guardian angel. Frankly, I find that a little hard to swallow."

"Not so hard, if you think about it. Anything happens to you, lady, anything at all, and all hell breaks loose. The entire Montenegro and Rangos organizations, down to the last man, will come gunning for us, not to mention Nicky Black and his own little team of ex-military buddies. Ivan does not want that, not in any form or fashion. We are not equipped for a mob war at the moment. Your husband-to-be has some very dangerous associates who are very fond of him."

Well, thank God for godfathers, Claire thought, appreciating Black's unheralded connections for the very first time in her entire life. Without them, she'd probably already be lying in a shallow ditch under a couple of feet of snow, nose to nose with the unfortunate real ATF guy, who hadn't been so lucky.

"So Petrov and Big Harold Fitch are in cahoots. Who would've thought it? Guess that's why it was a match made in heaven, right? What's the cargo? Guns? Fitch helping you guys smuggle guns down Mexico way? That it?"

Her new best friend, Misha, shrugged and stood up. "No need to worry about that. You need to worry about getting home to Nicky alive and well. That's my advice. Get the hell outta here because next time I might not be able to save your ass."

"Why don't I just arrest you now, just to get it over with? You can help me find my way outta here so I can get you down to the jail and locked up."

Misha stared at her but didn't take her up on the offer. "Don't think so. Okay, I better get going. You gonna be okay here for a while? Sorry, but I gotta take your weapon so Harold will know you're out of commission. I have to get back down there and tell the old man that you got away. They know you're resourceful. They'll believe me if I have your gun."

Claire considered all that for a moment and realized he was probably right. Besides that, she still had the .38 strapped to her ankle. Reluctantly, she handed the Glock over to him, butt first. "Get that back to me, you got that? It was a gift."

Misha took it and stuck it in his waistband. "I'll do my best. Think you can find your way back to your vehicle? You still dizzy?"

"Yeah, I am, and thanks again for clubbing me senseless and not killing me. You're a sweetie pie, sometimes."

"I didn't want them to think I had a problem with killing you. Or they would've done it themselves. Right then and there. Bullet in the temple. I didn't take pleasure in knocking you out."

"Well, that's a step in the right direction, I guess. Maybe I can return the favor someday. You know, slug you a good one up the side of the head but only to save your skin, of course." Claire sighed, suddenly just wanting to get out of that cabin and away from him, and the sooner the better. "I guess I do owe you, if you really are gonna let me go. Hey, this kid-glove stuff wouldn't just be a bunch of small talk to put me off my guard before you shoot me, would it?"

"Not to worry. I like your gumption. I see now why Nicky's so jealous."

Jealous? How the hell did Chicherin know that? Not that Black turned green-eyed every minute of every day, usually it just happened when Joe McKay was hanging around too much. "Thanks, think I'll wait on expressing any more gratitude until I actually walk out of here alive, though."

Claire watched him shrug into his heavy orange parka and pull on a pair of leather gloves. He jerked up the hood and tightened the drawstrings. "Look, I've got to take your snowmobile down there, or they'll know something's up. If you get lost in this blizzard, just walk with the wind at your back, and you'll eventually hit the road into town. Got that?"

"Yeah." She studied his face. "You sure about going back down there and telling them you screwed up and I got away? Sounds like you might be putting a gun to your own head."

"Lucky for me, they think they need me, and they're afraid of Ivan."

"So, what's the connection with the Fitches and the Petrovs? Might as well tell me that, too."

"Not if I want to stay alive. You better stay out of it, too, if you value your health. Ivan's afraid of Nicky Black's association with you. But the Fitches will put you down like a mad dog if they catch you again tonight, and they'll probably come looking the minute I tell them you got away. Take care, detective, and please, get the hell outta here while you still can. Tell Nicky I said hello. He doesn't care much for me, but he'll probably change his mind after tonight."

Then he opened the door, and was gone, leaving a swirl of snow and sleet blustering inside behind him. The flames darted and danced around and played shadow games on the walls. Then she was alone, and pretty damn shocked that she was. She stood up and punched in Bud's number, but the service was down. Probably because the storm was obliterating the signal. She tried Laurie Dale's number, and then Black's, then the sheriff's, but nothing was going through. So, it appeared that she and her headache were on their own in a snowy minefield of hillbillies and thugs, as per usual, when in life and death situations like this one. She stayed put awhile, trying to wait until her head quit spinning and she could walk straight. After the thudding subsided some, she put on the fleece jacket and then her heavy outdoor gear, pulled out her .38 and kept it in her hand. She sighed heavily, well aware she had a nice long trek ahead of her, wind and snow included, but resigned herself and headed out the door.

Before she got thirty yards away from the cabin, she was accosted by a shadowy figure in a black ski mask that came up quickly behind her and out of the dark night. Her assailant shoved her so hard in the back that she went down flat on her stomach, hit the ground, and got the air knocked out of her. She slid a few feet across ice crusted snow, fumbling to turn and get off a shot, which she did but she missed her assailant, and he was very quick or very practiced, or both. He had his knee on her back before she could draw in enough breath to fight back. He wrenched the gun out of her hand and twisted her arms brutally up behind her, where he secured her wrists with a plastic flex cuff, and then he was frisking her in a very rough and unfriendly but thorough fashion, a lot better than Percy Parker at takedowns. He was big, but not real tall, probably a little under six feet. So it wasn't Misha Chicherin, and unfortunately, it wasn't Bud, either. It appeared her nine lives had just dwindled down to a couple, possibly even the very last one, and that one was suffering some highly perilous circumstances at the moment.

Then she was jerked up by the back of her parka and prodded at gunpoint out ahead of her unknown captor. Her worst fear was that the man was Bones Fitch, but she didn't ask, didn't say anything, just tried to come up with a viable plan to get away. The hike was slow going because it was pitch black outside, but they were facing directly into the wind and the snow-blown drifts were very deep and getting deeper. He had stepped into a pair of crude snowshoes, but didn't offer her any. When she stumbled and landed face-first in deep snow, he just stood back and waited for her to wallow herself back up onto her feet. No gentleman, this guy, uh-uh. This went on for what seemed like five hundred miles. She was snow-blind for all practical purposes within the first few minutes; the darkness was complete and the harsh wind was flinging ice particles into her eyes, but he seemed to know exactly where they were going and prodded her on relentlessly with the business end of his gun barrel. On and on and on, in fact.

One good thing, and there weren't many good things going on at the moment, was that Bud and Laurie had no doubt already found her missing and were searching for her by now, thank God, and they would find the tracks they were leaving. But in the meantime, this tough guy was a serious menace that she had to deal with on her own. No rescuer flying in at the last minute this time. Not a chance. She had already decided that he wasn't out to kill her, or he would have already shot her dead with his long gun when she went down under that first brutal shove. So she still had a chance to survive, albeit not one of high percentage, and if she didn't freeze to death on their way to whatever hellhole to which he was taking her. Lady

Luck had been pretty good to her thus far in her life, but she had a feeling that lady had gone south for the winter and wasn't coming back to check on her any time soon.

When a dark mass that looked like a towering black mountain loomed up in front of them, he shoved her again and she slipped and sprawled forward, landing on her knees. When she gained her feet again, he prodded her toward a narrow crevice down low on the rock cliff, or whatever it was. At that point, Claire's heart absolutely stood still, because then she knew for sure. He had to be Bones Fitch, had to be. If all the scary stories about him were true, and they most likely were, then she was an absolute goner. She did not want to duck into that low hole that led to God knew where. Unfortunately, she had no choice.

Once inside, however, she realized that it didn't look like a cave, but maybe a mine shaft or something. When the guy behind her switched on a high-beam flashlight, she saw low tunnels leading off in three different directions. Despite the howling wind and pelting sleet outside, now that they were inside, it was very dark and very cold and very quiet. As he pushed her down through a passage that was so low that she had to bend over to walk through it, they finally ended up in a large open room that looked like it probably had housed a staging area for miners many years ago. A large fire pit encircled by stones was blazing high and warming the interior, and the smell of smoke was strong and caustic from the pall that drifted up and hung along the ceiling. It was furnished in a way, with an old couch and a couple of easy chairs, and a card table with two folding chairs. There were lanterns hanging around on the walls, providing a dim, flickering light. It was set up like a campsite with a Coleman's stove and two small pup tents with sleeping bags and air mattresses inside. What Claire stared at, though, were the small metal cages lining one wall. The guy prodded her at gunpoint to the nearest one.

"I'm not getting into that cage."

He didn't answer, just knocked her to her knees, shoved her inside with his foot, slammed the door, and set the padlock. After that, he stood outside her cage and stared down at her. He was dressed entirely in heavy winter camouflage clothing and wore a black ski mask and fur-lined cap.

He finally said something. "Know what? Thomas Landers really truly loved you. He told me he did. He cried about you sometimes. I promised him that I'd go get you, if anything ever happened to him. Then the bastard screwed me over, anyway."

Oh, God, Claire thought. Even in death Thomas Landers was putting her through hell. What had he been? A demon? And she had no doubt now. This guy was Bones Fitch, and he had brought her there to kill her.

"You shouldn't've ever had your boyfriend kill him. He was my best friend over in that hospital. And now Bones is really mad at you, too, now that I told him what you did to my friend." All riled up, it seemed, her captor jerked off his hat and ski mask and hurled them down on the ground, very angry, shouting angry words down into her cage.

Okay, he wasn't Bones at the moment. He was the other personality, the nicer one. The one he called Punk. But when she got a glimpse of his face, Claire's heart plummeted like a stone in a well. For such a raging, murderous, lick-happy lunatic, Bones/Punk Fitch didn't look half bad. In fact, he looked exactly like the buttoned-down, preppie-polite, Bud-friendly Patrick Parker himself. As she watched him warily, he shed all his outer wear and threw it aside, apparently the I'm-Gonna-Talk-Your-Arm-Off-Before-I-Beat-You-To-Death kind of psycho. "But you know what else, lady? It's been a real good night out there huntin' prey so far. Storm's a helpin' me sneak up on people. Caught me two real different types tonight. But you? You're the real prize. Bones is gonna love to get you. We can catch one of those goddamned Fitches any night of the week, but you're real special. Too bad Thomas can't be here."

Claire wondered if he could be reasoned with, or if he was too far gone. "Okay, I get it. You're not really Patrick, are you? You're Preston Parker but everybody calls you Punk."

"You're pretty smart, aren't you?"

"Apparently not. You've got me locked up in a cage, don't you?"

"You sure did fall for our little trick, didn't you? You thought I was my big brother."

"So you just made him up as a cover story after you escaped? That it?"

"Hell, no. Patrick was always my oldest brother, all through my whole life. Bones done killed him a long time ago, right where he sat watching the Rams play. We all look alike anyways. Everybody says so. Nobody could tell I wasn't him because Pa always made us keep to ourselves. Nobody knew it was Bones, neither, when he was pretendin' to be Patrick. Not even that Joe friend of yours."

"And Percy and the rest of the guys didn't notice your little charade? Not very observant little boys, are they?"

He grinned and sat down cross-legged on the ground right in front of her, the rifle across his lap. Like he was getting ready to tell her a campfire tale. "They knew, but they're all scared spitless of Bones so they do whatever he tells them to. And he told them he was gonna be Patrick until I got outta that hospital, and they better play along or he'd beat the life straight outta them. Then when I finally came home, Bones and me took turns bein' Patrick."

"So it was you all along when Joe and I came out to the quick stop that first time?"

"Nope, that there was Bones. He told me all about you, though. He thought you was real cute, said he wanted to catch you quick and put you in this here cage. It was me, though, when you came back with Bud that other day. We look almost exactly the same, don't we? We was gonna kill you both right then when you asked to go inside our trailer and make you pay for killin' Thomas and nosing around our place. Couldn't do it, though, 'cause I really did start to like that Bud guy you was with. Me and him are gonna be friends and hunt and stuff, once you're dead and can't tell him about me and Bones, and stuff like that."

After listening to that rather eye-opening, psychotic rendition of friendly chitchat, Claire decided it would be wise to keep her mouth shut. This guy, both of him, was a legit, card-carrying member of Crazytown USA, no doubt about it. In the dim light of the fire and the lanterns, his eyes reflected little white spots of light, as if burning inside with insanity. Entering into some kind of a heated, suicidal argument with him would certainly not be prudent. Doing anything at all with him would not be prudent, even breathing the same air. And this psycho was supposed to be the docile half of the cuckoo duo? Seriously? Sure couldn't swear that by her, no way. But if Punk was indeed the gentlemanly personality, the last thing she wanted was for his other, and hell of a lot more lethal, persona to come out of his sicko psyche and put the screws to her. She'd take her chances with Punk. Chances that wouldn't be so good, either, but better.

On the other hand, Patrick aka Punk aka Bones aka Preston was completely at ease now, gun at his side, leaning back on his palms, all anger swirling away like water down a shower drain, gone quickly indeed. He was now acting as if they were back munching delectable fried chicken and drinking hot chocolate at his redneck quick stop. His tone was ultra-pleasant, but the questions he asked, not so much. "How the hell could you treat Thomas like that? He was crazy about you. And it was real, real true love. But you didn't even care about him, did you? I hated his guts for leavin' me behind and I'm glad he's dead and all that, but listen, all Thomas wanted was a chance to be with you and make you happy. Just like I wanted to be with my girl. You oughta be ashamed of yourself. I knew you was a tease just like Landers said you was, trying to get men to look at you and take you to bed, ever since the first day you first came out to the store and asked Bones and the boys all those nosy questions. Even Bones fell for your crap."

Claire listened to him, but she was also looking around and assessing her chances for escape. That's when she saw another captive in a cage half hidden in shadows along the far wall. There was a man inside it, all right. A young man who looked a whole heck of a lot like a Fitch, but one she'd never seen before. At the moment, he looked as if he had been beaten into submission and couldn't quite focus his eyes. He was still fully dressed, lying on his side, blood coming out of his nose and mouth and wetting the front of his yellow Missouri Tigers sweatshirt. His breathing was shallow and wheezing, as if his lungs weren't quite working right.

Bones/Punk the Double Homicidal Maniac was still shooting the bull. "Know one thing I learned when those bastard Fitches put me in that god-awful hospital place? I learned that this feud thing goin' on between the Fitches and the Parkers was really dumb. Lots of silly stuff goin' on for no good reason. So I thought I'd come back here and me and Bones'd clean it up some, you know, help out our brothers a bit. Bones knew what to do, too. He said the only way to do that was to kill everybody in Fitchville. Just kill 'em all, everybody, men, women, children, and little babies. Just end it up right now, good and tight. Bones says that's the only answer to that kinda grudge fightin'. So that's what we're doin'. He says they deserve it anyways, 'cause they're the ones who put me in that hospital and kept me away from him."

He stopped, and stared at her without blinking for so long that she felt he might have gone unconscious. No such luck. "I could've killed you, too, real easylike, after Bones and me followed you and that other guy to that cabin a few hours back. Bones's out takin' care of him right now. He won't be gone much longer, though. He's gonna walk him out back to our dump site where nobody can find him and then shoot him. After they left, I just waited for you to come outta that cabin so I could catch you. And I'm gonna keep you alive till last and see what Bones wants to do with you. He'll be comin' back any minute now. He told me to bring you in here. He said we'd have lots of fun with you."

Well, Claire sure did hope that old Bones would stay somewhere in the back of this lunatic's brain a mite longer. She also hoped that meant that Misha was not dead and might get away and come find her. But right now and since she was dealing with the good, or at least, better part of the split personality, maybe she could win him over before Bones decided to pay her a less chatty and more deadly visit. "They're gonna find me, you know that, don't you, Punk? I didn't check in like I was supposed to, and so they're gonna know I'm in trouble and come looking for me. Bud and the whole sheriff's department and the FBI. I'm a police officer so they'll mobilize the whole damn highway patrol to search for me. It's only a matter of time before they find us here. Better let me go now before they track you down and lock you up again."

"They aren't gonna find us out here. Even Bud can't, and he's real smart, too. A good guy, and I'm sure glad he wasn't with you tonight, or we'd have to kill him, too. Then he couldn't go huntin' with me. Nobody's ever found us out here, not the Fitches, not our pa, not nobody. See, you gotta know the entrances, and Bones's got 'em hidden real good. So maybe you just oughta shut your trap now. Bones isn't gonna like your sass, no how. Just warning you. Better listen, too. Bones's not as gentle as me. He's gonna whup you up nice and hard, break all your bones up into little bitty pieces. That's what he does best."

Claire took that warning to heart, definitely. She felt shivers rising on her skin and skittering down her spine. She felt fear taking hold of her and not letting go. She had to get control of it. She was in a very bad spot, and she was completely on her own this time. She had better find a way out of that cage and out of that mine and in a great big hurry, too. As Punk moved away and headed for his other victim, Claire put her feet up against the bars and kicked the door as hard as she could. It didn't budge. Across the room, Punk was now dragging the captured Fitch out of his cage. His hands were already tied to-gether, but he had to be dragged, limp-limbed and only half-conscious, which was probably good. Punk hoisted the man into the air until he hung suspended from a hook drilled into the ceiling. His victim's eyes remained shut, his breathing labored. Claire hoped to God that he was unconscious and wouldn't feel whatever Punk was getting ready to do to him.

When Punk turned and looked at her, she stopped kicking on the barred door of her cage. "Hey, you, Claire Morgan, stop that kicking or I'm gonna cut off your feet." He frowned. "Hey, you ever hear a bone break clean in two. That pretty li'l snap it makes. It's like the finest music in the whole world. It's like playin' a fine-tuned instru-ment. That's what we call you guys in the cages, our instruments."

Then, and to Claire's absolute horror, Punk picked up a claw hammer off a table, raised it up in the air, and then brought it slam-ming down in a brutal blow on the man's left shin. She did hear the muffled sound of the bone giving way, and the pain brought the victim around. He shrieked in the most terrible way that Claire had ever heard.

"Stop it, Punk!" she cried desperately. "Just stop it!"

Punk did stop it. As if surprised, he turned around and stared at her, hammer still poised in his hand. "Why? Just 'cause Bones caught 'im don't mean I can't play on him some."

Queasy and trembling, Claire realized in that moment that she was utterly, completely helpless to save that poor man's life, or her own, and her voice showed it, wavering out weak and breathless and pleading and full of despair. "Yes, it does, yes, it does, Punk. Bones'll be mad at you if you take his fun away. He likes to do it himself, doesn't he? He won't like this one bit. Put him back in his cage. Come get me. You caught me."

"But I'm just now gettin' started. Be patient. We'll get to you in good time."

But he did stop his torture for a little while, and appeared to be standing there and thinking about what she'd said. Claire held her breath and hoped to hell that she had gotten through to him. If he would take her out, untie her hands, she could fight him, but she had to get out of the cage first. Then he called out, "I didn't used to hurt people this bad, you know, tie 'em up and beat on 'em, didn't even like it, but ever since I got out of that nuthouse and found my own true love had gone and got married to my own brother, that's all I ever wanna do. Just bust up folks, and I mean, bust 'em up good, too. Know what, I'm just like Bones now. He taught me how to hunt down Fitches just like he does. You know, it just makes me feel good to do it. So just sit back and relax. Your time's a comin' up soon enough. Bones'll wanna do you first, though. Or maybe he'll just keep you for a while and have some fun with you."

And then he went back to work, methodically inflicting damage on his barely conscious captive's body. Claire fought desperately to get out of the cage, kicking at the bars, but she couldn't break through. Finally, she just gave up and shut her eyes and tried to block out the moaning and groaning and cries of pain. She had seen plenty of awful things in her law enforcement career, but she had never witnessed anything like what Punk was doing to his helpless victim. The abuse went on awhile, with various bats and tire irons and hammers, in sort of a horrendously organized way, as if there was a method to his madness. Finally, Punk or Bones or whatever devil he was, stopped his gruesome work, now panting with exertion but smiling, always smiling. Then to her utter horror, he started licking the man's broken-up body, especially at the places where splintered bones had pierced the skin. Oh, God, oh, God. He was a sadist. A walking, talking abomination. He was worse than Thomas Landers had ever been. He took more pleasure in inflicting pain than killing his victim.

Punk continued undressing and licking the poor man for a long time. Claire spent that time frantically jerking and kicking as hard as she could on the bars. Nothing worked, the cage was way too strong. She stopped and tensed up to the consistency of set concrete as Punk approached her again.

"You enjoy that, Claire Morgan? Did you hear my pretty music?"

At that point, Claire didn't know what to do. Play along with him? Or just keep her mouth shut and hope he didn't get a hankering to play one of his creepy symphonies on her? She decided to play along.

"I heard a bone break when you hit him." She almost had to choke those words out, and then she hesitated, watching his expressions for guidance. This guy was a criminally insane psychopathic serial killer, and she was the only one around on whom he could take out his mountains of crazy. Across the room, she could hear a low moaning. His other victim had to be dying, had to be. No human being could endure such a beating and ever function normally again. He couldn't last much longer. She took a deep breath. In, deeply, hold. Out, deeply, hold. Okay, play along. She had to. What else could she do? Decision made, her voice still had a slight tremor when she spoke. "I liked it, I guess. It's different. I never heard any music quite like that before."

"You want to hear some more?"

Oh, God. Her bones were certainly next on his bone-breaking to-do list.

"Do you?"

Now his demented grin became dreamy, happy, appeared almost orgasmic. "Each bone makes its own sweet sound, kinda like different notes, and you can put 'em together once you figure it out. Bones told me that. He's better at it than me. He got lots of practice while I was locked up, but I'm getting better."

Claire breathed in deeply again, desperately trying to calm raw, ragged nerves, trying her best not to give in to pure mindless panic. She did not want the Bones personality to emerge, not here, not now. Dr. LeCorps made it clear to her that Bones was the brute of the family. But how could he do any worse than the terrible injuries she'd just witnessed Punk inflicting? She had to get him to let her out of the cage. That was her only chance. "Why don't you let me out of here, Punk? Let me watch you work, up close, where I can hear the music better."

Punk's eyes went extremely narrow, latched on her face, watchful, examining her in minute detail, no doubt thinking things over in his damaged, defective, demented brain, maybe even chatting about it inside his head with Brother Bones. Then he seemed to wake up from a short doze and laughed and shook his head. Claire's heartbeat wavered, not sure yet. "Don't think I oughta do that. Thomas Landers told me how tricky you are. He said you were always tryin' to escape when he had you tied up, and that you'd turn on him in nothin' flat. So I won't be taking no chances with you, no ma'am. But you can watch me all you want. I'm gonna go now and try to find me another Fitch to play you some tunes on. I try to catch us two instruments every night, you know, one for me to play with and one for Bones. That's how we gonna get rid of all of 'em. Now, if you'll excuse me, I gotta dump that guy over there. We got us a good place to put the bodies 'til spring. Nobody's gonna find 'em, not even Bud and those other cops. You wait right here, you hear?"

"Please untie my hands. It hurts me to lay on them like this. Please, I can't get out. Please take off the cuffs."

Punk thought about it, and then he walked around to the back of her cage, reached in and released her. "Now don't make me sorry I did this."

"No, I won't. Thank you."

Then he grinned at her, the whole time he was donning his winter parka and snow boots and gloves and ski mask and leather fur-lined cap. He headed outside without another word to her, his victim's broken body hanging limply over his shoulder, but she could see that the man was dead. God, now she'd seen with her own two eyes what Blythe and Paulie had suffered at his hands before he killed them. And how many others had died so cruelly in all the many years that Bones Fitch had been running loose and preying on innocent victims?

Claire renewed her efforts to get out, trying to pull loose the steel bars, using every ounce of her strength to dislodge them. They would not budge. She got her feet up against the door again and started kicking out with both feet, again and again, determined to get out before Punk returned. She did not want to be around when Bones emerged and took over. He would not mess around. He would not show mercy. He would not stand outside her cage and chat her up. This time Black was not going to come and rescue her, did not even know that she was in trouble. This time she was alone in the hidden lair of a psychopath with no way out. But she was gonna survive, damn it. She was not going to die in this awful hole. She was gonna get away. Somehow. Some way. She was not going down easy, no way, she was going to fight for her life. She was not going to let him kill her.

Chapter Twenty-five

By the time her captor stomped back into the cave, his coat covered with a crust of snow and ice, Claire was exhausted from kicking and jerking on the bars. Then the scariest madman she had ever run across walked right back up to her cage, smile still on his face. Not a good sign. Rigid with fear and tension, she waited for him to speak, terrified he had become Bones Fitch now, come back to take care of her once and for all.

"Couldn't find nobody else to play. Sorry 'bout that, ma'am. Guess you're gonna have to do. But just think how good you can hear the music, if it's your own bones I'm a snappin' and a poppin'. That's good, right? Maybe I'll go easy on you. Your bones are probably real slender and fragile and stuff, like Blythe's were. You know, easy to crack. But those kind sound good, too, once we got 'em all dried out and hanging up like wind chimes. But it's gonna hurt you, till you pass out all the way. Sorry, I hate to hurt you so much, you bein' Bud's friend, and all, but that's just the way it's gotta be. But then, after that, you won't feel a thing until you're dead and frozen up in the ice out there in the river." He gestured with his hand toward the shaft where he'd earlier disappeared with the body.

Long, rippling, and, yes, unspeakably horrendous shivers started shuddering their way down Claire's spine, like an endless undulating field of wheat blowing in the wind. The very calm and matter-of-fact way he had just described her demise was completely chilling, all right. And okay, now it was pretty damn clear that he planned to beat her within an inch of her life, strike that, beat her to death, and

sooner rather than later. Okay. Okay. Now she was in *big* trouble.
On the other hand, that meant he'd have to get her out of her cage in
order to hoist her up into his favorite pummeling position. At least,
that would give her a fighting chance to get away. She could probably
take this guy down. In a fair fight. Black had taught her a few new
boxing moves to go with her kickboxing prowess. Problem was, she
didn't think serial killers were into fair and gentlemanly rules of
engagement. Not from what she'd seen and heard thus far. But he
wasn't all that big or strong, and he sure wasn't that bright except in
planning heinous criminal deeds and escaping from the guys in white
coats who were probably still chasing him.

Maybe she could trick him. Wrestle his weapon away somehow.
Kill the damn bastard in the most horrible way possible. That one
sounded the best to her. Okay, that was her plan, as weak and unlikely
and impossible as it was. Now all she had to do was wait for him to
decide to release her from the cage and beat her to a pulp, and not
panic in the interim or in the aftermath. Stay calm and carry on, as
the British used to say during the war. Yeah, right. At the moment,
she heartily wished she *was* in England or at least had a grenade to
toss at the freak grinning through the bars at her.

"Where's Bones, anyway?" she asked him. Maybe distraction
would work. Chat, chat, and more chat. "I'd sure like to meet him
before, you, well, you know."

"Play bone music on you?"

Claire frowned. Maybe distraction didn't work with the criminally
insane. He seemed to have a one-track mind with Claire being his
next musical ditty. "Yeah. Guess that's gonna happen, regardless of
what I do or say, right?"

"Hey, it's gonna be so pretty. Really melodious, I promise. It'll
make it worth dyin' for. You'll be smilin' the whole time, promise.
Everybody that we've played tells me that they like it."

Yes, and she probably would, too, after he broke both her legs with
a Louisville Slugger and urged her to utter flowery compliments
about his musicality.

"So, come on now, Claire Morgan. Let's just get you out and
movin' over there and set you up and get all ready for when Bones
comes back." He was leaning down close to the bars now and insert-

ing the key hanging on the chain around his neck into the padlock. "Would you rather that I tie your arms up to that hook Bones put in the ceiling or strap you down on the worktable? You can choose. I don't mind. Whichever floats your boat."

"Whatever makes the music sound better, I guess."

Punk nodded agreement and pulled the lock apart, and then opened the door, still smiling and happy and nuttier than Mr. Peanut. She crawled out on her hands and knees, her legs cramping from being bent inside the small space so long. "I don't think I can walk yet. Give me a minute to stretch my legs, okay?"

"Sorry about that. I do want you to be comfortable. I promise. That was Bones's idea, you know, to put our musical instruments inside those old metal punishing cages so people couldn't really kick their way out. He's real smart."

Instruments, again. "Oh, I know he is. But so are you, Punk. But you don't know how much that I really like you. I knew it the first time I saw you out there with your brothers."

"You do?"

"Oh, yeah. Look, I'll show you."

Punk looked down at the doubled fist she held up, and then she smashed it into his genitals as hard as she could and then even harder into his nose when he bent over in agony. She heard the melodious crunch of his nose when it broke and welcomed the sound. Warm blood spurted out and hit her in the face and chest, and he staggered backwards, grabbing himself. But then he grabbed her parka with one hand as he fell, pulling her down with him. Claire really started punching him in the face then, aiming for his injured nose and front teeth, hitting him with both fists, but she couldn't break his grip on her coat. He hit her in the face, a brutal direct hit on her left eye. Stunned, she dropped back, unable to function for a few seconds. Quickly twisting around, he jumped on top of her and straddled her waist, the blood gushing from his nose and down over her face and hair.

"You bitch!" he screamed into her face. But then he calmed down pretty fast. "You hurt me bad, and Bones is not gonna like it. He's been taking real good care of me since I got back. But hey, did you hear that music when you broke my nose? Huh? Pretty, right?"

Claire was seeing double now, two of him, two of everything, very dazed and not quite thinking clearly. But Punk wasted no time. He jumped off her and dragged her over to the rope that had suspended the other man. He quickly wrapped it around her wrists, knotted it tightly, and then he wrenched her up with one hard jerk that nearly took her arms out of the sockets, and she was hanging in the air, her feet suspended about a foot off the floor. He stood in front of her, wiping blood off his face with a dirty white towel and then holding it against his wounded nose, but he was staring up into her face.

Still woozy, Claire started trying to loosen the ropes binding her wrists together, but he had the knots tied so tightly that it was already cutting off her circulation. He picked up an aluminum baseball bat from the table and held it up where she could see it. She swung her foot out at him, and managed to get him a good kick in the face again. He staggered back a few steps. If he liked broken bones so much, maybe she'd play a catchy tune or two on him before he finished her off.

Standing out of her reach, he wiped off more blood, soaking the towel. His voice was muffled. "You're pretty damn tough, know that? But you sure shouldn't've done that. Now you're makin' me mad."

"Untie me, and we'll see who's tough. C'mon, let's have a little cage fight, right here, right now. What'd you say? See who's really the toughest. You or me. Or are you too chicken to fight a woman? Do you have to tie me up to beat me?"

He laughed a little bit but he sounded uncertain. "You couldn't beat me at nothin'. You're just some skinny girl, and you don't have no badge and gun no more."

"I can fight, all right. Too bad you're too yellow to face me, fair and square."

At that, Punk frowned some more and thought some deep thoughts for a second, or two. "I'm not gonna fall for that shit. But know what? I'm a gonna leave you for Bones to play. Because, even though you really got me good, probably broke my nose, and all that, you do got some guts to you. Most of our instruments don't fight back, once we get 'em down here in those cages. They just hang there and take it and beg and cry. You're pretty damn different, but kinda stupid, too, 'cause you're just gonna make both of us real mad." Now he looked puzzled about it all. Glancing back toward the entrance to the shaft, he said, "Can't figure what's keepin' Bones. He shoulda been back by now."

"Maybe you oughta go out there and find him. Maybe he got lost in the storm. Maybe a Fitch shot him down and he's hurt and needs your help."

"Bones don't get lost nowhere. He don't get shot. He don't get hurt. He don't never need any help."

After that, Claire just hung there, hoping to hell Bones never came out to meet her. She sure didn't want to trigger that. She stared at him, still trying to work the knots free with her fingertips. They gave some but not enough.

Punk leaned against his worktable and stared up at her awhile, and then he said, "Know what?"

He waited as if she was supposed to take some kind of wild guess. She debated the wisdom of just waiting until somebody came and rescued her. *Who*, she didn't know, *when* she didn't know, but there were people out looking for her by now and had been for some time, she did know that much. She still had a chance. So she said nothing, and let him contemplate the meaning of life or whatever loony tunes he was playing inside his evil mind.

"Aren't you even gonna guess?"

"Not much point in it."

"Okay, then, I'll just show you what I done." He started unbuttoning his shirt, and Claire watched warily, hoping that didn't mean what she was afraid it meant. She had expected assault and pain and broken bones and lots of other horrible stuff, but not sexual assault, not rape. But, and lucky for her, Punk stopped when he got to his insulated underwear and just pulled the top all the way up to his chin. Claire stared at the scars on his chest, just above his nipples. ANNIE. It said Annie, all right, her birth name, the name Thomas Landers called her. Scratched out in some bizarre kind of homemade tattoo.

"Thomas did it, too, carved your name in his chest just for you, cut it with a needle. Then your boyfriend done gone and shot him dead. I'm gonna get him, too, when he comes out here lookin' for you."

· "Well, good luck with that. He'll kill you with his bare hands if you don't let me go."

Punk frowned. "Better not say nothin' like that to Bones when he gets here. He's real sensitive to that kinda thing. And he protects me from people like you."

So Claire just hung there, limp and completely unable to free herself. For the first time in her life, she realized that she was probably going to die. Right here, right now. Death was finally going to catch up with her in this awful place with this awful man. Her luck had run out. She was never going to get out of this alive. Never in a million years. She was never going to see Black again. Never see Bud or Harve or anybody else, not ever again. The revelation stunned her. She had always known she might get killed in the line of duty, that it was possible, but she had never allowed herself to accept it. Until now. Now she was accepting it. She was going to die the most cruel death imaginable, here alone with a madman. She was going to be beaten to death, just like the caged man and Blythe and Paulie and God only knew how many others.

Trying to swallow down the rising horror and accept her fate with some kind of courage, she began to hope that Punk or Bones, or whichever one of them killed her, would play his bone music staccato style and get it over with. But he had taken plenty of time with the other man, time she had witnessed and now would experience herself. But no, no way would she let that happen. She'd goad him into finishing her off quickly, if she had to. She sure didn't want to be awake and aware when the obscene body licking started. She resigned herself, tried to prepare for the first brutal swing of that bat, tried to control the paralyzing fear that was gripping her. She did not want to die, not here, not like this.

Then suddenly, in the utter stillness, in the endless waiting for the violence to commence, a voice rang out in the distance, echoing down the mine shaft, a woman's voice, like an angel calling down from heaven.

"Claire! Are you in here?"

"He's got a gun. . . ." Claire screamed to Laurie Dale, but that was all the warning that Claire could get out before he busted her mouth and nose with a quick jab of his fist. She felt an explosion of pain, went limp on the ropes, head lolling forward, only half conscious, but she heard him running. Heard multiple shots fired, heard somebody fall and crash into something. Then somebody was jerking her head up by the hair, and it was Laurie Dale's beautiful green eyes that Claire saw, worried and frantic and focused on Claire's face.

"Claire, Claire, can you hear me?"

Claire managed to nod, but then the ropes were being cut and she collapsed down into the FBI agent's arms. "I got him, Claire. He's dead. He's not going to hurt you anymore. Oh, God, look at your face. What did he do to you?"

"How did you . . . ?" Claire kept trying to talk, but her injured mouth wouldn't quite move the way she wanted it to. She could taste her own blood, warm and metallic and sickening.

Laurie was on her knees on the floor beside her now. "I came out to check on you when you didn't come back, saw the tracks in the snow leading down onto the Fitch property to some shack and then more footprints led me out here. C'mon, we gotta get you outta here and call this in."

Laurie dragged Claire up onto her feet, and Claire found she could walk and her dizziness began to clear a bit. Punk/Bones was laying on his back on the ground several yards away, the back of his head completely gone. Laurie was a good shot with that .357, all right, and thank God that she was.

"Think you can walk? I got the snowmobile right outside. All you have to do is get to it," Laurie said anxiously, still supporting Claire with one arm around her waist.

"Yeah, I'm okay, I think. I'm okay now. Thank God, you found me. He was gonna beat me to death. He had the bat in his hand."

"I was afraid something like this was gonna happen. I know the way these guys operate only too well. We're goin' in on them tonight, raiding Fitchville on the gun charges. . . ."

A sharp *blam* suddenly shattered the quiet and a slug slammed into the wall right behind them. They both hit the ground and scrambled for cover. That's when Claire got a glimpse of the man who'd fired at them. He was now kneeling over Punk's lifeless body, and when he looked up, Claire couldn't believe her eyes. Oh, God, Bones Fitch was *not* a figment of Punk's imagination as Dr. LeCorps had believed. Punk really did have a twin brother. Bones Fitch was real and alive, and he was back and he was armed and he was angry. She watched him throw back his head and wail plaintively for his dead twin brother. Laurie didn't need any more encouragement. She rose on her knees and got off a couple of quick shots, but Bones saw her and was too quick. He returned fire, hitting Laurie as she tried to scramble away. She was knocked backwards and fell on her side, her weapon skidding off on the dirt floor toward Bones Fitch. Laurie groaned and tried to push herself up, but then just collapsed and didn't move. Claire took off in the opposite direction and headed for the dark passage where Punk had exited with the dead man's body. Bones got off a shot at her just as she reached the first turn in the tunnel.

The shaft was low and narrow, and she heard another shot go off behind her, and then she heard the bullet ricocheting off the stone walls and knew Bones was hot on her heels. Good, at least he wasn't finishing off Laurie. She fled through the frigid darkness, unable to see anything, feeling her way along the cold damp rock walls with both hands, but she could smell fresh air and feel a breeze on her face and she knew that the passage was leading her outside the mine. She ran faster, stumbling on the loose shale covering the ground, cutting her palms on the sharp edges of the rocks, hoping Laurie wasn't dead, hoping she'd stay alive and get away somehow, but she could hear Bones Fitch coming hard down the passage after her.

Minutes later, she burst from a low arched opening and into the whipping blizzard winds outside. Icy sleet hit her and sent her backwards a step. She could barely see but realized she was up high on a cliff, a dead end with no way down. There was a frozen river below, one that was enclosed by high granite walls. She tried to run down the steep hill in front of her but slipped on the slick ground, her feet going out from under her, and then she hit hard on her side and slid all the way to the bottom on her back and then farther out onto the frozen river.

Another shot rang out behind her, and she tried to get up without falling and slide her feet out over the ice toward the opposite side of the river, but then in the reflected light off the snow she saw the dead bodies. They were all around her. Five or six bodies, at least, lying on the ice, some half in and half out of the water, like Paulie Parker had been, all frozen into stiff and grotesque human ice sculptures. She grabbed at the nearest one, shocked when she realized that it was Misha Chicherin. She tried to pull his legs out of the water and realized that he'd been wounded in the chest. Bones had shot him and disposed of him with the others. She dropped down behind him and tried to use his body for a barrier against the gunfire.

Then he made a little moan, and she realized that somehow he was still alive. She couldn't think about that very long because Bones was shooting down at her from the higher elevation, still up in the opening where she'd started her slide. His bullets were slamming into the ice all around her. She heard the crackling and sucking sounds as the ice began to give way under her weight as the rounds cut through it, and then the ice suddenly cracked wide open, and Claire and Misha both plunged down into the dark frigid water. She held on to him as best she could, trying to keep his head out of the water and break through the gradually splintering ice, trying to get them away from the shooter, but then Bones was out there on the ice with her, coming out toward her, only ten yards away, screaming curses, his shrill voice blown away on the wind. He had his gun pointing straight down at them, and then Claire remembered that Misha carried her Glock and the Beretta at his waist under his parka.

Frantically, praying that Bones hadn't disarmed him, she jerked at the tail of his coat, trying to find the guns, and when her fingers finally touched the icy grip of her Glock, she got hold of it, jerked it out, and aimed it up at the man above her, her back braced against Misha's shoulder, praying it would still fire, and then pulled the trigger and kept pulling it.

Bam, bam, bam, bam, bam, bam.

The slugs hit Bones Fitch dead center in his chest, all of them, in a tight pattern that sent him reeling backwards a few steps and then sprawling down on the ice. He broke through and floated there on his back. Panting, heart thumping, adrenaline surging through her veins, her waterlogged coat dragging her down, Claire tried desperately to get her arms up on the ice and pull both of them out, but she just couldn't manage it, she was just too tired and Misha and her wet clothes were too heavy. She hung on as best she could, her feet not touching bottom, grasping Misha's coat tightly, shivering and shaking with cold, and trying to summon enough strength to climb out of the water and onto the ice.

Then she heard the retorts of more gunfire not far away, and somebody calling her name. She hoped to God that it was Laurie Dale, still alive and looking for her. She lifted the gun in her hand somehow, and fired a couple of rounds up into the air to pinpoint her location and struggled to hold both of them out of the water while the ice continued to crackle and break up all around them.

Then Laurie was there, coming out toward her, wounded arm hanging uselessly at her side, but still up on her feet, her coat off and flung out for Claire to grab on to, and Claire did grab it and clung to it with all her remaining strength as she was slowly pulled in, ice breaking and coming apart in front of her as she moved through it and in toward the snowy bank. She had a death grip on the back of Misha's waterlogged orange jacket, her fist pretty much frozen into place on the handful of material she was clutching. But then she was out on the ground, gasping and shivering and trying to help Laurie drag the wounded man out onto the snow. Claire managed to tell Laurie to fire shots to summon help and hoped to hell Joe McKay was at home and could hear them echoing over at his place, and then she just collapsed on her back beside the unconscious Russian, sleet pelting her body. Laurie emptied her gun into the air and covered up Claire with her own coat and then stumbled off on foot to find the snowmobile.

After that, Claire just lay there alone in the dark, so very cold, completely still, as if she were already frozen like the other corpses in the water, thinking that freezing to death wasn't going to be so bad, if it was her time to die, and a lot better than her bones being smashed apart with a bat. In time, even those thoughts faded away and she began to feel sleepy and content, and slowly entered into a lovely dream where she was snuggled up close to Black at home in their bed, warm and cozy, his arms around her, where she always felt safe and secure and happy. That was the last conscious thought she had, except that death seemed to be slowly creeping up on her, pulling her away as the grim reaper was purported to do. Finally, those thoughts faded, too, and it was just cold and dark with the sound of wind and blowing snow, and then even that faded away, and there was only nothing, nothing at all.

Epilogue

Pacing the floor and worried sick about Claire, Nick Black hadn't been able to get hold of her or anybody else on their cell phones, the heavy snow making connections impossible for hours. He couldn't get her coordinates on GPS, either, and didn't have a clue where she was or what she was doing. But he wasn't willing to wait any longer and was ready to go out searching for her when his cell phone finally rang around two o'clock in the morning. Caller ID said that it was Claire. Damn it, she was way out of line this time. She should have called him and let him know where she was. What the hell was she doing out in a raging blizzard in the middle of the night?

"Claire! Where the hell are you? You all right?"

"Hey, Nick. Listen, it's Joe McKay. I'm at the hospital. . . ."

Black went rigid. "Where's Claire? Is she okay?"

"Well, actually she's pretty messed up, but she's gonna be okay, they think."

Black shut his eyes, and his heart pretty much just stopped. "What happened to her?"

"She got herself into some trouble with those maniacs she was tracking. I heard gunfire out in my backwoods, and I took off out there on the snowmobile to see what was going down. That's when I found them."

"Found who? For God's sake, Joe, tell me what happened!"

"Claire, and some FBI agent she knows named Laurie Dale. Claire was lying unconscious in the snow, wet and half frozen. God, Nick, I thought she was dead, for sure."

"Oh, God."

"Somebody worked her over pretty good. The Dale woman was gunshot but still on her feet, and some guy with them had been shot, too, and was barely breathing. I got them all back to my house as quick as I could and wrapped them up in blankets, and then got them down here to Canton County Medical in my truck. Claire's asking for you. Told me to call you and tell you that she was okay and ask you to come to the hospital."

"I'm on my way."

Despite the inclement weather, Black made it to the hospital in the Humvee in less than ten minutes. He pushed through the emergency room doors and found Joe McKay just inside the entrance, leaning against the wall and waiting for him.

"Where is she?"

"They just moved her into a private room, just down there." McKay pointed down the hospital corridor to his right. "Room 157. She's waiting for you. Afraid you'd be worried."

"Damn right, I'm worried. But thanks, Joe, for everything. I owe you."

"I better warn you, Nick. She doesn't look so good."

Black took a bracing breath. "Thanks again for getting her here. I mean it, Joe."

"I know. I just wish I'd been there when it all went down."

"Yeah. Me, too."

Black hurried down the hallway, pushed through another set of swinging doors and found Claire's room right next to the nurses' station. Claire was inside, sitting up in a hospital bed, her face turned to the window, wrapped up in electric blankets with a warming lamp focused on her. At first, he was relieved because she wasn't on IVs or flat on her back and unconscious. Then she turned her head and looked at him. Nick's stomach plummeted, and the floor seemed to drop out from under him. Appalled, he stared wordlessly at her. Her left eye was black and swollen shut, the other one getting there, her nose was packed with gauze to stop the bleeding, maybe even broken, and her bottom lip was stitched up and twice its normal size. Neither of them said anything for a moment. Black just tried to absorb the shock he felt on seeing the extent of the damage to her face.

Then Claire said, "'Sup, Black?"

Definitely not amused, Black moved over to the bed. "Oh, God, Claire, what the hell happened to you?" He reached out and picked up a strand of her hair. "You've got blood in your hair."

"It's not all mine. I got in a few good punches." Claire tried to smile, but it looked more like a painful little grimace. Her voice was hoarse. "Hey, I'm fine. Really. Just a little cold. Ran into some trouble tonight. Kept wishing that you'd show up and bail me out again but couldn't get through to you. Or anybody else. Big blizzard going on, and all that."

Black couldn't manage even the slightest smile. He kept shaking his head. "If I'd known you were in trouble, I would've been there."

Sitting down on the edge of the bed, Nick picked up her hand and pressed it to his lips. He tasted dried blood. God only knew whose blood it was. The knuckles on her hand were cut and swollen, but she still had on her engagement ring. It was caked with dirt and more dried blood. For a moment, he just felt ill, really, really sick, down deep in the pit of his stomach. Overwhelmed with helplessness and hopelessness and the inability to stop terrible things from happening to her, he just sat there and stared down at her injured hand. In that moment, he wasn't at all sure that he could deal calmly with the seriousness of the situation anymore. He wanted to slug somebody. He wanted to yell and curse and ram his fist through a wall. He wanted to beat whoever had done this to her to a bloody pulp. He tried to gain control but couldn't quite pull it off, so he just sat there and said nothing.

"C'mon, Black, please don't look like that. I'm okay. See. Just a little bit worse for the wear, that's all. I'll be okay after I get some sleep. I'm just really, really tired."

"You're not okay, Claire. You're terribly hurt. Your face alone looks like you've been hit by a damn truck." Suddenly, Black felt so angry that he could just barely contain it. He stood up. "Where's your chart? I want to see what they did to you."

Claire didn't answer, just sat there, all beaten and abused and watched him move to the end of the bed. He jerked out the metal chart and skimmed through the reports. Good God Almighty. Hypothermia, mild frostbite on her legs and feet, possible concussion, two cracked ribs, lacerated nose and mouth, cuts, abrasions, bruises, contusions, on and on and on. She was damn lucky to be alive. Then Black's fury got the best of him, and almost overwhelmed him completely, but he somehow managed to fight it down. It wasn't so easy. He wanted to explode and rant and rave and yell at her for putting herself into that kind of danger.

"Who did this to you?" His voice was now so low and controlled and gruff that he barely recognized it himself.

Claire was frowning at him, and it looked as if that effort was hurting her bruised, swollen face. "You need to chill, Black. Hey, you know that guy we were looking for? Punk Fitch? Well, I found him. And his very real twin brother, too. Guy named Bones. And get this. Bones has been impersonating Patrick Parker all the time Punk was in the hospital. Apparently, Patrick really was one of their brothers but Bones killed him and took his place somewhere along the line." She stopped there and wet her stitched lip. The talking was hurting her, all right, but she continued as if it weren't. "And he played that role pretty damn well, too, enough to fool me and Joe, and Bud, too. You see, all the Parker boys look a lot alike, especially with the beards they wear. His brothers were so deathly afraid of Bones while Punk was locked up at Fulton that they went along with whatever he said." She paused there, swallowed, wet her lips again, and shut her eyes for a moment. "You know, killing your brother in front of your other brothers is an awfully effective deterrent to ratting somebody out. The shrinks made the wrong call, too, with that split personality thing. Except that they both were homicidal maniacs, I'll give them that."

"Tell me everything that happened tonight."

Claire sighed and started to relate a very ugly story that began with his phone call to her earlier that evening. Nick listened, his frown growing deeper and more disbelieving as she talked, halfway shocked that she managed to escape alive from that hellish lair, or mine shaft, or whatever the hell it was. Despite her condition, Claire had been lucky, and extremely so.

Unfortunately, Claire was not finished. "And there's more. Your old Moscow buddy, Ivan Petrov? One of his guys sucker punched me, believe it or not. A guy named Misha Chicherin, or at least that's what he told me it was. He works for Petrov, and it seems Petrov is hot and heavy into a little gunrunning business down Mexico way with our pious little Fitchville friends." She stopped there, took a breath. "The FBI's been all over that with surveillance, and they're probably raiding the place as we speak, or will when they hear about what happened to Laurie Dale out there tonight. But Misha let me go because of you and your brother's connections. So you did save me in a way, so thanks for that. Misha wasn't so lucky. He might not make it. Last I heard he was still in surgery."

Nick said nothing at all to any of that, but he didn't like a single word of it. Claire laid her head back against the pillow and closed her eyes, as if all the explanations had finally taken their toll. She sighed heavily. "So, Black, how about we talk about the rest of this stuff later, huh? My mouth hurts pretty much now, and I am just so damn tired I can't think straight."

"I'm not sure you should go to sleep just yet. If you've got a concussion, you might ought to stay awake as long as you can. Just to make sure."

"Dr. Atwater said it wasn't that bad, a mild one, so I'll be fine. They're gonna give me sedatives so I can rest tonight and quit thinking about what happened. Don't think I need them, though. I can barely stay awake."

Nick leaned forward and gently fingered the giant bump and stitched laceration behind her ear. He felt his teeth clamp down hard and his fists ball up so tight that his nails bit into his palms. He was still so furious that those animals had dared attack her and lock her up in a cage that he couldn't even speak.

Claire opened her eyes again and studied his face. Her left eye was so swollen that he could barely see it. "You're mad, right?"

"Well, no. Not at you. What makes you think I'm mad?"

"Your jaw is clenching like crazy, and you haven't even tried to climb in bed with me, which is a first."

"Oh, for God's sake, Claire. How do you think I feel? Seeing you all beat up like this?" Black paced a few steps away from the bed, shook his head, and inhaled a couple of deep, calming breaths. After a minute or two, he turned back around. "I'm just glad you're here now, safe and alive. I'm not mad. I'm just upset that you got hurt again."

Claire watched him and then he watched her wet the stitches in her cut lip with the tip of her tongue again. She was in more pain than she was letting on. There was no way that she couldn't be. She had a couple of broken ribs, for heaven's sake.

"Oh, God, Claire, I just can't take seeing you like this. What did they do, just tie you up and hit you with their fists?"

"Kind of, I guess, but not exactly. I tried to fight back. I know I don't look like it, but I did get in a coupla good licks and a kick or two before it was over. They were going to beat me to death, but luckily Laurie Dale showed up and that didn't happen. I'm gonna have to buy her a great big thank-you present."

Yeah, luckily. After listening to that less than reassuring little speech, Black paced over to the window and stared outside at the falling snow. The wind was still gusting hard, billowing snow up in swirls and whorls around the light poles in the hospital parking lot. He had just about reached his breaking point, was maybe half an inch from losing his cool entirely. Fortunately, a nurse walked in and gave Claire some pills out of a little white cup, helped her suck water out of a straw, and then checked her body temperature. Black recognized her from his own stay at the hospital. Her name was Chris Dale Cox, and she was friendly and very good at her job.

"Well, now, we've almost got you back to normal," Chris was saying to Claire, switching off the warming lamp and patting Claire's hand. "You're almost there, detective. Just get a good night's sleep and you'll feel a whole lot better."

Claire appeared to be more concerned with her friends' medical conditions, which was par for the course with her. "What about Laurie Dale? You sure she's gonna be all right?"

"She just came out of surgery. They repaired the gunshot wound to her shoulder, and she lost a lot of blood before your friend, Joe, got her down here. She's in recovery now. She's gonna be fine. Her husband, Scott, and her parents are all down there with her."

"What about the other guy? Misha Chicherin?"

Hesitation. "I'm afraid that's still touch and go. The bullet missed his heart, so that's good, but it still did a lot of damage. The surgery is going well, and the good Lord willing, he'll pull through somehow."

When the nurse finished straightening the bedcovers and left the room, Claire shivered a little. "You see, Black? Everything's looking pretty good now. Laurie and I are gonna be just fine. Misha's gonna pull through, too, I know he will. So no need to get all bent out of shape and worry yourself half to death. I'm alive and talking and walking, so that's the important thing, right? Just in time for the wedding, too." Claire was trying to smile again, and it hurt her again. Which made him angry again. Good God, with all his money, his training, his security, his supposed ability to protect her, why the hell couldn't he do it?

"What am I going to have to do, Claire? Lock you up with me and throw away the key. Goddamn it, this is getting old."

Claire managed another weak smile and ignored everything he said. "You gonna get up in this bed and help me warm up, or not?"

Black was still fuming, but he wasn't about to turn that down, so he stretched out beside her on top of the warm blankets and pulled her close, then cringed at how cold her skin still felt to the touch. But inside him, frustration was building up with nowhere to go, and he was still so damn enraged that those psychopaths had put their hands on her and abused her that he couldn't think about anything else.

"Somehow you just don't seem overly happy to see me alive and breathing." Claire was half-heartedly joking again, but Black knew that she was also well aware of how he felt. He knew that. He just didn't think any of it was the least bit amusing.

"This is not funny. I could have lost you tonight. I was just sitting home working in my office, totally unaware that you were being beaten up and held captive by a couple of madmen. I had no idea that you were even anywhere near danger. You told me you weren't. I should've been there. Damn it, I should've come up there."

"No, you shouldn't have. I was doing my job, that's all, and it turned bad on me. C'mon, Black, when you called, I told you I was fine, and I was. Then. But some bad guys found me after that, but I'm here now, with you, safe and sound. Just a little cold and with just a little bit of a headache. It could've been so much worse. I could be in a coma again. I've been hurt a lot worse than this. That's the good thing, and you know it. You are definitely overreacting this time."

"Yeah, that's the good thing, all right. You're alive. It's just hard for me to stay calm after a bunch of guys beat the hell out of your face."

Claire didn't answer for a while, and then she spoke against his shirt, not looking at him. "I was there when he beat a guy to death, Black. I couldn't do anything about it. He had me locked up in that cage and I couldn't get out. I just had to listen while he hit that man over and over with a bat and then a hammer and then his fists. It was the worst thing I've ever heard. Just awful, the way that man suffered. I can't even stand to think about it."

Wincing at the pain and remembered horror in her words, all Black could think about was that it could have been her who died that way, that he could've found her body in that hellhole, dead and beaten beyond recognition. "Well, try not to think about it, okay? It's over now. There was nothing you could do. It's not your fault, Claire. You would have stopped it, if you could have."

Claire sighed some more and pressed herself in closer against his side. "Well, let's just talk about something else, think about something else. Plan the wedding, maybe, since we're just lying here and I'm too weak and sleepy to do anything else."

How Claire could continue kidding around after what she'd been through was nothing less than incredible to Black. She had just escaped a life and death struggle and barely survived to tell about it. But that had always been her way of coping. Then it occurred to him that she was probably making light of it for his benefit, trying to make it easier for him to handle. After that realization, Black felt himself start to relax. Okay, she really was all right. She was still breathing and not hurt terribly bad. Hell, she had been hurt a lot worse than this in the past, just like she'd said. The guys who hurt her were already dead, so he couldn't go find them and blow their heads off, which is what he really wanted to do. He had to live with what had happened to her, what happened to her all the time. He didn't like it, in fact, he hated it, but he had better get used to it if he wanted Claire in his life. And he did. That was the problem. A problem he couldn't quite seem to solve.

Although she had to be exhausted, Claire was still trying to stay awake and change the subject. "I know. How about us having a shooting contest as soon as I get outta here? Ten rounds with our new nines, and whoever wins gets to plan the wedding?"

And she was talking about the wedding to get his mind off her condition, too. And maybe her own mind off what she'd been through. That was pretty damn obvious. He played along, tried to make his tone light. "That's hardly fair, Claire. I'm a damn good shot with a handgun. I'll definitely win, and I thought you said that you wanted to plan everything."

"No way. I'm the one with the sharpshooting medals. You don't have a chance against me."

"I know what, sweetheart. Let's just be real quiet now and let you get some rest."

So they were quiet for a while, so long that Black thought that she had gone to sleep, but then she spoke, very softly, not looking at him. "I thought I was gonna die out there. I thought my life was over, that I would never see you again. I thought about how upset you'd be when you found my body." Beside him, her body began to tense up, and Black could almost feel her fear. "I pretty much made my peace, Black. I accepted that I wasn't getting out alive, that I was going to die. I've never felt anything close to that way before. I really, truly thought that I'd die alone in that awful place. Then Laurie came, and I thought it was all over and I was gonna live, that we had killed him, that everything was all right. Then the other guy showed up and shot her down, and I had to fight for my life again. I got him, though, shot him in the heart, but I was so tired then, Black. The last thing I remember was lying alone in the snow in the dark, just waiting to die."

Black squeezed his eyes shut, felt a shudder move deep inside him. He finally found some words. "But you didn't die, Claire. You need to quit reliving it, let it go. You're okay now, you're here with me, and we're going to figure out a way to keep you safe from now on. I'm going to do that, Claire. I've got to. This kind of thing cannot go on any longer."

Claire didn't say anything, but Black knew she was suffering now, reliving the trauma. He needed to do something to get her mind off what had happened. "I've got big plans for us as soon as I get you the hell out of this hospital."

"Yeah?"

"Yeah, I sure do. Plans concerning that trip to Tahiti. We're going, and I don't want to hear any argument about it. And we're going to stay there for a month, maybe two, maybe even a year. Hell, Claire, maybe we'll never come back. That suits me just fine. And we're going to get married there, too, maybe. I'm sick and damn tired of finding you all shot up or beaten up or lying half dead in some hospital bed." He stopped for a moment, but he kept his voice nice and low and pleasant. "And we're going to talk some more about that private detective agency I offered to set up for you. Okay? That's back on the table again, you hear me, Claire? And we're going to leave in the morning, first thing, as soon as you're warm enough and back up on your feet."

Claire said nothing for a moment, didn't even open her eyes. Then she said, "Okay."

Black wasn't quite sure he could believe his ears. "Okay? Just okay? That's all you've got to say to all that?"

Her eyes remained closed, but Claire found his hand and threaded her fingers through his, the strong sedative apparently beginning to take effect. Her voice was now slow and slurred and sleepy. "Yeah, that's all I got to say. Tahiti sounds nice and warm and fine with me. So I'm in. But don't forget Jules Verne, if we're really stayin' for a year. . . ."

After that, Claire slept deeply and peacefully without moving and hopefully without dreaming. Black lay there with his arm around her, her head resting against his chest, her arm across his waist, and he stared at the ceiling and then at her bruised face and then at her split lip and fought down more anger and regret and frustration. But he had been nothing if not serious. He had meant every single word he'd said to her. Tahiti sounded good to him, too, all right, very good. So did a wedding. Maybe elopement was the way to go, after all, fast and easy and alone and happy and lying on a private beach with Claire alive and uninjured for a change. No snow, no sleet, no broken bones, no guns, no crazy lunatics with baseball bats and hammers. Oh, yeah, he could live with that, all right. Maybe he'd buy a beach house there, one that was a million nautical miles away from her police work.

But right now, and as far as he was concerned, tomorrow morning and a flight to paradise could not come soon enough. After a very long time spent lying there and thinking things through, Black came to terms with what had happened. Okay. Good enough. She was all right. Things were going to turn out okay. It was going to take her some time to get over what happened, but maybe, just maybe, she had finally had enough, too. Now maybe he could get some rest. Maybe he and Claire could even have a normal life together someday. Yeah, maybe they could. Stranger things had happened. Sighing one last time, Black finally shut his eyes, and eventually fell asleep, still holding Claire in his arms.

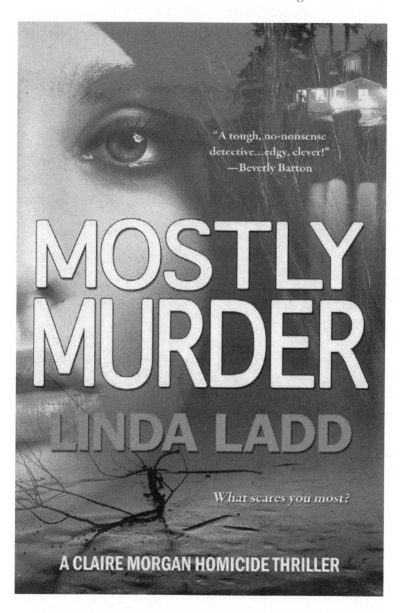

"A tough, no-nonsense
detective...edgy, clever!"
—Beverly Barton

MOSTLY MURDER

LINDA LADD

What scares you most?

A CLAIRE MORGAN HOMICIDE THRILLER

Prologue

A Very Scary Man

The first time the scary man realized that he liked to frighten people was when he was twelve years old. His little sister was his favorite victim because she was only six and small for her age. Late one night, he sneaked into the room where Mandy was sleeping so peacefully, snoring with little whiffs and snorts because of her allergies, and all snuggled up under the covers with her pink stuffed Easter bunny and her three favorite Barbie dolls. Earlier that day, he had waded through the brush lining the bayou until he finally caught a tiny black garter snake. So, now, at last, it was show time.

Grinning, trying not to laugh with anticipation, he opened up the white Kroger's plastic sack and dumped the wriggling little reptile onto Mandy's pink Cinderella pillow. He let out a loud hissing sound so she'd wake up, and then he took off for the doorway. But the snake had already slithered onto her and stopped right on top of her chest. He paused in the hall and waited with tingling nerves. Her *Snow White* night light was on beside her bed, and when she sat up, all flushed and sweet with sleep, she immediately laid eyes on the snake wriggling around on her blanket. The little girl let out a shriek like he just couldn't believe. She probably wet her pants, too, he thought, racing back to his own room, ready to put on the best acting job of his life.

The greatest lesson he learned that night was that if he was very careful and planned ahead, he could escape punishment for something truly horrible that he'd done. So, he was back in his own bed in his own room when his parents came rushing down the hall to see what was wrong with their little darling. He got up again, feigning sleepiness and concern like the little angel he wasn't, but he was laughing so hard inside when he remembered the absolute terror on his sister's face.

Unfortunately, he thought it best to go back to bed and pretend disinterest in Mandy's drama. So he had to miss all the screaming and sobbing and hysterics, not to mention his dad's frantic and comedic efforts to catch the harmless little snake. Truth was, of course, he really didn't want to hurt his baby sister. He loved Mandy a lot; she was just the most precious little thing in the world. But he loved to see the utter fear on her face even better, and that was the Gospel truth. He loved mind-boggling distress contorting anybody's face, actually. As long as they were absolutely terrified and showed it, it was good for him.

Keenly disappointed that he had been robbed of seeing the hour-long ordeal of rocking her back to sleep, he vowed that someday he wouldn't have to hide his secret obsession. Someday, somewhere, he would find someone that he could torment for his pleasure and never have to miss a single tear or shriek or scrambling flight away from perceived mortal danger. He would plan and plan and plan some more, until he could enjoy himself with no fear of capture or punishment or retribution or grounding. Yeah, and that day was gonna be so sweet. Oh, yeah. He could hardly wait.

And that day came a lot sooner than he expected, right after his Aunt Pamela and Uncle Stanley came to visit for the weekend, because they brought along their tiny little baby boy, Donnie, who was only eighteen months old. So the good thing about that was that the baby couldn't talk yet. Not a damn word, except for babbling for his mama and dada. Yep, he was the perfect little victim with his red curly hair and big blue eyes and chubby little cherub's face. His mommy and daddy loved him so much that they doted on him incessantly, snuggling him and spoiling him and kissing him and hugging him, as if he were the greatest kid ever born. Yeah, it was little Donnie this and little Donnie that and little wonderful Donnie, blah, blah, blah. It was downright disgusting.

Hell, his own parents had never treated him like he was their darling little angel. Of course, he wasn't an angel. He was a devil, really,
and proud of it, or maybe he was more like the murderous demons
he saw in scary movies. He had never killed anybody or driven
anyone nuts, not yet anyway, but he didn't really consider that to be
out of the question someday in the future. Not little Donnie, though,
not right now. He was way too little and sweet and innocent to kill,
and he was his cousin, after all.

When the adults decided they wanted to go out for dinner and
dancing at the country club, he was elated and quickly offered to
babysit the two little kids. His mom and dad and aunt and uncle
thought that he was just so loving and kindhearted to offer, which
gave him a really big edge on having two little victims to torment,
not to mention how he laughed inside his head at how stupid
grownups were. For obvious reasons, his sister begged to go along
with the adults, but they wouldn't let her, of course. But she wouldn't
tell on him; he had put the fear of God into her about tattling a long
time ago. So, instead, Mandy ran upstairs as soon as their parents
left and found a hiding place under her bed where he couldn't get at
her without poking her out with a broom handle. He didn't care. He
had somebody even better that he could make cry.

Angelic little Donnie didn't mind being left alone with him, not
at all. In fact, he ran over to him and held up his sturdy little arms
as if he wanted to be held. So he picked the toddler up and swung
him around and made him giggle with joy. But then, within moments, he felt *the need*, the one he just could not resist or control
anymore. Laughing, too, he tossed the little boy way up into the air
and suddenly screamed up at him like some kind of a crazy banshee.
For a second, the little kid just looked startled, but then he puckered
up and began to wail. The scary man caught his baby cousin and
cuddled him and rocked him until he stopped crying and was content again.

Once the child was calm, he put little Donnie down and left the
room to get something to eat. When he came back, the little kid was
playing with a toy that had holes where you inserted colorful little
balls to play music. He sneaked up behind the toddler and yelled

Boo! as loud as he could. The baby went completely rigid and then screamed so shrilly that the boy almost had to put his hands over his ears.

"Hey, now, it's okay, little sweetie pie. I didn't mean to scare you, shh, little guy," he crooned, scooping up the child and sitting down in the rocker by the fireplace. The baby settled down quickly; he guessed Donnie felt safe again. So he rocked the little tyke, who was really awfully adorable most of the time. But there was just something in the look in people's eyes when he scared them that he got off on. It was like they just froze into a statue for a few seconds, rigid and stiff and shocked, and then their brain shrieked out, "Hey, kid, run, run, get outta here fast!"

Oh, yes, he had plenty of that *malice aforethought*, like the lawyers on television shows always said. He liked lawyer shows, and he was smart, too, just like those lawyers. Straight A's in every subject. Maybe he'd become a lawyer someday. Still, that particular phrase intrigued him; it rolled off his tongue somehow and made him feel good. He looked up the definition in the dictionary, just to make sure it was apropos, and there it was, laid out for him in black and white. *Malice aforethought: a general evil and depraved state of mind in which the person is unconcerned for the lives and well-being of others.*

Okay, that's exactly what he had, that evil and depraved state of mind. Maybe he should call himself Malice Aforethought, or just Malice for short, give himself a name like the villains who battled the superheroes in the comics. Because that's what he came after people with, pure malice in his heart and mind and soul. Maybe he would call himself that, just for fun, and thus, his new moniker was born.

Malice grinned, thinking about the exact moment when his victims knew they were in trouble, right before they screamed or took off running or wept real live wet-to-the-touch tears. That's when that strange sense of joy erupted deep inside his gut. It was some kind of release, almost. Satisfaction, that's what it was. A burst of great personal gratification. He wondered if that was normal behavior, or if he might be a really bad person, or some kind of psycho, even. Then he decided he didn't care if he was or not, that it felt good and he was going to do it, whenever he knew he wouldn't get caught.

Yeah, he could even make it his hobby all right, just something to pass the time. He could gather scary things to use on people and figure out what kind of things gave people the creeps and watch murderers in movies and read gory books until he had his talents honed down to sublime perfection. Smiling to himself, he rocked little Donnie to sleep and then he laid the tiny boy gently in his portable crib and went to look for Mandy. After all, she was his favorite victim, and even more important, she was way too afraid to tell on him.

Linda Ladd is the bestselling author of over a dozen novels. *Remember Murder* marks her exciting return to the Claire Morgan series. Linda makes her home in Missouri, where she is at work on her next novel featuring Claire Morgan.

Visit her on the web at www.lindaladd.com.

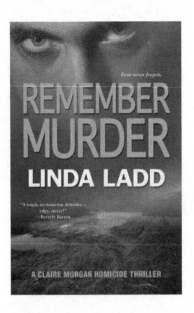

Fear never forgets.

REMEMBER
MURDER

LINDA LADD

"A tough, no-nonsense detective...
edgy, clever!"
—Beverly Barton

A CLAIRE MORGAN HOMICIDE THRILLER

Remember the Darkness

She can't remember why he chose her—or what he did to her.
But Detective Claire Morgan knows that something terrible
happened to her the night a deranged serial killer
escaped from the mental ward. Looking for pleasure.
Looking for pain. Looking for her . . .

Remember the Terror

Recovering in a lakeside resort, Claire hopes to sort through her
broken memories. But after suffering a temporary coma she can
barely remember her own lover, psychiatrist Nicholas Black.
Would she be able to recognize her abductor if she saw him again?
If he came back for more . . . ?

Remember Murder

If only she could remember his face or his voice . . .
if only she could comprehend the evil in his mind
or the depths of his cruelty . . . if only she knew
just how close he is—to her and everyone she loves . . .

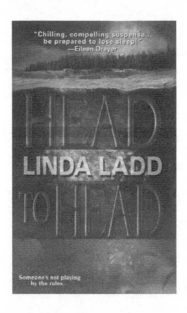

LINDA LADD

Someone's not playing
by the rules . . .

With Every Turn in the Case . . .

After moving from Los Angeles to Lake of the Ozarks, Missouri, homicide detective Claire Morgan has at last adjusted to the peaceful rhythms of rural life. Until a grisly celebrity murder at an ultra-exclusive "wellness" resort shatters a quiet summer morning . . .

With Every Twist of the Mind . . .

One of Dr. Nicholas Black's high-profile clients, a beautiful young soap opera star, has been found dead, taped to a chair at a fully set table . . . submerged in the lake. Back in L.A., Claire investigated the rich, famous, and the deadly—but she never expected the problems of the privileged to follow her to this sleepy small town. Just as she never imagined crossing the line with her prime suspect . . .

With Every Beat of the Heart . . .

Immersed in the case, Claire finds herself drawn to the charismatic doctor, spending more and more time in his company—and in his bed. Now, to catch a killer, Claire will have to enter the darkest recesses of the human mind. But is Black leading her there to help her . . . or luring her ever deeper into a madman's grip?

"A tough, no-nonsense detective with a
well-hidden vulnerable side...edgy, clever!"
—BEVERLY BARTON

EVERY
KILLER
HAS THEM...

DARK

LINDA LADD

PLACES

Missouri detective Claire Morgan is eager to get back to work
after recuperating from injuries sustained on her last job.
But the missing persons case that welcomes her home in the
dead of winter soon turns more twisted and treacherous than
Lake of the Ozarks' icy mountain roads . . .

The man's body is found suspended from a tree overlooking
a local school. He is bleeding from the head, still alive—but not
for long. Someone wanted Professor Simon Classon to suffer
as much as possible before he died, making sure the victim had
a perfect view of his colleagues and students on the campus below
as he succumbed to the slow-working poison in his veins . . .

Frigid temperatures and punishing snows only make the
investigation more difficult. And then the death threats begin—
unnerving incidents orchestrated to send Claire a deadly message.
Now, as she edges closer to the truth,
Claire risks becoming entangled in a maniac's web—
and the stuff of her own worst nightmares . . .

Die Young

Hilde Swensen is a beauty pageant queen with a face to die for and a body to kill for. But by the time Detective Claire Morgan finds her in a shower stall—posed like a grotesquely grinning doll—Hilde is anything but pretty. She's the victim of a sick, deranged killer. And she won't be the last . . .

Die Beautiful

Brianna Swensen is the beauty queen's sister—and the girlfriend of Claire's partner, Bud. She tells Claire that Hilde had plenty of enemies, including a creepy stalker, an abusive ex-boyfriend, and a slew of jealous competitors. But what she doesn't say is that they both shared a dark disturbing secret. A secret that refuses to die . . .

Die Smiling

From the after-hours parties of a sinister funeral home to the underworld vendettas of the Miami mob, Claire follows the trail with her lover Nicholas Black, a psychiatrist with secrets of his own. But it's not until she uncovers evidence of unspeakable acts of depravity that Claire realizes she's just become a diabolical killer's next target . . .

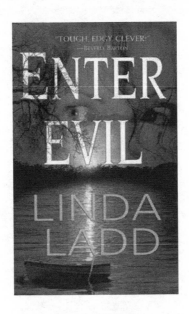

When the Mind . . .

His doctors are the best in the world, his father one of the most powerful men in the state. But they couldn't stop Mikey from succumbing to his darkest demons—the ones inside his head. The ones who told him it was time to end it all.

Plays a Deadly Game . . .

It should have been an open-and-shut case, especially since detective Claire Morgan's lover, Dr. Nicholas Black, recognized Mikey as a troubled former patient. Then Claire finds another body in Mikey's home. Curled inside an oven, charred beyond recognition, the method of murder mind-boggling . . .

of Murder

Claire's only lead is a beaded bracelet, believed to ward off the "evil eye," around each victim's wrist. But by the time she discovers what the dead were afraid of, she's trapped in a mind game of her own—with a brilliant sadistic killer. And this time, there's a method to the madness . . .